THE HARVESTER

The Burkes Series — Book One

Alexandra Burnett

Year of the Cat Books

If you purchased this book without a cover, you should be aware that this book is stolen property. It was reported as "unsold and destroyed," and the author has not received any payment for this "stripped book."

This book is a work of fiction. The names, characters, businesses, places, events, locales, and incidents are the products of the author's imagination or have been used fictitiously and are not to be construed as real. Any resemblance to actual persons, living or dead, actual events, locales or organizations is entirely coincidental.

Copyright © 2024 by Year of the Cat Books.

LCCN 2024905522

All rights reserved. Published independently by Year of the Cat Books, and any associated logos are trademarks and/or registered trademarks of Year of the Cat Books.

This is dedicated to my husband, John, who has supported me, encouraged me, and loved me through it all. I couldn't have done it without you!

Table of Contents

Chapter One	1
Chapter Two	8
Chapter Three	14
Chapter Four	19
Chapter Five	32
Chapter Six	33
Chapter Seven	40
Chapter Eight	49
Chapter Nine	57
Chapter Ten	59
Chapter Eleven	70
Chapter Twelve	76
Chapter Thirteen	83
Chapter Fourteen	86
Chapter Fifteen	89
Chapter Sixteen	91
Chapter Seventeen	103
Chapter Eighteen	109
Chapter Nineteen	119
Chapter Twenty	125
Chapter Twenty-One	134
Chapter Twenty-Two	141

Chapter Twenty-Three	151
Chapter Twenty-Four	155
Chapter Twenty-Five	166
Chapter Twenty-Six	170
Chapter Twenty-Seven	172
Chapter Twenty-Eight	178
Chapter Twenty-Nine	184
Chapter Thirty	188
Chapter Thirty-One	191
Chapter Thirty-Two	198
Chapter Thirty-Three	213
Chapter Thirty-Four	214
Chapter Thirty-Five	216
Chapter Thirty-Six	217
Chapter Thirty-Seven	235
Chapter Thirty-Eight	238
Chapter Thirty-Nine	245
Chapter Forty	252
Chapter Forty-One	256
Chapter Forty-Two	266
Chapter Forty-Three	276
Chapter Forty-Four	287
Chapter Forty-Five	288

Chapter Forty-Six	301
Chapter Forty-Seven	305
Chapter Forty-Eight	307
Chapter Forty-Nine	314
Chapter Fifty	315
Chapter Fifty-One	317
Chapter Fifty-Two	322
Chapter Fifty-Three	324
Chapter Fifty-Four	327
Chapter Fifty-Five	334
Chapter Fifty-Six	338
Chapter Fifty-Seven	345
Chapter Fifty-Eight	356
Chapter Fifty-Nine	362
Chapter Sixty	365
Chapter Sixty-One	372
Chapter Sixty-Two	377
Epilogue	386
The Harvester Soundtrack	391
Sneak peek into book two: The Siren's Storm...	
Acknowledgments	
About the Author	

Chapter One

Business at the café had finally slowed down. The lunch crowd had dispersed, and Danielle was finally getting a moment to sit down and enjoy a cup of tea. With her feet propped up on one of the chairs, she looked out the window at the people walking by. La Jolla wasn't like the city, where people were always in a hurry. The folks out here took their time and didn't always frantically look at their watches every few seconds. Danielle appreciated that. She wasn't particularly drawn to the hustle and bustle of San Diego. La Jolla was relaxed and provided a kind of solace for her.

Who doesn't like solace, she thought. Just then, the little bell on the café door jingled.

"Hey, Dani," a woman's voice said.

Danielle, lost in thought with her tea, kept her gaze on the window.

"HELL-O, Danielle!" the woman spoke more forcefully.

Danielle looked over to the door and saw her best friend, Carrie, giving her a questioning look.

"Oh, hi, sorry. I guess my mind was wandering a bit. What are you doing here? It's Monday. I thought you weren't coming by until Saturday?"

"I decided to take the rest of the day off, and I figured I'd drop by for a bite. I didn't really get a chance to eat lunch."

She immediately walked up to the counter and started eyeing her options. Carrie was always a fan of the desserts and pastries and had the metabolism for them. Danielle had always been a little jealous of her friend in that sense. Carrie could stuff her face with the most fattening things you could imagine and not gain a single pound. She was shorter than Danielle, about five foot-four and probably weighed one hundred and ten pounds soaking wet. Whenever they stood next to each other, Danielle–a long five foot-nine–always felt like an Amazon towering over her. Her frame was very delicate, like one of those ballerinas inside a music box.

By looks, Danielle and Carrie were complete opposites. Carrie had dark espresso brown hair that was layered from her chin down past her shoulders. Her skin was more olive-toned, passed down through a long line of Mediterranean heritage, whereas Danielle had a fairer complexion. One of Carrie's best attributes, the one that had men babbling a new kind of gibberish when they saw her, were her eyes. They were like bright green emeralds sparkling and entrancing. One smile and a wink and the men were bewitched.

"Are you going to have your usual?" Danielle asked.

"Actually, I think I want to try something different today."

Carrie was hovering over the glass case, trying to choose which tasty treat she wanted. Danielle turned her attention back to her tea. The drink was starting to get cold, which wasn't ideal for orange spice, but it was autumn, and even though the weather wasn't chilly in the slightest, it was that time of season. It could be one hundred degrees outside, but if it was anytime between September to February, she was going to have hot chocolate, hot tea, or hot cider if she wanted it, end of story.

Danielle was nearly finished with her tea when Carrie sat down to join her. She gracefully seated herself in the chair, her movements slow and fluid. On her plate she had a huge piece of chocolate hazelnut cheesecake, accompanied by a tall glass of milk.

"Care, that's what you always get. Are you sure you know what different means?"

Carrie just smiled with that *I don't care what you think* look on her face. "You know, you should be flattered that this is what I always choose to get. It's one of the café's best desserts and probably the best one you've created yourself," Carrie said very matter-of-factly. "Besides, Ralph is whipping me up some sort of savory crepe concoction. I don't even know what he's putting in it. I told him to surprise me, so see, I *am* trying something different."

If they had been children, now would be the moment when Carrie stuck her tongue out. Danielle called out to the head waitress, "Nina, mark today on the calendar. This will go down in history as the day Carolina Marossi allowed someone else to make a decision for her." Nina began chuckling as she pulled out a big Sharpie and walked over to the calendar by the register.

"Oh, ha, ha, Danielle. You should start preparing your stand-up routine for the comedy clubs." The two of them both started laughing. They were always able to do that to each other, even if the joke had the wit of a five-year-old. "Besides, you're a fine one to talk." Danielle just lightly rolled her eyes in response.

At that moment, Ralph—Danielle's sous chef—brought out Carrie's crepe. The thing was huge, but then so was Carrie's stomach. Carrie picked up her fork and cut into it to see what surprises Ralph had hidden inside. Steam came billowing out of the crepe along with seasoned chicken, sun-dried tomatoes, ricotta and asiago cheeses, baby spinach, and caramelized onions. The smell intoxicated Carrie, and she took her first bite.

"OH MY GOD!" she said with her mouth full of crepe. "Ralph, this is amazing!"

"Thank you, dear, but the credit doesn't go to me. All I did was cook it—it's Dani's recipe."

Ralph was a tall man in his fifties with a little extra padding in the middle. His hair was peppered and thinning just a bit, but he was still a very handsome man. Danielle had first met him when she put an ad in the paper for a cook a few years ago. She had pulled together enough money to open her very own eatery and was even lucky enough to have gone to an excellent culinary school on a scholarship, thus making tuition less of a headache. Her parents were pretty thrilled about that, too. She had worked all sorts of odd jobs through high school, and when she got to college, she was actually getting to work at a real restaurant as a real chef. Well, a cook, but nonetheless, she was doing what she loved. She saved every penny she earned to check mark her goal on her list.

Ralph proved to be just what Danielle was looking for. He was charming from the get-go, but his cooking skills were impressive as well. Anything Danielle threw at him, he was able to replicate, and that was extremely important. If she hired someone who couldn't make her dishes as well as she could, then there was no way she was going to let anyone eat her food. It had to meet her own expectations. The opinion of the public was everything, and if the customers didn't like the food, then you were out of business.

Carrie whipped around to look at her friend, eyes wide, ready to pop out of her head. "This is yours? How come I've never tasted it before?"

"It's relatively new and getting you to eat new things can be a pain sometimes." Carrie looked at Danielle with a mock hurt expression, as if Danielle had just insulted her.

"I don't know what you're talking about, and frankly, I resent that comment, madame." Carrie was always good about adding dramatic flair to her dialogue—she said it was an Italian thing. Anyone else would be thrown by it, unsure if Carrie was actually serious, but Danielle knew better. She started laughing at her friend again. Carrie gave her an evil glare as she took another bite of her crepe.

"Mmm. You're lucky this is so good, or I'd be mad at you right now," she said, again with her mouth full as Danielle smiled and looked back over to the window. "You look a little tired. Have you been getting enough sleep lately?" Carrie studied her friend carefully as she continued to eat.

Danielle let out a big sigh and turned back to face her. "There's just so much I still have to do before the festival Saturday night. The worst part is I can't make all of the food early, because it won't be fresh."

"What all do you have left to do?" Carrie had already scarfed down the crepe and was now working on her cheesecake.

"Well, I need to double check my inventory for all of the ingredients for what the cafe is going to provide," Danielle said, as she began the checklist on her fingers. "I have to call the electrician and make sure that all of the square's power sources are inspected and have all of the hanging lights and lanterns installed. I have to make sure the other businesses are on schedule with their plans for the festival and verify that the live band we've booked has all of their equipment and playlists together and their stage area is erected according to standard safety codes."

"Did you volunteer for all of that, or did you get roped into it?"

"A little of both, I guess."

"I'd bet my red stilettos that everyone knows what a perfectionist you are, so they dumped it on you. And they know you can't say no."

"That's true, I do have a hard time saying no, but once I get started on something, I have to make sure it gets done right. I guess you could say the square and I have a symbiotic relationship."

"If you ask me, the other businesses need to be pitching in more. You'd think that Mr. Cline would make more sense to be handling the lighting and stage than you." Carrie wasn't wrong, but Danielle was what some might call a micro-manager. That was something the friends had in common.

The Fall Festival was an annual tradition that her square had been putting on for the past few years. All of the businesses got together and found ways to provide their own services that would benefit the festival. With Danielle having a café, she was in charge of the confections. She had to make larger orders for her essential ingredients, but with the sales at the festival, she always profited.

Other owners, like Emmett Cline's hardware store, sponsored games for the people to play. They had dunking tanks, basketball hoops, face-paint stations, you name it. Many of the townspeople volunteered themselves to run the different booths, and there were even some who had specialty hobbies, like juggling, knife throwing, and sketch artists who would do caricatures. Even though it was overwhelming, Danielle loved putting on the festival, but there was still so much to do.

Remember, check one box at a time. Don't think about the list as a whole, just one at a time.

"Well, if anyone can pull it off, it's you," a male voice carried across the room. Both women snapped their heads around to see a man at the back of the café. He was leaning against the side of the counter with a pleasant smile on his face.

"Neil, I didn't even hear you come in."

"I came in through the back, since I have crates to give you. I brought the fresh apples and berries that you ordered."

"Did you happen to bring my onions, bell peppers, and baby spinach?" Danielle pulled out a chair, motioning for Neil to come and sit down at the table.

"Of course I did. Have I ever disappointed you?" Neil crossed the room to join the two ladies and smiled a little bigger, knowing what Danielle's answer would be.

Neil Ghering was Danielle's one-stop shop for produce. His store was catty-cornered from the café in the square, and he specialized in organic fruits and vegetables. His stock was always fresh and flavorful, and she got a great discount from him on her orders.

"So, what are you doing for the festival?" Carrie chimed in. Her voice always took on a flirtatious quality whenever he was around.

"The same as every year—bobbing for apples." He flashed a smile back at her, then quickly turned his attention to Danielle again.

Carrie's expression seemed perturbed, and Danielle was sure she knew why.

"Let me know if you need someone to sample your goodies before the festival—I'm always happy to help."

Danielle laughed and rolled her eyes at him.

Neil feigned a voice of innocence, "What? I'm totally serious. If there's anything you'd like for me to taste, I'm your man." Danielle laughed a little harder this time, and Neil began to chuckle along with her. Carrie didn't seem too amused.

"Alright, then I'm off," Carrie said abruptly, as she stood up from her chair. Danielle knew that her ego was a bit bruised, but she also knew that Carrie would get over it. It was only a matter of time when she would decide to move on to someone less difficult. Her friend had a limit to her patience, and it was soon to be maxed out. Though they had known each other for quite a while, Carrie had been very casual with her flirtations, never having dedicated more than a slight effort with Neil, and whether she actually wanted to date him, which Danielle didn't believe so, it was more of the fact that she couldn't hold his attention. It was certainly something she wasn't accustomed to.

"I think I'll head out, too. I know you're a busy woman, and I wouldn't want to delay you. Miss Marossi, shall I escort you to your car?"

Carrie softened again as she took Neil's arm, and they left the café.

Danielle looked at her watch and realized the time. It was only three-thirty p.m., but it felt like nine. Her feet were really starting to hurt, and all she could think about was taking a long, hot bath. Saturday was still five days off, but to Danielle, time was running out.

Chapter Two

Saturday was here, and Danielle had miraculously pulled everything together. There hadn't been a single hitch, and she prided herself in that. She hated stressing, but it always worked well for her. Carrie had arrived early to help with the set up. Ralph had been at Mon é all day with Danielle baking the festival menu, which was consisted of warm apple cider, pumpkin cupcakes with cinnamon cream cheese frosting, and caramel and candied apples. The food looked perfect and tasted even better. Carrie, of course, had stolen a few of the cupcakes, claiming a test was needed for 'quality control.' The quality must have been questionable because she conducted three.

Twilight was approaching, and everyone's booths were up and running. People began to show up, and soon, the streets were filled. Kids were running down the street with sparklers in their hands while their parents socialized. Couples were strolling hand in hand, laughing and giggling together.

As sweet as the picture was, there was a small pang deep inside Danielle. As far as men in her life went, there weren't any. Of course, she had her father, her brother, and Ralph, who she embraced as an uncle, but men to be romantically involved with? No. And even though Neil made jokes here and there of the flirtatious nature, their relationship was purely platonic.

Besides, she considered herself far too busy to worry about relationships. The café took a lot of work, and considering that's where she spent most of her days, the inflow of suitors wasn't that much. Sure, there was the occasional male customer who would come in and do a bit of flirting, but nothing ever came of it. She just wasn't really interested in any of them.

Much to her chagrin, Carrie would drag her to the clubs in the city, but the nights always turned out uneventful. Danielle loved dancing but wasn't crazy about men inviting themselves to dance *with* her. She didn't want to meet anyone or be pulled into a slow grind with some drunk, egotistical tool. The only thing Danielle cared about was moving her hips to the beat, to feel the bass pulsing through her bones. Any wandering hands that started a frisk were quickly rendered useless for the next five minutes.

One night, Carrie had dragged Danielle to one of the pretentious clubs that she loved to frequent. They were always brimming with lawyers, stockbrokers, bankers, and executives of all types. Essentially, any job that required being a douchebag. Carrie mainly went to make connections, though not typically of the love variety. As an Assistant District Attorney, she believed she should continually add to her ever-expanding list of contacts, should she need a favor. Carrie also enjoyed having her drinks paid for. Sure, they could go to a lower profile club or bar and get plenty of offers, but Carrie liked knowing her wannabe beaus were good for it.

Danielle, on the other hand, was not so fond of it. Carrie loved the attention, practically craved it, whereas Danielle preferred to be left alone, or at least not bombarded with potential suitors. Suitors, of course, meaning men who wanted to get into her pants. Some of them were lucky enough to gain Carrie's interest. None of them earned Danielle's... except one.

It was the first—and last—time Danielle had given her approval to any of the men she had met at The Lion. He had approached her like a wolf in sheep's clothing, and Danielle had been a stupid sheep.

"Pardon me, miss?"

Danielle turned to face the stranger tapping on her shoulder. "Yes?" she asked, already skeptical, waiting to hear what self-assuring pick-up line he would use. *'Have you ever had the caviar at Joffrey's?'* or *'You would look even more beautiful in the glow of the sunset from my boat.'* It was nauseating. Carrie ate it up—Danielle passed the plate and the bullshit they were dishing.

"I'm sorry to bother you," he had started, looking quite nervous as he continued, "but, well…" He shifted his weight back and forth and looked as though he was battling with his courage.

He was wearing a fine suit, minus the jacket, that fit him like it had been tailored. His royal blue power tie stood out against the crisp, white dress shirt. The black leather belt accentuated the lean line of his waist and hips, promoting his fitness. Danielle acknowledged to herself his attractiveness.

"I mean, I'm sure you get hit on a lot. Hell, probably by every man here," he said, looking around the room, still showing his nerves. "I just, well, my friends bet me I was too much of a chicken to tell you."

She raised a brow at him. He certainly didn't look the poultry type. "To tell me I get hit on a lot?"

"What?" he asked, seemingly flustered, then muttering to himself, "Damn, I'm really screwing this up." Finally, he gathered some fortitude with determination in his bright blue eyes. "I just wanted to say that I think you are so lovely, which I'm sure you already know—I mean, you already know you're beautiful, not that you knew that I think you're beautiful," he rambled, then blushed at the realization, "but I wanted to tell you, anyway."

The handsome man looked relieved, glad that he'd finally gotten out his proclamation. He flashed a bright white smile at her, revealing his dimples, then turned to leave, denying Danielle the chance to form a response. She wasn't sure what to make of him. He hadn't tried to impress her with his job or materialistic things like the others. That, alone, made him stand out.

After taking just two steps, he turned back to Danielle. "While I'm embarrassing myself, would you possibly want to get coffee sometime?" He flashed that charming smile at her again, and this time, she felt its effect, enough so that she surprised herself by saying yes. He hadn't asked for dinner, or drinks, just coffee. It was refreshing. Had Danielle known the kind of man he truly was, though, she would never have accepted the date… and probably would have told him where he could piss off.

The Harvester

"Hey, I brought you something." Neil pulled Danielle from her thoughts as he strolled over from his booth. "Even though they're the main theme of your spread, I wasn't sure if you'd actually tried my apples." He tossed one her way, and it fell perfectly into Danielle's hands.

"Actually, not this time. I didn't want to waste my inventory, and you know Carrie did plenty of 'taste-testing' for everyone."

She smoothed her hands around the apple, inspecting it. At that moment, Danielle's stomach growled loudly, and she felt herself blush a bit. She hadn't eaten in quite a while, being too distracted with the festival. Danielle took a big bite, which made a loud crunching sound. The apple was very juicy and full of flavor, and Danielle wasn't sure if she'd ever had an apple that tasted this good.

"Neil, this apple is fantastic—it's perfectly ripe."

"Well, it is the harvest season. I'm glad you like it, because that's my last apple. All of the bobbers have wiped me out."

"Me, too. My caramel and candied apples ran out within an hour. I've got Ralph in the cafe whipping up some more cupcakes to fill the void."

"Danielle, you've done it again," Mrs. Cline interjected, "Your food is to die for! I'm hosting Thanksgiving dinner this year, and I would love to serve these cupcakes. Is there any chance you'd let me borrow the recipe?" Mrs. Cline was Emmett Cline's wife and being that they were fellow business owners in the square, and the fact that Mr. Cline would always offer his services to help Danielle when she had repair problems in the café that she couldn't fix herself, Danielle was not going to refuse her.

"Of course, Margaret—anything for you."

"Oh, dear, you are just an angel sent from heaven." Margaret Cline gave Danielle a light touch on the hand and a polite kiss on the cheek.

Neil entered the conversation again, "I'm going to shut down early and see if I can't help out somewhere else. I'll catch you later." He strolled back over to his booth and started to close shop.

By ten p.m., the festival was over, and Danielle had sold every last cupcake and all of her cider. The visitors had all cleared out, and she and the other owners began the clean-up, which usually took about an hour, not including the cleaning she was going to have to do inside. She had already sent Ralph and Nina home, since they'd helped so much in the kitchen, continuing to bake through the evening. Danielle felt bad that they didn't get to enjoy the rest of the festival. That was the nature of the beast, though.

"Man, I'm exhausted." Carrie let out a huge sigh as both women plopped down onto chairs inside the café.

"Me, too. I love it, but I'm definitely glad it's over. I can finally relax."

"It was so magical with all of the lights and smiles and laughter. It reminded me of a scene straight out of a movie you'd see on the Hallmark Channel."

"Well, they never show people having to pick up after the magic. I still have to clean the dishes and machines in the back."

"Do you want some help?" Even though Carrie made the offer, Danielle could tell that she wasn't really up to it. Her friend was being polite by the suggestion, but Carrie actually did look exhausted, and Danielle wasn't about to make her stay. She still had to drive back to the city to go home.

"No, that's okay, I've got it. I don't want you falling asleep at the wheel trying to make it to your apartment."

"Are you sure?"

"Yeah, I'm sure. I promise I'll be fine."

Carrie stood from her chair and slung her purse over her shoulder. "You'd better call me the moment you get home, understand?"

"Yes, ma'am, I understand," Danielle replied with a smile.

The girls said their goodbyes, and Danielle started her chores. It was eleven forty-five p.m. by the time she was done with her work, and she was beat. Her feet were killing her, and all she wanted to do was lay down and go to sleep.

She walked out the door, locked up, and started heading to her car. She always parked in the alley next to the café because it allowed more parking for the customers in front and it was only fifty extra feet. Danielle had her head down as she fiddled with her keys, trying to pick out the one belonging to her car from the rest.

As she rounded the corner of the alley, she tripped over something. She crashed to the ground, nearly face-planting into the asphalt. Luckily, she was able to direct most of the blow to her hands, throwing them out in front of her instinctively. Despite using her arms to brace herself, the momentum was too much to keep her face from hitting some gravel. She had scraped up her palms pretty bad and gashed her head above her right brow, and it burned like hell.

Danielle had the wind knocked out of her, and she desperately started gasping for air. When she caught her breath, she looked behind her to see what had caused her to nosedive. She was blinking furiously to make out the object. The pain had caused her eyes to tear up, and she couldn't see much, not to mention the alley was quite dark.

Slowly, her vision came back to her, and when she realized what she was staring at, she lost her breath again.

Chapter Three

It was a body. She had tripped over a dead body. As the words cemented into her brain, she started to panic. She could see the large pool of blood that looked eerily black in the darkness. The woman was laying there on her back with a decent sized hole in her chest.

Oh God, what if the killer was still in the alley? She was frozen in terror, afraid to turn around. He might be there, waiting to attack. The fear was sending her to the extremes of paranoia, and that thought got her legs moving.

Get up, Dani, get up! she screamed inside. *Oh God, just run, you idiot!*

She could feel something viscous running down from above her temple past her eye. Her cuts stung from exposure to the air, and her body felt like a lead weight. The door to the café was only twenty feet away—give or take—but it felt like an eternity, each second in slow motion like a Slasher flick.

Miraculously, the keys were still in her hand. She fought with them trying to get the right ones in the locks. This was the first time she regretted having so many, and it didn't help that her hands were shaking violently. Once the last key was in, she threw open the door and slammed it shut, racing to get all of those damn locks in place, which now she was grateful for again. She frantically patted herself down searching for her cell phone.

"Shit!"

The battery was dead—she had forgotten to charge it. Danielle ran to the café's phone and ducked behind the counter. For a split moment, she went completely blank. What was the number she was supposed to call? She could feel herself starting to get light-headed and realized that she was beginning to hyperventilate. She forced herself to breathe deeper and slower. She couldn't call the police if she passed out, and she *needed* to call the police. 9-1-1! That was the number. Danielle punched the number keys hard and was clutching the receiver so tightly her knuckles were turning white.

"9-1-1, what is your emergency?" The voice of the woman on the line was calm and slow. *She's too relaxed,* Danielle thought, although she figured they had to be or else they might scare the callers even more, and she was frightened enough as it was.

"Please send someone right away. I think a woman has been murdered."

After she had been reassured twice that the police and paramedics were on their way, Danielle tried to focus on her breathing again. She felt something else wet running down her face. Tears were streaming, although she hadn't noticed before. She started wiping them away and then realized her hands were on fire. The salt from the tears had brought it back to her attention. She winced when she looked down at them. They were cut up pretty bad, and she felt other surges of pain rise up. Her knees were aching and her head was throbbing.

She heard the sirens in the distance and ended the call with the operator, who had stayed on the line with her until the police arrived. Danielle decided that she needed to regain her composure. The police were no doubt going to ask her a lot of questions, and she needed to have her wits about her when they did. Being a stuttering, weepy mess was only going to make their jobs harder and the night last longer. She heard the squad cars pull up and knock on the door. She continued to sit there behind the counter.

"Ma'am, it's the police. Please open the door." When Danielle didn't move, the officer spoke again, "Ma'am, we need you to open the door." Time was moving in slow motion. Even though they claimed to be the police, Danielle couldn't make herself move.

"Burke, I need to see you in my office." The police captain, Roy Jensen, called out his request through the department. The man was not known for being soft spoken.

Detective Adam Burke looked up from his desk to see that the captain had already headed back to his office. The man didn't wait for anyone, apart from Mrs. Jensen. Adam didn't know if he was about to be reprimanded for something, but he didn't care. It was almost midnight, and he was staying late to finish some paperwork. Oh, how he hated paperwork.

His partner, Ben Anderson, finally had the chance to take his wife out on a date without their four- and two-year-olds. Even though he was only thirty—the same age as Adam's older brother—he had a sagely maturity about him. He told Adam that marriage and kids will do that to you. He was like a brother to Adam, even though he already had three. These outings were few and far between for Ben, and Adam couldn't make his partner suffer with him. Besides, it wasn't like he had anything better to do. However, regardless to his lack of a social life on a Saturday night, that didn't change his detest for it. The abrupt meeting with the captain was a much-needed break from staring at the files. Adam walked into Jensen's office and closed the door behind him.

"Captain?" he asked.

"There's been a murder at a little café in La Jolla called... Damn, where are my glasses?" The captain started combing through the papers that were spread all over his desk.

A lot of the boys gave him hell for needing them, cracking jokes about being an old fart and such. Jensen didn't care what they said, he just hated having to need them to read. Putting them on and taking them off all day was a huge pain in the ass, and he was always misplacing them. Finding the glasses, the captain put them on and started adjusting the distance of the paper with the name written on it.

"Ah, here we go. It's called, Mon Félicité. I want you to get over there and take lead of the investigation."

Adam blinked for a moment, slightly confused at what Jensen had just said. "La Jolla? Why are you sending me there? It's not our jurisdiction. Surely the blues over there can handle it." What the hell would he want to go to La Jolla for? Adam stuck to the city where the major crime was. That's the way he liked it—he could make a real difference here.

"It's not your average death by robbery or something. Based on the call I just got, the victim's body has been mutilated in a unique way, making it a special case. They're out of their element and asked for our help. You said you're ready for something more challenging, so here you go." The captain sat down in his seat, hands folded together, "Or how about, because I said so?" The captain leaned forward, reading over some papers. When Adam didn't start moving for the door, Jensen spoke without looking up, "Is there a reason why you're still standing there, Burke?"

"Captain, I really don't think it's necessary for me to go out there. I still have those reports you wanted finished today, and I'm not even close to being done." As much as Adam hated paperwork, he also didn't like being behind. He couldn't move on to the next case if the previous wasn't finished. His parents had taught him and his siblings that follow-through was important. It said a lot about one's character, providing the information on whether that person was dependable, efficient, and trustworthy.

"Anderson can finish them tomorrow." Captain Jensen was still looking at the papers on his desk. "Besides, do you really want to sit there and fill out reports?" and before Adam could even respond, he added, "I didn't think so."

"Captain—" Before Adam could get out another word, Jensen shot up from behind the desk, ripping off his glasses with a spark of fury in his eyes.

"Burke, is that your name on the door?"

"No, sir."

"Whose name is on that door?"

"Yours, sir."

"Yes, it's mine. Frankly, you should be damned glad I'm putting you on lead, but if you think you know better than me, then by all means, go finish your damned paperwork. And then you can finish *everyone's* damned paperwork for the next damned month." Jensen eased down into his chair, leaned back, and laced his hands. "What's it going to be, Detective?"

Chapter Four

Adam cursed the captain from behind the steering wheel as he drove out of the city. As he turned onto one of the little boulevards of the square, red and blue flashed brightly into the night. The closer he got to the café, Mon Félicité, he noticed that the responding officers were clustered in front of the door. *Why the hell are they just standing there?*

Adam parked on the opposite side of the street, got out of the car, and made his way over to the scene. Some of the officers were over by the alley, as well as two paramedics. It looked as if they had already begun to probe the body looking for evidence. As Adam approached, one of the blues headed over to him.

"Are you Detective Burke? We've been waiting for you." The man had an exasperated look on his face, but Adam could tell it wasn't directed toward him.

"Yes, are you the one in charge here?"

"Charlie Mendez," the officer said, as he shook Adam's hand. "I'm glad you're here."

"What's going on? Why is everyone standing at the doorway?"

"The woman who called in the murder won't let us in. It appears she's too scared to reason with."

"Who's the woman?" Adam asked.

"We're pretty sure she works in the café, considering she has keys to the place, but other than that, we don't know. We can't even get her to speak, much less tell us her name."

"She's probably in shock. I'll see if I can coax her out. Do you mind?"

"By all means," Mendez said, as he gestured his hand toward the building and stepped back, as if to grant Adam a path.

Adam stepped in front of the other officers, forcing them to back away. He was sure that if she was truly scared, all of them crowding around the door was only going to make it worse. Adam pulled out his badge and held it up for the woman to see. "Miss, I'm Detective Burke with the San Diego Police Department."

Danielle poked her head out from behind the counter. There was something about the man's voice that eased the paranoia. Or it could've been that he introduced himself as a detective and not just an officer. It seemed too specific to be untrue. She slowly began to stand up, moving with caution, as she walked toward the door. Every few steps she would hesitate, then start moving again. When she made it to the door and began to reach for the locks, she stopped. Adam saw her eyes move down to his hip. She was staring at his gun with terror across her face.

"I know you're scared, but I'm here to protect you. In order to help me do that, I need my gun. Tell me if you understand."

Finally, she nodded her head, but continued to stare at the weapon. Danielle had never been around guns before, so the idea of it possibly being used in front of her gave her so much anxiety it was staggering.

"Okay," the detective said, as though he were caving to end a stalemate, "here's what I'm going to do. I'm going to give my gun to this officer here." He slowly pulled it from its holster and handed it to one of the other officers.

Danielle's face eased a bit.

"See? No weapon. I'm just a guy who wants to help you. Will you let me help you?"

She nodded again but still didn't move. Her brow furrowed, and she blinked rapidly, as if rationality was warring inside her head.

"Sweetheart, I need you to open the door. Otherwise, I can't help you. You're perfectly safe now. I promise I won't let anything happen to you. You have my word."

Danielle stared at the man standing at her door and started to calm down. So much for being level-headed. Even though the other officers in uniform had identified themselves, she hadn't been able to make herself let them in. But there was something about this man that put her at ease. She moved closer until her still-shaking hands were on the locks. Her eyes never left him, as they scrolled—studying him.

He was tall, about six foot four, and he had dark, sable brown hair that was grown out just enough to have its own little curl at the ends. His eyes were a steel gray suit, like none she'd ever seen before. The color reminded her of a cool winter day. The image in her mind made her relax a bit, and it was as if she could feel the crisp, cool breeze blowing on her. The fear and anxiety had made her pulse race and her entire body to flush in a heat from the adrenaline.

With bloody, unsteady hands, Danielle slowly unlocked the door and opened it. As she stepped out, she let out a deep, ragged breath and then collapsed.

Sweetheart? Where the hell had that come from? He had no time to think about it as he caught the waitress in his arms as she fainted. She was crashing from the adrenaline rush. As he held her, he noticed that she had blood smeared on her cheeks. He began looking her over. There was no doubt that the blood had come from the cut in her forehead and the exposed layers of skin on her palms. It looked as though something had seriously cut into her right palm. It was then that he began to see the rough, jagged outline of keys in the torn skin. He could see long streaks slicing through the blood on her face and realized they were tear tracks. She must have been wiping them away, and as a result, spread the blood all over like war paint.

As he scooped her up and carried her over to the ambulance, he studied her harder. Despite the red markings on her face, he could tell she was beautiful. Her skin looked soft in the moonlight and her long, caramel blonde waves swayed with each step he took. One of the paramedics held out his arms for Adam to pass her off, but he didn't immediately react. He wasn't ready to let go of her, which was odd. He didn't even know this woman, yet he already felt protective of her. After all, he was the only one she had agreed to open the door for, and he had promised her that he wouldn't let anything happen to her. She clearly decided to trust him, and Adam felt that he should keep his word.

"Detective?" asked the paramedic, as Adam raised his gaze to the man. "Can I check out the young lady?"

Adam, still holding on to her, laid her on the gurney the paramedic had placed outside the ambulance. The man started checking her pulse, making sure her heart rate was leveling out. "How long do you think it'll take for her to wake up? I need to question her and find out what the hell happened here."

"It looks like she just fainted from an adrenaline crash and possibly exhaustion. She should come out of it relatively soon."

Adam was reluctant to leave her there, but he needed to assess the crime scene. "Let me know the minute she wakes up."

"Sure thing," said the paramedic.

The yellow tape had already been put up, and Adam ducked below it to get in the alley. The woman lying motionless on the ground had a puddle of blood encompassing her from above her shoulders to her lower abdomen. As Adam put on his rubber gloves, he did a full three hundred-sixty degree walk around the victim and then crouched down to get a better look at the woman.

Her eyes were wide, expressing her last moment of fear, which was now permanently cemented on her face. The captain wasn't kidding when he said she was mutilated. There was a huge hole in her chest, revealing the true disturbing nature of this killing. Her heart had been cut out. This had been done with a purpose, but what? Why here, in

La Jolla? It's not like it was known for having high crime rates, especially murders.

He turned around to face Officer Mendez. "Tell me what we know."

"We didn't find any identification on the body, so we're running her through the missing persons database by her physical description. We did, however, find something that will intrigue you." Officer Mendez pointed deeper into the hole in the chest cavity. "We didn't want to move anything until you and CSU got on the scene. The killer managed to keep it from getting soaked in the blood."

Adam knelt and retrieved a paper origami heart.

"What is it?" Mendez asked.

Adam unfolded the paper, quickly inspected it, and then handed it over.

Mendez read the hand-written note aloud. "Number one was quite fun, but I won't be done until I've won."

Short and sweet, Adam thought.

"Won what?"

"That's what we have to figure out."

"*I won't be done*..." Mendez quoted again and momentarily paused. "Does this mean..." he trailed.

"With only one body, we can't officially call it, but based on that..." Adam said, as he stood and gestured to the note. "Yes, I think we might have a serial killer here."

Adam looked the woman over again. She had long blonde hair that was now matted with blood and cold, dead hazel eyes. She was dressed in a crimson negligee night gown that came down to her ankles. The skirt was flowing out away from the body, and her arms were outstretched in a high V, fingers left loose and dainty. It was obvious that the woman had been posed, but for what, Adam wasn't sure.

He bent down to get even closer to the body and picked up two distinct aromas. There was a heavy scent of alcohol, wine most likely, coming from her mouth and the smell of something almost sweet.

"I want the photos from CSU as soon as possible and make sure a blood sample gets to the crime lab. We may have to try to pull dental records. I'd like a time of death, and I want a check run for anything unusual in the autopsy, like any drugs or sedatives. I can already tell you that there's alcohol in her system, but I want to know how much and the exact substances he used."

"Yes, sir. We'll do a preliminary and then have everything sent to your department and medical examiner," Mendez replied.

"Has CSU already dusted for fingerprints?"

"Of course, and everything's clean. He was most likely wearing gloves."

"I'm hoping she scratched him, giving us some DNA to work with."

"I did notice dirt under her fingernails, but she's lying in an alley, so that may not mean anything."

"Excuse me, Detective," the paramedic interjected, "the woman is awake now if you're ready to talk to her." He motioned his head to the ambulance, signaling for Adam to follow.

"Thank you." Adam pulled off his gloves and put them in his pocket. "Mendez, keep me posted and make sure that note gets tested, too."

As Adam approached the ambulance, he noticed that the woman had a lock of hair in her fingers and was twirling it around nervously. He couldn't help thinking it was sort of endearing.

Get your head straight. This isn't the time to be thinking about things like that, he said to himself. In fact, he shouldn't be thinking like that at all.

When Adam stopped in front of her, her long legs dangling from the edge of the ambulance, she stopped twirling her hair and looked up at him with big doe eyes. She had gauze and bandages wrapped around her hands and a single Band-Aid on her forehead. In that moment, Adam felt the urge to hold her in her arms again and comfort her. Instead, he decided to cut to the chase.

"Miss, can you tell me your name?"

"Danielle Walsh."

"Miss Walsh, tell me what happened tonight." His voice had become very stern and serious. Adam had his pen and notepad out, ready to take down her statement.

"The square had our fall festival tonight, and after it was over, I went back inside the café to clean up."

"What time did the festival end?"

"At ten o'clock, and all of the business owners cleaned the streets until eleven."

Adam was scribbling on his note pad, not even looking at her when asking his questions. "What time did you finish cleaning the café?"

"I think it was eleven forty-five. I shut off the lights and locked the door. I was walking to my car, and the next thing I knew I was on the ground. I wasn't looking where I was going, and I guess I tripped..." she swallowed hard as her eyes glanced to the dead woman still lying on the ground, "over her."

Adam could see that the sight was sickening her. "Don't look over there. Just keep your eyes on me, okay?" he gently instructed.

Danielle nodded in agreement.

"Did you see anything out of the ordinary, anyone suspicious-looking hanging around here?"

"No, nothing. The streets were empty when I was leaving."

"What about earlier during the festival?"

"No, I know the majority of the people that were here, and it couldn't have been any of them."

"In my line of work, Miss Walsh, that doesn't mean anything. You never truly know what someone's capable of."

His words made Danielle's blood run cold. It was clear that he'd seen crimes like this before.

"Is there *anything* you can tell me about the victim or the crime? Was the woman maybe a customer of yours? Can you give me a name?"

Danielle spoke with defeat in her voice, "Actually, no, I don't know who she is. I've never seen her before in my life, and I certainly have no idea why this happened."

"So, you know nothing?" The detective was staring at Danielle with different eyes. The ones she had seen earlier, when he was trying to coax her outside, had been soothing and safe. Now his eyes were cold and calculating. She didn't like the feeling they gave her or the attitude he was giving off. He was looking at her like she was a waste of his time, which she didn't appreciate.

He continued to ask her questions that she didn't have the answers to, and both of their frustrations were starting to show.

He let out a big sigh, "Well, we're sure to crack this case wide open with all of this extensive information," he mumbled, sarcasm coating his words.

Danielle couldn't believe what he'd just said. She didn't need this, and it was time for her to put him in his place. She came off the edge of the ambulance and stood directly in front of him, only mere inches from his face… close enough to slap that asshole look right off. "Excuse me, *Detective*, but I'm trying to cooperate as best as possible. I'm cut up, bruised, bleeding, and exhausted. My head feels ready to explode, and all I want to do is go to sleep and forget that this ever happened. I'm sorry I don't have all of your answers, but it's not my responsibility to do your job for you."

His expression was stone. Danielle was sure he thought she was just another weepy, fragile woman—considering she *had* been when he'd first arrived—but now that she was rational again, she wasn't going to be the frightened and docile damsel in distress, and she did not need to be rescued. If he thought that of her, then he could go to hell.

Suddenly, a grin crept onto his face. Either he liked being told off, or he was an even bigger jerk than she'd thought. Fed up, Danielle started to walk past him, heading for her car. The detective put his arm out to catch her at her waist, stopping her from storming off.

"May I ask where you're going?" His tone had a hint of amusement in it.

Danielle glowered at him. "I'm going home, Detective, since I don't have any *'case cracking'* information for you."

"I'm going to have to insist that you have an officer escort you home."

She raised an eyebrow. Insist? Did he honestly think she was going to take orders from him? His eyes were no longer cold, but instead had a mischievous quality, like the two of them were sparring.

"That's quite thoughtful of you," she said, adding her own dose of sarcasm, "but I think I'd rather drive myself home. I wouldn't want to imposition you anymore than I already have." She stared hard at him for a moment. Finally, the detective dropped his hand back to his side and handed her his card.

"If you think of anything, you can reach me at this number."

Danielle reluctantly accepted it, doing her best not to snatch it and reveal her attitude, then walked away with her head high.

As Danielle walked to her car, Adam called Mendez over, "Follow her home, and make sure she gets there safely. You aren't to leave until you hear her door lock."

Adam could feel the intensity in his eyes as he spoke. Mendez nodded and headed to his squad car, and Adam looked back to see Danielle. Damn, she had long legs. He wasn't sure if he'd seen any as sexy as hers, and they weren't even in top condition since she had bruises and scrapes covering them.

She was wearing a simple white cotton shirt—which now had spots of dirt and blood on it—that fit her so perfectly as it followed the hourglass curve of her waist, and a pair of denim shorts that accentuated her hips and the length of those long, long, *long* legs.

She was taller than most women—her head actually reaching his chin—and he found that attractive. He was used to having to crane his neck far down to kiss women. Not that he would be kissing her.

Adam wasn't expecting her to be such a spitfire, either. She had been so afraid and vulnerable before, unable to respond out of fear, but then out of nowhere, she called him out on his behavior, and it took him by surprise. He had seen the loathing in her eyes—those beautiful eyes that were rimmed with green and gradually blended to that same caramel color as her hair—before she walked away. God, that had affected him. He didn't want her to hate him, which shouldn't matter and never had before with other women, but with Danielle Walsh…

He had become so calloused over the years—dealing with murder and death on a daily basis—that he forgot what it was like for ordinary people. What she just went through was pretty traumatic, and he had insulted her by showing zero compassion for her feelings. Adam walked back over to the body, and at that moment, he looked at Jane Doe's face and realized that he was standing in the same spot Danielle had been when she'd stared back at the woman's lifeless eyes.

Adam let out another sigh. Yep, he was definitely an asshole. He deserved her hatred even though he didn't want it, but he was afraid that if he had comforted her the way he'd wanted, things might've gone somewhere they shouldn't, and that was the last thing he needed. He'd never gotten involved with a witness before and wasn't about to start.

He was all about the job and fooling around with women involved in his cases was unprofessional. He'd seen it many times before with other cops. The woman was usually an emotional wreck, depending on the circumstances, and looked to the investigator for comfort, turning him into her knight in shining armor and clinging to him like plastic wrap. Adam hated watching those women get their hearts broken when they realized they were nothing more than a fling—a woman seeking comfort and offering her body to her hero, just to have him take what he wanted and leave. It disgusted him. Any thoughts he had about Danielle Walsh had to go this minute.

———

Danielle watched the patrolman following her from her rearview mirror, and she couldn't keep the scowl from forming on her face. Where did that detective come off? She didn't need his stupid escort. She was perfectly capable of making it home on her own without his help. He was rude, arrogant, and a complete jackass. Just thinking about it made her rage inside.

She pulled up to her apartment building and parked in her spot. As she got out of her car, she noticed that the policeman was parking as well. He followed her to the front door of the building and patiently waited for her to unlock it. Her building was rent controlled, so in order to get in, you had to know the access code, have a key, or get buzzed in by a tenant. Danielle looked at him questioningly, raising an eyebrow.

"I told Detective Burke I'd make sure you got home safely," Officer Mendez, according to the name printed on the tag, replied to her unspoken question.

"I do appreciate that, Officer Mendez, but I'm here now, so you're welcome to go home." She walked to the elevator and pushed the up button. When the doors opened, she stepped in, and the officer followed.

Before she could even give him the confused look again, he responded, "That includes seeing you to your door, ma'am."

The officer had a very serious expression on his face, as if he'd been given a precious assignment to carry out. Danielle thought it was a little over the top, but also admired his dedication. *If only more people could be that way,* she thought.

She pressed the button for the fifth floor. When they reached their destination, she stepped out into the hall, Officer Mendez close on her heels. She inserted the key and was turning open the lock slowly. Her hands were still in pain, even though the paramedic had bandaged them and given her something to take for it. The drive home was no piece of cake, either. Just holding the steering wheel had made her want to cry.

Danielle opened the door and flipped on the lights. Officer Mendez poked his head in and scanned the room, searching for something, although Danielle didn't know what he expected to find. Once he was satisfied, he gave her a quick nod and asked, "Is there anything else you need, ma'am?"

"No, thank you, Officer Mendez. You've done more than enough."

"Please, call me Charlie, and are you sure? There's nothing I can get for you?" His eyes showed concern like she was a delicate vase about to break.

"Yes, Charlie, I'm sure. You really didn't have to go through all this trouble, you know."

"I'm just doing my duty, ma'am, and it was no trouble at all." Danielle noticed that Charlie was beginning to blush a bit, as a subtle smile appeared. "Besides, it was Detective Burke's orders."

That jerk really ordered it?

"What exactly did he order?" She was intrigued to find out what Detective *Jerk*—oh yeah, that was his new name—had commanded.

"I was to follow you home, see you to your door, and make sure you locked it behind you, *or else*." He chuckled the last bit.

She couldn't help but ask, "Or else what?"

Charlie smiled a little bigger this time. "He thought you might ask that. He also said to tell you that it's not something a lady should hear."

She frowned a bit, feeling like she was being left out of a joke. How did he know she would ask?

Charlie's blush returned. "He wouldn't have needed to give me a reason anyway."

Now it was Danielle who was blushing. She wasn't used to this kind of flattery. She wasn't used to any kind of flattery. Carrie always said Danielle was blind to it, but she honestly didn't see it. "You're very kind, and again, thank you."

"It was my pleasure, ma'am." Officer Mendez waited for Danielle to close the door and turn the locks before he walked away. After unplugging the apartment phone, Danielle trudged through the living room and headed straight for the bedroom.

God, what a night, she thought.

It was one in the morning, and she was completely drained. Inside her apartment, she felt safe. It was familiar and comfortable, and everything else faded away. The whole thing already seemed made up in her mind. Usually, Danielle would wash her face and carry out her nightly routine before heading to bed, but tonight had been so chaotic and intense, that she just walked to her bed and flopped down. She didn't even bother to strip out of her dirty clothes. The second her head hit the pillow, she was out.

Chapter Five

He smiled as he placed his prize on the new shrine he had created. Oh, how beautiful it looked. It was even more beautiful when he had felt it pulsating in his hands, slowing by the second, until at last, it stopped. He shivered with pleasure as he poured himself a glass of wine. The killing had gone perfectly, and the police were as stupid as he'd hoped they would be. He crossed the room to sit in his master chair and continued to stare at the shrine.

Poor girl, he thought, *she brought it upon herself.*

She looked like his angel, but he knew better. He knew what she really was—a liar and a whore. Who did she think she was, tempting him like that? Pretending to be an angel, *his* angel, was punishable by death.

He took a sip of his wine and chuckled. He never knew smiting could be so much fun. This had to be a short celebration, though. He had a lot of preparations to take care of to keep everything on schedule for the next one.

Chapter Six

The next morning, Danielle woke up to someone pounding on her door. She looked over at the clock, which read eight-thirty a.m. She normally didn't sleep this late, but right now, that's all she wanted to do. Her eyes burned from the poor quality of sleep she had gotten. Even though she had slept solid, not even rolling over once in the night, she felt like she had closed her eyes for one second and then opened them again the next, only to find it was already morning. She hated that. In her mind, that was the worst kind of sleep you could get. She felt robbed of her peace and rest.

Thump, thump, thump! The banging at her door persisted, and Danielle decided if it was going to stop, she'd have to answer it. As she got closer, she could make out the voice of a woman on the other side of the door.

"Dani, open up, *please*! Open the door, Dani!" It was Carrie.

Danielle released a heavy sigh. "Crap." She whimpered to herself because she knew what was coming. She didn't know how Carrie found out, and she didn't really care. She was just dreading the dramatic monologue Carrie was going to unleash on her. At this moment, Danielle regretted giving Carrie a key and the access code. She slid open the chain—the only thing that had kept Carrie from bursting in—and unfastened the lock, opening the door. The second they met eyes, Carrie pushed the door the rest of the way open and threw herself at Danielle, locking in a hug, holding on to her with a vise-like grip.

"Oh my God, sweetie, are you okay?" Within a second, Carrie's words came rushing out non-stop, her tone changing back and forth between worried and angry. "Dani, I was so scared! Why didn't you call me? I can't believe someone was murdered outside the café. How come I had to read about it in the paper this morning, huh? I must've called you fifty times, but you weren't answering your phone... I'm so mad at you for staying by yourself. I'm so mad at myself for letting you!"

Carrie let Danielle go and walked past her to the kitchen. She immediately opened the fridge and went for the milk, still chattering away as Danielle closed the door.

"Do you know how freaked out I was? Last night, I thought, 'Okay, maybe she just forgot. I'll fuss at her tomorrow for making me wait up,' but when I called, you didn't answer the phone, so I thought you had turned it off. Then, I tried your landline, but you didn't answer that, either. I'd decided I was really going to chew you out. Then, this morning, I practically choked on my orange juice when I read it on the front page of the *Tribune*, hence the aforementioned fifty missed calls."

"It's already in the paper?"

"Murder in La Jolla? Uh, yeah, it's in the paper already—front page." Danielle wasn't sure why she was surprised. Carrie was right—something like this happening here was unheard of, so it was bound to get quite a bit of attention from the media. Still... the front page?

Carrie opened one of the cabinets searching for a glass. When she turned around to face Danielle, she froze. Her hands let go of the milk jug and the glass, both dropping to the hardwood floor and bursting everywhere. She gasped as she brought her hands up to her mouth. Carrie's eyes grew wide and then began tearing up. It was the first time she had actually looked at her friend since she had walked in the door, and her anger vanished.

When Danielle got home last night, she had gone straight to bed and hadn't looked in a mirror. In fact, she hadn't looked in a mirror since she got ready for work yesterday morning. Did she look that awful? Carrie burst into tears as she walked back over to Danielle, taking her into another hug. Apparently, she *did*. Carrie began talking between her sobs. "Danielle," sniff, "what," sniff, "happened to you? Should we go," sniff, sniff, "to the hospital?"

"No, I'm sure if that was necessary, the paramedics would have taken me last night," she said, as Carrie burst out into a new sob. "Carrie, I'm fine. It's just a bunch of scrapes and bruises." Carrie pulled back to inspect for herself, still sniffling. "It's not that bad," said Danielle.

"Danielle, have you not seen yourself? You look like you've just come from a scene in a horror flick."

Danielle walked into her bathroom and flipped on the switch. The light seemed brighter than usual. After her eyes adjusted, she saw what Carrie saw—what Detective *Jerk* and Officer Mendez had seen. Her face was smudged with dirt and reddish-brown streaks of blood, which matched her once white shirt. Her hair was wild and tangled, desperately needing a brush run through it. She looked down at her hands and saw that the gauze bandages had gone from white to light-pink, where her cuts had probably bled through during the night.

She was horrifying. She looked like she had been beaten—only in reality, her assailant was the street. She had done this much damage? *Well*, she thought, *it was actually that body she had tripped over that caused the damage, not because she was clumsy*. The words hit her—*that body*. Danielle could feel the acid rising in her throat. It was real. Last night had really happened.

Carrie appeared in the mirror's reflection of the doorway. "Let's get you cleaned up, okay?" Her voice was so soft and maternal.

Danielle nodded her head and sat down on the commode.

Carrie was soaking a washcloth in hot water, as she asked, "Are you able to talk about it?" She began to wring the water out, and Danielle winced in anticipation of the heat. Carrie was leaning over her, one hand holding the rag, and the other one peeling back the Band-Aid on her forehead. She didn't go for the cut immediately, but instead started wiping Danielle's cheeks.

Danielle let out a huge sigh, "I'm not even sure what happened—everything is kind of a blur. The only information I actually know is that a woman was stabbed outside, and I tripped over her trying to get to my car." Danielle finished the story for Carrie, whose face changed every few moments from horrified to incredulous to angered, then horrified again.

"I honestly don't know how you're functioning right now. I would probably be catatonic," Carrie said.

"Well, I didn't really have a choice. This crazy lady was beating down my door this morning while I was trying to sleep." Danielle grinned at her friend, who wasn't grinning back. "So, sue me for being concerned about your well-being. I'll make sure it never happens again." Carrie went back into melodrama mode with her exaggerated motions and gestures. "Actually, you can't sue me because I'm the best damned lawyer in San Diego and I would kick your ass."

Danielle kept on smiling, "Yeah, I love you, too."

"You're damn right." Carrie had her hands on her hips as she let out a huff. She was wearing a fitted, collared shirt with a decorative belt that went around the center of it. It was emerald-green, and the belt was brown, adorned with different shades of green jewels. Her jeans were the darkest wash of blue you could find, and they always seemed to be dressy, which was kind of an oxymoron. In all actuality, blue jeans were meant to be casual, or at least that was their original purpose, but Carrie had a way to make everything she wore look fancy. You wouldn't catch her dead in a pair of sweatpants and a baggy shirt. She was wearing tall, brown leather boots that had a good heel to them, which brought her only slightly closer to Danielle's height. "Okay, now go soak in the bath, because Lord knows you need one, and I'll clean up the mess in the kitchen."

Danielle was too worn out to argue with her. It wasn't that Carrie was wrong, it was just that Danielle liked to oppose her out of spite whenever she got particularly bossy. Today was an exception, though. Danielle went into her bathroom and turned the hot water on. Just the steam alone was refreshing, and she was already anticipating how relaxing the whole dip would be. She climbed in the tub, easing herself down into the water. She was careful not to submerge her hands or her knees. Instead, she just sat there, soaking the warmth into her aching muscles. It was a good thing she had a loofah brush so that she wouldn't have to get her hands wet. She felt dumb using it to wash her hair, but it saved her some pain.

When she was good and clean, she reached for her favorite fluffy towel, one of those oversized bath sheets that were twice as big as regular towels and wrapped herself up. After she combed through her hair, Danielle stepped back into her bedroom.

Her dirty clothes were missing from the floor. She looked around and saw an outfit laid out on the bed and next to it was a note:

Dani, I'm running your clothes down to the dry cleaners. Hopefully, the blood stains aren't completely set. I've taken the liberty of picking out something for you to wear today, and don't bother choosing something else because you know I'll make you wear mine anyway. I'll be back soon.

Ciao, Bella.

Carrie always did like dressing people up.

Danielle looked over the outfit. It was a plum-colored cotton dress with a sweetheart neckline. A deep eggplant-colored satin sash wrapped around the waist and tied in the back. Danielle loved this dress, and Carrie knew it. It was pretty and feminine, yet still comfortable, and right now she needed both.

After seeing how grotesque she had looked, she needed a confidence boost, but she also didn't want to go to the nines. Carrie had picked out some black shoes that had a low heel, which were surprisingly comfortable. Danielle paused a moment, considering her knees. Luckily, the dress was just long enough to cover the tops of them where the abrasions were. The cuts were actually quite minimal after she had cleaned the dirt and blood out of them. Now, they were only slightly red. There wasn't any way to disguise the bandages on her hands, though.

Danielle was finally dressed and ready for the day. She had made the part in her hair a little deeper so that when she swept it to the side it would conceal the bandage on her forehead. She kept her make-up natural and applied a light coat of gloss to top it all off and looked herself over. She felt a million times better. It was amazing what one little dress could do.

Just then, Carrie came in the front door. "Dani, are you dressed?" she called out, as she walked to the back of the apartment. As Danielle came out of the bedroom, Carrie said, "I see you approved of what I picked out. Are you feeling gorgeous yet?"

"Yes, thank you, you're the best. I don't know what I'd do without you, Care."

"Stop that, or you're going to make me cry again," Carrie said, as she started fanning her hands at her eyes, and the two women started laughing. "Are you sure you want to go into work today? No one would blame you for wanting to stay home."

"I'm sure. I really have some work to get done, and that's also going to include damage control. I think if my customers see me at the café today, it'll be better for business. If I don't go in, people are going to get even more concerned and might stop coming for a while. If I'm not scared to show up, then there's no need for them to be scared, either."

"Then, I insist on driving you. I don't want you leaving there by yourself. I already talked to Ralph while you were getting ready. He agreed and said he would bring you home. Don't fight me on this," Carrie warned and pointed a finger at her.

"I'm too tired to fight you," she conceded with a smile.

As Danielle and Carrie walked into the café, everyone stopped what they were doing to turn and look at the two women. Danielle could feel all of the eyes in the room on her, and it was making her nervous. She didn't like unwanted attention, and right now, she definitely did not want any. After a few still moments, the chatter started up again among the customers. She caught little bits and pieces of their conversations, picking out words, like "murder," "witness," "victim," "body," and "dangerous." The last word Danielle had heard added to a whispered question of the safety at the café. It was time to acknowledge it and address it with the customers.

"May I have your attention?" Everyone's eyes, again, fell on Danielle, so she continued, "I want to let you know that the tragedy that occurred here last night was indeed unsettling, but it has nothing to do with the café. It was an unfortunate circumstance and nothing but coincidental in it taking place here." Danielle turned the serious tone lighter. "Now, I want everyone to enjoy because breakfast is on me."

Smiles returned to their faces and even a few cheers rang out. Danielle wasn't in the habit of comping meals, but she decided in this case it would be a wise business move. Even though most of her customers were regulars, she couldn't afford to lose any of them. Danielle's customers turned back to their meals with lighter conversations.

Phew, that went smoothly.

At that moment, Ralph stole her away to the kitchen. "Dani, I don't care what happens, you will always have me to back you up. You can count on it."

"Thanks, Ralph, I really appreciate that." She was truly touched by his loyalty.

"The free breakfast applies to me, too, right?" Carrie had her pitiful puppy eyes already set for dramatic effect.

"When does it *not* apply to you?" Danielle asked, although her question was more of a statement. Carrie just smiled and gave the nod to Ralph to fix her up something.

Chapter Seven

Adam didn't much care for working on Sundays, but this new case needed a lead or Jensen would have his ass for breakfast on Monday. He sat at his desk combing through new piles of information. The missing persons database hadn't provided a name for their Jane Doe, and the lab results for any toxins hadn't come back yet. He was leaning his elbows on his desk with his hands clenching his hair.

"You're going to go bald if you keep doing that." Ben Anderson, Adam's partner, walked up from behind and gave his friend a smack on the back.

Whereas Adam kept his hair slightly grown, Ben's light ash brown hair was short, which didn't allow him to yank on it in frustration—not that he ever would. It was a dumb habit Adam had developed over the years, and Ben loved teasing him about it.

"I hear Jensen assigned you lead on a new case." Ben sat down at his desk across Adam's, who didn't look up from the papers or even acknowledge his partner's presence. "Hey, man, aren't you happy about it?"

"That's not it. This case is just... I have no leads yet, and I'm waiting for some more statements to come in from La Jolla."

Ben's denim blue eyes showed his confusion. "La Jolla?"

"Some sick bastard murdered a woman there last night after a festival. Due to the nature of the killing, the call came here, and Jensen handed it to me. Well, us, I guess. By the way, Jensen wants you to finish the paperwork from the Lee case."

Ben leaned back in his chair and let out a low sigh. "So, that answers my next question. Alright, finish filling me in on the La Jolla case first, then I'll get the Lee reports done." Adam began telling Ben about the dead woman and the waitress from the café. "So, what's the victim's name?"

"I don't know yet. I'm waiting on dentals to come back."

"Nothing from missing persons?"

"No, which means she probably hasn't been gone long enough for anyone to call in."

Just then, a voice interjected, "Actually, we do know," said Detective Lewis Randall. "The vic's name is Ashley Cairnes. She's twenty-two years old and lives on the opposite side of town. Her mother just reported her missing not even thirty minutes ago. According to Mrs. Cairnes, Ashley was supposed to call her Friday after work. When she didn't, her mother assumed she had been held up and would call her later. She said she'd called Ashley's phone repeatedly, but it always went to voicemail. She called Saturday to report her missing, but of course, that precinct had to tell her that she couldn't be declared missing until after forty-eight hours. She called again this morning despite that, and since you had that Jane Doe come in last night and an alert put out, that precinct sent it to us." Randall handed Adam a piece of paper. "We just ran her name through the DMV's database and got a picture of her driver's license."

"You're right, that's definitely her," said Adam, as he passed the printout over to Ben. "Have you already notified her family?"

"No, I wanted to wait and check with you two first since it's your case. Plus, I don't like breaking that news unless I'm sure." Adam and Ben nodded their heads in agreement. They had both made their share of those calls and it never got easier. "Do you want me to call the mother now?"

"Actually, if you could get me Mrs. Cairnes address, I'll go speak to her in person. Thanks, Randall."

"You got it." Detective Randall did an about face and headed off to his own desk.

Adam handed the crime scene photos over to Ben. "I've been staring these down all day—I need a pair of fresh eyes."

Ben began flipping through the photos. "Jesus, I see why we got the case. This guy completely removed her heart. Did you say that the waitress found the body?"

"She did more than that—she tripped over it and landed right beside it."

"Damn, I bet she had nightmares. She must have been scared out of her mind."

Adam winced.

"What did you do?" Ben asked. "I know that look, it's the one that means you did something wrong." Adam told Ben the conversation that he'd had with Danielle. "Man, you really know how to piss off women."

"You say that like I make it a regular habit or something."

"I'm just saying you can be a real asshole when you want to be. If I were you, I'd apologize to her before Lacey finds out."

He rolled his eyes at his partner. "Do you really have to tell your wife everything?"

"What can I say, I'm weak. She can tell when I hold something back, and she'll get it out of me eventually, so there's no use in fighting it." Ben chuckled and then went back to inspecting the photos. "Has the lab already completed a semen test?"

"Yes, and nothing came back."

"Really?" Ben said with surprise. "Given the way she was dressed, I would've assumed some sort of sexual assault."

"I know, me too." Adam was silent in thought for a moment when he remembered more. "I haven't even shown you the best part." He handed a photo of the origami heart note—that was now sitting down in evidence—to Ben. "It seems we have a poet on our hands. Apparently, this is a game to him."

Ben read the short verse and then let out a small sigh. "Serials, they all think they're natural born writers. The good thing about them is that they usually leave a pattern to follow. The bad thing is that they're totally screwed up in the head."

"The bad thing is that it's never just one body. So, you think he's going to be a serial, too?"

Ben nodded his head in agreement. "So, what does he mean, 'until I've won?' Won what?"

"I have no fucking clue. All I know is that he's not going to quit until he gets it, and right now, we have no way to stop him."

Both men were silent for a moment, thinking to themselves. Adam, still frustrated, was getting stir-crazy. He needed to do something besides sit at his desk. "I'll be back later. I have to go for a drive."

Whenever he hit a wall, he got in his car and drove around the city to clear his head. Sometimes he felt caged at the station, so getting outside made him feel free, and that usually got the brain flowing again.

Over the next few hours, things finally seemed like they were back to normal. Danielle's routine was just like any other day, and the whole ordeal was just a hazy nightmare. Carrie had decided she was going to spend the day with her and provide any assistance she might need. She wanted to support her friend, even though Danielle insisted she was fine. Danielle may put on a brave face and a hard shell, but inside, she had a lot of emotions roiling around inside, and Carrie knew that eventually, she would have her breaking moment.

It was close to one p.m. by the time the morning and lunch crowds slowed down. Danielle was crouched behind the counter taking an inventory of what was left of her treats and what needed to be whipped up for the dinner and dessert crowds. Carrie was standing by the register chattering away, but she didn't have Danielle's full attention. Every once in a while, she would throw in an 'mmhmm' and a 'yep' just so Carrie would think she was listening.

As the bell on the door jingled, Carrie stopped talking completely, and then whispered, "Hot damn!" Danielle, clipboard and pencil in hand, kept focusing on the task before her, brain still on autopilot for conversation. "Dani, you have to check out this fox."

"Carrie, I'm busy right now. You saw him first, so go ahead."

"Dani, you haven't even looked at him. I'm telling you, you want to see this."

Slightly exasperated, she turned her eyes to her friend. "Care, I'm not interested."

"Excuse me, miss, I'm looking for the owner of this establishment."

It was a man's voice, and Danielle could tell immediately that he was charming. The sound was rich and smooth with a hint of flirtation. That voice probably buckled a few knees on a daily basis.

"I'm with the San Diego Police Department, and I have a few questions."

Carrie made a quick assessment and already decided who this sexy cop was. "Ah, you must be Detective Burke. I've heard so much about you." She moved away from her post to shake his hand, giving a sly smile and looking him over. The detective raised an eyebrow and gave a grin of his own.

"Is that so?"

Danielle rose from behind the counter. Carrie was right, it was Detective *Jerk*. Oh, how she did not want to see him right now. He was nothing but a reminder of last night, and that was something she didn't want to remember. But today, she wanted to assert her power. There was no way she was ever going to let herself be vulnerable around him again.

"It's a pleasure to meet you, Miss..." the detective trailed off, waiting for her to insert her name.

"Carolina Marossi, but you can call me Carrie."

―――

So, this was Carolina Marossi. Adam had heard of her through reputation. With his precinct being out of her district, she had never taken cases of theirs, but nonetheless, she was fairly well known for her win-rate within the pool of assistant D.A.s.

"Carrie, do you know who the owner is?" Adam asked almost seductively. Just then his attention turned to the caramel-haired beauty. She had just popped up from behind the counter, giving him déjà vu.

"You're looking at her," Danielle said with a touch of coldness.

Adam's sweet waitress was in fact the owner of Mon Félicité. He wished he hadn't been such a dick to her last night, but there was nothing that could be done about it now. All he could do was continue the investigation and be as professional as possible.

"Do you have a minute?" Rather than answer, Danielle lightly huffed in clear annoyance.

Adam pulled out a chair for her to sit in at a table in the far corner. He didn't want their conversation to be open for all to hear. As Danielle stepped around the counter and into the dining area, Adam couldn't help but stare. The purple dress she was wearing was hugging her curves and turning him on. Last night, he had thought she was beautiful even when she was covered in dirt and blood, but now that she was cleaned up, she was absolutely gorgeous.

He remained standing until she sat down, showing at least some sign of gentility. He needed to get his thoughts under control so he could get this second interview done.

"I see that you made it home okay." He was trying to start out the conversation with some pleasantries before they got down to business.

"Yes, I did. Officer Mendez followed your orders to your exact specifications. Although, I must say that I'm surprised you had him flatter me so much. He was very sweet, and even though I resented you for sending him after me, I was grateful that he was there. So, I guess I should thank you."

Adam nearly broke the pencil that he was holding in half. Had Mendez really hit on her? What the hell did that guy think he was doing? Adam definitely did not give him those orders. Maybe his waitress was just goading him. He supposed it might have been her way of striking back at him for his previous attitude, but she couldn't have been sure whether it would work on him. Of course, it did, and that pissed him off.

"You're welcome, Miss Walsh. I do what I can." He quickly flashed a smile to show her that her comment didn't bother him... which was a lie. "Now, I know we went over a lot last night, but I wanted to talk to you again after you'd had some sleep. Many times, witnesses will remember new things each time they're questioned. After the trauma wears off, the mind allows you to recall things better than you would have been able to at the time."

Danielle raised her eyebrow at him and asked, "Just how many times do you plan to interrogate me, Detective?"

"As many as necessary, Miss Walsh, and don't think of it as interrogating. I'm merely getting your story." Adam hadn't planned on getting any more statements from her, yet he just told her he'd get as many as he wanted.

They went through the entire line of events all over again. He asked her to describe everything to the tiniest detail, in case it contained a clue. After the first forty-five minutes, Danielle leaned back in her chair, looking tired.

"Would you like some tea or coffee? I have to take a break and get some caffeine flowing through me." When she leaned back, he noticed that her dress moved just a fraction higher above her knee, which caused him to lose all concentration.

"I'm sorry, what?"

"I asked if you wanted something."

Did he want something? Yeah, he wanted something, and it was making him crazy.

"I'll take some coffee, please."

Danielle sat there waiting, but he was silent. "Is there a certain way you'd like it, Detective?" If she only knew the thoughts that her questions were generating in his mind, she'd probably slap him good and hard. Adam just needed her to get out of the chair and walk away so he could breathe for a minute. She was driving him to distraction, and he needed to focus on something else.

"It doesn't matter, however you want to fix it." His words came out rushed, and he pretended to be too focused on his notes to look at her.

The Harvester

Danielle left the table and went behind the counter to start working on their drinks.

———

She sighed as she reached the back where the coffee and cappuccino machines were. Her head was starting to pound, and she wasn't sure if it was due to recalling last night's events or having the detective around. Danielle began making her orange spiced tea and was so lost in thought that she jumped when Nina walked up to her.

"I'm sorry, I didn't mean to scare you. I was just checking to see what orders on the inventory I need to tell Ralph to make." Nina had a sweet apologetic smile on her face. She reminded Danielle of a dainty fairy out of *Fantasia* or something. She seemed to have the quality of innocence you'd find in a fairytale story, and Danielle thought she'd go great in a Disney movie.

"Ugh, dammit, I totally forgot to finish. I started the checklist and then *he* walked in…"

"It's okay, I can wrap it up really quickly and help Ralph get started. I've been wanting to help more in the kitchen anyway." Nina started to beam.

"Anytime you want to learn from Ralph or me, just say so. I'm more than happy to teach you."

Nina's grin got bigger and she was practically jumping up and down with excitement.

"And thank you for finishing this—I can use all the help I can get today."

"No problem, boss, and by the way," she began whispering, "if he was sitting that close to *me*, I'd be forgetful, too." And just like that, she whirled around and started her chore before Danielle could protest.

She took a minute and studied the detective as he sat at the table, pouring over his notes. Since it was Sunday, he was wearing a tee shirt that was just tight enough to accentuate his muscles. She hadn't noticed how big his arms were last night, although checking out his body wasn't at the forefront of her mind. Still, looking at them now, they seemed hard to miss. His butt didn't look too bad either in those jeans.

Danielle giggled to herself, *Good lord, woman, get over it. An ass is an ass... no matter how nice his butt may be*.

Chapter Eight

Danielle had just put the food and drinks on the table when, without warning, the door flew open and in rushed a man—a tall, very handsome man. His baby blue eyes scanned the room in search of someone.

"Danielle! Oh, thank God," he said with such relief it was almost believable. *Great*, she thought sarcastically, *this was just what I needed*. He didn't wait for an invitation to approach, but instead took long strides across the dining area to reach her. He also didn't wait for permission to touch her.

"I heard what happened, but the details were so limited... I had to see for myself that you were okay." He gripped Danielle's arms in a way that suggested far too much familiarity, and those blue eyes roamed over her looking for, what she could only guess, were any injuries.

His face wore a mask of worry and concern, and Danielle fought hard not to roll her eyes at him. She also fought the urge to rip his hands off her. She settled for subtly stepping back out of his grasp. Unlike Carrie, Danielle cared about making a scene in front of others, and she refused to do it, especially not for him.

Trevor Whitman was great-looking and had the ego to back it up. His sandy blond hair was always meticulously coiffed without a single strand out of place. His facial features were sharp and streamlined. Danielle classified him as a pretty boy, almost too attractive. Even the most beautiful women would still feel insecure of their ability to keep him at their side.

He was tall and lean and extremely fit, perhaps obsessively so. He worked on sculpting his muscles every morning after waking and every evening before bed—no matter what. When he was finished, he would marvel at himself in the mirror for at least five minutes before being satisfied with his reflection.

Yes, Trevor Whitman was the epitome of a narcissist. Danielle wasn't sure if he was that talented at hiding it or if she had been too busy to notice. It had been nearly a year since she had met Trevor and three months since she had dumped him.

Adam took one look at the guy who had just rushed into the café and had him sized up. He was wearing dark brown loafers with a matching belt for his fitted khaki trousers and a casual baby blue button up, sporting the recognizable emblem of a man on a horse. His ensemble screamed 'tool.' He might as well have jumped right out of the Ralph Lauren catalogue. Adam doubted he wore anything but designer labels. Hell, he probably had a subscription to *Forbes* magazine because odds were that he worked in the financial district.

His hair was immaculately in place, and if Adam had to guess, he probably spent fifteen minutes on it just to make it so. Adam spent all of fifteen seconds on his hair. All he required was a quick run through of his fingers. Done.

He tried not to notice the way he touched Danielle and his dislike of it. The guy was probably her boyfriend. A woman as beautiful as her wasn't typically single, and pretty boy over there probably gave her anything and everything she asked for. The more Adam read her body language and facial expressions, though, the more he questioned the nature of their relationship. She had stepped out of the man's embrace, the movement suggesting a discord between the two, and Adam became more assured in his speculations from her icy response.

"Now that you have seen for yourself, you can be on your way." The peacock didn't seem the least bit deterred.

Adam leaned toward Carrie, who had been sitting at the table with them, and whispered, "Who is that?"

Carrie kept her irritated, if not tempestuous gaze on the man. "No one of any importance."

The Harvester

"Can we talk? Please, Danielle, you know how much I care about you." Trevor stepped forward, closing the distance she had previously put between them, and placed his hand on her shoulder. Still not wanting to make a scene, Danielle decided not to shrug him off.

"Trevor," she said, lowering her voice, so that nosy eavesdroppers couldn't hear, 'you know there is nothing to talk about. What's done is done. You need to accept that."

He exhaled sharply from his nose as he delivered her a tight-lipped smile, a smile that did not reach his eyes. It was as though he was holding back some less than pleasant words. He was clearly frustrated with her, but he said nothing of it. Instead, he shoved his hands in his pockets and said, "I'm glad you're okay." He sharply pivoted and walked out the door.

The nerve he had, Danielle thought, *coming in here, pretending to give a damn*. Had she been alone right then, she would have screamed out her anger. But she wasn't. Detective *Jerk* was still here. Ugh, this day could not end fast enough. Her attention went back to the other pain in her ass.

"That friend of yours..." he started to say.

"Isn't relevant to your case," she said, as she took her seat again, "so perhaps we should stick to questions that are."

It seemed to Adam that neither of the women were going to tell him.

"Fair enough," he said with a nod. He would humor her for now. If he decided that that information was pertinent at a later date, she *would* tell him.

The plate she'd placed in front of him was filled with an enormous turkey sandwich and the cup had something other than coffee steaming up. He looked at her inquisitively. "What's this?"

"Taste it first. I think you'll like it." Danielle had a confident smile on her face as she watched Adam hold the cup up to his lips.

"It's not poisoned, is it?" he joked, as he prepared to take a sip.

"Damn," she said, snapping her fingers, "I knew I forgot something."

He gave her a smile before he took a drink. He gave no reaction, and Danielle was a little too interested in what he thought.

"It's a chai latte. I know you said coffee, but I thought this might soothe you better. The flavor is relaxing in its own way, but you're still getting your caffeine. Plus, the bit of sweetness compliments the savory notes of the sandwich."

"I look like I need soothing?" His tone was easy, but his eyes were hard.

"You seem wound a little tight. So, do you like it?"

"It'll do," Adam said, placing the cup back onto the table.

―――

It'll do?! Danielle couldn't believe the nerve of this guy. Here she was being cooperative—again—and even feeding him, and all he can say is *'It'll do?'* Danielle had to tell herself to calm down and get through this. Carrie would have immediately, and pointedly, informed him of his insult and what he could do with it—and was probably dying to—but she knew not to fight Danielle's battles. As soon as this was over, she'd be one step closer to never having to see him again.

After he devoured the sandwich that she didn't bother to ask his thoughts on and the latte that *would do*, Danielle was ready to get him out. Everything was pretty much finished at this point, and she was just waiting for him to leave. Danielle left him at the table and headed to the back to get herself another cup of tea. She was hoping that her absence would give him the hint that they were finished here.

As if he'd read her mind, he got up from the table, but instead of walking to the door, he walked over to the counter. Nina was at the register, grinning like a schoolgirl. Danielle couldn't blame her since he was smiling back at her with dimples that could melt hearts.

He laid down some money on the counter, winked at Nina, and headed for the door. Danielle was outraged. This was the final slap in the face that she could take, and he was going to get his. She grabbed the money off the counter before Nina had time to put it into the till and stormed after him. His hand had made it to the door handle when she exploded.

"What the hell is this?" She had the twenty-dollar bill clutched in her hand, practically shaking it at him.

"It's money for the food." It was too much money.

"I don't need your money. When I give something, I don't expect anything in return. If I was going to charge you for the meal, you'd have known it."

"Don't you give people food in exchange for money? That's typically what an eatery does." Now he was deliberately goading her. Danielle's eyes narrowed sharply on the detective.

"In the past twenty-four hours, I've been insulted more times than in my entire life. I have done everything that you've asked of me. I've answered all of your questions, put up with your badgering and rude remarks, and even accommodated you, and you can't even say thank you." Her chest was heaving as she breathed. She'd gotten herself so worked up that she hadn't taken a breath in her rant. He was silent for a moment and then took a step toward her, putting them close enough together to make her heart race for a whole new reason. She could feel herself panicking inside. What was he doing? Why was he standing so close?

He touched the side of her arm, giving her goosebumps, and leaned a little closer. He softly smiled as his eyes searched around in hers. "Thank you, Miss Walsh." His voice was deep and husky, the sound seducing her ears. Danielle fought the urge to let her knees buckle, though she wasn't sure how long she could hold out. He turned for the door again and walked out. She hated that he'd had that kind of effect on her. He must have noticed because she was positive that she could see his smug grin through the back of his head.

When she turned around, Carrie and Nina were both standing in front of her with giant smiles on their faces. "Oh, cut it out, you two are ridiculous. You look like giddy schoolgirls."

"I think he has a thing for you." Carrie looked at Nina, and they both synchronized a head nod.

Danielle scoffed. "No way, not possible. Weren't you listening to him? He's rude, arrogant, selfish, and an all-around jackass. What on earth would make you think that he has a thing for me?"

"Well, for someone who is such a 'rude son of bitch,' he seemed pretty damn pleased at the knowledge that he had been the topic of conversation."

"It's called an ego, Care."

"Boss, it's like on the playground when a boy pushes a girl. He does it because he likes her. He can't let it show, though, because it would allow for the possibility of rejection, so instead he lashes out in the opposite way to keep his feelings safe and pride in-tact." Nina was working on a psychology degree.

"This isn't elementary school, Nina—we're grown-ups."

Carrie tagged in again, "And tell me, Danielle, what men do you know who actually behave like mature adults?" As she was about to answer, Carrie rushed to add, "And you can't say your father or Ralph."

Crap, Danielle had nothing. Carrie was making it harder for her to argue.

"So, you're telling me that Detective *Jerk* is 'pulling my pigtails,'" Danielle gestured with air quotes, "because he has a crush on me?"

"Yep."

"Well, I'm not letting him pull on *anything*."

"Actually, I think he'd rather pull *off everything*." Then, Carrie added after a slight pause, "And I think you'd let him." As she turned around and headed off to get herself something to drink, Danielle stood in place, her eyes widening and her mouth dropping just a bit.

The Harvester

"Absolutely not, Carrie. I don't go for guys like him." She was going to battle this one out.

"You mean tall, gorgeous, sexy guys?"

"No, I mean conceited men who think they can get any woman they want. They go around winking and smiling, expecting panties to drop left and right. It's disgusting and a complete turn off." Her voice grew louder and more venomous with each sentence, and her hand gestures became wild. Jesus, she was acting like Carrie.

"Are you sure you're not describing someone else—maybe projecting him on Detective Burke?"

She rolled her eyes and scoffed. "Please."

"So, you're telling me that you don't find him attractive—not at all?" By this time, Carrie had seated herself at a table with some milk and cheesecake, patiently waiting for Danielle's response. Danielle began to wonder why she hadn't started eating—Carrie was never one to hesitate when it came to food. Once it was in front of her, she dove in.

"No, I don't think he's attractive. He has nice eyes, and that's about it," she lied.

Carrie picked up her fork and took a small bite of her cheesecake. "Eww," she said, as she made a gross face.

"What? Is there something wrong with it?" Danielle was sincerely concerned. She couldn't stand her food not tasting like perfection.

"Yes, it tastes like you're feeding me bullshit," Carrie said matter-of-factly, "and frankly, I don't much care for it."

How typically theatrical, Danielle thought. Carrie pushed the plate away from her and sat looking at Danielle, waiting. Even though Carrie was right, Danielle wasn't about to cave. She'd been pushed this far, and she didn't feel like losing. This was one of the fights Danielle was going to win no matter how much she had to lie to spite Carrie. Why was that woman always right?

"Truth is all I'm serving right now."

"I'm not finishing this until you confess," Carrie said with more sternness.

"Then, I guess you'll be needing a to-go box."

Nina stood off to the side, watching them argue through metaphors. To her, they were definitely the strangest debate methods she had ever witnessed.

Carrie suddenly smiled and laughed lightly, "Okay, sweetie, whatever you say." She walked over to her friend and gave her a hug, then waved goodbye as she went out the front door. Danielle hated when Carrie used her condescending voice with her reverse psychology crap. She stood there with her hands on her hips, glaring at the cheesecake.

"I'm just going to go put this in the fridge," Nina awkwardly laughed. "We both know she'll end up eating it." She tiptoed to the table and back like she was walking in the line of fire. Danielle didn't object and instead, let out a short huff. She had a restaurant to run, damn it, and she didn't have time to let Carrie or anyone else annoy her.

Chapter Nine

"That bitch," he hissed after the café door closed behind him. Trevor couldn't believe how ungrateful she was. He had come all the way down to her pitiful little restaurant to comfort her, and she had the nerve to send him away? What did he have to do to make her see that she needed him? He had half a mind to tell her how lucky she was that he was giving her any thought at all, but he didn't. He couldn't, not if he wanted her to ask him to come back. Some people might phrase it as to take him back. Just the thought left a foul taste in his mouth. He had never once uttered such repulsive words. He hadn't needed to.

Women didn't leave Trevor, he left them. They were the ones to plead with him to stay, not the other way around. Yet, here he was, pleading with Danielle... continuously. It disgusted him. He loved women, and they loved him. In fact, they loved him so much that they overlooked how he continued to love other women. He did who he wanted when he wanted, and when he was tired of screwing them, he moved on. Danielle had been the only exception. Her legs hadn't immediately uncrossed for him, which presented her as a refreshing challenge. She was much more guarded and didn't hang on to his every word. She wasn't besotted like the rest of them and clearly didn't understand the gift of his attention. The fact that he chose her to be the woman on his arm was quite the compliment, yet she seemed completely oblivious to it.

Danielle's beauty was worthy of his consideration, and her independence made her intriguing... for a while. Trevor was confident that she would crave him like oxygen, and he was delighted about seeing it happen, but she never did. Oh, she cared for him, but she wasn't in love with him, and it angered him. The game of possessing her undying devotion was getting tiresome, but Trevor couldn't seem to let it go. He had to win. Unfortunately, he got caught with his pants down—literally—and since Danielle wasn't another one of his obsessively infatuated lovers, she didn't turn a blind eye to his infidelity.

Then, the unthinkable happened—she broke up with him. *She* broke up with *him*. *Him!* No one had ever dumped Trevor Whitman—ever. All of that time wasted. No, she couldn't leave him. He would make her see.

Chapter Ten

God, he'd wanted to kiss her. She was so angry, spitting fire at him, and all he could think about was kissing her so deep she'd go mute. Adam was pretty sure just touching her arm had done the trick. It took all of his energy to turn around and walk away. After all, he did have some work to do. He was still at square one with no leads. He was definitely going to need help on this one. His partner was back in the city finishing the work that the captain had threatened Adam with. He and Ben were a team, and Adam needed his partner's brain since his didn't seem to be working right. He drove back to the station to meet up with him and form a game plan.

As he headed back into the city, Adam started thinking about the photos again. There was something there—a clue, even if the tiniest. He kept seeing Ashley Cairnes's lifeless body in his mind, the way she looked angelic if you discount her pain-stricken face.

"That's it!"

Adam came bursting through the station doors and went up to the fourth floor where homicide was located. Ben was still at his desk typing when Adam entered.

"Get the pictures," he said loudly.

Ben whipped his head up, startled, though he'd never admit to it. The urgency in Adam's voice got Ben moving, shuffling through papers for the photos.

"I take it your drive was successful?" Ben handed over the stack to Adam, whose stride was so fast, Ben thought he might actually tear up the floor.

Adam flipped through the photos, pulled out one, and slammed it on the desk. "Tell me what you see."

"Alright, the guessing game, my favorite," Ben said, as he leaned in to get a better look. He remained silent, studying the photo before he made any guesses. He could tell Adam was getting impatient. Just then, Adam stuck his thumb over the girl's face, covering it from view.

"What does she look like?"

Ben studied for another minute and then it hit him. "An angel."

"Exactly."

"What does it mean?"

"It means he has an actual motive as opposed to random murder. Is Jimmy here? I bet he could give us a good profile on this guy."

"I'll find out. By the way, the toxicology report came back. It was negative for Rohypnol. This guy is anything but typical. One thing the report does say is that there was alcohol in her system. The alcohol content in her blood stream was high, and Douglas said her stomach was filled."

"Does the report say what kind of alcohol?"

Ben raised an eyebrow and began flipping through the file. "Uh, let's see, it was some sort of wine, and it says there was enough residue on her lips and inside her mouth to do a comparison to what was in her stomach." He closed the report and set it back down onto the desk. "Do you think the wine means anything?"

"Maybe, maybe not," Adam said. "Let's see if Jimmy's here. I really want to get his thoughts."

"I'll call him up."

Adam sat down at his desk and read the coroner's report along with the autopsy pictures of the corpse. It was noted that there was faint bruising around the wrists and ankles where she had been bound with rope. She hadn't been tied up for very long, so the bruising was probably from the slight struggle she had been able to produce under her condition. A few moments later, Ben was off the phone. Apparently, Jimmy was out of town and wouldn't be back until tomorrow.

"Hey, it's already six o'clock. I think I'm going to head home. You're welcome to come over for dinner if you'd like."

Adam shook his head and smiled. "Nah, that's okay. I think I'll go get a beer or something. Besides, I know Lacey's dying to scold me, and I'd rather save that for another time."

"You're hoping she'll forget, aren't you?"

"Yep."

"Not a chance," Ben said, as he patted his partner on the back and left.

Instead of leaving the station, though, Adam decided to give a visit to Douglas, the medical examiner at the precinct. Maybe if he talked to him in person, it could make something connect. Luckily, Douglas was still there when Adam walked through the door of the morgue.

"Ah, Detective Burke, are you here about the girl?" Douglas asked, as the two men met to shake hands.

"Yes, I read your report, but I wanted to come down and see you."

"You're hoping that you can make sense of it all if we talk it out," Douglas stated rather than asked.

"How did you know?"

"You're not the only one, kid." Robert Douglas was in his early fifties, just barely old enough to be Adam's father. He and his wife didn't have any children of their own, and Adam wondered if that was why he referred to everyone younger than him as '*kid.*' "I'll go pull her out." The wheels squeaked as he rolled her to the middle of the room underneath the bright light that made her already colorless skin look even more devoid of pigment. "Okay, what would you like to know?"

"Just start from the top," Adam said, as he stood over Cairnes's body.

"As I put in the report, I swabbed for any semen, which is standard for female homicides, but it came back negative. I couldn't find any DNA other than her own. There were no fingerprints on the body, no hair follicles or epidermal tissue, absolutely nothing that I could use to run backgrounds in the criminal database."

"And that's assuming he is even in the system. I think he might be a first-time offender."

"Well, for a beginner, he did a damn good job not leaving any physical evidence behind. I found small fibers of rope on the skin of her wrists and ankles, which suggests she was bound, but the markings are so faint, I almost didn't notice. This leads me to believe that she didn't put up much of a fight. There was no blunt force trauma on the skull, so to me, that rules out the possibility of being knocked unconscious."

"So, you think she was drugged."

"Yes, but my toxicology tests were all negative for the standard drugs."

"What does that mean, then?"

"It means I'll have to run more tests, and since I have no idea what I'm looking for..."

"How much time?" Adam was searching Douglas's face, praying he'd give Adam the answer he was hoping for.

"Honestly, Burke, I'm not sure. It could be a few days or a few weeks, there's just no real way to tell."

Shit. That was definitely not the answer he wanted.

"Okay, well, what about the weapon he used? Have you been able to narrow down the possibilities?"

"The only thing I can tell you is that it's probably some sort of saw. I was able to immediately rule out types of knife blades because of the kerf marks that were left on the bones and the fact that the hole is completely symmetrical. There's no way anyone could freehand a perfect circle like this." Adam studied the fatal wound in Cairnes's chest, associating a visual to go along with the information Douglas had just given him. With no physical evidence or strong suspect leads, this case was going to be a bitch to solve.

———

Adam threw his keys on the end table as he entered his apartment, and he immediately headed to the refrigerator and grabbed a beer. The sound of the pressure release and the bottle cap hitting the counter was soothing to his ears. This case was frustrating him. He still felt like he was floundering in the water with nowhere to go.

He flopped down onto the couch and turned on the TV. He began channel surfing, looking for something, anything to take his mind off the case. Who was he kidding? To take his mind off Danielle Walsh and off those big, beautiful golden topaz and green eyes a man could get lost in, those pouty, kissable lips that were just begging to be nibbled, and Jesus, those full breasts, curvy hips, and tight—yet round—butt that dared him to grope every inch. His attraction to her was undeniable, and Adam was pretty sure she was attracted to him, too. He could tell by the way she'd looked at him when he'd touched her. She'd looked startled, as if something intimate were happening. Oh yes, he'd noticed the sudden dilation of her eyes and subtle quickening of her breath. When he'd touched her, his intent had been to get her all flustered—which he'd succeeded—but not fluster himself as well.

Adam took a few sips of his beer and kept clicking the channel buttons on the remote control. Scrolling through the guide blindly, Adam's mind began to wander. Images of Danielle kept creeping into his brain, all showcasing different, alluring traits of hers.

Her hair was probably as silky and soft as it looked. He started picturing himself running his hands all through her locks, sensually combing each tendril. Then, the picture in his mind zoomed out, showing the two of them embracing each other. Her long legs were wrapped around him, gently squeezing. He didn't know where they were, but did it matter?

A soft light created a luminescent glow to her skin, drawing his undivided attention to her unclothed body. She was magnificent. His hands were still in her hair as she leaned her head back, closing her eyes. He wanted to touch her so badly, but he couldn't seem to remove his hands from the caramel silk running between his fingers. He was just going to have to use his lips instead. He kissed her neck softly, slowly working his way down her throat to her collar bone.

Adam drew his arms closer together, pulling Danielle's body up against him. Her breasts pressed into his chest, and her nipples hardened. The feel of them mashed into his pecks was extremely arousing. She was so warm as her hands slid along his arms and across his back. He could feel his own temperature rising. In fact, he could feel the blood pulsing through his veins and down to his shaft that was growing taller by the second. Those sun-kissed thighs squeezed tighter, causing Danielle's feminine folds to kiss his cock.

On a ragged sigh, Adam cursed, "Ah... fuck."

That sweet, little spot was hot on his skin, and Adam shuddered. His breathing intensified, and he dipped his head down to pull a breast into his mouth. He heard a soft catch in her own breath as he swirled his tongue around the perked nipple and suckled her. Using his teeth, he nipped the pearled, rosy bud, rolling it over and over.

Without notice, Adam's hands were freed from the invisible shackles that were hindering his exploration, and he immediately knew where to put them. He slid one down her throat—following the same path his mouth had taken—and between her breasts, then made its way to the one that was being neglected. Her skin was as soft as corn starch and felt heavenly to his fingers as he palmed and massaged her.

Adam's other hand traversed down her back, tracing the length of Danielle's spine and filling his grasp with a round cheek. He explored the fullness of it and its curve as it became her thigh. Sliding his hand back around, Adam gently touched her sex from behind. A moan escaped Danielle, telling him her approval of his touch. He slid his fingers up and down her folds, teasing her and causing her to drench him. She was so damn wet. Delicate fingers fisted his hair, yanking his mouth away from Danielle's breast, forcing him to look into her hypnotic, wanton eyes. She crushed her lips to his, swallowing him in an intense kiss, her tongue swirling with his. She was overwhelming him. Her moans into his mouth were about to set him off, and he wanted nothing more than to plunge inside her and feel her sex strangle his cock. Adam grabbed Danielle's hips to lift her onto him...

"But wait, there's more!" the announcer of the infomercial yelled at him. Adam nearly shot up off the couch. He had been so lost in the erotic fantasy, that the host's obnoxiously cheesy, over-the-top shout had startled him back to reality. Adam had sat through a five-minute commercial and couldn't even recall the product they were selling.

"Shit," he said, as he shook his head. He needed to get her out of his mind.

Danielle locked the door and kicked off her shoes. It had been a long day, and all she wanted to do was sleep. Ralph had dropped her off after they closed the café for the evening. He had insisted, and Danielle wasn't about to argue. She viewed herself as a big girl who could handle things on her own, but she wasn't going to turn down Ralph's offer. The truth was it made her feel a little safer, though there was nothing to indicate that she was in any danger. Still, she felt better anyway.

She decided she'd hop in the shower before she went to bed. She was hoping that the hot water would melt away the stress and stiffness she still had in her muscles. As Danielle began to disrobe, her telephone rang. She was the only person at the ripe old age of twenty-eight that she knew of who still believed in landlines. She had grown up with them, and she found it practical to have both options, in case the other failed. She went over to the nightstand where the phone was sitting and reached out to answer it.

"Hello?"

There was no one on the line. *It must have been a wrong number*, she thought. She hung the receiver up and walked back to the bathroom. Again, the phone rang. This time, when Danielle answered, there was a delay before the caller hung up. Now she was getting annoyed. Who still prank-called people? Everyone has caller ID these days, so it would seem pointless to waste time with it., but the name came up as unknown.

Once more, Danielle headed to the shower to wind down. The phone rang a third time. "Alright, that's it." She stormed to her bedside this time and yanked up the receiver as she shouted, "HELLO?! What do you want?" How did they even get her number? It wasn't listed.

"Dani, should I call back tomorrow?" She looked down at the caller id. It was her mother this time. Danielle's stance eased a bit.

"Oh, Mom. I'm sorry I yelled."

"Is everything okay?"

"Yes, I just had someone prank call me a second ago, and it got me agitated. What's up?"

"Well, I just thought I'd check in on you and see how you were doing. Your dad is still a little edgy about the murder being so close to you. And after all, it was just last night."

Thanks for the reminder, Mom, she thought.

"I know, but tell Dad everything's fine. The police are working on it, and I know it has nothing to do with the café. It was some sicko who happened to choose my alley, that's all."

"Do something for me, honey. I know you're a self-reliant woman, but please don't be so much so that you let pride cloud your judgment. I'm not saying that you need anyone to help you. I'm just saying you should accept the offer if it's given."

"Mom—"

"Danielle, everyone needs help sometimes. Now, promise me." Her mother's voice became very stern.

"I promise."

"Well, we love you, and we expect to see you next weekend, okay?"

"Yes, ma'am," Danielle said, smiling.

"Bye, honey."

"Bye, love you, too."

Finally, she was able to take her shower. She turned the water on slightly hotter than usual for her newly accrued aches and pains, and as she waited for the temperature to climb, she assessed herself bare in the mirror. Cuts and scrapes were already dulling to softer shades of pink, and purple bruises were fading to green on the outer edges, but still Danielle scowled. Her body looked like artwork created by a mischievous toddler who had gotten ahold of some Crayola markers and gone to town scribbling hideous mixtures of colors in giant splotches all over her skin. She might as well be one of those beat up, bruised peaches at the market that everyone avoided. On the plus side, they looked worse than they felt. Those huge indigo polka dots had lost a considerable amount of tenderness, and Danielle could only pray that

The Harvester

the grotesque color palette marring her—which looked like a violet rendition of Starry Night—would diminish just as quickly.

She caught sight of her scowl in the mirror and rolled her eyes in self-mock. There wasn't much she could do about the marks, and they would go away eventually, so it did no good to waste time forming frown lines, which *would* be permanent. Besides, it's not like she was trying to impress anyone, right? *Right*? An image flashed in her mind—Detective *Jerk*. As quickly as it had entered, she pushed it right back out.

"Ugh, absolutely not," she said and shook her head. Danielle returned her focus to the much-anticipated shower as she stepped over and into the porcelain tub. At that moment, she couldn't care less about her water bill. Ah, it felt good. Moving under the spray, she took her time letting every strand of hair and every inch of skin be drenched in the warmth.

She began working her hair into a lather with the shampoo, and the continuous motion became hypnotic, causing her to zone out. After double of the normal amount of time, she turned and tipped her head back to let the suds wash away. As the water and shampoo mixture ran down her body, she started to imagine the sexy detective's hands taking its place, warm and comforting, gently caressing her skin, like he'd done today at the café. It was the slightest touch, but it had sent shivers down inside her.

He was standing behind her with his body molding to hers, slowly kissing her jawbone down the length of her neck and to the top of her shoulder. His lips left sensual burns on her skin with every kiss he planted. The burns felt like an intense heat warming her, making its way to her core, which was already beginning to ache with need. The detective's arousal became very apparent as it rose and pressed itself in the crevice between her round cheeks. Its presence, alone, was a cruel tease. All of the possibilities of where it could venture and how close it stood was enough to make Danielle weep.

Those strong hands of his began massaging her breasts, rolling her pink nipples between his fingers, making them as hard as his erection.

A deep inhale of steamy air drew in and forcefully out of her mouth. Then, Danielle's heartbeat started picking up speed as one of the detective's hands slid down her flat belly and cupped her between her thighs. A finger swirled through her small patch of soft curls and began dancing with her clit.

Oh, holy shit.

Just the contact on its own threatened to make her come. The pleasure he was evoking had her legs quivering with every twirl and flick of his finger. A shaky arm braced against the cool, white tiled wall, while the other reached behind and found the nape of his neck, clinging for support.

She could hear him breathing in her ear, yet he said nothing. She said nothing. This wasn't about talking or emotions, it was simply and purely about actions and pleasure. Pleasure that was intensifying deep in her and quickly rising to the surface. One finger, then two slid inside her folds, and Danielle found out how wet she really was—and it had nothing to do with the water. Her slick arousal ran down with every exploratory turn and thrust of his fingers inside her. Her hand no longer clung to the back of the detective's neck, but instead kneaded it roughly, mimicking the timing of his movements inside her.

Her erotic senses were on overload. She had one breast being palmed and tweaked, two masculine digits swimming around inside her, a thumb torturing her clit, and a solid, thick shaft molding into her backside. The slightest movement of his hips—that's all it would take—and he could be pushing inside her.

Oh... God!

Danielle's panting was heavy, and she was surprised she was still standing, although in a moment she wouldn't be. It was getting harder for her to breathe, and she wasn't sure if it was because of the steam rapidly filling her lungs with each ragged breath or the detective's delectable fondling—most definitely both. Danielle could feel the wave racing upon her. Sheer seconds away. An outstanding orgasm was about to rock her body into tremors. Almost there... Almost there...

Something strange happened. The luscious heat of the detective's hands, lips, body, embrace... were leaving. No. No, no, no, no! What was going on? His physical touch was leaving, abandoning her. No hard, masculine body working her over, seducing her. Why? The confusion and frustration were about to cause tears to spring from Danielle's eyes. Someone was taking her pleasure from her. Someone was trying to hurt her, hurt her with—coldness? Maybe freeze her to death? She opened her eyes to find the source, only to realize that she had spent so much time fantasizing, that she'd used up all of the hot water.

She let out a small growl. She hated cold showers, and she wasn't even close to being finished. Hell, she still had to condition. She was going to have to wrap it up before she froze.

She became a member of a race car pit crew, she was going so fast. She rinsed, soaped, and shaved in under three minutes. She hurriedly grabbed for a towel to prevent goosebumps, then dried off and slipped into an oversized cotton t-shirt. When she crawled into bed, she stared up at her ceiling for a minute or so. Why had she started thinking about him? She didn't *want* to think about him.

As she reached across to turn out the lamp, she muttered, "Damn Carrie."

Chapter Eleven

Danielle woke up feeling quite refreshed. It was six a.m., and she was ready to go. The café didn't open until seven, and Danielle wanted to dive into her work. It only took her fifteen minutes to get ready since she had showered the night before, and she would make herself some breakfast at the café while she prepared for the day. She drove herself today, wanting to get back to her regular routine as quickly as possible. It wasn't that she didn't appreciate her friends' help, but she hated being a burden.

Ralph hadn't arrived yet, and Nina had the day off for school since Danielle didn't want to overwork her. For the days Nina was at school, Danielle took over waitressing and hosting duties. Most people gave their order at the counter, but they also had the option of sitting down with a menu if they were new or having a hard time deciding on their meal. In those cases, Nina or Danielle would make sure that the customers weren't neglected and that they were well accommodated. She knew how important customer satisfaction was, and she'd be damned if anyone ever left unhappy.

She was in the kitchen when a voice startled her. "Hey, Danielle."

"Oh, hey, Neil—you scared me a little. I wasn't expecting anyone."

"I'm sorry, the last thing I want to do right now is scare you. I'm sure you're still pretty shook up about the other night."

"A little, I guess. I'm trying not to think about it."

"Do the police have any idea who did it?"

"I'm not sure. The detective in charge questioned me a few times—"

"A few times? Is he the same one who interviewed the rest of the square yesterday?"

"Yes. He's kind of a jerk."

"Do you need me to set him straight?" Neil asked with a playful smile.

She smiled back. "No, but thanks for the offer. Besides, I can't have you getting arrested, or who else would I get my produce from?"

"Aw, how sweet. I do love loyal customers." They both shared a laugh. "Look, I just came by today to see how you were doing. I figured yesterday you probably had enough people in your face, and I wanted to wait, give you time to breathe. Do you need a hug or something girly like that?"

His face showed his discomfort with the idea. She could see that he felt uncomfortable with touching on what he thought might be an emotional topic for her, too. It surprised her that he wasn't the soothing type.

"Ha, ha," she genuinely laughed, "I'm not that fragile."

"Yeah, I didn't think so. Well, I've got to head back over to the shop. Let me know if there's anything you need. You know I'm always happy to help."

"Of course, I appreciate that."

———

The week went by with no news from the police or Detective *Jerk*. Danielle visited her parents for the weekend while Ralph ran things at Mon Félicité. It was a wonderful escape, and even her siblings, Kyle and Alaina, showed up for the get-together.

"Sweetie, it's so good to have you home." Her mom hugged her from behind as she sat at the kitchen table. She was preparing dinner for the family. Danielle had offered to cook, but her mother refused. She wanted to give her daughter a break since all she did was cook, day in and day out.

"It's good to have all of you kids home." Her father smiled as he gave Kyle a firm pat on the shoulder. Seeing everyone gathered around the table was making Danielle nostalgic. She felt like she had traveled back in time and was a kid again with no worries in the world. This was exactly what she needed. For the first time, she didn't think about the murder or the café or anyone. She was completely focused on her family.

"Alaina, when's the next time the dance company goes on tour?" Alaina was part of a successful dance troupe that put on performances in San Diego, as well as toured other parts of the nation. Danielle had once been involved with dance, but cooking soon became her world. Alaina had stuck with it and now was an accomplished principal dancer.

"We head out next week. We're doing this round of concerts mainly in the southwest. We're going to L.A. first, then up to Salt Lake City. After that, we'll hit Denver, Dallas, San Antonio, Albuquerque, Phoenix, then back home."

"Damn, how long are you going to be gone?" Kyle looked exhausted just from listening to her schedule.

"About two months. We'll spend a week in each city, that way we don't get worn out too quickly. Plus, the last week will act as a small vacation before we start working on our next show." Danielle was glad her sister was going to be gone for a while. Her big sister instincts were kicking in, and she didn't want Alaina to be worried and lose focus. She was being silly, though—there was absolutely nothing to be worried about. Still…

"Dani," Kyle said, as he snapped his fingers at her.

She realized she had missed part of the conversation. "Sorry, what did you say?"

"How's the business?" he repeated.

"It's fine, why?"

"I was just wondering if the whole *thing*, as Mom likes to call it, brought down some of your profit?"

"Kyle!" Laurie yelled at him in a harsh whisper.

"What, are we just going to pretend that it never happened—never talk about it?"

"Yes, that's precisely what we're going to do. I don't want to hear another word about it."

"Seriously, Mom—"

"Kyle," their father spoke in the tone that he only used when he was dead serious. That's when the kids knew that they'd better behave or face the consequences.

The kitchen was silent for a moment, until the egg timer rang. Dinner was ready, and Danielle was famished. She hadn't eaten a whole lot the past few days, and her appetite seemed to be returning to normal. The Walsh family dug in and continued with their regular conversations, telling stories and cracking jokes, and spent the rest of the weekend laughing and playing games. Yep, this was exactly what she needed.

The week dragged on and on for Adam. Jensen was breathing down his neck, and the killer hadn't made any moves, which was odd, considering the analysis Jimmy Tharp, the department's criminal psychologist and profiler, had come up with Monday. He had looked at Adam's notes, studied the photos, and checked out the autopsy report.

"He's angry," Jimmy had said.

"Can you be more specific?"

"This murder was done out of hate. I'm not surprised one bit that he made sure this woman was conscious when he started killing her. I can tell you right now this guy is a sociopath with psychopathic tendencies. He's probably a narcissist, as well."

"What is he angry about?"

"At this point, I can't answer that, but I can shed some light on your angel theory. Good catch, by the way." Jimmy picked one of the pictures from the pile and laid it out for the two of them to view. "I believe you're right about the arms representing wings, because of the angle at which he arranged them and the curvature of the hands."

He knew it—Adam knew he had been right.

"Now, if you ignore the blood in her hair, you can see that it's fanning out, giving the impression that either she's floating or wind is blowing over her."

"It's the same with the skirt of the negligee. He's got it flowing outward from her legs," Adam said, as he drew an invisible outline on the photo with his finger.

"Exactly, he's made this woman look ethereal and heavenly—meant to be worshipped."

Adam looked at Jimmy, confused. "I don't understand, you said he did this with rage. Why would he pose her as a '*divine being*?' Angels are supposed to embody beauty and love and innocence."

Jimmy smiled and pointed a finger at him. "You've got it."

"Got what?" He was beginning to get frustrated. He wished Jimmy would just lay it all out there.

"Innocence, yes, but look at what he dressed her in, a revealing piece of lingerie."

"How do you know she wasn't already wearing that?"

"Trust me. I'd bet on it. You can tell by the fact that her gown is red. If she were a true angel, he'd have dressed her in white. That's the way painters and sculptors have depicted them throughout history. White is seen as a symbol of purity. Red, on the other hand, is a color of sin. The killer is telling us that this woman was sinful. Maybe he feels she was impersonating a heavenly being. And that's why, drum roll please…"

Adam scowled, giving Jimmy the signal to get on with it before he lost his temper.

"Okay, okay," Jimmy cleared his throat, "and that's why he removed her heart. For an impure creature to pose as an angel is absolute blasphemy in his mind. To him, she is evil for committing such a sin, and therefore, he can't allow her to have a heart—she has no right to it. This is how I'm interpreting it."

Adam couldn't believe the insanity. "Because, what, demons don't have hearts?" Adam's question was sarcastic and incredulous at the same time.

"He's dehumanizing her, justifying his reasons for doing this. This man has no remorse and no concern for human life."

He trusted Jimmy's analysis. He was rarely wrong about his profiles. It was amazing the insight and accuracy he could gather from such little evidence. It astonished Adam every time. He ran his hands over the top of his head, letting out a deep breath. "Fuck."

"Look, Burke, Jensen said this case was a high priority, so I'm on call for you until this guy is caught."

"Thanks, man. Let me know if you come up with anything else."

"Same."

Adam came back to the present. Since their conversation Monday, Jimmy hadn't uncovered anything new with the killer's psych profile, and Adam was not any closer to solving this case. Jimmy had guaranteed him that the killer would strike again, but *when* was the question. Adam knew if he didn't figure something out, someone else was going to die.

Chapter Twelve

Two weeks had passed now since the murder, and life was back to normal for Danielle. It was Sunday, and she was looking forward to tonight because it was movie night at the park. It had been so long since she and Carrie had gone to one, and she decided that it was time to resume the tradition. Luckily, Carrie didn't have any plans and was just as excited as she was.

Danielle had been working throughout the day on the goodies she was going to bring to the movie for them to eat. Tradition called for something salty and something sweet. Her savory snack would be her garlic butter and cheese biscuits, then some white grapes for a light flavor to cleanse their palates, and she would follow it all up with peanut butter and chocolate ganache bonbons. Danielle even had their thermoses full of milk chilling in the fridge.

Ralph took notice to her happy disposition. "You seem extra chipper today." She had been dancing around the kitchen, listening to music as she cooked her food. She truly believed her dishes came out better when she jammed in the back.

"Is there a reason why I shouldn't be?" she said, as she shuffled around the kitchen, snapping her fingers to the beat.

Ralph chuckled. "No, I suppose not. It was just an observation, not a critique. Believe me, I'm glad you're back to doing your goofy dances. I was actually starting to miss them." He made some fake sniffles and sad eyes as he teased her.

Danielle laughed. "You just wish you had moves as awesome as I do."

Ralph rolled his eyes and chuckled some more.

"I know I do."

Danielle stopped shaking her hips and turned toward the kitchen door. He was standing inside the doorway, arms folded across his chest, grinning from ear to ear. "Please, don't stop on my account," Detective *Jerk* said.

She could feel herself getting hot. She was embarrassed that he had been watching her dance and mad at the fact that she was embarrassed. It was her damn kitchen, and she could do whatever she wanted. Her kitchen was her sanctuary, and she was pissed as hell that he'd barged in without an invitation.

"Detective Burke, what a pleasant surprise," she said in a sarcastic monotone. "What can I do for you this time?"

"I was in the area and decided I was hungry for one of your delicious sandwiches."

She raised an eyebrow. "A sandwich?"

"Yes, a sandwich." His expression had changed to casual.

"And since you were in the neighborhood and were already going to order a sandwich, you might as well check up on me, right?"

"Maybe—we'll see."

"Well, how about you take a menu," she said, as she pushed him out the door, "and seat yourself right over there for me, okay?" Danielle was already back in the kitchen before she ended her last word. She watched him walk over to his table and sit down. She couldn't believe he actually went to the table she told him to. He was leaning back in his chair, one hand holding his menu and the other propped against his face, which was grinning again.

After a moment, he put down his menu and looked to the kitchen door. Danielle quickly turned away. By the look of it, he was ready to order, but she decided she'd make him wait. It went against her code of great service entirely, but this one time she would bend the rules.

Finally, after a good ten minutes, Danielle came out into the dining area and over to his table. He was waiting there patiently for her. *Ugh, what an ass.*

"Well, Detective Burke, what'll it be?" She stood next to him with her hands on her hips, hoping that she was making him as uncomfortable as he had done to her during their last encounter.

"Aren't you going to write this down?"

"Oh," she said playfully, "that won't be necessary."

"Okay." He pulled her down onto his lap, cupped her face with his hand, "then I'll have this." He moved in to kiss her...

Danielle was still standing over him at the table waiting for his order, only now she was breathing a bit heavier.

Adam's eyes narrowed at her. "Are you okay? You seem a little winded."

"Yes, I'm perfectly fine. So, what do you want?"

He stared at her for another second, then gave his order, "I'll have the Monte Cristo sandwich."

"It'll take me fifteen minutes to make. Are you sure you want to wait that long?"

"I don't have anywhere I need to be, so I'd be more than happy to wait for one of your sandwiches."

What was he doing? Was he being extra complimentary toward her to make up for insulting her food the last time? *Ugh, what an ASS!*

———

Fifteen minutes later, as promised, Danielle came to his table with his sandwich. It was piled high with turkey and ham, and the cheese was melting all down the fried bread and onto the plate. She had dusted the powdered sugar generously over the top and had given him a large side of raspberry jam. Adam's mouth was watering. After she set the plate down, she didn't walk away. He knew she was waiting for him to taste it.

He picked up one of the monstrous halves, dipped it in the jam, and took a huge bite. Dear God, this had to be the best sandwich he'd ever eaten. As he chewed, she put down a glass of water in front of him. He reached for it the second it hit the table. He took a couple of gulps and set the glass back down, then looked up to see her smiling smugly back at him.

Before he could even compliment her, she said, "I know," then began to walk away from his table. She knew how good her food was, and he was feeling ashamed for not acknowledging that previously. Instead, he'd been an ungrateful jerk. "Oh, and don't forget to eat your pickle intermittently. It balances out the richness."

Adam didn't waste any time with his lunch. When he'd finished, she came over to take away his plate. Scooting out the chair opposite to him with his foot, he said, "Sit down with me." When she hesitated, he said, "Come on, I promise I'll behave." He gave her a boyish grin as she reluctantly sat down.

"Is this the part where you check up on me?"

Adam decided not to answer her question. "How are you?"

"I'm great, how about you?" Her voice was perky and bright. If she was having a hard time, she definitely didn't want him to know it.

"I'm fine, thank you."

After an awkward moment of silence, she said, "Well, it's been lovely chatting with you, but I really do have some work to get done." There was the perkiness again.

Before she could stand up, Adam put his hand on top of hers. "Have you been getting any strange or threatening letters?" She looked shocked, clearly not expecting him to be so direct. He had decided not to beat around the bush and just go ahead and ask.

"No... Not really."

He cocked his head slightly. "What do you mean, not really?"

"I mean that for the most part, everything has been normal."

"For the most part?"

"Yes."

He was starting to get exasperated. "Danielle, tell me." Her eyes dilated ever so slightly in response when he said her name. He hadn't asked permission to address her informally, but it sounded so good to his ears.

"It's nothing. Someone prank called me the other night."

"When?"

"Two weeks ago—Sunday night."

"The night after the murder? What did they say to you?" Adam could hear the concern growing in his voice.

Danielle must have, too, because she was looking at him oddly. "They didn't say anything. The first time—"

"There was more than one?" His hand, still on hers, began to tighten.

"Yes, two. When I answered the first time, the line was dead."

"And the second?"

"The caller stayed on the line for a moment and then hung up."

He sharply exhaled and released her hand, sitting back in his chair. He hadn't realized that he had leaned into the table. "I want to look at your cell phone records. Maybe we can trace the owner of the number."

"They didn't call my cell phone." Danielle continued before Adam could look any more confused. "It was my landline."

"You have a *landline*? How old are you, Grandma?" He hadn't intended to tease her, but it just slipped out.

"Detective, you know perfectly well how old I am. Besides, you're no spring chicken, either."

"Is that so?"

"That *is* so. You have to at *least* be thirty-two." Adam might've been offended at her intentional jab... if she wasn't so damn cute.

"Well, I hate to break it to you, sweetheart, but I'm also twenty-eight." He gave her a boyish grin when she looked disappointed about her inaccuracy. He needed to get back on track, though. Bantering with Danielle wasn't what he should be doing. "Do you at least have a caller ID box to go with your rotary phone?"

"Rotary? Now who's old, Grandpa?" She had him there. Knowing the term for something so obsolete was definitely revealing. "And yes, I do, but the calls came up as 'unknown,' so it didn't display a number."

Damn it. Another dead end. "What's your phone number?" He sighed when she raised a questioning brow at him. "I want to see if there's any way to do some sort of reverse trace."

She continued to look skeptical.

"Sweetheart, if I wanted your number for *other* reasons, I'd already have it. Trust me."

The Harvester

Danielle practically fumed at his *confidence*. She would probably call it arrogance. *Get back on track.*

"You should have told me about this sooner."

"Why?"

She knew damn well why. The question was why was she being so stubborn?

"Because what if that was him? He's still out there. You do realize that, don't you?"

She stood from her chair, seemingly defensive. "I promise you, Detective Burke, it was nothing."

She walked away, and Adam quickly followed. "I'm not trying to scare you—"

"Good, because you're not."

"But you should be more logical." He was about to follow her into the kitchen again when Danielle stopped and turned to face him. He was expecting to see her boring holes into his head with her eyes, but instead, she smiled.

"You're absolutely right, silly me. I'll be super careful the next time I answer the phone, I promise."

Now *he* was trying not to glare at *her*. She was purposefully being a smart ass. "If you think a murder outside your café and mysterious phone calls are a coincidence, then you're fooling yourself."

She took a deep breath, then grabbed his arm and escorted him to the door. Evidently, he'd pissed her off again.

"Look…" When she reached for the handle, Adam gently took hold of her wrist to stop her. "I wasn't trying to insult you, but—"

She exhaled a soft sigh. "Detective, I appreciate your concern, honestly, I do, but I'm fine. I just want to move on from it."

He saw the genuineness in those amber-green eyes and let her open the door, releasing his hold on her. She pulled the door open and leaned back to let him pass by, but instead, he stopped directly in front of her. He could see her pulse quickening in her neck. Standing that close, he could smell her. She smelled sweet, like vanilla, and it was making him hungry… in more ways than one.

"Will you do something for me?" he asked.
She sighed. "What is it?"
"Don't let your pride make you careless."
Her eyes widened in reaction to his words.

Chapter Thirteen

Everyone was gathering around the park for the movie. This week's showing was *Funny Face*. Carrie and Danielle both loved Audrey Hepburn. She was always stunning, no matter what style she was sporting. They had agreed that she was the only woman who could have bangs that short and still look beautiful. Not to mention, she was wonderful to watch. She made you believe that she *was* the character she was portraying. Everything from sweet and innocent to sassy and carefree, you believed her.

"Hey, Dani, look," Carrie said, as she tiptoed forward, "no one's taken our spot." Carrie was having some issues taking normal sized steps in her shoes. She was wearing tall wedge sandals, which she usually didn't have a problem with, but the ground at the park was more uneven, causing her to wobble here and there.

Everyone in the park, including them, was wearing shorts and t-shirts. Even though it was autumn, it was still plenty warm outside. Like a ripple effect, blankets flew through the air as people settled down in their spots. Danielle and Carrie always sat under the big tree, where they had more space to themselves. The two of them were notorious for talking during these movies, primarily because they'd already seen them at least a hundred times. They'd quote lines, eat and talk with their mouths full, and laugh their heads off at different things.

"What time does the movie start?" Carrie asked, as she positioned their own blanket.

"Seven-thirty, so we have ten minutes to kill." Danielle felt uncomfortable using that expression now. The girls sat down and started unpacking the picnic basket.

"So," Carrie said, as she took a bite of her biscuit, "anything interesting happen today?" Danielle knew she was trying to act nonchalant, but it was obvious she was digging for something, so she decided she'd play along.

"No, not that I can recall."

"Hey, do you smell that?" Carrie started looking around and sniffing the air.

"No, smell what?"

"I think I smell fire, oh, no wait, it's your pants."

Danielle laughed as she rolled her eyes. "Did Ralph call you? I swear he's as bad as Nina."

"Okay, so quit torturing me, what happened when Detective Sexy stopped by?"

"'Detective Sexy?'"

"Hey, it's better than your nickname for him." Danielle recapped the conversation that she and Detective Burke had, although she left out the fantasy part. She wasn't ready to admit that Carrie might be right. "Oh my God," Carrie laughed.

Danielle looked at her waiting to be let in on the joke.

"Seriously, Danielle, are you that dense?"

"What are you talking about?"

"He wasn't *in the neighborhood*," Carrie said with her air quotes, "or doing some *follow up*."

"I know he wasn't *in the neighborhood*, but he was definitely there to follow up. He asked me specifically about threatening letters, which means he probably knows something and is keeping it from me."

"He probably doesn't have enough to tell you yet."

Danielle just shook her head and started picking out her own food.

"Anyway, he showed up today because he needed an excuse to see you." When Danielle didn't respond, Carrie added, "And you're glad, too."

She snapped her head up, "No, quite the opposite—he has done nothing but frustrate me."

"Yeah, sexually." Carrie added jokingly, "Hey, is that why you've been so irritable?"

"Shut up and eat." Danielle was scowling at Carrie, who was giggling her butt off.

After an hour and a half of singing, dancing, and lovely notions of 'happily ever after,' the end credits were rolling, and the audience was dispersing. Danielle and Carrie packed up their things and headed to the car. Danielle had gone home before the movie, so that she could change clothes, and then she and Carrie picked up the food at the café on their way to the park.

Once they had pulled up in front of Danielle's building, Carrie put her Audi in park and turned to Danielle. "I didn't want to say anything earlier, since I'd ruffled your feathers, but I agree with Detective Burke."

"Agree about what?"

"You really should have told someone about those calls, and I know you don't think they were a big deal, but the chances that someone prank called you the day after—"

"I know, I know."

"And you also know I'm a worrier, so just be careful, okay?"

"Everyone seems to be telling me that lately. I promise my guard is up," Danielle said, holding up her hand in the Girl Scouts honor sign.

"Okay, now give me a hug so I can go home before I get emotional."

The two of them laughed and said goodbye. Carrie waved as she drove away, and Danielle headed inside to her apartment. As she was entering her door, she heard everyone's voices playing in her mind. She wasn't being careless, but she didn't want to overreact. Danielle washed her face and got into bed. Catching some Z's would be the best way to block everyone out of her head.

Chapter Fourteen

He marveled at himself in all of his naked glory, his most recent conquest laying sated in his bed, oblivious to his self-worship. He smiled at his reflection as he flexed various muscle groups, feeling himself over with his hands for proof of what he saw, of what women felt when they touched him.

He was amazing, they said. He already knew that. Every time they raved about his physique, it made all of his hard effort worth it. It was no easy feat looking like a god, and they should be grateful for it. He deserved no less—no less than willing, if not begging, to be taken, whether it be the honor of making it to his sheets or bent over in the bathroom of whatever night club he chose to visit.

They all spread their legs for him, each one eager to receive him. They'd give him whatever he wanted, and he would fuck their brains out. It was a win-win. If they were a good lay, he'd continue to see them. If not, it was one and done. Yes, women loved him… except one. His frustration mounted as he simmered in the disbelief of what he considered inconceivable, and he couldn't let it go.

Landing her hadn't been easy. She was already guarded enough when she'd agreed to their unofficial first date. The night they'd met, he'd watched her from afar and decided based on his observation of her body language and attitude that she would present a challenge. His usual tactics probably would have worked on her friend, but she was going to require something different.

Normally, he would flash his best smile, shower her in compliments, and boast his status and accolades without concern for modesty. Not this woman. No way in hell would that work. He needed relaxed charm and hints of wavering confidence to portray the 'nice guy' persona that she was more likely to respond to. And it had worked… to a degree.

He'd had to keep up the shtick much longer than he'd originally anticipated. Even after they became a couple, it had taken over two months to get her under him. If she were anything less than gorgeous, she wouldn't have been worth the wait. He hadn't starved, though. He'd had plenty of other snacks to tide him over in the meantime... and during... and after. He had an appetite that he'd never before apologized for until her.

Her long hours had cancelled more than a few dates, but from time to time, she would drop by his office to bring him a treat, usually his favorite—chocolate chip cookies—to make up for it. After the last three missed dates, though, not once had she shown up. She was too busy, or so she'd led him to believe. How was he supposed to know that she'd wanted to surprise him? She wasn't a spontaneous person, so the fact that she had shown up unannounced caught him completely off guard.

She had brought his favorite cookies, however, neither of them had expected her to walk in and catch him stealing cookies from someone else's jar, half naked on his desk. The pastry box hurled toward him, narrowly missing his head. It was amazing that he was able to dodge it and keep going. It almost ruined his orgasm. She'd already run out of the room, so why not finish? Waste not, want not.

If he hadn't already invested so much time into making her his, he would've walked away without so much as a backwards glance, but he wasn't finished with her. She still wasn't in love with him yet, which meant he didn't hold the power in the relationship. He *always* held the power.

At first, he tried reasoning with her, get her to see it his way, thinking he could explain how it was as much her fault as his, because relationships were a two-way street, and his needs weren't being met. They should both accept responsibility for their faults and move past it. She *didn't* see it his way.

He'd had no choice but to do the one thing he'd never done—apologize. To his utter shock, though, she didn't accept it. What else could she possibly want? Didn't she understand how incredibly big his gesture was? Evidently not.

Trevor's reflection was scowling back at him now, causing deep creases on his face, and he cursed Danielle for it.

―――

Rrring, rrring.

Danielle reached for her cell phone to turn off her alarm. Was it morning already? Her eyes were still heavy, and the room looked unusually dark.

Rrring, rrring.

It wasn't her alarm, she realized. It was set to a soothing song by *Air*. Danielle hated to be awoken by loud buzzers—they were too obnoxious. Her eyes were starting to adjust to the black in the room as she looked at her cell phone again. Four-thirty a.m.

Rrring, rrring.

It was now that she realized the ringing wasn't coming from her cell phone. Danielle's hands searched clumsily now, desperate to make the noise stop. Finally, she grabbed the receiver of her telephone. "Hello?" Her voice sounded groggy and confused. "Hello?" She thought she could hear someone breathing, but she couldn't be sure, then *click*. The line went dead.

Chapter Fifteen

The morning air was crisp and fresh, the sun coming up over the horizon. Patricia Hoffstedt and her dog, Trip, an enormous Great Dane, were taking their morning walk through the park. As a puppy, he would weave back and forth through Patricia's feet, causing her to trip over him constantly, thus earning him the peculiar name.

As they headed down their path, Trip stopped abruptly and sniffed the air, with Patricia almost toppling over him. Why did he stop? Patricia began to assess his condition but didn't see anything sticking out of his paws or anywhere else. *Hmm,* she thought, then *whoosh!* Trip shot off into a heavy run. She almost went flying into the dirt but had the good sense to let go of the leash.

The Great Dane was already out of sight. It was a good thing she was wearing her good running shoes. She began jogging ahead in the direction he had sprinted. She wasn't that concerned about Trip taking off. She had trained him well, and he was very mindful with the exception of this morning. She kept her pace, jogging down the dirt path that ran all through and around the park. In the distance, she could hear Trip barking loudly. She stopped running, took a few breaths, and put her fingers to her lips. When she whistled, she could hear the loud echo spread through the air, but Trip didn't come. Patricia blew another deafening whistle, but still nothing.

"Ugh, damn dog," she muttered, as she started running again. He definitely wasn't getting any Beggin' Strips later. Trip's barking got louder, and Patricia knew that she was getting closer. Finally, she saw him over by the big tree. What was he doing? He was just sitting there, staring at the tree, barking. She slowly walked over to him and crouched down.

"What's wrong with you, boy, huh? What are you fussing at, a squirrel?" Patricia patted her dog a few times when he started whimpering. "What?" Trip stood up on his hind legs, then dropped back down, barking more emphatically. Patricia stood up and walked around him to get a better look at the tree from the other side. When she looked up, she gasped, and then let out a blood-curdling scream.

Chapter Sixteen

The entire park was blocked off with yellow crime scene tape, denying access to anyone without a badge. Flashes of light were going off every two seconds from the Crime Scene Unit's cameras. The air wasn't chilly, but the sight of the gore in the tree made Adam shiver. He thought back to that phone call he'd received early this morning.

"Hello?" Adam had answered with sleep in his voice.

"Hey, man, are you awake?" It was Ben on the other end of the line.

"I am now, what's up?" Adam said, still groggy.

"We've got another one."

Adam shot up from his bed. "Who?" His words came out urgently. *Please don't let it be—*

"We don't know yet, but you should head over here as soon as you can."

Oh, thank God.

Ben had seen Danielle's picture from the café's website, so he'd have known if it was her. Adam startled himself with the words of prayer and gratitude that had sprung into his head. It seemed a bit extreme to be that anxious over a woman he barely knew.

"Okay, Detective, we're done with the pictures. The scene is all yours," said a woman from CSU.

"Thanks, how soon can I get prints of those on my desk?"

"It'll be at least an hour, maybe two."

Ben walked up to Adam and offered him a cup of coffee. This wasn't how he had expected to start the week. He accepted the hot drink and took a few sips before Ben started the breakdown. He had already been at the station when the call came in from the first responders about the body and the hysterical woman who had found it. The two men approached the body and looked at each other. Adam had worked a lot of homicides, but this one was, by far, the most creative and sick.

The killer had strung the poor woman's body up in the tree without losing his theme. Like Ashley Cairnes, this one was dressed in a long, red satin negligee, and her arms were spread into wings, which he'd fastened to the branches with rope. He'd, of course, removed her heart as well, and Adam could see the note sticking out of the cavity. He passed his coffee back to Ben, as he walked forward—putting on a pair of gloves—and then climbed up the small ladder to reach it.

"Another note?" Ben asked, as Adam unfolded the origami heart and read.

"Yes, although it's more like a love letter."

Ben's brows furrowed, "What does it say?"

"Here, see for yourself." Adam swapped the note for his coffee and walked a few paces away from the tree.

"'*Number two just won't do. She isn't you... so I must pursue.*' Who do you think he's talking about?"

"I'm not sure, so let's talk about what we *do* know. The victims are both women in their late twenties, blonde, and equal in height at about five-nine," Adam said.

"And, of course, we won't know until the autopsy comes back, but he probably drugged her, too," Ben added.

"But what else? We still can't prove that Cairnes was drugged. There has to be something else, a clue we're overlooking." Adam looked back up at the woman hanging in the tree. "Jesus, can someone get her down and get a body bag or a sheet or something?" He couldn't look at that image anymore. What was going on with him? He'd never been so squeamish before. Ben called over some people to cut down and bag the body. They already had all of the pictures they were going to need.

"Hey, are you alright? You've been acting strange lately."

"I'm fine, it's nothing," Adam replied in a tone that suggested Ben drop the subject.

The funeral home Adam's precinct used had arrived to pick up the body for transport to the medical examiner's office. Two men brought a gurney and bag with them to set the body on and pack up. They would be the ones to deliver the woman to Douglas, wherein he would get started on her autopsy and blood work.

Adam stood to the side and watched them cut her down and begin to bag. CSU began collecting the rope for evidence and had already bagged the killer's note. He studied harder, leaning close, as he scrutinized the lifeless body. There was something about her… Just like Ashley Cairnes… but what was it? Adam closed his eyes and sniffed. A scent lingered in the air around the victim, sweet and delicious like…

As they were about to zip the body bag, he stopped them. "Wait!" The two men—startled—looked at him and then stepped away. "Ben, call the station and have someone check the autopsy report from the first victim."

"Am I having them look for something in particular?"

"Yes, chemical compounds, specifically vanilla."

"Vanilla?" Ben asked with a bit of disbelief.

Adam hadn't made the connection before, but now looking at this Jane Doe and remembering the photos of Ashley Cairnes, the similarities were unmistakable. Both women had wavy blonde hair… just like Danielle's. They both had hazel eyes, they both had the same coloring, same height, same facial features… It was like he was staring down at *her* lifeless body. The thought was sickening him.

It was Danielle who the killer was really after. He wanted to scare and torture her, knowing that she was sure to see these murders in some form or fashion. But why the park? Did she come here often? The first murder was right outside the café, where Danielle was sure to notice, which also meant that the killer knew Danielle was inside that night and could have easily waited in the alley to kill her. Instead, he chose to kill other women. Women who looked exactly like her. It was like a twisted prelude to the main event.

Adam could feel his blood pressure starting to rise. This discovery also meant that he was going to have to tell Danielle the significance of her role in all of this and probably put her in protective custody. He was pretty sure that her being the primary motive and possibly next victim of the killer, he wouldn't have any problems getting her in. He was not looking forward to breaking the news, though. He wasn't sure how she was going to react to the whole thing.

Adam called Douglas immediately to inform him of the new body that was being sent his way. His second call was to Jimmy, the profiler, who was still on-call for the case. He told him about the second victim and the circumstances and asked him to look over the pictures of the new Jane Doe and compare them to Cairnes. He also let Jimmy in on his theory about Danielle being the center of the murders, told him that he could find a picture of her on Mon Félicité's website to examine with the other girls. Now, he had to go see Danielle.

* * *

Danielle had had a hard time falling asleep after that call. The breathing she heard through the phone had creeped her out, and she was ready to admit that it wasn't pranksters or coincidence. *Did* she have a stalker? Was it Trevor just going overboard? The number on the caller i.d. came up 'unknown' again. She dismissed the idea. Trevor did call her and text, but he had never taken it as far as to disguise his phone number. She had stopped answering and replying months ago. She had already said everything she'd needed to right after the break-up. There was nothing left to talk about, no matter what Trevor thought. Besides, he never called her landline. Probably because she had never given it to him.

Since she was wide awake, she got ready for the day and headed to work early. She was going to call Detective Burke later, at a more decent hour, and tell him about it. She had promised to be cautious and practical and to not let her pride haze her judgment.

As usual, once she arrived at Mon Félicité, she started preparing the morning pastries and breads. She had the coffee and cappuccino machines ready to go for the early customers and went ahead and made herself a big mugful. Even though she was fully awake, her body still felt tired. It was barely after seven when the first customers arrived, some of which were her regulars. The Jacksons, for example, came in every morning like clockwork. They were an older couple, already retired with nowhere to be, but they always came in at opening. They said they wanted to have first pick.

An hour had passed already, and Ralph was just making it in. When he made it back to the kitchen, he stopped just inside the door, "Good morning." He was looking at her oddly.

Danielle let out a small sigh. "Morning, Ralph."

"Are you okay? You look exhausted."

"I'm fine. I just lost a bit of sleep last night." She didn't feel like worrying any more people than she had to. Just then, the bell on the front door jingled, and to avoid any further conversation about her lethargy, she left the kitchen to greet the guest. She didn't normally run away from Ralph, but she wasn't the best liar, and if they remained on the subject, he might crack her.

With the kitchen door swinging behind her, she stopped short when she saw Detective Burke, and it smacked her in the rear. The force shoved her forward, and there was no real way to recover from it, so she kept walking. She might as well tell him about the call while he was here.

She met him at the counter. "Detective," she greeted, "I'm actually glad you're here."

He raised a dark brow at her, in question.

"I was going to call you later." Danielle lowered her voice to a whisper and leaned closer. "I got another call last night."

"What time?" His voice was serious.

"Well, technically, it was this morning, about four-thirty." She heard him sigh an expletive and knew there was something he wasn't telling her.

"We need to talk in private."

She noticed he was holding a file folder in one hand. He must have found some new information, after all.

"Do you have an office here?"

"Yes, it's through the kitchen, this way."

As they walked through the swinging door, he held it open and then guided her with his hand lightly on her back. His touch sent a shiver down her spine. Was he being a gentleman?

Danielle's office was small, but cozy. Aside from her desk, she had a few filing cabinets, some lamps, and a small sofa. She had spent many nights there, especially in the beginning when she was just opening the café, and the make-shift bed had really come in handy. It was plush, but still firm enough to get a decent night's sleep. Those times had been pretty hard and demanding.

Trying to start a business from the ground up didn't allow a whole lot of free time, and the café was the number one priority in her life. Luckily, it had taken off and was doing very well. Carrie said that Danielle couldn't use it as an excuse anymore for avoiding men, but she just didn't understand the pressure.

She had poured all of her money and energy into Mon Félicité and made many sacrifices, like putting relationships on the back burner, which, according to Trevor, was why Danielle couldn't place all of the blame on him for their break-up. At the end of the day, the café had been a higher priority than their relationship. His excuse had been neglect, but Danielle knew deep down that he would have done it no matter what. She was actually grateful that she'd discovered his true nature sooner rather than later. True, she hadn't been in love with Trevor, but it still hurt. To be betrayed by someone you thought you could trust… If she were to be honest with herself, she was still a little gun shy from the whole experience. The one exception she had made, and it had blown up in her face. Needless to say, relationships remained on that back burner.

She sat in her chair behind the desk while Adam remained standing. From where she was sitting, he looked so commanding in stature. His broad shoulders and chest boasted confidence. His deeply developed muscles displayed his strength. This man exuded power, masculinity, and sex appeal. She could feel herself staring a little too intently at him

The Harvester

and cut off her gaze. She cleared her throat. "Would you like to sit down? The sofa's pretty comfortable."

"Thank you, but I'm fine for now." Oh man, he *was* being a gentleman, which gave Danielle the impression that something must be very wrong.

"So, what do you need to speak to me about?" She was nervous to hear his answer. *Please let it be good news. Maybe they finally caught him.*

"We now know the motive behind these murders—"

"Murder*s*?"

"We found another woman this morning."

Okay, now she was getting freaked out. She felt her breath catch in her throat.

"Danielle, you're highly involved in this, and I'm going to have to show you things you won't want to see."

She wasn't sure why, but she started feeling defensive, as though she was being blamed. "How am I highly involved? I know absolutely nothing about this or what's going on. I didn't even know the first woman, and I probably don't know the second one." That sentence made her sick.

"Look, I know this is confusing, but I want to prepare you for what you're about to be told. I need you to be calm and focused, okay?"

She nodded her head hesitantly, as she eyed the folder in his hands. He opened the file folder and laid everything out on her desk. Danielle wanted to puke. She was so out of it that first night that she hadn't remembered the woman looking that way. She had been scared out of her mind and was just trying to run to safety. Looking at the photos now brought back all of the images from that night that she'd apparently repressed.

The detective started explaining all of the notes, including the toxicology and autopsy reports, as well as a psychological profile. He went over the killer's signatures and then dropped the biggest bomb on her. "These murders are about you."

"What?" she asked, incredulous.

"The killer has a clear obsession with you, which he has made evident in his choice of victims," he said, his words stunning her into silence. "If you look at them, you can see the similarities. Their hair is the same color of blonde and texture, their eyes are the same hazel, their height, their skin complexion..."

"No..." She lightly shook her head. She was swamped in disbelief. This couldn't be happening.

"All the same as you. He's gone as far as to make them smell like you. Add that to all of the physical likenesses... Danielle, they *are* you."

"*Stop!*" She didn't mean to snap at him, but she didn't want to hear anymore. She might as well have been looking at herself. Suddenly, the last part of his statement caught her attention. "What do you mean they smell like me?"

"Both women had traces of vanilla extract on them, noted here." He pointed to a line on the first victim's autopsy report. "I noticed the scent on the first victim, but it didn't mean anything to me at the time. When I smelled it on the second woman, though, that's when it all made sense."

She burst up out of her chair, "No. No, none of this makes any sense. It's completely sense*less* and evil and sick!" She was beginning to get worked up and remembered what he had asked of her, so she forced herself to breathe. "And how would you know I smell like vanilla?"

"It's hard to miss."

They'd only met on three different occasions, and he remembered how she smelled? She wasn't sure if she should find it flattering or creepy. Regardless, she felt herself blush. There was her answer.

"I know these pictures are hard to look at, but I need to know if there's anything, anything at all, that means something to you."

Danielle sat back down, reading over the love notes and inspecting each photo, trying to fight the nausea. When she came to the photos of the second woman, she felt her hands starting to shake. "I know... I know this place. Carrie and I watched a movie last night at the park. We sat under *that* tree. We always sit under that tree. Oh, Jesus, first the café, and now my place in the park. He's following me, isn't he?" She left her desk and started pacing around the room.

"It looks that way. Do you know anyone who might have a grudge against you?"

"No, no one," she replied, eyes focused on her steps, shaking her head continually.

"Are there any boyfriends I need to know about?"

That question made Danielle stop in her tracks and look at him. For some reason, the inquiry seemed too personal. Was she embarrassed to admit that she didn't have anyone special or that she was glad she didn't? She refused to accept either. She didn't have the time or desire to be in a relationship, and allowing the slightest ghost of a thought in her mind that she was happy to be available because of this man was outrageous. He may be sexy and gorgeous, but the idea of the two of them together was absolutely absurd.

"No, no boyfriends."

———

Adam felt relieved by her answer and mildly disturbed at the reaction of pleasure he got, knowing that she was single. "Good." Damn, he couldn't believe he had let that slip.

"Good?" she asked. He was lucky his head had been down, or she might've seen the panic in his expression.

"It's helpful in the elimination process," he said to cover his response. "What about any exes? Any past relationships that didn't end well?"

Danielle was quiet with hesitation, and her eyes now purposely looked away from him.

"Danielle? It's time for full disclosure. You can't hold anything back from me or else I can't stop him."

She released a heavy sigh. "About three months ago, I broke up with someone."

"How long was the relationship?" Adam was taking notes in his pad to be sure he didn't miss anything.

"A little over six months." She was choosing not to elaborate. If he had to ask her every miniscule question it took to get all of the answers, he would.

"And why did the relationship end?"

"I discovered monogamy wasn't in his vocabulary." He could hear the hurt underneath the vague answer. He kept his gaze cast down at the pad, so that she wouldn't see the anger that was rising.

"He sounds like an asshole."

"Yeah," she laughed humorlessly, "he told me it was my fault because I wasn't making enough time for him anymore, time for 'us.'"

Adam's head snapped up, eyes wide in disbelief. "Excuse me?"

"I suppose it was partly my fault."

"In what way, exactly?" Adam couldn't believe what he was hearing and was beginning to lose his composure.

"I let myself believe that he was different from all of the others. I should've known better."

"Stop," he commanded.

Danielle was slightly taken aback, finally looking him in the eyes.

"Do not, for one second, take any blame for him. There is no excuse for his behavior, and he is solely responsible for his own actions. So, let me guess, this prick was the same guy that was in here when I came to see you two weeks ago?"

"That would be the one. He seems to think he can win me back."

"How so?"

"He sends me flowers and gifts, telling me how much he misses me, and his voicemails and texts promise that I'm the only woman he wants. Occasionally, he'll show up unannounced to talk about 'us' or just pretend to run into me on accident."

The revelation alarmed Adam in more ways than one. "How long has this been going on?"

She stalled in giving her response. "Um... ever since we broke up."

Adam's temper was boiling. He stepped in close to hold her gaze. "So, he's been harassing you for three months? Danielle, tell me you have a restraining order against him."

She went quiet again.

"Are you kidding me?" he shouted, incredulous, as he took another step toward her. "Why the hell not?"

"First of all, stop yelling at me," she countered, "and second, a restraining order seemed a little extreme." She stood tall and stiff, defending the decisions she had made on the situation.

"A little extreme? He's been stalking you."

"Annoying me is more accurate. He hasn't done anything to scare me or harm me in any way. His ego is just bruised. He'll find a shiny, new toy or two and forget all about me. Besides, he can't possibly be obsessed with me."

"Why is that?"

Danielle answered him very matter-of-factly, "He's too obsessed with himself."

"Well, right now, he's my number one suspect."

"Don't be surprised if he has alibis for both nights. I have no doubt that you'll find at least one 'witness' to account for his whereabouts," she said resentfully.

"Regardless, we're going to put you into protective custody. You'll have someone with you at all times, that way if the killer makes a move for you, we'll know it."

"No."

"Danielle—"

"You are not locking me up in some safe house somewhere for God knows how long. I have a business to run and obligations, and I am not letting some maniac disrupt everything I've worked for."

"This is serious," Adam said with a scowl.

"I'm well aware of that." Her hands rested on her hips, taking on a defiant stance.

"Are you?"

Danielle glared at him. "I'm *not* going."

"Sweetheart, you don't have much of a choice," he said with a condescending tone and a smile to match.

"Like hell I don't. I know my rights, and you cannot force me to do this."

He had been hoping that she would be more cooperative about it, but it seemed as though she wasn't through fighting him. Her hands fisted tightly as she glowered at him.

"This isn't over, Detective," she spat, as she stormed past him to gather her purse and keys.

He let out a sigh. "Where are you going?"

"I'm going to go speak to your boss," she answered with venom.

"By all means, I'll drive you there myself," he said, smiling.

"Thank you, but that won't be necessary. I'm perfectly capable," she said, as she rifled through her purse.

Two full minutes passed. "Are you sure about that?"

Danielle didn't respond. She didn't even turn to glare at him. He figured she probably didn't want to see the smug grin on his face. Was it childish of him, sure, but she made it so easy to tease her. Adam had no doubt that she was cursing herself for being unable to produce her keys. After another two minutes ticked by, she had no choice but to give up. She grabbed her purse and shot him a look that dared him to say something as she made her way to the office door.

"After you," he said, moving out of her path. Danielle didn't say a word, just continued past him in a sour state. Adam watched her as he trailed behind and he was beginning to notice that anytime Danielle was angry, she swayed into her hips more forcefully when she walked, and he just couldn't help himself from looking. The curve of them was very pleasing to the eye.

Chapter Seventeen

When they arrived at the station, Danielle was still huffing and puffing. She had played the silent game with Adam on the drive over, stewing while he called the precinct to let the captain know to expect them, and as they entered the building, she still had that sexy sway in her steps, which apparently, he wasn't the only one who noticed. Many of his co-workers stopped mid-conversation to scope Danielle in full. He wanted to deck all of them.

As they walked through homicide, more men ogled, and Adam's glare, being as intense as it was, suggested every man in that room would do well to back off. There was one detective, in particular, however, who was notorious for being a ladies' man that didn't seem to pick up on the signal.

"Hello," he said with a sly smile, "you must be Miss Danielle Walsh." Mitch Corolla darted in front of them from his desk, looking at Danielle like a dog sniffing for a treat. "I'm Detective Corolla, but you can call me Mitch."

He took her hand as if to shake it, but instead held it up and kissed the top of it. "It's a pleasure to meet you, and I want you to know that I will assist you in any way that I can. Here's my card—you can reach me day or night for any needs you might have."

Adam was ready to smash his face in.

"Thank you, that's very kind." Danielle accepted the card and smiled.

Adam was dumbfounded—he couldn't believe she actually took this creep's number. He hoped that she was just being polite.

"It's not a problem at all," Corolla said, as he went to kiss her hand again.

Adam didn't give him the chance. He put his arm around Danielle's waist and began walking ahead, taking her with him and forcing

Corolla to let go. His agitation level was steadily rising. What the hell did that douche bag think he was doing, hitting on her like that? It was neither the time nor the place. To Adam, it would never be the time. That guy was shameless, and if Danielle wanted to, she could have him charged with sexual assault. He wouldn't mind if she did. It might teach Corolla to keep his hands—and lips—to himself. Then again, Adam scoffed to himself, she probably wouldn't. If she wouldn't take out a damn restraining order on a stalker, he doubted she would bother punishing a slime-ball like Corolla.

At last, they made it to Jensen's office. Adam closed the door behind them to keep others from listening in on what was none of their business. He pulled out a chair for Danielle at the desk and then went back to lean on the door, arms folded. He was still sour, but he knew once the captain talked to her he'd start feeling better.

"Hello, Miss Walsh, I'm Captain Jensen. I understand you wanted to speak with me. What exactly can I do for you?" The captain shook her hand and pulled off his glasses as he sat down at his desk. It seemed that he had attempted to organize the space a bit. Was it because they were having company?

"Yes, sir, I wanted to talk to you about Detective Burke," she said.

Adam could hear a bit of disdain in her voice when she said his name. She was sitting up tall and proper, which he assumed was her way of asserting her own dominance.

"What exactly is the issue?"

"He is challenging my civil rights, trying to force me into lockdown. I have a business to run with people depending on me, and I can't just drop everything. I refuse to be put into a safe house surrounded by bodyguards day and night and cutting myself off from the world."

Jensen focused on Danielle, silent for a moment. "And what would you like for me to do?"

"I ask that he be reprimanded and dismissed from authority for his behavior."

Jensen sighed and stood from his chair, "I'm afraid I can't do that, Miss Walsh. Your protection is our number one priority right now, aside from catching this lunatic. Being that you are the center of the killer's motivation, it would be laughable to just let you walk around exposed and vulnerable, knowing that you might very well be his next victim."

"Laughable?" Danielle was surprised by the captain's choice of words.

"You see, if the press found out about you and the manner in which you're involved, they would have a field day. I don't know if you've read the papers, but they've already dubbed him, the Harvester. If they knew that we just left you out in the open, without taking any measures for your safety, well, that would look really bad for the San Diego Police Department."

She was stunned by what she just heard. So, this was political? Fine, she'd go political all over their asses.

"And I wouldn't bother going to the mayor," said Jensen. "He, too, wants this guy to be captured and not have any more casualties."

She couldn't believe what she was hearing. She was in America, right? The land of the free? Captain Jensen was standing tall, his hands behind his back in a military-type stance, now asserting his own authority. "Miss Walsh, I encourage you to stop fighting and accept our help. It's for your own well-being. We just want to protect you."

"That's funny because it seems more about protecting yourselves."

"Miss Walsh, as police officers, we have taken an oath to protect and to serve. We protect the innocent, such as yourself, and serve justice to the criminals that would do harm. You of all people should know that publicity can make or break you. If the public were to lose faith in our ability to follow through with that oath, the trust would be gone. That would surely be the result if you were harmed or killed due to us not taking every precaution to care for your life."

She crossed her arms over her chest, almost pouting. Captain Jensen definitely had a way with words. It was hard to protest to such a compelling argument as eloquent and heroic as his.

"Fine, but I have demands." Jensen raised an eyebrow. "No safe house or bodyguard entourage, you must let me continue my work as normal."

"Agreed." Danielle smiled at her seeming victory. "Detective Burke will stay with you," the captain added.

"I'm sorry?" Danielle asked, unsure if she'd heard correctly.

"You have a new roommate, Miss Walsh."

She jumped up from her chair. "No, no, no, he's not living with me. He can surveil me from a car or something."

"My dear," Jensen's tone was much more fatherly and assertive now, "I believe I have been very accommodating in compromising with you, which if you ask anyone here is not something I do often. Pairing Detective Burke with you will allow me to have a pair of eyes on you at all times while still giving you your freedom." Jensen paused for a moment, and then a light bulb switched on in his expression. "Besides, I believe there could be another advantage to this. We know the killer is aware of you and where you go. Without a doubt, he knows where you live. If we pose Burke as your boyfriend—let's say a whirlwind romance—it may just draw the killer out." The captain seemed quite pleased with himself. "Yes, he'll become jealous and emotions cause carelessness."

Detective Burke pulled away from the wall after hearing Jensen's decision. "Captain, how am I supposed to work on the case if I'm under cover with her all day?"

"You can work on it from her apartment, when you're not out in public. Besides, Anderson will be assisting you from the station with some extra men." Danielle opened her mouth to protest, but Jensen cut her off, "And that's final. Ah, I'm glad we were all able to come to an agreement."

"Captain—"

"You wouldn't be questioning me again, would you, Burke?" Jensen stared hard at the detective, who decided to keep his mouth shut. "Well, you two kids have fun. Remember, whirlwind romance—make it look real." When neither one offered acknowledgement, he narrowed his gaze. "Got it?"

So, Danielle thought, *we've gone from Siberian isolation to using me as bait?* Jensen had insisted on her protection being of the utmost importance, yet now he was going to dangle her in front of the killer's nose, so to speak. She wondered if the captain recognized what a contradiction that was.

―――

Son of a bitch, Adam thought.

How was he going to live with her? He'd never lived with a woman before and especially not one that was off limits. He'd have to kiss her for show—which of course there were worse things—but when they were alone in her apartment, he'd have to remain professional. Hands off. He couldn't allow anything real to happen between them.

Jensen dismissed them, putting an end to the discussion. His attention was already needed somewhere else, and it was clear that his word was final. Adam escorted Danielle to his desk. Ben was at his own, looking over his copy of the case file. He quickly closed the folder, no doubt to conceal the gruesome photos from Danielle. Considerate, but unnecessary. She had already seen the photos back at the café with Adam.

"This is my partner, Detective Anderson."

"Ben. It's nice to finally meet you, Miss Walsh," Ben said, as he shook her hand and gave her a warm smile.

"Please, call me Danielle."

Adam cut the pleasantries short. "Did you get anything back about tracing those calls?"

"Yes, and it's a no-go. According to the phone company, it's called a 'trap and trace'. They can't trace an unknown number to a landline if there wasn't a trap in place, and even then, it's practically impossible. It would take a handful of extremely specific variables to come together, and it's never happened, hence why they said 'impossible.'"

Fuck. That would've been a vital lead. Now, he had to go follow up on a different one, one that he wasn't particularly looking forward to. It was time to pay a certain jerk-off a visit.

"Ben and I are going to run an errand."

Ben raised a brow in question, but didn't ask aloud. He must've known there was a reason why Adam wasn't revealing it and would fill him in on the way.

"Okay, then you can drop me off at the café on your way." She was apparently still bitter about their meeting with Jensen.

"No, you're staying here."

"What for?"

"Because outside of this station, you don't go anywhere without me."

"Then, let me come with you."

"Out of the question."

Danielle huffed her exasperation and perched her hands on her curvy hips. "Why?"

Adam didn't see a point in telling her that he was about to go interrogate her ex, and he certainly didn't want her anywhere near Trevor. She was going to stay put until he came back for her. "This is something I have to take care of first. I would feel better having you here, where you will have some protection until I get back." His gaze shifted to Corolla's desk, where the horn dog sat, practically salivating. Adam's eyes narrowed on him, causing Mitch enough discomfort to look away and get back to work. He wasn't particularly happy with leaving her in his presence, but should Jensen see him trying to fraternize with her, he would make sure Corolla was buried in paperwork.

Chapter Eighteen

Trevor Bryan Whitman was the epitome of self-entitlement. For some odd reason, he seemed to think he was above the law, which he had made evident when he'd directed Adam and Ben to schedule an appointment with the receptionist for their questioning. When Adam had informed him that they could "talk" in his office or down at the station, Trevor just laughed.

"Officers," Trevor responded, purposely demoting their titles of authority, "I'm extremely busy and really don't have time to entertain this. If you want a meeting with me, you need to see Becky about reserving something."

Adam followed Trevor's line of sight to the busty brunette sitting behind an oversized desk that he highly doubted she had any use for. Without a word, Adam strolled over to her, flashing her that charming smile of his. "You must be Becky," he said, as he shook her hand. "I hear that you're the woman I need." A pink blush overtook her face, and she let out a slight giggle. "I'm Detective Burke."

Still blushing and grinning from ear to ear, she asked, "What can I do for you?"

"Becky," he began, increasing the volume of his voice so that it would carry, "I need you to clear Mr. Whitman's schedule so that Detective Anderson and I can question his whereabouts at the time of the brutal murders of two young women." He asked the favor in the most polite and casual manner.

Becky's face dropped, her eyes wide and mouth agape. Her head whipped back to Trevor, who was now blustering.

"What the hell do you think you're doing?" he shouted.

"Making an appointment," Adam said very matter-of-factly. Trevor looked as if his head were going to explode, and Adam was sure he could see steam coming out of his ears.

"You can't just waltz in here and accuse me of murder."

"I haven't accused you of anything," Adam continued in his nonchalant manner. "Yet."

"Becky," Trevor said, trying to recover his cool, arrogant tone, "you will do no such thing." He then addressed Adam again, determined to win the pissing contest after being challenged on his own 'turf,' "I don't have to say a goddamn word to you." He folded his arms and puffed out his chest, trying to establish dominance again. It didn't work. Adam could see the fear he was trying to hide.

"Mr. Whitman, you can either chat with us here, or we can handle it in an interrogation room." Ben wasn't as tauntingly passive-aggressive as Adam. His tone was all business.

Adam smirked at Trevor, spinning his handcuffs around his finger. Trevor's eyes narrowed on both Adam and Ben before he stalked off to his office. He left the door open in silent acquiescence as an invitation for them to follow. Adam had been banking on him not catching their bluff and that they could only force him to come to the station if they had a warrant, which they didn't. They could only suggest it. Whether or not he was smart enough to determine the distinction was his own fault. Warrants weren't as easy to come by as the television shows made it seem. As long as they didn't arrest him under false pretenses, they weren't breaking any rules.

Trevor took his seat in his chocolate leather chair behind his high-priced mahogany desk, attempting to regain his composure of power. Adam and Ben chose not to sit in the small chairs reserved for the clients. It was clear that the size was strategically chosen to make Trevor seem larger and in control. He scowled at their decision to remain standing.

"So?" he asked in agitation.

"So," Adam began, "two women were murdered within the past two weeks. One was outside the café, Mon Félicité, and the other was at La Jolla Shores Park."

"And?" The jackass showed zero compassion for the slain women.

Adam couldn't believe Danielle had dated this guy. What could she have possibly seen in him? Money? Looks? He definitely had both. Adam shook the idea from his head. He felt deep down that she wasn't the type to be seduced by materialism. The dick probably lied to her about who and what he was.

"What the hell does that have to do with me?"

Adam ignored his question. "Where were you on the nights of Saturday, September sixth, and last night?"

Trevor snorted. "You think *I* killed those women? What's my motive?"

Ben opened the manila folder he had been holding and placed a photo of each victim in front of Trevor. His reaction to the photos was an uneasy surprise, which he quickly tried to mask.

"I can think of a motive." Adam pointed to the picture of Ashley Cairnes first. "Take a good look at her." Adam gave Trevor a minute to examine the photo. "Now, look at her," he instructed, pointing to the picture of victim number two, as Trevor spent less time on the second photo, clearly impatient. "Would you say that they look somewhat similar?"

Trevor huffed. "Maybe... somewhat."

Ben placed a picture of Danielle in front him. "Would you say that she, too, looks somewhat similar?" he asked, and Trevor's eyes widened with recognition.

"I would say she bears a striking resemblance," Adam answered.

"Uncanny," Ben agreed.

"And," Adam added, "I have it on good authority that you've been harassing this woman." He touched Danielle's picture markedly, as though to punctuate his statement.

Trevor jumped up from his chair. "She said I was harassing her?"

"Aren't you?"

"No!" Trevor shouted his denial.

"The long list of text messages, phone calls, and intentional run-ins would suggest otherwise."

Trevor finally dropped his act. He fumed, his face enraged. "I don't care what that bitch said. I'm not a fucking stalker, and I'm certainly not stalking her!"

"Here's that motive you asked for," Adam began. "You got caught with your dick out, so she dumped you. You couldn't handle it. You started calling and following her around. When she didn't take you back, you got pissed, obsessed. You decided to use that anger to punish her by murdering other women who look like her."

"WHAT?" Trevor was leaning over the desk, his hands slamming down, covering the photos. "You think I'm killing women because we split up?"

"Not because you split up—because she *dumped* you." Adam made sure to accentuate 'dumped'. He knew it would piss off Trevor and right then, and that's exactly what he felt like doing.

"This is ludicrous." Trevor shoved himself upright and away from the desk.

"People have killed for less."

"And," continued Ben, "with the nature of your relationship with Miss Walsh, both past and present..."

"It's not looking too good for you," Adam finished.

Trevor shook his head in adamant denial. "No. No, this is bullshit."

Adam shrugged his shoulders. "Then, where were you those nights?"

"None of your fucking business," Trevor snarled.

"We're making it our business," said Ben. "Where were you?"

Trevor's jaw clenched and he fisted his hands. He was holding something back. "I was at home," he said through tight lips.

"Was anyone with you who can corroborate that?"

Again, Trevor held back. Adam had a strong feeling that Danielle was right, and he'd probably had a woman underneath him, but why he wasn't forthcoming was odd. This guy seemed like the type to boast his exploits. Unless... she was an exploit that he couldn't boast.

"Well, maybe a holding cell will jog your memory." Adam moved to round the desk, continuing the bluff, handcuffs at the ready. Panic got the truth out of him.

"Kimberlee Vance... I was with Kimberlee Vance."

Adam and Ben looked at each other. "Vance? As in—"

"Yes," Trevor hissed.

The CEO of this particular brokerage firm was Richard Vance, Trevor's boss. The man was beyond wealthy, which no doubt helped his third wife see past the male pattern bald patch on the back of his head that his salt and pepper hair seemed to be running away from. His gut and cigar-stained teeth were sexy, as long as they came with cash, cards, and jewels. The twenty-four-year-old graduate from Gold-Digger University was as cliché as they came. Platinum blonde hair, big breasts, and tan, flawless skin. Bleach white smile, lips so glossy you could see your reflection, and the intellect of a gnat. The ideal arm candy and trophy wife for any man over the age of fifty, including Richard Vance.

Trevor was nowhere near fifty, but he was handsome and fit enough to make her stray, and Kimberlee was a tight body with a pretty face, a stacked chest, and, evidently, pliable legs. It was no wonder Trevor hadn't wanted to share that bit of information. Screwing the boss's wife wasn't something anyone would want to advertise.

Adam thought back to his conversation with Danielle. She had told him that Trevor had insisted she was the only woman for him, yet here he was, having to use a secret lover as an alibi. He scoffed. *Piece of shit.*

"We'll see if Mrs. Vance corroborates your alibi."

"You need to be discreet about this, am I clear?" Trevor said insistently to Ben, narrowing his eyes to near slits. *Still trying to be the big man in charge*, Adam thought. Neither of them acknowledged his demand.

"In the meantime," Adam picked up, "you aren't to leave town."

Trevor scoffed and rolled his eyes in response.

"And," Adam added with unmistakable menace, stepping so close to Trevor it caused him to back into his leather chair.

Trevor was tall, but Adam still had a few inches on him, and the fact that his overall bone structure and muscle mass dwarfed Trevor's, Adam used his larger size to intimidate him and end the debate on who was in charge. Trevor was certainly no match in physical strength, no matter how much he worked out. There simply wasn't enough of him.

"You are to never contact Danielle Walsh again. You will not call her. You will not text her. You will not drop by, and you sure as hell will not touch her... ever." He growled the last word harshly through his teeth. "You *will* stay away from her, and should I find out you went anywhere near her—that you so much as breathed her name—our next meeting will be very different." Adam's words dripped heavily with pure malice—an undeclared promise of pain should Trevor disobey. "Am *I* clear?"

Trevor swallowed a hard lump in his throat, a sign that he understood the silent threat perfectly well. He then gave an almost imperceptible nod of acknowledgement, no doubt inciting complete unadulterated rancor down to his core. He had turned out the beta. Though despite the unfavorable outcome, he still had enough bravery to express his vehement disdain for Adam through the glower of his baby blue eyes. Adam, every bit the alpha, held his gaze for another minute, cementing his dominance over the asshole while Ben collected the contents of the folder.

The two of them walked out of Trevor's office without a word, leaving him to silently fume. As they began to pass Becky's desk, she stopped them.

"Um, excuse me, Detective Burke?"

"Yes?"

She stood from her desk and came around to stand close to Adam. She smiled and bit her bottom lip. "Here's my number." She had written it down on the back of one of Trevor's business cards, and Adam noticed that her cleavage was more prominent than it had been before.

"In case you have any questions or need something... in particular. I'd be happy to help." She arched a brow to articulate the insinuation of sex. Adam absolutely would not pursue—his rule still in play. Besides, Becky offered no temptation for him. Sure, she was attractive. Adam had a feeling that it had been a requirement for her to have earned her 'position,' which just happened to be outside Trevor's office, no doubt in plain view. He also had no doubt that Trevor had put her in many different positions, maybe even over that unnecessary desk. Yes, she was easy on the eyes, but there was only one woman that tested his resolve, and Becky didn't stand a chance at measuring up.

"Thank you," Adam said, as he took the card. He gave her no flirtatious smile, no suggestion of accepting her offer. He did not want to encourage her by telling her he would keep it in mind or that he really appreciated it. Becky didn't seem the least bit deterred, though. She probably didn't get turned down very often, Adam thought.

He and Ben continued their exit of the brokerage firm, more than happy to leave the slime-filled building behind them.

"You're not going to make me have to tell you to calm down, are you?" Ben asked, pulling at Adam's attention.

"What are you talking about?"

"Back there, you came damn close to issuing a legitimate threat to Whitman, and right now, you look ready to kill, which I'm going to go out on a limb and say Whitman again." Ben was right, but Adam wasn't going to say as much.

"I'm fine... don't worry about it," Adam said automatically. Yes, he had been ready to kill Trevor Whitman the second he had referred to Danielle as *'that bitch.'* He'd already wanted to maim him when Danielle told him about Trevor's cheating earlier today. Hell, even before that, when Trevor had dared to put his hands on her at the café. Adam hadn't liked that at all.

Five minutes ago, though? Oh, Adam had been far past dislike. A rage had been boiling inside him. The restraint it had taken not to reach over the desk and slam Trevor's face into it had been beyond difficult. Gathering the strength to fight the urge to break that pretty boy face with his fist—the sheer willpower—was nearly impossible. Adam had half a mind to go back and do it, too. The better part of him knew what the consequences would be if he did, though. It would quite possibly land him with a suspension and most definitely a lawsuit and charges for assault.

"Yeah, okay," Ben said with a light chuckle. "Whatever you say."

Something must have happened on that errand, Danielle thought, because Detective *Jerk* had returned to the station in an even fouler mood than he'd left in. Now that her own irritated state had just increased, she wasn't inclined to ask about his, and she doubted he would have told her if she had. From what she had gathered thus far, he wasn't the openly communicative type. She would probably have to waterboard him just to find out his favorite color. The thought of his torture over something so trivial made her chuckle.

"What?" he asked.

Danielle didn't know he had been paying any attention to her. He had barely spoken a word since he and Ben walked back in. In fact, he'd damn near ignored her completely, which she thought was rude. This man was such a contradiction. His attitude said one thing, but his eyes said another. Though he was being silent and aloof, she almost thought she had seen relief on his face when he had spotted her. Relief to see she was exactly where he'd left her maybe? That relief had turned into razor sharp, darted glances around the room—particularly in the direction of Mitch Corolla's desk—as he hoofed it straight to her. Mitch was currently out of the station, and something told Danielle that it was lucky for him.

It hadn't escaped her attention earlier when Detective Burke had displayed a sort of possessiveness over her at the slimy, barely-understated advancements of Corolla. His hand around her waist, pulling her away with him had said as much. She didn't want to acknowledge the butterflies his touch had caused low in her stomach or that she'd liked the idea of that possessiveness. She could also be completely wrong and overanalyzing it, she realized.

Not long after the two detectives had left, Corolla made attempts again to engage her in conversation, which she had in no way been in the mood for. It wasn't just because she was still pouting over the sudden—and forced—change in her life, but rather that the man tirelessly making suggestive innuendos was creeping her out. If Danielle could describe Mitch Corolla in one word, it would be *greasy*. He oozed it with every word that came out of his mouth and coated her in a thick film that seemed it would be nearly impossible to wash off. Danielle would definitely need another shower tonight.

"It's nothing," she said with a hint of a smile still curving her lips, thinking about the torture.

Detective Burke raised a brow in disbelief, but he didn't push. He gathered up his copies of the case files and his laptop before they headed out.

"I'll call you tonight with an update," said Ben.

He nodded. "Sounds good."

"Danielle, it was nice to meet you," he said, as he shook her hand, "and don't worry. You're in good hands with this guy." He delivered a heavy pat on his partner's shoulder with a wide grin, like he knew something she didn't.

"It was nice meeting you, too. You're *probably* right."

Ben let out a small laugh at her comment. Detective *Jerk* didn't seem to think she was very funny, though. He whipped his head to look at her. Surprise was in his expression at her gall to make such a jab. He turned to glare at Ben when he heard the sound of his snicker.

"C'mon," was all he said. She must have struck a nerve, but at the moment, she couldn't seem to make herself care. He continued to scowl as they exited the department and didn't let up until they got to his car. What was his problem? Was he always like this? Was this all because of her comment? *What a baby,* Danielle thought.

Probably? Adam thought. She sure knew how to kick a man in the balls. He was going to have to let it go, though, and quickly. Pretty soon, he was going to have to pretend to be in love with her, and it wouldn't do for him to be ornery. He needed to lift his mood, but that was easier said than done when every man in the room was appreciating Danielle's figure again as they made their way to the doors. He had no claim to her, so it was absurd for him to be feeling so territorial, so bothered by their lingering glances. Regardless, his face kept its dark look.

Chapter Nineteen

Danielle made him stop by the café first after they'd left the precinct to tell Ralph that she was taking the day off, but that she would be back tomorrow. There were some things she needed… like her keys. Since she wasn't in a rush this time to defy anyone, she took her time searching her office. She whispered prayers as she scoured the floor, the couch, and her desk. She rummaged a second time in the top desk drawer, as if they might appear out of sheer will. Her fingers knocked something across the drawer that made a familiar jingling sound.

"Oh, thank God!" she said. She didn't remember putting them in her desk, but her thoughts had been a bit scattered over the past week, so anything was possible. She gathered some papers to take home and then locked her office.

The detective was waiting in his car for her. He had reluctantly agreed when she argued that it wasn't necessary for a police escort to her office. She had also made the point that it would be better to wait at least a day to spring their *relationship* on everyone. It was incredible enough as it was, but to leave with him and come back the same afternoon in love? One hundred percent unbelievable. Danielle had doubts that they were going to be able to pull it off at all.

"Maybe you should take tomorrow, too," Ralph suggested, as he followed her out of the kitchen. "You just spent the last few hours at the police station because of these murders. That has to be weighing on you, hon."

"I promise I'm fine. I just need a couple of hours to myself."

Ralph gave her a look that said he didn't believe her and that he wasn't going to let it go.

"Okay, I'll think about it," she compromised.

Just then, the bell on the door jingled and in rushed the detective. Set determination took root in his eyes as he crossed the dining area at a clipped pace. Ugh, she groaned internally, he was supposed to wait outside for her. Then, Danielle grew concerned. Had something happened? Had the killer struck again?

"I'm off the case," he said, as he came to a dead stop right in front of her. That sure wasn't what she was expecting to hear.

"What? What do you mean—"

"I stepped down."

She shook her head. She was so confused. "Why would you—"

"Because I have feelings for you."

Her eyes widened with shock as she released a breathless, "What?"

"I have feelings for you, Danielle. I haven't been able to stop thinking about you since we met. That could cloud my judgment and jeopardize the investigation. I had no choice but to hand it over to someone else." He took a step even closer to her. "And... I think you have feelings for me, too."

She felt like a deer in headlights. She had no idea what to say or do. She couldn't think. His unexpected confession had just sent her thoughts flying all over the place.

"I... I..." she stuttered, still trying to form a response. Without warning, Detective Burke snaked an arm around her waist and pulled her into the hard plane of his body. Just as quickly, he cupped her cheek, his large hand covering her jaw and reaching into her hair to barely tickle the nape of her neck. Then, he kissed her, and Danielle's breath abandoned her. His lips were warm and tender and commanding all at once, and she felt heat shoot straight to her core.

He broke the kiss and searched her eyes. "Tell me you feel the same way." Deep pools of steel gray held her captive.

"I..." she began, still breathless. Her mind continued to be too flustered to find the words. Her body, on the other hand, knew exactly what to say, as her hands found their way to his chest and lightly gripped his shirt. Her gaze fell to his lips, then flicked back up to those pools.

Apparently, that had been answer enough because he smiled and kissed her again, deeper this time. Danielle's grip tightened on the starched cotton dress shirt, her hands practically fisting the material, and she felt herself lean into their kiss and even closer into his body. Their lips remained locked for a good ten-count before sense returned to her, and she pulled away.

She was fully aware of the room now, and all of the stunned faces, including Ralph's. She felt a deep, crimson blush heat her face as her gaze caught the looks from the patrons in the café. Many of the women were also blushing, accompanied by girlish smiles. Ralph's expression was one of disbelief at what he had just witnessed.

"Do you think I could steal you away for a little while? I think we have some things to talk about."

"Yes, actually, I'm taking the rest of the day off." She was finally getting her brain back.

Ralph cleared his throat. "So, I take it I won't see you until Wednesday, after all?"

"Umm…"

"Would that be okay?" Detective Burke asked.

Ralph shrugged. "She's the boss, not me."

Danielle didn't feel she was in the right state to be making decisions. "I'll, uh, let you know later," she answered.

Ralph suddenly smiled.

"What?"

"Nina is going to hate herself for missing this."

Embarrassment flooded Danielle's face again at the reminder of the passionate moment she'd just had in front of everyone. She couldn't think of anything else to say, so she turned and headed for the door. The detective followed close in tow, then passed her just enough to get the door for her. More of that chivalry. Where was it back at the station?

As he walked her to her car, he laced his fingers with hers, and more of those butterflies tickled, their wings fluttering heat in her. Just the act of him holding her hand could get her this aroused? She felt like a teenage girl experiencing things for the first time. Every look, every touch creating a flurry of feelings, both physically and emotionally.

She reached for the car door, but he turned her to face him. "The seed has been planted."

"What?" she asked, confused.

He leaned in, ensuring that his profile hid hers from the street and any passersby, and whispered in her ear, "Our cover has been established. Make sure from now on that you maintain your role in this." He gave her a quick kiss, then opened the door for her to climb inside. Realization hit her like a ton of bricks. "Hurry up and get in, or your expression is going to blow it. I'll follow you to your place and then we're going to get to work."

After she got seated behind the wheel, it took everything in her power not to slam the car door. She forced a smile and patiently waited for him to return to his own vehicle. Oh, how badly she wanted to peel out and leave him behind.

The drive back to her apartment had been an angry one. Danielle was seething inside. She was furious with him for pulling that stunt, and more furious with herself for not seeing it for what it was. She had taken everything he'd said and done at face value. She was as bad as the people they were trying to fool. Why had she fallen for it so easily? Was it because... maybe deep down...

She could feel her eyes begin to water, and she nearly slapped herself. She refused to even let the question finish forming. "Never," she said to herself.

Once they were behind closed doors, away from the public eye, she unleashed her ire. "Don't ever do something like that again." She glared hard, willing him to burst into flames from the power of it.

"Like what?" His response was so casual, it infuriated her all the more.

"You completely blindsided me back there. The plan was to wait until tomorrow. I wasn't prepared at all—"

"That was the point."

"What do you mean?" she asked, perching her hands on her hips.

"Taking you by surprise made it more authentic. We couldn't take the chance of it sounding scripted." He had yet to look at her. He was too busy dropping his stuff on her living room floor. Before he and Ben had come back to the station, he had gone by his own apartment and packed for their semi-permanent sleepover.

Detective *Jerk* had brought two duffel bags with him. One was filled with everyday items, and the other, smaller one was carrying weapons and ammo. He set down his bags next to the couch and started opening the one with the firearms. He placed them on the coffee table and began dismantling and cleaning them.

"Do you really think all of those are necessary?"

He had a couple different guns with him, not to mention extra handcuffs, magazines, and a knife.

"I like to be prepared, too," he said, as he sat down on the couch. "Besides," he steered back to the original topic, "we had just talked about it. It's not like you didn't know it wasn't true."

That was the thing, though. She kind of... sort of... *had* thought it was true. Danielle felt a strong wave of embarrassment flood through her. At that moment, she was glad he wasn't looking at her, otherwise, he might've seen her foolishness written all over her face. He was right, they *had* just talked about it. She couldn't believe how gullible she was.

"Well, 'from now on,' Detective Burke," Danielle reprised, "you will consult me first. No more surprises." He looked at her now. He put down his tools and walked over to her. Danielle was still standing near the door, and he got so close to her, that she nearly backed right into it.

"Considering how much time we'll be spending together, you should probably start calling me Adam."

Danielle's pulse picked up speed. Up to this point, she'd refused to address him that way. It was on the card he'd given her the night of the first murder, but it hadn't seemed appropriate. Even when he had begun to call her by *her* first name, she couldn't bring herself to do so in turn. It felt too personal, and she had been doing her damnedest to avoid getting that intimate with him.

"Especially if we're going to convince people we're intimate." He was staring straight into her eyes now, and she wished he'd go back to avoiding her. His stormy gray irises were putting off an intensity that she couldn't decipher.

"Also, we shouldn't tell anyone that this is a ruse—not your family, not Ralph, not even Carolina Marossi. We need everyone to think it's real. The killer might know you personally, which means he might know your friends and family. If they don't believe it, he won't. Not to mention, if you do know him, we can't let him find out. You can't trust anyone, Danielle."

Those steel gray eyes were searing her, and she could feel herself getting hot. As if he sensed it, Adam backed away and headed to the couch again to clean his guns. She finally took a breath when he left her. She hated it when he stood that close to her. It made her feel things. She let out a small sigh. Carrie was going to give her so much hell for this. The '*I told you so*'s were going to be endless.

Chapter Twenty

The hours passed by, and around six p.m., Danielle decided she was starving and was ready to make dinner. She pan-grilled some lemon pepper chicken and served it with new potatoes and a Caesar salad. She didn't feel like cooking anything too complicated and was especially grateful that she had a bottle of wine. After the day she'd had, she needed something to help her unwind.

Dinner went well. They talked some more about their likes and dislikes, and Adam even told a few jokes, which were actually funny. As she got up to do the dishes, he stopped her.

"Go sit down, I'll do these."

She wasn't used to other people cleaning up after her, and it felt strange. She decided to go ahead and open the wine, pouring herself a glass of sweet red Zinfandel. She then remembered that her brother, Kyle, had sent her home with some beer. Despite her objections, he had promised that it would convert her. She went to the fridge and grabbed a bottle for Adam. He was nearly done towel drying when she offered it to him.

"They can finish air drying, come on," she said.

He took the bottle from her hand, and barely touching her fingers with his, caused her spine to tingle again. "Thanks, I didn't figure you for a beer kind of girl." Adam used the bottle cap opener at the end of her corkscrew and let the little metallic circle clink onto the counter. He took a sip and smiled. "It's good."

"I'm glad you like it, and no, I'm not a beer kind of girl. My brother made me bring it back from our parents' house last weekend."

"I'll make sure it doesn't go to waste, then," he said, as he took another sip. They both plopped onto the couch and resumed their conversation. By the time nine rolled around, Danielle had gone through the bottle of wine. She was starting to feel good, and she noticed Adam was only on his second beer.

"Would you like another?" She realized she was tipsy, possibly too tipsy, since it sounded to herself as if she were trying to get him drunk.

"I'm good for now, but thanks." He gave her a little smile, and she felt the red flush in her cheeks. She needed a distraction. She turned on the TV—the most reliable distraction—and channel surfed until she came across a *Lethal Weapon* marathon. It was only halfway through the first movie, and she was thankful that Adam didn't object.

Not even forty-five minutes later, Danielle was out. Adam was so into the movie, also glad for the distraction, that he didn't notice she was asleep until she fell onto his shoulder. After all, she'd had an entire bottle of wine by herself, and with a day like today, he couldn't blame her. Finding out you were the obsession of a serial killer still on the loose was a lot to take in, not to mention having to suddenly dive into a fabricated, serious relationship with a complete stranger and allowing said stranger to live in your home. Adam actually admired how well Danielle was handling the very recent upheaval of her life.

He raised his arm and moved it behind her, allowing her to slide down to his chest. Her hair had fallen in her face, and he swept the waves from her eyes, pulling the rest away across her neck. Moving in her sleep, she reached her arm across and held onto his shirt. He had turned into a pillow, which he didn't mind one bit. Her body felt good against his, and he wanted to enjoy it just a little while longer.

Suddenly, Danielle awoke, looked at Adam, and smiled. Until dinner, he hadn't seen her truly smile. It was beautiful. It pulled at something inside him that he was unfamiliar with. As she began to rise up, though, he noticed that her smile looked less sweet and more seductive. She crawled across him until she was fully straddling his hips. What was going on? He definitely hadn't expected this. Hoped, maybe, which he knew was very wrong to even entertain. It was the total adverse to the logic of his rules and reasoning. Hoping was a gateway that would lead to more dangerous thoughts like wishing… like wanting… like taking. She took him by surprise even more when she pulled her blouse up over her head and tossed it onto the floor. He was instantly aroused and could feel his blood heating.

"Danielle—"

"Shh." She leaned in, taking his face in her hands and kissed him with intensity.

After the two seconds of initial shock wore off, Adam began caressing the smooth skin on her back and then moved his hands lower to squeeze her ass through her tight jeans. Danielle let out a soft moan and deepened their kiss. That sweet sound drove him to make his own primal growl. His hands became greedier with the need to grab the full scope of her rear. They needed to feel the soft skin underneath the denim.

God, she was sexy. He twisted her under him on the couch, carefully placing his weight. He saw pure lust in her eyes, those eyes that threatened to devour him. His hand ran down the length of her as he went in for another kiss and pulled her leg up to wrap around him. Their tongues were dueling with each other, both hungry for the other.

Adam sat up long enough to remove his own shirt before Danielle yanked him back down. Her chest was heaving, and his focus followed. Her breasts were rising and falling with each panted breath. He cupped one in his hand, feeling the intricate design of her lace bra. He began to gently massage it and redirected his kisses to her neck. He could feel her pulse pounding against his lips. She let out another soft moan, causing his hands to work harder. As hot as she looked in that black lace, he quickly determined that it was in his way and it needed to come off—now. As he went to unhook her bra, he heard the loud pop of gun shots.

Adam jolted awake by the noise. The marathon was still going, and Danielle was still asleep in the crook of his arm.

Fucking hell, he thought, raking a hand through his hair.

It had only been a dream. A dream that both his mind and his body seemed to think was real, since he had a raging hard on. He gently scooped up Danielle and carried her to her room. It was dark, but he didn't want to turn on the lights in case they woke her up. He pulled back the sheets and laid her down on the bed. He covered her back up and walked out of the room, closing the door behind him. Falling back down onto the couch, Adam let out a deep breath. This was the second time he'd fantasized about her, only this one was much more real. He needed to get his shit together.

The next morning, Danielle woke up in her room. She hadn't remembered getting into bed, although she had drunk that entire bottle of Zinfandel by herself. She shuffled into the kitchen and found Adam sitting at the table with a mug of coffee. She inhaled the heavenly aroma and already began to feel refreshed.

"Morning." His voice lacked any sort of cheer, which she took to mean he wasn't really a morning person and would explain why he'd left off the 'good.'

"Good morning," she said, wanting to lighten it up.

He was acting very reserved, even though they had gotten to know each other a little better last night. She had to remember, though, he wasn't in the comfort of his own place and was probably a little thrown off.

"How did you sleep?" she asked, as she went to the coffee pot and began making herself a mug. She felt the dull pain of a minor hangover. Given the fact that she was rarely ever plagued by them, she chalked it up to the combination of the alcohol and the stress of yesterday's events.

"Fine, you?"

"Fine, thanks." Even though she'd slept okay, being awake was not, but she wasn't about to embarrass herself by revealing her intoxication-induced headache. She just hoped that he didn't think she was an alcoholic.

Why do you care what he thinks?

Danielle noticed that she was still wearing her clothes from yesterday. If she had put herself to bed, there's no way she would have worn those jeans and blouse to sleep in. That meant Adam had probably dropped her off in there. Thank God he wasn't a pervert and tried to undress her. She started to picture what that would be like, and when he spoke again, she jumped.

"We're going to be staying in today."

"We are?" She was a bit surprised by that plan. "I figured you would want to be out in public to bait the Harvester."

"We have plenty of time for that."

Plenty of time, her mind echoed. Did that mean that he anticipated it would take quite a while to catch him? It was such an open-ended statement.

"I want to take advantage of the time and work on the case as much as I can. When you go back to the café, I'll be benched during the day."

Danielle thought she detected some resentment in his comment. Well, it wasn't her fault that he was sidelined to be her bodyguard. She certainly hadn't asked for it. She decided to let it go, though, before she got herself worked up. It really didn't matter.

Adam dove in immediately, leaving her alone to decide what to do with her time. If it were any other day, she might've gone to the beach or the park to read a good book, but going outdoors without him was not an option, and she certainly couldn't go back to the park anytime soon.

Her other go-to was staying inside, putting on her cozy sweatpants, and binge-watching movies all day. However, this wasn't an ordinary day off. There was no way she would be able to relax and treat it as one. So, that left only one option.

―――

Something smells delicious, he thought, as his head lifted and his nose sniffed the air. Adam's mouth began to water as his stomach growled. His watch said it was ten forty-five a.m. It seemed his bowl of cereal and coffee had worn off already. It really hadn't been that long since he had eaten—only three hours—but his body was reacting to the savory aromas like one of Pavlov's dogs.

He turned in his seat on the couch to look over to the kitchen. Curvy hips swayed to an inaudible rhythmic beat, one that appeared up-tempo to Adam's eyes. Damn, it was sexy, and kind of adorable. He smiled as he watched her groove. Danielle must have taken a shower at some point because she was no longer wearing the clothes from yesterday that he had to put her to bed in. She had on a graphic t-shirt and a pair of denim shorts, both accentuating her assets. Then again, everything accentuated her assets.

The music pouring from her earbuds made her completely oblivious to her surroundings, including his approach. He reached out to touch her, then hesitated. Where could he touch her that would be safe? What part of her body could he put his fingers on that wouldn't send vibrations through him?

Adam's dilemma came to an abrupt end. Danielle had turned without warning and nearly jumped a foot into the air, releasing a small scream in surprise. Then, her wide eyes quickly narrowed into a scowl, which was likely due to the chuckle coming from him.

"What the hell, Adam?!" she said, as she slapped his chest in reprimand, as though it was a natural reaction to strike after being startled. "You scared the daylights out of me."

He couldn't stop laughing. The angry face she was making was too cute.

"It isn't funny, you jerk."

"Sure, it is." She went to swat him again, but Adam caught her hand instead. He clasped it with both of his and placed it gently on his chest, where she had intended to strike again. "I really didn't mean to scare you, I promise."

Adam had subdued most of his laughter, but he was still sporting a boyish grin, which Danielle had to admit was *maybe* sort of, kind of charming.

"So, then why were you standing behind me like a weirdo, huh?"

"Something smelled delicious. I called to you, but you couldn't hear me with your headphones in your ears."

"Oh, sorry," she said, a little sheepishly. He stepped even closer, still holding her hand in place, and she could feel his heartbeat. It was strong and steady. She was glad that he couldn't feel hers because it was quickening to the point of erratic as the heel of his palm brushed past her cheek to remove one of her earbuds.

"So, what are we listening to?" he asked rhetorically, as he placed the earbud in his own ear. A smile tugged at the corners of his mouth, as though he were trying to fight it. "Marky Mark, huh?"

Danielle's face flushed a bit. "Yes, so? It's a good song." Why did she sound so defensive?

"I'm just surprised is all, and you're right, it is a good song. You do have some good gyrations." There was that boyish grin again.

Danielle rolled her eyes at him. "It's 'vibrations,' and you know it."

"My mistake. I'm sure your vibrations are just as good." His heartbeat was still steady beneath her hand, while hers was still fluttering in her chest, and it was starting to make her squirm.

"Pervert."

"Tease."

She felt a full-on blush of crimson spread across her cheeks. She pulled her hand free and averted her gaze.

"I made some quiche, but I wasn't sure which style you prefer, so I made both Lorraine and Florentine," she said, taking her other earbud out. She wasn't about to risk touching Adam. He could remove his himself.

"You could have just asked me. Either would have been fine. You didn't have to go to any extra trouble."

"It wasn't any trouble, really."

"In that case, I'll have a slice of both."

"Sure," she said, turning to the cabinet. She retrieved her pie server and a plate.

"Danielle, this isn't the café. You don't have to wait on me," he protested.

"I don't mind. I guess you could say it's second nature to me."

―――

She handed the plate and a fork to him. Steam still billowed from the enormous slices she had cut, and Adam's mouth started watering again.

It didn't take him long to devour his hearty helping, and he was completely stuffed. Danielle had gone back to the kitchen to work on something new, so he jumped back into the case, his attention completely focused. Every once in a while, he glanced to the kitchen to get a peek at her. She was wearing her earbuds again, but she didn't dance. Adam realized whenever he looked at her that that was what he was looking for. He wanted to see Danielle dancing again. He wanted to see her enjoying herself. Had his comments earlier embarrassed her? She was clearly making a conscious effort not to shake her hips. Those hips... He needed to get those thoughts out of his head.

Sometime later, a plate lowered between Adam and his computer.

"Break time." Her smile was so honest and sweet. He couldn't help but smile back. "Cranberry orange scone."

He took a bite and gave his seal of approval. She beamed at the praise, and he felt something tighten in his chest. For the rest of the afternoon, she brought him plate after plate, each one with something new.

"Are you planning on feeding all of San Diego?"

"I know it's a lot of food. I compulsive cook when I don't know what to do with myself or when I can't relax. I guess it distracts me from thinking about things."

Things like serial killers, Adam thought.

"I drive," he offered.

"Where do you go?"

He shrugged. "Nowhere, anywhere... I just drive. I don't really think about it." Just like his drive after the first murder. He hadn't thought about where he was going, but he'd ended up at Mon Félicité anyway. He hadn't intended on seeing Danielle so soon, but there he'd been.

He looked at his watch. It read four-thirty in the afternoon. He could go for another break.

"Do you want to go?"

Danielle thought about it for a moment. "That would be nice, actually. I don't have anything in the oven right now, and I wouldn't mind getting some fresh air... Do you think we could end up at the market? I need to pick up some things for dinner."

He chuckled. "Sure." What else could she possibly make? They had enough food to feed an army.

Chapter Twenty-One

The drive had done Danielle some good. She had been cooped up in her apartment all day, and though she had been baking the entire time—which she loved—she had felt a little like a bird in a cage. She'd needed to stretch her wings.

Going to the market together had also done some good for their cover. The short outing provided an opportunity to display some affection in public, going on the assumption that the killer could be watching them.

Adam had been a complete gentleman and opened her door for her, held her hand at any chance, and looked at her adoringly. Was he like this in real life with the women he dated? They probably swooned over him, regardless. The idea of it sparked something inside her—something resembling… jealousy? No, she had no right feeling jealous. His past played no part in her present, not really. Danielle couldn't stop herself, however, from picturing him with some faceless woman, doting on her, holding her, kissing her… She gave her head a mental shake. Could she be more pathetic? She needed to get a hold of herself. They weren't friends, and they weren't lovers. They were partners, of a sort, to get a job done. The reminder of that jump started her resolve.

———

Adam had actually enjoyed their little interlude. He was, by no means, a PDA, lovey-dovey kind of guy, but behaving that way with Danielle had felt… good. Lacing their fingers together to hold hands, stealing kisses, touching her whenever he wanted—oh yes, it had felt good. Now that they were back at her apartment, though, it meant it was back to 'hands off.' *That was a good thing,* he thought. If he had to be all over her all of the time, he might not be able to hold back.

As per usual, her cooking smelled amazing. He found himself anticipating the spread that she was preparing for dinner. He had offered to help, but she declined. She was very meticulous in her method.

"It really is sweet of you, but I already have everything on schedule, so there's not really anything for you to do."

Adam felt disappointed. "Can I watch you, then?"

Danielle laughed nervously. "You don't have to do that."

"I know I don't have to. I want to," he said, as he leaned over the counter.

She let out another nervous laugh. "Why?"

"Because you always look happy when you cook." He smiled mischievously.

She turned around quickly to hide her blush, using the excuse of finding her skillet. "Okay, sure," she said with her back to him.

Adam truly enjoyed watching her. He was impressed with how fluid and seamless she was as she went back and forth between each dish. Her timing was impeccable on arranging everything to be completed at the same time, and she did it without breaking a sweat.

"Danielle, this is incredible." They had sat down for dinner, and he wasted no time.

"Thanks, it's actually Carrie's mother's recipe. Chicken Milano with parmesan risotto. The broccoli is just steamed with some lemon juice. Nothing special."

"Everything you make is special."

Her cheeks turned bright pink, and Adam was quiet as he momentarily studied her. "Why are you blushing so much today?"

———

Danielle felt even more embarrassed. "Why are you complimenting me so much today?"

Adam took another bite of his dinner. "Should I not?" He was so casual in his manner, like it was any other normal conversation.

"It's not that, it's just… different—kind of unusual for you."

"How would you know what is usual for me? We hardly know each other," he said very matter-of-factly.

Oh no, she thought. Had she just offended him? Did she just ruin all of the progress they had made today? She felt anxiety trying to settle in.

"I'm sorry."

He's sorry? What for? she wondered. After all, she basically just told him he's typically a rude person.

"I've clearly given you a lousy impression if you had already come to the conclusion that I'm an asshole by nature."

"No, Adam, I didn't mean—" she protested, waving her hands in denial.

"It's okay. It's not something I haven't heard before from women. I just hadn't intended for you to be one of them."

She wasn't sure what to say. Could she really keep refuting it? There was truth to what he'd said, but not necessarily to the degree he was suggesting. She wanted to turn the conversation around. What better way than to make a joke out of it?

"*Asshole* is a little strong. Let's settle on *jerk*." She gave him a playful smile, and he laughed.

"I'll take it."

Danielle capped off dinner with cheesecake shots drizzled with a raspberry compote.

The rest of the evening was casual, as though they had been doing this for years. They had done the dishes together and even sat down to watch Monday Night football. Danielle felt herself relaxing. In fact, she was so comfortable with him already that she put on her favorite sweat pants and an oversized t-shirt that always ended up falling off one shoulder.

She wasn't a major sports fan, but she liked watching the Chargers every now and then. This particular game being broadcasted was between two teams that she knew nothing about, so it didn't appeal to her in the same way, but Adam was clearly the type to watch any team of any sport and enjoy himself. Watching his reactions to the various plays and calls was very entertaining, especially when penalty flags were thrown. There were a few times when Danielle had to hold back a laugh.

It wasn't until a laundry detergent ad came on that she realized she had a hamper full of clothes that she needed to wash. Her mind had been so congested with everything that had transpired that she'd completely forgotten about some of her regular, everyday tasks. Plus, Adam had his clothes from yesterday that she could add to her load.

She left him to the game and began gathering all of her garments. It was then that she realized she had no idea where his clothes from yesterday had gone. *Probably in his duffel bag*, she thought. Without thinking, she began sifting through it, looking for the items. One white dress shirt, a black jacket, and slacks to match. She also found a pair of wadded up dress socks. Danielle rolled her eyes. *Men*, she thought. His jacket needed to be hung to avoid wrinkles.

Actually, she should probably have it dry cleaned. She would hate for something to happen to it if she tried to clean it herself. She began to check the pockets for pens or paper—anything that seemed important.

When she came to the inner breast pocket, a thick paper rectangle met her fingers, and she pulled it out to look at it. It was Trevor's business card, which meant that Adam had been to the firm to see him. That must have been the 'errand' he had gone to do when he'd left her at the station because they had been together every moment since.

Danielle remembered how he had come back so hostile. Originally, she had thought it was her and their situation, but now knowing that he had met Trevor, it made perfect sense. Trevor could have that effect on people. Now, she was curious as to what had happened to put him in that state.

She had seen Trevor's business cards plenty of times, enough to know exactly how they were laid out. The front was black with gold lettering and the back was solid white with his phone number. He purposely didn't include it on the front, so that you would have to look over both sides of the card, making it stand out in your memory. She turned the card over and saw that his number was scratched out with bright pink ink. A new number was written in its place in a feminine script along with a name and a message:

Call me anytime. –Becky

———

Adam had been so engrossed in the game, he hadn't been fully aware of where Danielle had gone. He just knew that she wasn't next to him anymore—and he didn't like it. It was odd, but having her near seemed to put him at ease, and he really wanted her close. He got up to look for her. There were only so many places she could go in the apartment, so it was silly to even feel the need to find her.

The moment he turned around, she looked at him with a face he couldn't quite read. She was holding something small in her hand, his jacket pooled at her feet as though forgotten.

"So, I take it you met Trevor?"

He noticed the casual smile she was forcing on her face, but he didn't understand why. "Yes, Ben and I had the pleasure," he said sarcastically. He was trying to amuse her, but it didn't appear to be working. He was hoping that she would give a genuine smile at his jest, instead of the fake one.

"I guess that's why you left me at the station."

Why did she seem upset?

"Yes."

"What did he have to say?"

He moved around the couch to walk closer. He didn't like the distance that was currently between them. "He denied stalking you and having anything to do with the murders."

"Yeah, I figured as much," she muttered. Her gaze kept going back to the item in her hand. "So," she paused for a moment, "who was his alibi?"

Was this why she seemed so bothered, hearing about who he was sleeping with?

"Kimberlee Vance."

"Oh," she said, genuinely surprised. Then, she plastered on that phony smile again. "See, I told you he would have an excuse." Danielle's eyes flicked down to the card again. "Here," she said, as she stepped forward and handed him the card. Her gaze didn't quite meet his.

The back of the card was face up, meaning that was what she had been looking at every time her eyes left him—where Becky's thinly veiled message was written. When she truly looked at him again, he saw her eyes were getting glassy, and she was clearly struggling to tamp down her emotions.

"I should have asked before I went through your pockets. Sorry."

Adam understood now. He took the card from her and tore it up. Her brow furrowed in confusion, as he walked off to the nearest trash can. "I take it she was the one?" he asked gently when he had returned to her. He knew he didn't need to clarify. Becky was the woman Danielle had caught Trevor with. He wanted to comfort her, but he didn't know how, or if she would even want him to. "I'm sorry he hurt you."

She swallowed hard, as though she were pushing every bit of feeling she had down deep and gave a casual shrug of her shoulders, folding her arms over her chest like a shield. "It doesn't matter."

She's wrong, he thought. It *did* matter, because he hated to see her in pain. He hated that she was *still* pained, and he absolutely despised the man that had caused it.

"Well, don't worry," he said with a playful smile, as he moved in closer and took a lock of her hair in his fingers, "I prefer blondes anyway."

Danielle's fluster was more than discernable in her reaction to his admission... and his arrogance.

———

"Why would I be worried?" she asked with artificial annoyance, as she freed her hair from his hold and put some distance between them. She didn't wait for an answer, but instead turned her back on him and returned to her basket of laundry. A second longer, and Adam would see Danielle's embarrassment overtake her. Had her self-consciousness been that glaringly obvious?

The instant she had seen the unabashed invitation, all of those feelings of hurt and humiliation came flooding back, along with the memory of Becky and Trevor intimately entwined. What nearly brought her to tears, though, was the vision of Becky with Adam. It had made her heart clench in her chest, confusing her. The unwarranted pang of betrayal was absurd. Adam didn't belong to her, so why did she feel it? Was she muddling the truth with the charade, or was it strictly because the woman brazenly offering herself was the one—most assuredly of many—that her ex-slime ball boyfriend had cheated with? Danielle surmised—with insistence—it was the latter.

If that were so, then why did Adam's allusive words of reassurance give her relief and satisfaction? Why did his intimation incite a certain heat down inside her? The provocative way he'd touched her golden waves, that wickedly confident smile, evoked panic and excitement throughout her body, all suggesting she *wanted* that charade.

Chapter Twenty-Two

"What time do we need to be at Mon Félicité?"

Danielle had just emerged from her bedroom and made it to the kitchen, still in the process of waking up. She had lost some sleep thinking about the man on her couch. "What? Oh, um..." Her brain wasn't ready to start at full force. She needed a minute to have some coffee and ease into the morning. Adam, however, looked raring to go. "I can be ready in an hour. Would you like some breakfast?"

"I already ate."

Danielle couldn't help but note the agitation in his voice. Was he upset about something? "Is everything okay?"

Adam quickly cut her off before she could inquire any further. "Everything's fine," he said, forcing a smile.

It sure didn't seem fine, whatever it was. It was clear, though, that he wasn't going to tell her anything. She sighed internally. Was he reverting back to his old self, when they had first met? Was this his true self? Could the man from yesterday have been for show, even in the confines of the apartment when the two of them were alone—when there was no one to persuade? Perhaps. To her, it made no sense to do so, but as Adam pointed out, she hardly knew him.

She wasn't going to let him bring her down, though. She had plenty of other things to focus on, like feeling nervous about being lovey-dovey with him in front of her friends and customers. What if they saw right through it? Would she be able to be convincing enough? Could Adam? Probably. He was pretty damn convincing yesterday, and especially their show at the café when he had practically swept her off her feet. She was still somewhat bitter about that, primarily at herself—about how unbelievably naïve she had been.

He was waiting for her in the living room while she finished getting ready. Maybe if she spiffed herself up a little extra today, it might make it easier for him to put on a good performance. Plus, she was still feeling a little insecure. Ever since she found that note, her confidence had been taking a beating. He'd had done his best to lift her up, but could those have been hollow words? Her pride needed a do-over from the sweatpants and t-shirt. She had nothing to prove, but it demanded it from her, nonetheless.

Danielle decided to wear the royal blue dress shirt with the plunging neckline, her sleek gray pencil skirt, and some black heels. This outfit always made her feel like a sexy, empowered businesswoman. She pinned her hair so that the waves swept more to one side, leaving part of her neck exposed. She put on the finishing touches with some simple sapphire earrings and necklace.

When she emerged from the bedroom, Adam looked her over in silence. She wasn't sure what to make of it. Was he pleased, displeased?

Remember, she thought, *it doesn't matter what he actually thinks. He has to act pleased, regardless.* Besides, Danielle knew she looked good, and she felt good, and *that* was all that mattered.

"Are you ready to go?"

"Yes," was all that she offered him. She was being childish, she knew, but his shortness from earlier still lingered with her. He got up from the couch as she grabbed her keys from the hall end table. After she locked the door behind them, Adam took her keys.

"I'm driving."

"Then, why are you taking my keys?"

"I don't want you to get rebellious on me."

She rolled her eyes at him and walked to the elevator.

When they stepped out of the main door to her building, a gust of wind blew into her, making her break into shivers. Adam turned her to face him and started rubbing the sides of her arms to warm her. It was sweetly considerate and seemed genuine, second nature, even. After a few moments passed, he took her hand, and they walked down the street to where his vehicle was parked. It was your typical black sedan, as standard as they came, but sportier—probably to impress the ladies. *It's such a bachelor's car,* she scoffed to herself. He opened her door and

The Harvester

helped her climb in. Her skirt made it a little harder to maneuver, but it was worth it.

The drive was short but still oddly quiet. His reservation was confusing. What was wrong, she kept wondering. They parked outside Mon Félicité, and he assisted her again. She was ready to walk inside when he entwined his fingers with hers. He leaned in and whispered in her ear, "Let's turn that frown upside down."

Before she could ask his meaning, he pulled her in close, pressing her body to his, and nearly kissed the breath out of her. Danielle had to stifle the moan of approval that threatened to escape her. She couldn't allow it to meet his lips, or he would feel the truth. She couldn't allow it to meet his ears, or he would hear the truth. He would be able to see right through her and know the veritable arousal he was stirring inside her.

"That's better," he said after pulling away from her. His own smug smile indicated that he had gotten what he wanted.

And so the play had officially begun. It had really started the second he had 'confessed his feelings' and kissed her in front of the crowd at the café two days ago. Today was different, though. Today, it was more than infatuation and feelings, more than flirtatious suggestions. Today, it was love every minute of the day until they were back at her apartment. Adam was making a routine out of opening doors for her, and she figured his job was going to be to master the role of the perfect boyfriend.

Danielle laughed to herself and thought, *Yeah, if only.*

Everyone inside did a double take when they saw the two of them together, hand in hand. Nina was manning the register when they approached. Her eyes were about to pop out of her head and then she oddly began to blush. Danielle wasn't sure why, then saw a huge grin on her face. Nina was blushing out of excitement—too much of it, at that.

"Well, hello," she said with a little surprise and giddiness.

"Hi, Nina. How are things going this morning?"

"Great, just great!" If Nina was trying to contain herself, she was doing a poor job.

"Is Ralph in the kitchen?"

"Yes, yes. I'll let him know you're here," Nina said, as she started backing away. It seemed as though she didn't want to turn around only to discover that she'd imagined it.

Danielle looked at Adam. "I don't think she's going to need any further convincing."

"Mmhmm," he said.

She could tell Ralph was getting closer when she heard, "What surprise?" Nina was practically pushing him through the swinging door. "Oh, hello, you two."

The lack of a reaction from Ralph left Nina dumbfounded. Her head whipped back and forth between him and the unlikely couple.

"You didn't tell her?" Danielle asked.

"Tell me what?"

"Nah, I figured I'd let her see for herself."

"Good to see you again, Ralph," Adam said, as he shook his hand.

"Likewise, Detective."

Nina was still trying to absorb the situation. "But when? How?" The question wasn't posed to anyone in particular, but more so to whomever would answer her first.

"On your off day," replied Ralph.

"You've known for two days, and you didn't say anything?"

"It was quite a show, too," Ralph teased Nina.

Danielle blushed again at the memory of it. How off-guard and completely enveloped in the moment she had been.

Nina was still dying to know more. "Seriously? What happened?"

Ralph answered first again. "Oh, the detective here came gallivanting in, confessing his affections and basically frenched Danielle in front of everyone." His voice was sarcastically casual, as though the entire event was no big deal, and his smile had a dual purpose of taunting Nina and embarrassing Danielle, which worked well.

"And then he whisked her away... and here we are."

Nina looked like a bomb ready to explode confetti hearts and glitter everywhere. "Oh my god, that is so romantic!" she swooned. "I can't *believe* I missed it! This is what I get for being a responsible adult and going to class," she pouted sourly, throwing up her arms, then crossing them like a child.

She's right, Danielle thought. It *was* romantic, incredibly so… *And incredibly fake*, she reminded herself. Yes, the most romantic thing that had ever happened to her in her whole life, and she couldn't even enjoy it. She sighed to herself. Nothing like that would ever really happen, especially not to her. That was the stuff of fairy tales and romance novels, not real life.

"Are you okay?" Adam asked, bringing her thoughts back to the group.

"Yes, I'm just dreading the bookkeeping that I'm about to do," she lied. Well, a half-truth anyway. The accounting and reconciling wasn't her favorite part of owning her own business, but it was necessary. She couldn't afford to hire someone full time to help with that side of things, and besides, she wanted to make sure that everything was done properly.

"Ralph, I'm going to be working in my office all day, so I thought maybe you could teach Adam some things in the kitchen." Adam looked at Danielle with protest.

"Sweetheart, I don't think Ralph wants me loitering around the kitchen. I would just get in his way."

"Nonsense. My paperwork is tedious and dull, and I know you'll be bored. Ralph, do you mind?"

"Not at all. It's fine with me."

――――

Why Adam hadn't wanted to let Danielle go, he didn't know. When she had pulled her hand from his hold, he had felt its absence, and his agitation came back. She had sensed it earlier at the apartment, and he had lied to her. His grouchiness had stemmed from his irritation with himself. He had spent too much time thinking about her last night. Fantasizing about her more, but in a new way. He didn't just make love to her now. Now, he held her, laughed with her, and showered her with sweet kisses, all while clothed. It was as if... as if they were in a real relationship, a real couple doing 'couple things.' That's what irritated him the most. Fantasizing about rolling around naked with her was already difficult enough, but throw in feelings and it was too much. Thoughts like those were too risky—thoughts like those threatened his control.

Shaken from his thoughts, Adam took his first real look around the kitchen. There were a multitude of stove tops and ovens. In the far corner was an industrial sized dough machine and at least two stand mixers that he could see. To contrast all of the steel and brushed nickel, there were splashes of color in all of her décor. Anywhere that would allow for it, there it was. It truly made the place brighter, not just to the eyes, but to the spirit. It didn't feel as cold and hard.

Continuing his assessment, Adam's attention was drawn to a corkboard on the wall. It had different messages of positivity tacked to it.

'Winners never quit and quitters never win,' '11:59 is the end of one and 12:00 is the start of another,' 'Don't reach for the stars, grab the universe,' and his personal favorite, *'Kicking ass and taking names.'* Then, something in particular caught his eye.

"What's this?"

Ralph walked over to see the item in question. "That's a picture from Danielle's first baking competition."

Adam studied the photo closer. An adorable little girl with wavy, caramel hair, an enormous grin, and a twinkle in her eye posed with a trophy. Her apron was speckled with flour and batter, some even making it to her rosy cheeks. She was beaming with joy as she held her prize close.

"She took first place," Ralph added with pride.

"How old was she?"

"Ten, I believe."

"How big was the competition?"

"You'd have to ask Danielle, but I think it was somewhere around thirty kids. That was after qualifying, of course. The ages ranged from nine to twelve."

"Not bad."

Ralph chuckled. "Not bad? Son, that's damn impressive. To have that kind of determination and self-discipline at that age is amazing. Most kids don't have the patience it takes to dedicate their time and focus to something as precise as baking. It's not like cooking, which is more accepting of experimentation. Baking is a science. Obviously, you must do some experimenting with ideas, but it's far less forgiving if you make a mistake."

Adam continued to study the picture. For some reason, he was embarrassed to admit how in awe of her he was... and how much disappointment he felt of not having known her, which in his mind made no sense. That face, though. He couldn't look away from the warmth of it.

Adam smiled to himself, because in all honesty, that radiant light that was smiling back at him told him that no matter how old they were, he would've been drawn to her regardless.

"So," Ralph began, bringing Adam back to his senses, "where would you like to begin?"

———

Danielle had been in her office for about an hour working on her accounting and profits figures. On any given day, she could knock this stuff out in about three hours, but today she wasn't even a quarter of the way through. She was having a hard time focusing with everything that was going on. Between a crazed serial killer stalking her and a man who made her crazy living with her, she considered herself lucky to have any brainwave activity.

She got up from her desk to file the papers she'd finished in the cabinets. She always kept hard copies. Carrie said she was living in the Stone Age, but computers had the ability to crash, and Danielle didn't believe in putting all of her eggs in one basket. When she turned around, she jumped back and gasped. Neil was standing in the doorway.

"Jesus," she laughed, "do you enjoy scaring me?"

"I promise, I never mean to, but it *is* funny." He gave her a big smile and a wink.

That seemed to be a popular opinion these days. "So, what's up?"

"I was checking to see if you had your list ready for the upcoming week's produce." He walked into the room and leaned on Danielle's desk as she went to sit back down in her chair.

"I'll have to ask Ralph. I'm sorry I don't have it, but it's just been kind of crazy, you know?" she said, as she leaned onto one elbow with her hand on her forehead.

"Yeah, I heard about the other woman. How are you holding up?"

"Fine, I guess, considering."

―――

Adam heard laughing coming from Danielle's office, and it wasn't just her feminine voice. There was a masculine timbre mixed with hers. When he rounded the corner and made it to her doorway, he saw a blond man sitting on Danielle's desk, though not Trevor. Had it been, Adam wouldn't have been able to restrain himself from making good on his threat. Regardless of who he wasn't, this man was a little too close for Adam's liking.

He knocked on the door frame, "What's so funny?" He made himself sound genuinely interested.

"Oh, hey," Danielle said with a hint of laughter still lingering, "It's nothing really, just an old anecdote. Have you met Neil?" She got up from her desk to greet Adam.

"Yes, when we interviewed all of the merchants in the square after the first murder." He stepped forward to shake Neil's hand.

"Neil gives me the best deals on produce for Mon Félicité." The two men shook hands and gave slight head nods but didn't exchange any words. There was an awkward tension beginning to build in the room, so Adam decided he'd intensify it.

"Sweetheart, let me know when you're done in here. I have something I want you to taste." He pulled her in with both hands on her waist and kissed her softly on her lips, making sure he took his time with it. As he pulled back, he looked at Danielle, who seemed completely flustered.

"Um," she paused, clearly having trouble thinking, "yeah, sure. I'll be right there. I just have to give Neil my, um, produce list for next week." Her words were breathy, and Adam was feeling quite pleased with himself. He walked out of the office and headed back to the kitchen.

―――

Adam surprising her with that kiss made Danielle lose her train of thought. She hadn't expected it, and as a result, she reacted like a befuddled teenage girl. Again. She turned to Neil, who was looking at her with one eyebrow raised.

"Sweetheart? Did I miss something?" His voice wasn't as pleased as Nina's. "Isn't that the same guy you said was a huge asshole?"

She decided to go with Carrie's and Nina's explanation. "Yes, well, it turns out he was behaving like that to push me away, but..."

"But what?"

"He decided not to fight his feelings anymore."

"And what about you? I thought you loathed him?" His eyes were narrowing in on her, suggesting he wasn't buying the act.

"Part of the reason why I thought I despised him so much was because even after he was so curt toward me, I was still attracted to him and it scared me. Once we became honest with ourselves, we were able to be honest with each other, and we fell." She was laying the mushy dream eyes on thick.

"Fell? *In love*? Danielle, you barely know him. Don't you think you're rushing it a bit?"

"Neil, I know it sounds absurd, but you don't decide when or who you fall in love with. It just happens, sometimes without warning. Trust me, I would normally be in the skepticism boat right there with you, but… when it's real, you know it, and there's nothing you can do." Damn, she was better than she thought she would be. So good, in fact, that if Mon Félicité ever went out of business, she thought she could possibly start an acting career.

"Wow, I'm not really sure what to say… Except, it's good to see you smile. I just hope you don't end up getting hurt."

"Thanks, and I won't. Now, let me get you that list."

Danielle gave Neil her order and said goodbye. She was going to have a talk with Adam about that kiss later. She was pretty sure he'd done it in front of Neil blatantly, which was childish, especially since hers and Neil's relationship was nothing more than casual friends. Was it possible that he was jealous? She felt her stomach flutter for a moment, then she snapped herself back to reality. *Pfft*, she scoffed, not likely. Regardless of any jealousy, if he was going to kiss her, he needed to be doing it in a more public area with a larger audience. That was the whole point, wasn't it?

Chapter Twenty-Three

Danielle walked into the kitchen with her hands on her hips. "So, where's this *thing* you wanted me to taste?" She didn't look too pleased with Adam, although it was quite the contrary when he'd kissed her. Well, they needed the practice, and if it happened to be in front of Neil, then so be it. Adam was going to have Ben run a secondary background check on him later, too, to see if any dirt came up.

Ben was still digging deep into Trevor Whitman's life. He had a surprise interview planned for Kimberlee Vance tomorrow. Adam wished he could be there for it, just to see her reaction. Would she corroborate Trevor's story? She may admit to sleeping with him, but that didn't mean that she was actually with him those nights. Did he think she would lie for him?

Adam had to stay with Danielle, though, and he certainly wasn't going to take her with him. Judging by her reaction with Becky's number, Kimberlee Vance could act as another reminder of Trevor's infidelity, and Adam wasn't going to subject her to any pain that might bring her.

"It's over here, come on. I really think you're going to like it."

She looked over at Ralph with a questioning glance as she walked to Adam. Ralph gave her a nod of approval, so whatever it was must have been decent.

"Alright, close your eyes."

She hesitated for a moment, then complied. He put a spoon up to her lips, and she sipped the contents.

Danielle detected an assortment of flavors—garlic, butter, cream, thyme, nutmeg, salt, pepper, lemon, and a little white wine. She recognized the cream sauce Adam had made. It was the one she used when she made shrimp fettuccine. "Wow, I must say I'm impressed."

"He did it all by himself—I didn't even tell him what to make. He just looked through your recipes and took it from there."

"I didn't realize you could cook," she said to Adam with intrigue.

"I never said I couldn't. You seem to enjoy cooking for us, so I didn't say anything."

"Well, from now on, you're more than welcome to cook at home," she said, smiling.

"At home?" Ralph seemed unsure about what he was hearing. "Are you two living together?"

"Well," she said, as she turned on the dreamy eyes again when she looked at Adam.

"Dani, could I speak to you for a moment?" Ralph had his *'father'* expression on his face.

"Sure." She felt like she was in trouble, even though she hadn't done anything wrong.

"I'm going to finish getting lunch ready while you two talk," Adam said, as he gave her a little peck.

She felt herself blushing again. She and Ralph stepped into her office, and he closed the door.

"What's going on with you?"

"What do you mean?"

"I don't oppose the two of you getting involved, but living together?"

"I know it seems a little fast—"

"A little? Try zero to ninety."

Danielle couldn't think of a reasonable—plausible—explanation to give him. Ralph studied her for a minute and sighed.

"Even though I think this is strange, I've never seen you this happy, and I know you're a big girl, but I just want to make sure you know what you're doing."

He'd never seen her this happy? What was he talking about? She'd been perfectly happy before this.

"I do, I promise."

Ralph gave her a big hug, and they went back to the kitchen. Adam had plated the shrimp pasta and was about to take it out into the dining area. He gave her a wink, and she smiled, following him.

Instead of sitting across the table from her, he scooted his chair right next to hers. They talked as they ate, and he told more jokes to get her to laugh out loud. People needed to take notice of the two of them, so making noise was the best way to get their attention, and it was the *only* noise he could allow himself to make with her.

To cleanse their palates after eating the rich pasta, Danielle made them some fruit smoothies. It was mid-afternoon now, and the cafe was dead.

"Is it usually this slow?"

"On weekdays, yes, but weekends are busy pretty much all day. I'm sure Ralph and Nina had their hands full while I was gone."

"Do you ever get bored doing this every day?"

"There are always things that need to be done around here, and I don't have enough time to be bored. Besides, these lulls are the only times I get to myself. I love my customers, and I'm grateful for their business, but right now is my time to relax and prepare for the dinner and late crowds. When I get home, I'm so tired that I crash soon after. You have no idea how much energy it takes to run this place."

―――

Had he struck a nerve? He delicately placed his finger under her chin. "I'm sorry, I didn't realize. I know you work hard. It just came out wrong." He gave her a soft kiss.

She instantly cooled off and blushed, yet again. Adam wasn't entirely sure why he'd kissed her. There wasn't anyone around to see his little display of affection. Nina and Ralph were in the back, and there were no customers. Perhaps, it was purely to calm her down. Plus, it would be good to make it second nature for them. Even though the *'relationship'* was new, people might get suspicious if she was turning red every time he kissed or touched her. Adam knew he'd enjoy breaking her of that habit.

"It's okay," she said with a soft smile. Ah, that smile. The subject changed as they went back to a casual mood. "I still need to tell Carrie about us. If she finds out from someone else, she'll kill me. I've already warned Ralph, and especially Nina, to keep their mouths shut for now."

"I have an idea. How about we invite Carrie out to dinner? It would be good for us to get more public exposure as a couple."

Danielle thought it over for a minute. "Sure, but let's not tell her you're coming."

"Why?"

"I want it to be a surprise. With the ribbing I'm going to get, I should get a little fun, too."

Adam wasn't sure what she meant about the ribbing, but based on her tone, he decided not to ask.

Chapter Twenty-Four

The only thing Adam told her about the evening was that they were going to Blue Star. This meant she was going to have to wear something very nice. Blue Star was one of the finest restaurants in San Diego. The food was to die for, or so she'd heard, and the ambience was supposed to be magical, almost dream-like. She had no idea how Adam was able to get them a reservation last minute like this, even on a weeknight. She also felt a little uneasy about him taking her there. She knew it wasn't cheap, but he seemed like a prideful man, and there was no way she was going to bring up the expense with him. Even so, she had to admit to herself that she was excited.

Danielle stood in her closet, critiquing her wardrobe. Ugh, what was she going to wear? There were a handful of outfits that she could choose from, but she wasn't sure if she should go with conservative or sexy. After ten more minutes, she threw her hands in the air. "Just pick something!" She needed to hurry up, the reservation was for seven o'clock, and it was already six-fifteen p.m.

She reached for the conservative black dress that she usually ended up wearing for the majority of her nights out, but at the last minute, she grabbed the sexy red dress that she never wore. It was well fitted and shorter in length, accentuating her long legs, and had long, draped sleeves. The neckline cut into a low V, and the back opened up all the way down, stopping right above her derriere. If that wasn't enough, there was a sparkled embellishment at the stopping point to make sure your eyes didn't miss it. With the sleeves being draped, the back hung loosely, as well, not daring to touch her skin. The dress was a splurge that Carrie had talked her into. Danielle had never had a good reason to wear it, not even when Trevor took her out, but tonight...

She emerged from her bedroom to find Adam patiently waiting on the couch. His eyes didn't fall onto her until he stood. He was frozen in place as she closed the distance between them. She began to feel self-conscious as he slowly looked down and then back up her body, and the intensity in his eyes made it hard to tell what he was thinking. She would almost say he looked angry, but as his gray eyes met hers again, she saw what appeared to be a flash of something else. It was more like heat, and after his jaw clenched tight with a kind of restraint, she decided that the sexy red dress had been a good idea.

———

Adam's mouth went dry, and he lost all capability to move. The closer Danielle got, the harder it was for him to breathe. He couldn't take his eyes off her.

Mmm, he thought, as that Pavlovian response kicked in again—this time to a delicious body—overriding the cottonmouth.

Oh, the things he wanted to do to her—he couldn't imagine where to begin. At least he didn't have to completely keep his hands to himself. "Shall we?" he nearly choked out, as he headed for the door. He turned the knob and stepped back to allow her to walk through, and that's when he saw the back of her dress—or lack thereof. Adam could feel his arousal growing in his slacks. He could only hope that he could get it under control before she noticed.

When they arrived at Blue Star, the valet was waiting to open Danielle's door. As Adam tried to hand the guy the keys, he noticed that the young kid—probably making his way through college—was staring a little too hard at her, especially her backside. When the guy didn't acknowledge his presence, he grabbed the pervy valet's hand and closed it around the keys, squeezing until a whimper escaped the little punk. He let go and gave a deadly look to the valet, who quickly backed away to take the car.

As they entered the front doors, he noticed that she was swaying into her hips the way she did when she was angry. *She must use the same walk for when she's feeling sexy*, he thought. They were quickly seated near the center of the dining room, which Adam had specifically requested. The restaurant had a dance floor in its center. The construction and decoration of it created a sense of gliding among the night clouds, perfect for inspiring romance.

Danielle's face lit up when she saw the starlit ceiling and turned to smile. Adam couldn't help but smile back at her. The delight he saw in her eyes made him feel.... good. He had brought it to her. He had been the cause of the upward curling of those beautiful red lips.

―――

"Adam, this place is beautiful, thank you." Danielle felt like a young girl on a date with a boy—nervous and excited. It was silly, but she couldn't help it.

"*You're* beautiful."

She could feel herself blushing right on cue. Why did she always react that way?

"I'm sorry I didn't say so sooner, but..."

"What?"

Adam smiled and slightly chuckled at himself. "That dress can easily render a man speechless." He was looking right into her eyes as he said it. And three, two, one... blush. "Come on," he said, as he grabbed her hand.

He led her to the dance floor where the band was playing the old crooner tune, *"Misty"* by Johnny Mathis. The velvety vocals of the singer captured Mathis's perfectly. Adam held her hand in his while the other made its way to the small of her back, pulling her in close. Butterflies were flying chaotically in her stomach.

"You look very handsome yourself, by the way."

"I know."

She let out a small laugh at his playful self-reverence, and he laughed along with her. "Do you have any new information about the case?" Even though she was curious, the question was more about finding something objective to discuss. Her skin was starting to feel hot, and she knew the change in topic would cool it off.

"We're not going to talk about that." His expression stayed exactly the same, his voice remaining calm and smooth.

"We're not?"

"No, we're going to dance." The two made several laps around the floor, all the while, absorbing the romantic dream-like atmosphere. When the song finally drew to a close, Adam dipped Danielle in a slow, sensual circle, her back arching from left to right, her hair nearly brushing the floor, and her hips pressing into his. When he pulled her back up, his lips were mere inches from hers. The heat in her skin spread like wildfire down her body. They were no longer dancing but standing still on the floor. Her breaths became heavier, and she couldn't slow them down. Was he going to kiss her? He brought in the hand he'd been holding and kissed the top of it.

Guess not.

"Thank you for the dance," he said, smiling as he took a step back.

"Sure." There was a slight tone of disappointment in her voice. She broke her gaze from him and looked around the room. Everyone was staring at them, including Carrie. Her mouth was hanging wide open. How much of that had she seen? It didn't really matter, Danielle guessed, since Carrie had to be convinced anyway, and by the look on her face, she was sure that Carrie wasn't going to be much of a challenge now. Hell, she might be as easy as Nina was.

The couple met Carrie at the table, and Adam pulled out both ladies' chairs. There was that chivalry again, and *again,* Danielle thought about the nameless, faceless women receiving his acts of consideration. Cue the spike of jealousy—cue the chastisement.

"Well, Detective Burke, this is such a pleasant surprise," Carrie said, smiling as her eyes darted back and forth between them.

"Please, call me Adam, and that's what we were going for." He held his palm up for Danielle's hand.

"So," Carrie said with a slight pause, "when did *this* happen?" She gestured with her hand at the two of them.

"We wanted to tell you as soon as possible because Danielle said you'd kill her if you were the last to know, and I can't have that," said Adam in a playful tone.

"I know, Care, it is fast," said Danielle, as she looked over to him and teased, "but he just couldn't stay away from me."

"The same goes for you, sweetheart," he said.

Carrie recovered herself and now presented a look of expectancy. "Well, then I guess I'll take this opportunity to tell Danielle 'I told you so.'"

"And I knew you would," Danielle said, as she rolled her eyes at Carrie.

"What exactly did you tell her?" Adam asked.

"Oh, just that you had a thing for her." Carrie then added with a sly smile, "And that she had the hots for you… from minute one."

Adam looked at Danielle and started smiling smugly. "Is that so?"

Before she could even form a response, Carrie threw in, "Oh, yeah. Bad."

Damn it, Carrie, shut up!

"Well, how could she not?" he joked.

"Besides," Carrie said, "that dress proves it."

Danielle didn't think Carrie could sound any loftier if she tried. Adam raised an eyebrow in question.

"This is the first time she's worn it."

Danielle was going to kill her.

"And how long has she had this dress?"

Carrie looked at Danielle and saw the look of murder on her face. She might as well tell him if she was already going to die.

"Let's just say it's not new."

"Then, I guess I'm a lucky guy." He squeezed Danielle's hand. She prayed that he didn't bring this up later. She was already embarrassed enough as it was.

"Miss Walsh, I do believe you owe me a piece of cheesecake. Adam, if you'll excuse us, we're going to go powder our noses," Carrie said, as she grabbed Danielle's hand. He rose from his chair as the women left the table and headed for the ladies' room.

It was one of the most ornate bathrooms Danielle had ever been in. Crystal chandeliers matching the ones in the dining room had been incorporated, continuing the starlight theme. Carrie pulled her to sit on the deep blue velvet chaise, then grabbed her shoulders and exclaimed, "Oh my god, are you kidding me!"

"What do you mean?"

"What do you mean, '*what do I mean*?'" Carrie was shaking her now. "A few days ago, you *hated* the guy, and now you two are *dating*? Tell me what happened in the last forty-eight hours to bring on this one hundred-eighty-degree flip?"

Okay, it's time to bust out those acting skills full throttle.

"There was a second victim. The killer had her in our tree at the park."

"*In* our tree?" When Danielle didn't elaborate, Carrie gasped, "Oh my god, you mean... she was hanging in our movie tree?"

Danielle nodded for confirmation.

"When?"

"Two days ago."

"But that was Sunday. You're telling me he did this the same night we were there?" Danielle didn't have a chance to respond. "And I'm just now hearing about this?" Carrie was legitimately upset, as opposed to her usual theatrics.

"I'm sorry. I know I should have told you, but things started happening so fast, one after the other. I feel like everything has been a blur, and I haven't had a chance to actually think."

"Okay, I suppose I can understand that. So, then what happened?"

"When Adam went to the scene, the woman reminded him of me, and it scared him." That was partly true. Danielle actually had no idea if it had truly affected him that way.

"Reminded how?"

"She resembled me—in fact, both women did. The police think the killer is picking out women who look like me and murdering them in places that I go."

That was probably more than she was supposed to be sharing with Carrie, letting her know that she was tied to the murders, but she had to clue her in a little if they wanted her to believe their story. A simple "just because" explanation for Adam's constant presence wasn't going to cut it.

Carrie was speechless, which didn't happen too often. "I think I'm going to be sick," she said after a moment.

"Tell me about it."

"You're oddly calm about this."

"I guess with Adam around I feel safer, more at ease. When he realized how relieved he was that the victim wasn't me, he decided that he wouldn't waste any more time. He removed himself from the case so that there was no conflict of interest and told me how he felt about me. I couldn't help it. I just melted." Danielle's voice transformed from solemn to wistful.

Carrie still had a grip on Danielle, completely enveloped in the story. Finally, she started to relax. "Well, I guess now would be the best time to have a cop for a boyfriend."

Oh no, would Carrie figure it out?

Suddenly, she whipped her focus back to Danielle. "Did you sleep with him?"

"What? NO!" Danielle exclaimed, as Carrie arched her brow giving a look of disbelief. "No, Carrie, I didn't sleep with him. Stop looking at me like that."

"Well, if you had seen what I saw earlier, you'd have a hard time believing you, too."

"What does that mean?"

"Oh please, Dani," Carrie said, as she rose off the chaise, "I thought he was going to rip your dress right off you. Why do you think everyone was staring at the two of you?"

Danielle could feel her face getting red and her heart beating faster. "Carrie, I promise you, if we had slept together, I would tell you."

Carrie's eyes were still skeptical, but she finally relented. "Well, when you do, you had better tell me, you hear?"

"Yes, I hear you," Danielle said, as she rolled her eyes and laughed.

Inside her head, though, she wasn't laughing. Now she was going to have to make up something to tell Carrie to keep her believing their story because there was no way Carrie would buy them living together as a couple in love and not having sex, and she had no intentions of crawling into bed with Adam. Ugh, she hated lying to her, but Carrie couldn't know the truth. It might put her at risk, and she wasn't going to put her friend's life in danger.

"I need to live vicariously through you because God knows I don't have a love life of my own right now." Carrie was usually a nun when she was in the middle of a big case. There wasn't time for relationships, or at least that's what she said. Danielle could easily accuse Carrie of using the same excuse as she did. She wasn't even sure why she hadn't before, but that was a battle for another day.

Even though Carrie insisted Adam's passion was there, Danielle couldn't trust it. What if he was just a *really* good actor? After all, he had convinced the hell out of her at the café. There was no acting, though, when it came to his skills as a kisser. She had to admit he was pretty damn good at it. How many cases had he done this for? That thought burned her up.

Quit it, she said to herself, *you're being idiotic.*

After all, it's not like they needed to sleep together for their cover story. It couldn't happen because that's all this was—a story. Some kisses and hand holding were enough. Danielle was determined to keep it at that. Anything more, and it would lead her down a dangerous path where she was sure to get hurt.

The women rejoined Adam at their table, and once again, he rose upon their arrival. Why did he have to be such a gentleman? He was making it harder for her to quash her attraction to him.

The three of them spent the rest of dinner drinking wine and laughing as they shared stories, particularly ones about Danielle and Carrie getting into all sorts of shenanigans. Adam didn't take Danielle for a shenanigan type of person. According to Carrie, she wasn't uptight one hundred percent of the time.

"How else do you think she releases it?" Carrie giggled. "Well, this was really nice. I enjoyed getting to know you, Adam."

"Likewise, it was a pleasure," he said, as he moved in to wrap his arm around Danielle.

"Maybe we could go dancing next time, although it would probably need to be after the trial," Carrie said.

Danielle began to wonder how good of a dancer he was. She already knew he was good at the slow, romantic, and seductive style—oh, yes, he was good at that. She could feel her temperature begin to rise as she thought back to earlier in the evening and the way he touched her—the way he moved her.

"Maybe. Well, I guess we'll head home then," he said, as he pulled Danielle even tighter to him.

"Pardon?" Carrie asked, an espresso-colored brow arched in disbelief, as if she didn't trust what her own ears had heard.

"Oh…" Danielle could feel the anxiety clawing around in her stomach, and her speech almost stumbled over the lump she was trying to swallow.

Danielle could tell that Adam sensed how nervous she was getting, and if *he* could, then Carrie would certainly notice. If that happened, she might see through their cover and at this point in time, it was vital for as few people to know about it as possible.

"Danielle was kind enough to humor me and let me stay with her. Since I have a good deal of free time now, I want to spend as much of it with her as I can."

She found her nerve again. "He had a bunch of vacation time built up…"

"So, I figured, why not?" he finished.

Carrie was wearing the same look of shock as when she'd seen Danielle and Adam dancing. If she'd been taking a drink, she probably would have started choking on it.

"Wow… that's… wow."

Danielle was pretty sure that this bomb hit Carrie big. It wasn't very often that she was at a loss for words, especially since she was a lawyer. She was known in the courtroom for her articulation and elocution.

"You probably have a few concerns, Carrie, but I promise my intentions are pure. Scouts honor." Adam turned his gaze back to Danielle. "I don't want to be without her." Damn, he really was good at this. If she didn't know better, she'd have bought it all over again.

"This is so unlike you, Dani," Carrie started, then changed the shocked expression to one that seemed pleased. "I'm glad. It's about time you unclenched."

Adam let out a snicker, but Danielle wasn't very amused by Carrie's comment. She was burning holes in the back of Carrie's head as they made their way out of the restaurant. As they stood waiting for the valets to bring around their cars, a light breeze blew over her, making her shiver and sending goosebumps racing all over. It wasn't too surprising with so much skin exposed. She was practically half naked in that dress.

Adam took off his suit jacket and put it around her shoulders. He pulled her hair out from underneath the weight of it and brushed the tendrils back. There were those butterflies again. The entire world was fading out, and the only thing Danielle could see was Adam's cool gray eyes that were transforming into a storm, threatening to thrust her into the gale.

Danielle swallowed hard as Adam grabbed the lapels of his jacket and pulled her into a kiss that made her legs feel like Jell-O. His lips were soft on hers at first, then grew in intensity. His tongue made its way into her mouth, exploring. Her hands placed themselves lightly on his chest. Her brain was complete mush—she had no control over her limbs. It was remarkable that she was even still standing.

Adam slowly pulled his lips away from hers, and Danielle had to fight back a whimper. The kiss had only lasted about ten seconds, but it felt like an eternity. The world slowly came back into focus, and once again, all eyes were on them.

One of the valets pulled up with Carrie's car.

"O-kay," said Carrie with a smile indicating that she was trying very hard to hold back something—a squeal maybe. "You two kids have a great night. Oh, and, Dani, I'll be expecting that call tomorrow." She gave Danielle a wink and then disappeared into her car.

Chapter Twenty-Five

The drive home was quiet. Danielle spent the entire car ride gazing out of the window. Had he offended her in some way? Adam couldn't think of anything in particular that might have upset her, maybe except something Carrie had said. He thought back to Carrie's triumph over the cheesecake bet, which was an odd thing to bet on. Was she right? Had Danielle really been lusting after him since they met? He'd admit it, he had been for her. There's a chance that Carrie was wrong, and Danielle really didn't want anything to do with him, but for the sake of the cover, she had to let Carrie think so.

On the other hand, he thought, she looked embarrassed as if Carrie had told a secret that was supposed to stay between girlfriends. And then there was the way her eyes and body reacted to him. She was practically panting at the end of their dance and his kiss... He was pretty sure if he hadn't been holding on to her, she would've fallen over.

And sweet lord, that dress! Carrie had said—practically out and out—that Danielle had worn it just for him. It meant she hadn't worn it for Trevor—not for any other man. If she wasn't attracted to him, at least on some level, she wouldn't have bothered, would she? It was excruciating for him to not let his hands roam over every inch of the soft fabric and the body it was clinging to. If they hadn't been in public, Adam didn't think he could've stopped himself.

"Why are you smiling?" Her voice brought his focus back to the present. Was he smiling? He hadn't realized it. Apparently, she was done staring out the window, ignoring him.

"Nothing in particular," he said, as he looked over to her. She raised her eyebrow in skepticism but gave up. She probably knew he was lying but didn't want to know the truth. It was better that she didn't.

They made it back to the apartment, and Adam conducted a preliminary search before relaxing. When he determined the place was

The Harvester

safe, he locked the deadbolts. He'd added an extra one, so now she had two. If anyone wanted to break in during the night, they were going to have a hard time. Adam began removing his shoulder holster with his gun.

Danielle did a double take. "Were you wearing that the entire time?"

"Yes, you didn't notice when I took off my jacket?" he asked, as he set them down on the coffee table.

"No, I guess I didn't." Her eyes seemed to be darting around the room now, as if she couldn't look directly at him. Had the kiss distracted her that much? She didn't even notice in the car, though how would she since she barely gave him a glance?

After a moment of silence, he decided to direct the conversation. "I think Carrie bought it. Although, you know her better than I do, so would you say that tonight was a success?"

"Yeah, I'd say so." It looked like she was keeping something to herself, but he didn't push. "So, what's the next move with this?"

"The next move?" he asked, confusion on his face as he sat down on the couch.

"With our *relationship.*' I need to know what the boundaries are." She was still standing, her arms now crossed over her chest like a shield.

"I don't know. I've never done this before." Adam would swear on his life that there was a look of relief in Danielle's eyes. "Do you need some boundaries?" This whole situation would be easier if she said yes. There's no way he would go against her wishes, and that should make the urges easier to control. A voice in the back of his mind wanted her to say no.

"How else do you think she releases it?" Carrie had said. Oh, he could think of a few ways he could make Danielle release. And a few reasons why he shouldn't.

"Yes."

Damn. No, this is a good thing.

"We probably should set some up, you know, just as a guideline."

"Okay, so what's first?" he asked, as he leaned back into the sofa and put his hands behind his head.

Um... Damn it!

Danielle hadn't even thought up any yet. Her mind was lost in the car, so she'd wasted that time. The kiss kept replaying in her head and how badly she wanted to do it again. She needed to put some space between them, so she made her way to lean against the bar top connecting to the kitchen.

"Well," she swallowed to buy some time, "our sleeping arrangements will stay the same. Me in my bedroom, and you on the couch."

"Of course." He looked so relaxed, and that pissed her off. He should feel as tense and uncomfortable as she did.

"I also think we should discuss how physical this needs to be." She thought for sure that question would at least get some sort of reaction out of him.

"Okay, how physical do you want to make this?" Adam didn't flinch.

She was trying to form her answer but wasn't sure how to say it. Hell, she wasn't sure what the answer was.

"I'm going to have to ask you, though, to try not to sleep with me," he said, grinning.

Well, that made her mind up right there. Her hands moved to rest on her hips, and she rolled her eyes at him. "That's awfully presumptuous of you." This felt like a challenge, and she wasn't going to back down. The battle of *who couldn't care less* was on. Adam stood up and moved to her, once again trapping her from escape. Danielle could feel the bar top pushing into her back. His body was practically pressed up against hers, and his eyes were trying to penetrate hers... and her clothes.

"Is it?"

Dear. God. He spoke in a low, seductive voice, and his words were filled with confidence. No—arrogance, she decided. He was trying to break her just to prove a point to his ego that he could and then he would no doubt turn her away. Oh, two can play at this game.

I. Will. Win.

"Yes, it is." She put a hand on his chest and moved to walk him back to the couch. She stopped him before it hit the backs of his legs and started with her own sexy voice. "Do you think that every time you touch my hair..." she traced a few fingers through his own, starting from his temple to behind his ear, "every time you touch my skin..." she ran her hand down his chest, "every time you kiss my lips..."

She purposely left the question hanging, and since he didn't have jacket lapels, she settled for his necktie and grabbed it, pulling his lips to hers. She choreographed the kiss like a slow, provocative dance, each movement with its own purpose. It might have been a while since Danielle had dated, but one thing that she was always good at, no matter how much time passed, was kissing. It never failed her. She ended the kiss with just the slightest bite of his bottom lip.

"Do you think that every time you do those things to me," she continued with her wanton tone, "I'm aching for more?"

Adam didn't respond. He just stared back at her, eyes hooded with lust. *Just a little further,* she thought.

"Adam?"

"Yeah?" he responded, sounding out of breath.

"Will you do something for me?" she asked, as she drew him closer by the grasp she held on his tie.

"Yes."

Gotcha!

"Get over yourself," Danielle whispered in his ear and shoved him down onto the couch. She left him slack-jawed as she strutted to her bedroom and shut the door.

Chapter Twenty-Six

He paced back and forth in front of his shrine, each step heavier. Satisfaction and frustration were at war in his head. The killing had gone splendidly down to every detail. Seducing and drugging the woman had been a piece of cake. He didn't even use his best lines, and he had her ready and willing to go home with him.

"I'm just dying to see your place," she'd said. And die she did, just like that whore deserved.

Getting her body up into the tree was no simple task, but he'd managed to get it done quickly, and when he was finished, oh, it was a work of art. He'd fixed her at all the right angles to showcase his talents. Would his angel be impressed? He certainly hoped so. After all, this was for her. These women had the gall to walk around looking like her and then offering themselves up like sinful sluts. They were sullying her reputation, and it was his job to protect her—his job to punish them.

He chuckled as he continued to think back to the second murder. Number two presented herself as a *modern woman,* which meant loose. Yes, that whore got what she deserved.

This cop was a problem, though. How dare he try to steal his angel, kissing her and touching her? He wanted to cut the detective's hands off. That would teach him not to play with what was his. Alas, he had to keep his distance if he wanted his plan to unfold without any hitches.

He hadn't anticipated for a romance to take hold of his angel. Clearly, she was being seduced by the detective, who was going to corrupt her. He couldn't allow her to be tainted. She belonged to *him*!

He reached out to touch a picture of her—one of many. In fact, the entire room was covered with his angel. He traced the outline of her hair and sighed. She couldn't possibly be falling for the detective's lies…

could she? He smiled wickedly as his resolve strengthened. No, he'd help her see. He'd make her see.

Chapter Twenty-Seven

Ben waited patiently in the foyer of the thirteen-million-dollar estate. Richard Vance spared no expense on anything, and this house was proof of that. The ten thousand square foot home was enough to house at least two families, yet Richard and Kimberlee were the only occupants. The four spare bedrooms were used for party guests after their frequent soirees and Kimberlee's girlfriends to crash in following a late night of drinking frou-frou cocktails and a few bottles of wine. Nine bathrooms were incorporated throughout, leaving it impossible for someone to not be able to find a toilet when they needed to purge the excessive amounts of alcohol they had consumed.

Behind him were three glass French style doors that opened to the main patio, where the outdoor pool lay straight ahead. Beyond the perfectly manicured lawn and garden was an amazing view of the San Diego skyline. From that vantage, Ben could only imagine how beautiful the sunsets were that served as the backdrop and how incredible the gorgeous colors would be as they reflected on the waters of the bay.

Ben had done his homework and researched the address. The miniature mansion also came with a tennis court, an indoor pool, a covered patio and cabana, two living rooms, and a large kitchen covered in marble and granite—a kitchen that was completely unnecessary. The probability of Mrs. Vance ever cooking a single meal on her own was minuscule. Going on the assumption that they had a staff to maintain the home, the cooking would have been done by one of the employees or some sort of high-priced nutritionist chef.

More likely than not, the Vances went to expensive restaurants every night where they could be seen by those who were deemed important. Yes, the only use Kimberlee could possibly have for that kitchen would be to chill her wine and store her corkscrew.

"Thank you so much for waiting, Detective."

The Harvester

Upon Ben's arrival, Kimberlee had excused herself to freshen up. *Bullshit.* There hadn't been a need to. She didn't look any different than when she had first let him in—perfectly styled hair, form-fitting dress and stilettos, all impeccably coordinated, and make-up perfected down to the last detail. Her entire appearance suggested she had plans, but Ben wondered if she was even planning to step outside the house. It was nine in the morning on a workday, but there wasn't an office waiting for her arrival. No desk to file her nails at, and no coworkers to gossip with at the water cooler. Mrs. Vance's paycheck came directly from Mr. Vance. Her job was to be a trophy wife, and she was fulfilling those duties diligently.

"I hope I'm not keeping you from anything," she said with artificial concern.

She had just wanted to make him wait fifteen minutes to emphasize that her time was more valuable than his. She held the power to dictate his schedule, a power she no doubt used consistently. It implied her superiority over others. Richard undoubtedly controlled most aspects of her life, so any piece of control she could take for herself, she did. In this instance, it was her time that Ben was asking for, so she would make him earn it.

"Not at all," he said. It was the truth. Talking with Kimberlee was at the top of his to-do list—everything else came second. "I just need to ask you a few questions relevant to a case that I'm working on."

"I'll help in any way I can, though I can't imagine what it could be about."

"Please remember that I need you to answer honestly."

"Of course, Detective," Kimberlee said, looking somewhat offended.

"Where were you on the nights of September sixth and September twenty-first?"

"I was at Lotus Blossom Med Spa," Kimberlee answered without hesitation.

"Are you sure?" Ben kept his head down as he wrote in his notepad.

"Yes, I go every other weekend, unless Richard and I have plans, but what does that have to do with anything?"

Ben was going to be as blunt as possible to see what kind of reaction he could get from her. He was looking for any sort of tell. "Do you have a sexual relationship with Trevor Whitman?"

"Excuse me?" she gasped.

He had definitely succeeded in catching her off guard. "Do you have a relationship, sexual or otherwise, with Trevor Whitman?"

"Absolutely not! I don't even know who that is." That sugar sweet voice turned to fury at his inquiry, and she took a step back, as if to put more space between them.

"He works at your husband's firm."

"Lots of people work at Richard's firm, that doesn't mean *I* know all of them. Why would you even ask me such a thing?"

"Well, Mr. Whitman claims that on both of these nights he was with you, and we need to confirm the legitimacy of his alibi."

"His alibi... For what?" Kimberlee shifted her weight. She was no longer angry, but cautious in her questioning.

"For multiple homicides. He's a person of interest in the murders of two women." Ben continued to study her expressions.

"Oh my god, he murdered two women?" She looked genuinely surprised... and possibly scared?

"We're not certain, which is why it's important that we verify his claim of having been with you."

Kimberlee shifted her weight again and crossed her arms over her chest. "It's like I said, I don't know him."

"Then, you have no issue with me confirming with the spa of your stays there on the days in question?"

"None. You will see that I am booked there by myself as always."

"We'll see." The veritable shock and offense in her expression at the nerve he had to doubt her was anything but subtle.

"Why do you suppose he would say that the two of you were together?"

"How the hell should I know? If he's a killer, he's already screwed up in the head." Ben wasn't going to get anything else from her. She was closing up tighter than a clam.

"Hmm," he resigned, "you could very well be right."

Kimberlee now looked pleased with herself, as if she had just solved the case for him.

"Thank you for your time, Mrs. Vance."

"I love my husband, Detective," she added, pointedly.

Ben took one last glance at the beautiful estate in his rearview mirror as he headed down the front drive. Kimberlee Vance had all but slammed the door in his face after she reluctantly took his card. No doubt, it met its untimely end in the trash, the shredder if she were clever.

"I love my husband, Detective."

Ben scoffed. *Loves his money is more accurate.* There was most certainly a prenuptial agreement, and if she got busted having an affair, she would likely lose everything. Ben's gut told him she was lying, but he had no proof. It was possible that she was fully aware of everything at stake should she commit adultery and was too smart to chance it.

After all, studies showed that the majority of women craved financial security above all else, and with Kimberlee being the wife of a man thirty plus years her senior, it was safe to say that she was a part of that majority. He would see if there were any cameras at Lotus Blossom Med Spa to determine if she was telling the truth or just looking out for number one.

Ben knew that Adam wanted Trevor to be the Harvester, but he wasn't too sure. It was obvious that Adam loathed the guy, which, in Ben's mind, meant the cover story wasn't too far from the truth. Adam's actions at the brokerage firm were an indication that he couldn't stay objective, not when it came to a certain tall, blonde bombshell. He had never seen that kind of behavior from him before, which undoubtedly stemmed from Trevor's less than complimentary words about her and his overall general attitude.

The agenda had been officially changed. Now, Ben had to go to the spa to gather any evidence they might have to either verify or disprove Kimberlee Vance's claims. Whether or not they would comply willingly was the question. They could demand him to get a warrant before they provided any records, which wasn't the end of the world, but it *was* another speed bump to slow him down.

Fortunately, Ben dodged the *speed bump*. After verifying her identity and getting her consent, he was able to get his hands on the reservation logs and video footage from all of the security cameras at Lotus Blossom. Even though there were only two dates in question, Ben decided to check out Mrs. Vance's other weekend stays. He pored over the videos but found nothing. Not once did she meet with someone else in the lobby, nor by the pool, or the spa. No one else was seen entering her room from the hall cameras. There were other guests staying in the rooms on either side of her, but they appeared to be women. There was *zero* proof to support Trevor's claims of being with her.

Now, as far as his claims of sleeping with her, Ben had little doubt in his mind, but that wasn't the issue. The issue was that he wasn't at the spa during the times of the murders, and in the law's eyes, that's all that mattered.

The agenda had been officially changed *again*. With nothing to substantiate Trevor's alibi, Ben's next stop would be to the district attorney's office for an arrest warrant. Considering the priority level of this case, Ben was confident it wouldn't take too long to get the D.A. and a judge to sign off on it. Captain Jensen had emphasized what the importance was to many 'people of influence' of getting it solved. Hell, it would probably be expedited, and Ben would be making that next trip to the brokerage firm as early as tomorrow.

It was a good thing Adam was tied to Danielle for the time being for Trevor's sake because if Adam were to be involved, the jackass would probably end up a eunuch. Ben laughed at the thought and then laughed even louder. Finding castration funny was funny in itself.

―――

Adam had been waiting, practically on the edge of his seat, to hear from his partner. His visit to Kimberlee Vance was this morning, and he was a little more than curious to find out what she had to say about the tryst. A soft buzzing vibration came from his pocket, and he fished out his phone. It was the call he had been waiting for. Walking into Danielle's office, he answered, skipping a greeting.

"So?" He listened as Ben gave him a rundown of his conversation with Mrs. Vance, the trip to Lotus Blossom, the warrant, and what their next move for the investigation would be. Adam knew arresting Trevor was the first order of business. "I want to be there tomorrow."

"That's not a good idea."

"Why?"

"You *know* why."

"Two is better than one with this guy. He's too arrogant. The only way he's going to sweat is if we both put the pressure on... I need to be there for this, Ben." There was a long pause, then a heavy sigh blew through the phone.

"Interrogation room only."

Ben was sidelining him from taking part in the arrest. As bad as Adam wanted to be the one to slap the cuffs on Whitman, he had to respect his partner's decision.

"Was that Ben?" Adam looked up from his phone, having just ended the call, as Danielle entered her office.

"Yes. I need to go by the station tomorrow." She began to groan, ending in a full on pout. He knew she really didn't care for sitting there, waiting around for him when there were better, more important things she could be doing with her time. "I know, but it's something I have to take care of." He smiled as he reached out, wiping away a smudge of flour from her cheek, causing her to flush in response.

Chapter Twenty-Eight

He had been waiting in the room for nearly thirty minutes by himself, another forty-five before that in a holding cell. The room was anything but inviting with the drab concrete walls, a cold metal table that he was currently shackled to, and the giant mirror that reflected a man who was filled with anger and humiliation. His fresh, crisp white shirt was becoming more wrinkled by the minute, and he didn't even want to think about the filth that his tailored Gucci pants had been subjected to from sitting on the concrete bench in the aforementioned cell.

The whole scene played out in his head, as it had been doing since the moment he had arrived. The surprise of seeing the detective that he had labeled as 'the composed one' being accompanied by two extra police officers. The inability for comprehension as the unfashionable—and uncomfortable—metal bracelets were tightened around his wrists. The inexorable denial that took hold of his mind as he was given a recitation of words. To top it all off, the mortification as he was escorted from the building, leaving a trail of whispers and penetrating stares in his wake, in what had to be the worst kind of walk of shame.

His career—his life—was effectively ruined.

The knob of the door turned and in walked 'the composed one' *and* 'the aggressive one.' What were their names again? He hadn't deemed it necessary to remember them from their first visit, and he had immediately thrown away their cards after they had left.

Aggressive hadn't been physically violent, but it was in the tone of his words, the look in his eyes that had suggested the volatility that lay just below the surface, waiting to break free at any moment. The same ferocity still lived in those eyes today as he calmly made his way to his seat.

"Mr. Whitman," *Composed* began, "do you know why you're here?"

Trevor thought about what he had been previously told. If he were smart, he'd be timid and compliant. "Yes, you morons seem to think I killed some women." So much for that plan.

"That's putting it mildly."

"How about butchered?" *Aggressive* suggested.

"Why don't you tell us again where you were during these murders."

"I already told you where I was," Trevor sneered.

"Right," *Composed* said, as he opened a folder, "you were with Kimberlee Vance?" Trevor remained silent as he glared at the two detectives. "Do you have any proof, maybe some receipts or witnesses?"

"When you're fucking your boss's wife, you tend to make sure that you *aren't* seen together. Besides, I don't need a witness. Maybe if you two would do your jobs right and ask her—"

"And therein lies the problem, Mr. Whitman."

"What does that mean?"

"It means we did ask her." The two detectives just stared straight at him, waiting for him to catch up.

"Wait... no, no, wait a minute. I was with her. We were at—"

"Lotus Blossom Med Spa?"

"Yes!"

"You told us you were at home, meaning you lied to us previously. Who's to say you aren't lying now?"

"I'm telling you the truth this time. I was at the spa."

"I checked, and there is no record of you staying there. You're also nowhere to be seen on any of the security cameras."

"Because I was in fucking disguise! I used aliases."

"And what were the names of those aliases?"

Fuck! At that moment, Trevor couldn't remember a single one. He had purposely avoided using the same one for this very reason—to make it impossible to prove they were meeting in secret.

"It's like I said," he reiterated forcefully, "when you're fucking your boss's wife, you cover your goddamn tracks!"

"Well, unfortunately, Kimberlee denied even knowing you, much less being in your company those nights."

"She's lying!" Trevor yelled furiously. He could feel himself starting to panic. *That little bitch!* She wanted to protect herself so badly that she would lie, knowing what was at stake for him? *Just you wait,* he thought. *You're going to get yours, slut.*

"Just like Danielle Walsh was lying about you stalking her?" *Aggressive* taunted, but this time, he was missing his arrogant smile. In fact, he looked something close to incensed, just like he had that day back at the firm. Why? Why was this guy so worked up about…

Ah-ha.

"Yes," Trevor replied, casually, "just like Danielle." The detective's eyes narrowed hard on him. "But, if that whore wants to lie, fine."

"Watch your mouth," *Aggressive* growled through gritted teeth.

Trevor just smiled. "Don't worry, Detective. I'm not referring to sweet Danielle. She's anything but. It actually took quite a while to get those long legs to open up, but once they did, man oh man… well, you know," he said with a nod, as he casually gestured to *Aggressive* with a small wave of his hand. Though the size of it was insubstantial—thanks to the hand cuffs—it spoke volumes.

White hot fury burned in the detective's eyes. "It seems you've forgotten the agreement we made the last time we spoke. I suggest you think extra hard to remember because you don't want me to repeat myself."

Trevor pretended to search his brain, then shrugged and smiled, as though he had come up with nothing.

"That's enough," *Composed* firmly interjected. "Mr. Whitman, I don't think you fully comprehend the situation you're in."

"Actually, I think I do. Let's cut through the bullshit, guys. Regardless of what that bitch says, and even the lack of proof of me being at the spa, you have no *real* evidence that I killed those women. You're clearly grasping at straws, so stop wasting my time with this joke of an interrogation. There's no point in continuing." Then, Trevor added, smugly, "And, without any evidence, you can't hold me here."

"Actually," *Aggressive* mimicked, "motive and probable cause says we can."

Trevor glowered. "You're lying."

"You certainly do say that a lot. Do you enjoy it, or is it that we've met the extent of your vocabulary?"

"Don't bother, Burke," *Composed* said, never taking his eyes off Trevor. "You're pointlessly wasting Mr. Whitman's time, remember? He's in a hurry to get back to his cell."

Trevor began sputtering incoherent profanities. Neither Adam nor Ben were fazed by it. In truth, they'd heard far worse before. Adam couldn't care less what Trevor called him, but listening to him talk about Danielle like that had inspired so much hostility. Adam was known for being cool and collected. He rarely flew off the handle.

Ever since he took this case, though, his temper had been on a low boil just below the surface, ready to spill over at a moment's notice—and he knew it had everything to do with the woman he was confined to close quarters with.

Like a fly, Trevor's ranting buzzed in his ears. Oh, how he wanted to swat that fly, and after five minutes of the relentless tantrum that had no end in sight, it was apparent that Trevor needed more time in his jail cell. They weren't getting anywhere.

"Is Danielle just doing this to get back at me? Is that was this is—fuck a cop and get him to harass whomever she wants? And don't bother denying it, either. I know you're screwing her! Hell, who knows how many of you she's fucking just to get her stupid, petty revenge."

Adam had finally had enough. Without warning, he stood and walked around the table to his suspect, who slowed his monologue with each of his steps, warily watching and confused.

Trevor's head violently slammed down, the force of it echoing in the small room.

Wham!

"Hey! What the hell are you doing?" Trevor screeched in surprise. His right cheek was pressed hard against the cold metal table, unwillingly held in place.

"Repeating myself," Adam growled and leaned down to hover above Trevor. "You better listen and listen well, you piece of shit. Danielle is no longer your concern. You will not speak about her in such a way again. If you're even a fraction as smart as you seem to think you are, you'd do well to remember this time." Adam's tone was so menacing that all Trevor could do was gawk. It took a good minute for his thoughts to gather again.

"I want to call my lawyer! I'm going to sue your ass for assault!" Adam showed no outward reaction as he unchained Trevor's cuffs from the table.

"Go ahead," he responded, as he lifted the slime ball out of the chair and headed for the door. His grip on Trevor's arm was unnecessarily tight—just enough to make him uncomfortable without leaving any marks. It wasn't like there was anywhere for him to run, not to mention, he was no match for Adam in pure strength.

"You're only proving my point."

Yes, he was, but not the way he should have. He should have been levelheaded and played off Trevor's filthy comments and false inference of their relationship. Adam just couldn't talk about Danielle like that. He couldn't bring himself to say anything crass or lewd, even if it helped their cover. Instead, he had let his possessiveness do the talking for him. *Whatever works*, he thought.

Two officers were waiting outside the interrogation room as Adam dragged him through the doorway. "Take him back to holding," he ordered, as he roughly passed Trevor off.

One of the officers silently accepted the command with a nod. "Come on, let's go," he said to Trevor.

"Just you wait! I'll have your badge for this, asshole!" Again, Adam showed no cause for concern, which only seemed to enrage Trevor more.

He remained stone faced, as he watched them escort Trevor down the hall. Trevor, on the other hand, had seething hatred blazing in his eyes as he got one last look at Adam before the elevator doors closed. Then, and only then, did Adam allow his emotions to surface. He wanted to punch something, throw something, shoot something, because he knew they could only keep Trevor under lock and key for forty-eight hours.

Trevor had been correct in his claim that they had no real proof that he was the Harvester, and without it, Adam would have no choice but to let him go. His jaw clenched in frustration at the thought of Trevor walking out of the station freely.

Chapter Twenty-Nine

Danielle wished that Adam had left her at the café every passing second for the last ninety minutes. In fact, she downright despised him for bringing her here—and leaving her here. Detective Greasy had been leering at her since he had come back from lunch, then took his time sauntering over, so as to not look too eager. *Mission not accomplished.* She was sitting in Adam's chair, minding her own business, when he had approached, trapping her at the desk. He was grinning like an idiot, and she whimpered internally in dread of the coming interaction.

He'd rambled ad nauseam about all of the cases he'd closed, bragging about how modest he was. She decided he wasn't intelligent enough to recognize that oxymoron. Thinking to impress her, he prattled on, pausing only briefly for a confirmation that she was listening to his heavy ego stroking. She had tried to tune him out, even though it was rude, but his sleazy smile and wandering eyes had caused her to stay sharp.

She was going to kill Adam. Kill. Him. She didn't know how yet, but he was going to make this up to her one way or another.

A loud voice carried down the hall, through the department doors, stealing her focus. A man was screaming like a lunatic, issuing a threat about taking someone's badge. It almost sounded like... Trevor? Could it have been? It certainly was something he would say, trying to maintain what a big shot he was. Danielle snorted and rolled her eyes.

"It was a pretty big deal."

Her attention came back to a different self-absorbed man. She had become distracted by the disturbance, resulting in her brief exit of the already unwanted conversation.

Corolla was waiting for her to acknowledge his statement in agreement. "You know?"

Since she hadn't been paying attention, she wasn't sure what to say. Sure, she could go along with it, but she didn't want to encourage him. She needed to think of some sort of excuse to get away. She was at her limit. There was one surefire method, but she didn't generally like using it. It was kind of a cheap cop out. In this situation, however, she was willing to pull it out of her arsenal. Desperate times called for desperate measures.

'I just started my period.' Want to see a man put some distance between you, tell him you're bleeding profusely from the place he's trying to get to. He'll jump back a few hundred feet and into a hazmat suit like you have the bubonic plague.

Danielle didn't get the chance to use it, however. As she was preparing to gross him out, someone interrupted.

"Can I help you with something?"

Corolla jumped at the deep voice that boomed so close behind him. The question was no doubt rhetorical. She knew what Adam was really saying was, *'Back the fuck off.'* His arms were folded over his broad chest, a deep scowl pulling at the corners of his mouth. Yep, that's *definitely* what he was saying.

How had he gotten to them so fast? She had just been looking at the doors not one minute ago from Trevor's outburst, and Adam had been nowhere in sight.

"Miss Walsh was all by her lonesome, so I thought I would keep her company," Corolla said, as he turned to face Adam, feigning good intentions.

"Did she ask for your company?" When Corolla didn't answer right away, Adam continued, "I would recommend you give some company to your own case." Finally, he turned his eyes to Danielle. They still had so much ire in them. "We're leaving."

"O-okay." Why did she respond like she was in trouble, caught doing something she shouldn't have been? She was the victim in all of this, after all. If anything, he was the one who should be in trouble for even allowing the possibility of this situation to happen. She was going to let him know, too. Later. Danielle may have hated being around Detective Greasy, but she wasn't cruel. She didn't believe in deliberately insulting someone to their face. If she had informed Adam of his cruelty for dragging her here, resulting in her being stuck with Corolla, then she would have been doing just that.

Adam moved into Corolla's personal space, forcing him to step back and allow Danielle to get up from the chair. Finally, she could breathe. He waited for her to round the desk and pass by him before he moved away. Once they were outside, he stopped her.

"I'm sorry if he was bothering you. If he's making you uncomfortable in any way, tell me. I'll personally see to it that it stops." The aggression in his voice and body was still prevalent, and Danielle felt as though it was up to her to calm him down. The scolding she was going to give him had lost its necessity. He was clearly on edge.

"You can make it up to me later."

Adam raised a brow in question.

"Besides, I was just about to handle him before you showed up."

"Oh?"

"I was going to ask him where the tampon machine was."

Adam blinked in shock and then erupted in laughter—not what Danielle was expecting. Still chuckling, he pulled her in and sweetly kissed her. *Definitely* not what she was expecting. He had a gleam in his eyes, as though he was proud of her. *My man is proud of me*, she thought, smiling inside. What a ridiculous thing to get excited about, and oh yeah, Adam wasn't her man. Not really.

"I guess I won't worry so much next time."

He was worried?

"There won't be a next time," she said, poking a finger into his hard chest. "I won't let you leave me all alone."

―――

All alone? Adam thought. The context in the way she said it, her tone, felt akin to abandonment, the word usually associated with hurt or sadness, longing for what was missing. Was that how she had felt? Had his absence affected her the same way hers affected him? Did she actually... *miss* him? Why did the thought make him happy?

As though she realized the connotation of her words, Danielle rushed to edit herself. "I mean, you will not leave me stranded again." A second passed, then two. "Since I'm stuck going anywhere and everywhere you go," she added, still trying to recover from the implications of her previous statement. It was clear she was becoming uncomfortable—from her statement *and* from his silence. Adam decided to put her out of her misery and spare her from the embarrassment she was so obviously experiencing.

"Let me help you make dinner and it's a deal," he said with a casual smile. The tension in her body eased as she smiled and shook his hand.

"Deal."

Chapter Thirty

Trevor had never been a day-drinker. He was too busy making money... until now. His job was hanging by a thread. Vance didn't fire him, but he was on a mandatory hiatus for an indeterminable amount of time. Unpaid. No one wanted a suspected murderer on their payroll.

He seethed as he knocked back the last of his whiskey, the ice clinking against the glass. Now realizing it was empty, he walked over to his bar and poured another two fingers, swirling the liquid as he plopped back down onto the couch.

The past seventy-two hours had been a nightmare. Getting arrested and hauled in for questioning and then being held in a filthy cell for two more days with no privacy. The only pleasure he'd gotten was seeing Detective *Aggressive*'s face as he was forced to release him. Oh, and his face when Trevor talked about Danielle in bed. That had been quite entertaining. He still planned on pressing charges on the detective for assault.

The dickhead cops weren't what he was seething about at the moment, though. No, his burning hatred was directed at one person. Kimberlee Vance. Had it not been for her, those aforementioned dickheads wouldn't have been able to hold him without something substantial. Hell, they wouldn't have even been able to arrest him.

She had lied, knowing full well that they'd been screwing like rabbits every other weekend at that spa for the past two and a half months. Fuck, she was willing to let him go down for murder just so she could keep spending her husband's money!

Unfortunately for Trevor, being good at keeping their hook-ups hidden from the world was biting him in the ass. He was the planner, the one with the knowledge and experience to pull it off. Trevor handled it all while Kimberlee didn't have to do a goddamned thing... which was unfortunate for *her*.

From the moment he'd seen her, Trevor knew he would get what was under the too-short, extremely tight skirt. The looks she gave him encouraged him to, but seeing as how she was his boss's current trophy wife, measures needed to be taken to ensure his job security.

Richard Vance was rich as hell, but regardless of his wealth, there was no way on Earth that a young, pretty piece of ass like her was satisfied by an ugly, wrinkled, old dog turd like him, and before Trevor chanced giving her some satisfaction, he needed to see who else was giving it to her because he was sure as shit he wasn't the only one.

It only took a week for the private eye to bring Trevor video evidence of her other indiscretion. It was surprising to him that she hadn't already been busted. She was too careless with her meeting places, not paying a bit of attention to who might see her. Trevor didn't let her know what an idiot she was, nor did she question why he set up all of their rendezvous. It was one less thing she had to do, not that she did much of anything.

Dumb cunt. She had no idea the mistake she'd made. He was livid with her for denying his alibi, but the fact that she didn't take any of his calls to even attempt to explain herself, not that it would've done her any good, pushed him past livid and into enraged. If she wanted to screw him, fine. He would fuck that gold-digging slut one last time.

Trevor took another gulp from his glass. Pretty soon, Vance would be opening an e-mail with a very special video starring his whore of a wife and the personal trainer. Trevor rolled his eyes at the cliché. That pretty little prenup was going to be null and void. He just wished he could be there to see her down on her knees, begging and pleading. He'd had her down on her knees plenty of times, begging and pleading, but for an entirely different reason.

Even *if* Kimberlee was smart enough to figure out that Trevor was the one who set her up and told Vance about their romps, there was no way she could prove it, all thanks to his ability to hide their dirty, little secrets. Yes, he wished he could see Richard Vance kick her ass out onto the street. That brought a smile to his face.

Chapter Thirty-One

Adam had been on edge ever since Trevor walked out of the precinct with his *'smug grin plastered all over his damn face.'* At least, that was how it had been relayed to her. Once again, Danielle had been forced to go down to the station with him—so much for their deal—but this time, she was allowed to wait in Captain Jensen's office. Adam must have said something to him about Detective Corolla for her to get such an invitation.

If she had thought his mood was foul the first day he met Trevor, it was exponentially worse the day they were forced to release him. Though they still didn't have any proof, Ben was able to get a detail placed on him. They were aware of everything he did, every place he went. If he was going to make the decision to come near her, they would know about it.

It had been almost two weeks since the second murder and still no moves from the killer. She was hoping that he had given up on his game, but the voice inside her head told her that it was doubtful. She sat at her desk updating the books, going over the profits and the budget. Luckily, this whole thing hadn't affected her business. It might have helped that the police didn't release the specifics of the case, like how the entire thing was centered on her—that she was the object of the killer's affection. Make that *obsession*.

The media had been begging for scraps, but the police stayed tight-lipped. The truth was they still didn't know enough to tell. Adam said forensics was still running lab tests, and until they got something back, there wasn't much they could do. Everyone who even played a minor role in Danielle's life had been questioned and interviewed. They were told it was just a routine follow up from the first murder outside the café.

With nothing to do but wait, she tried to focus on the café and push everything else to the back of her mind. She had never realized how monotonous her days were until Adam showed up. Every day it was the same thing, wake up, go to Mon Félicité, work all day, then go home. Having a shadow made the time creep by more slowly. Danielle thanked her stars that Ralph was able to take Adam off her hands and occupy him in the kitchen. He popped into her office with his experiments more than she would have liked, but at least he wasn't hovering anymore.

The story they were telling everyone for the reason why he hung out with her all day was the same as they'd told Carrie—that their relationship was a conflict of interest in the investigation, and he had to step down from the case. He had that vacation time to burn, etcetera… His love was so strong that all he wanted to do was stay by her side.

Barf, she scoffed.

It was *so* romantic that it was ridiculous. The idea that he felt that much love and devotion for her? Now *that* was laughable. That was another reason her days were longer, she had to concentrate to put on a show for everyone, yet not lose herself in it. Often, she would find herself slipping into the false reality, which caused a knee jerk reaction, compelling her to distance herself. It was exhausting. The sexual tension was still there waiting for them every night when they got home. Danielle had to watch what she said to avoid setting Adam up for some hot comment, getting her all flustered. She was sure that he was doing it to irritate her.

The only real relaxation they had was watching movies together, but she made sure she sat as much on the opposite end of the couch as possible. The only time she sat close to him was the night they watched *The Ring*. She had curled up into his side, holding on to his arm. Actually, it was more like gripping his arm so hard, she was going to cut off the blood flow.

"Sweetheart, I'm going to need my arm working if I'm going to throw you at the demon girl when she crawls out of the television," Adam had said.

"Some gentleman you are," she said, punching him in the arm.

"Ow," he managed to get out through his laughter, which made her laugh.

Danielle's attention came back to the present. She was still in her office with the record books open on the computer screen in front of her. It was ten o'clock, and she was ready to call it a day. Mon Félicité was closed, and Ralph and Nina had gone home for the day. She was surprised that Adam hadn't protested to staying so late. Usually, he would've been pressuring her to leave at least an hour ago, but instead, he was sitting in the dining room, waiting. He must have gotten the message not to mess with her today. She had really wanted to get the numbers in the system, but now, she didn't care. She just wanted to go home and kick off her shoes, drink a glass of wine, and take a hot bath.

Danielle rose from her chair and arched her back. A few loud pops sounded as her joints cracked in relief from sitting all day. The need to use the bathroom just hit her now that she was standing. She hadn't even realized she'd been holding her bladder for so long or how badly she needed to go. She walked a little faster than usual on her way to the bathroom. Adam was munching on some crackers as he lounged in one of the chairs. He looked tired, and she empathized with him. She decided she would make him some tea when they got home to help him sleep.

When she walked back through the dining area from the restroom, Adam's head was starting to loll. Yeah, she would definitely make him some tea. On her way through the swinging door of the kitchen, her skin prickled with goosebumps. There was a breeze blowing on her, but it wasn't coming from the air conditioner. Her eyes landed on the door that went to the back alley. It was hanging wide open. Her pulse was quickening, and something heavy was squeezing all of the breath out of her lungs.

Okay, don't panic, don't panic.

With light footsteps, she slowly walked toward the door. She saw the block that housed her knives and grabbed the largest one she could find. She continued forward, eyes leery, and swallowed loudly like she was pushing down a lump in her throat the size of an apple. With the knife raised in her hand, she stuck her head out of the door, ready to start slashing. There was no one in sight, and she backed into the kitchen, locking up the alley door. Still, there was no way she was going to put down her knife.

It's definitely time to go, she told herself.

Danielle walked back into her office to grab her purse and her coat. She wasn't even going to save her files or shut down her laptop—she only cared about getting the hell out of there. As she was collecting her things, one hand for grabbing and the other for wielding the knife, she noticed something on her desk that didn't belong there. The childhood photo of her winning her first cooking competition. This should've been on the corkboard in the kitchen.

The gears in her mind were still turning, trying to make sense of it, when she noticed something underneath it. She slid the photo to the side. Danielle dropped her things and picked up the foreign object with a shaky hand. Her eyes went wide, and this time she lost all of her breath, which made it very hard to scream. In her hand she was staring at a picture of herself in her pink lace bra and panties, putting on a pair of boxer shorts as she got ready for bed.

Finally, she found her voice and let it out. Adam came bursting through the kitchen and into her office with his gun drawn. "Danielle, what's going on?" he rushed out.

"Why?" she yelled, as her eyes began forming tears. "I don't understand, why me?"

He looked at the photo in her hand and released it from her grip.

"He's been watching me in my apartment, Adam, through my window!"

After he cleared the office, the kitchen, and then double checked the alley, he took the knife that was still in Danielle's shaky grip and pulled her into him. The second he wrapped his arms around her, she broke down and cried. She'd said she would never expose herself to him

The Harvester

like that again, but she couldn't stop the tears. She was terrified, and it was time for her to act like a grown-up and admit that she needed him.

"Shh," he cooed, "it's okay, I'm here."

Still crying, she clung onto his shirt and buried her face in his chest.

He tightened his arms around her and gently stroked her hair. "I won't let him hurt you, Danielle. I promise."

The sobs finally slowed, but she didn't release her grip on him. She looked up at him. "He was in here, Adam, so close to me. How easy would it have been for him to kill me?" There was a pained look on his face.

"I know. I'm so sorry, Danielle."

She sniffled a few times. "Why?"

"The whole point of me being here is to protect you, and I let you down. What if..."

She saw his jaw clench so hard she thought he was going to break his teeth. "No, don't do that."

He didn't say anything—he was clearly angry with himself.

"Adam, take me home. I want to go home."

———

He constantly kept one hand on her as she locked up the café. She had turned pale white and looked one hundred times more exhausted than before. He was such a piece of shit. His one job, and an easy job at that, was to keep her safe, and he couldn't even do that right. Adam finished his earlier question in his head... *What if he'd taken you from me?*

Just the thought hurt like a blow to the gut. She was in danger of being killed, and he was in danger of falling for her. Being with her, day in and day out, had become so easy and comfortable. He knew her likes and dislikes, her quirks, her mannerisms. He hadn't even known that much about any of the women he'd legitimately dated in the past. With Danielle, though, he knew everything that made her who she was—sweet, adorable, sexy, smart, tough... take your pick.

His eyes were in constant motion, examining their surroundings for anything or anyone that bothered him. When they got up to the apartment, he kept Danielle close behind him until every room was checked out. She tossed her keys and purse onto the kitchen table and trudged to the couch where she flopped down, her arms draped over her face. Adam sat down beside her and took off her shoes. As he started to massage her feet, she let out a deep moan. He knew her feet were always aching, no matter the day, and right now, he wanted to do anything he could to make her feel better.

"I'm so angry," she said, as she let her arms fall to her sides. "He's taken both of my homes away from me. I don't feel safe anywhere now."

He stopped the foot rub to pull her up to lay on him. They stretched out on the couch, and he put his arms around her again, twirling a lock of her hair the way she did when she was anxious. Within five minutes, Danielle was fast asleep, and Adam soon followed.

———

Adam woke up from a dream that could only be described as a nightmare, which he didn't care to think about or it would make him sick. All the lights in the apartment were still on, and he could feel a crick in his back intensifying. He carefully removed himself from underneath Danielle and headed to the kitchen. He searched the cabinets for some Ibuprofen and popped a few of them in his mouth. He turned off the lights on his way back to the couch and gently scooped Danielle up and took her to the bedroom.

When he laid her down on the bed, she whispered something—eyes still closed—startling him a bit. He hadn't realized she was awake. "Don't leave me."

He was glad for that because he didn't want to leave her. Adam slipped into bed beside her and let out a sigh. The mattress felt so good to his spine. The couch was comfortable enough, but it wasn't meant for sleeping on weeks at a time. Danielle rolled into his side, cuddling up close, and he surrounded her with his body, creating a protective barrier. She let out a sigh of her own, and he gave her a soft kiss on the forehead. Her hair smelled of pears, and her skin had her signature scent of vanilla. Both were extremely soft, and he thought he could touch them for hours.

Adam thought back to his first fantasy of Danielle when she was wrapped around him, and his hands were combing their way through her hair and exploring her body. It wasn't good to be thinking about it because it made him crave her all the more, but it was hard not to, and God, she felt so good next to him. Sleep and arousal were playing tug-of-war inside of him, but finally sleep won out, and Adam rested his head on Danielle's and drifted off.

Chapter Thirty-Two

The next morning, Adam awoke to find Danielle still in his arms, and he felt himself smile. She was breaking down his resolve, whether she knew it or not, and he needed to hold it together. They couldn't have a real relationship, especially not now, and maybe not ever. Would she even want to? Something told him that she would, and the smile came back. Damn it, he had to stop doing that.

She slept for another forty-five minutes before she woke up and came into the kitchen. He was cooking breakfast for them—the scent of scrambled eggs and toast filling the apartment—and he'd already poured glasses of orange juice and set the table. She closed her eyes and inhaled, and Adam could swear he saw her mouth begin to water. When was the last time she had eaten?

"Good morning, did you sleep okay?" he asked, as he plated the eggs and toast.

"Good morning, and yes, actually, I did." She stretched her arms high over her head and went to sit down.

"I thought so."

"Why?"

"You didn't move an inch. You slept in the same position all night and into the morning. Do you want butter?"

"Butter?" she asked with confusion.

"For your toast. I also have some jam out. I assumed since it was in the fridge that you liked it."

She gave her head a slight shake, as if trying to clear through the fog. "Um, yeah, I do, thanks." A look of discomfort formed on her face, "Thanks for staying with me. You really didn't have to." She wouldn't look him directly in the eyes. Instead, she began eating her breakfast, hoping it would end the topic.

The Harvester

"Of course I did. What kind of a man would I be to refuse?" he said nonchalantly.

She didn't give a response and continued eating.

"Oh, by the way, you need to pack a bag."

She finally looked at him. "Why?"

"I'm taking you to my parents' house in Oceanside," Adam said, as he took a swig of his juice.

Then, Danielle took him by complete surprise. "Okay."

"Wow," he said with raised brows.

"What?"

"I was just expecting more of a fight from you."

"Well, first of all, it's not like I actually have a choice. I'm sure you'd make me go no matter what, and secondly, I need to get out of here." She went back to eating the rest of her breakfast. He knew he should be glad that she didn't resist, but he'd prepared a speech that now he couldn't use.

―――

Danielle was so run-down, she didn't care about anything. She wanted to get away from everyone and everything—she wanted relief. She knew that wouldn't be completely achievable until the killer was caught, but some time away would help. *It's funny*, she thought, *the one person she vowed to never take her guard down for is now the only person that she could let know how scared she is.* Even if she were allowed to tell her friends and family what was really going on, she would have to keep a brave face—they couldn't see her like this. Adam made her feel safe—despite his silent self-berating over what happened at the cafe last night—and his assurance was the one she could really trust. Dealing with stuff like this was his livelihood, and she would be more inclined to believe any affirmations he gave her.

"Alright, I know how you like to be in constant control, but I want you to know I already took care of everything," he said, as he took their plates to the sink.

"I don't always—"Danielle let out a sigh of defeat as he raised an eyebrow at her. "Okay, so what did you take care of?"

"I talked to Ralph and let him know that you were stressing out so much it was making you sick, so I was going to take you away for a few days for some R&R, but I didn't tell him where. He's going to run Mon Félicité while you're gone, and before you start protesting about burdens and stuff, he said he was more than happy to do it."

Ralph. That man was a saint. Danielle didn't know what she would do without him.

"So, when do we leave?"

"As soon as you're dressed and ready to go."

"Wait, am I allowed to leave town?"

"I already got the okay from Jensen. After last night, he agreed that it wouldn't be a bad idea."

After a long, hot shower, she felt better, like some of the anxiety had already washed away. She pulled her small suitcase out of the back of her closet to start packing. She wasn't even sure when she'd used it last—vacations were not common for her. She packed all of her toiletries, a pair of jeans, some shirts, and even a casual dress. It wasn't until she was reviewing her bag that she realized all of the underwear that she had packed were either lacy or barely there. What had possessed her to load up on sexy bras and panties? Okay, that was a dumb question, but she knew that nothing could happen between them. Still, she didn't replace them.

Adam walked out ahead and held the front door of the building open as she stepped onto the sidewalk. She was developing his habit of scoping the surroundings—always on alert. He was probably less conspicuous.

"Do you think he knows we're leaving?" she asked.

"I doubt he's watching you every minute. I don't think we'll have to worry about him following us." Just then, he pulled her in for a long, sensual kiss with one hand holding his duffel bag and the other completely wrapped around her waist to hold onto the opposite hip.

The Harvester

Danielle had to concentrate not to drop her suitcase. After he finished, he gave her an extra peck before he pulled away.

"Just in case he *is* watching," he said with a mischievous grin. "It's nice to know I've finally kissed you enough to stop you from blushing."

Really? She wasn't sure how she'd pulled that off.

"I think you were secretly sabotaging yourself so that you could get as much of this as possible."

She just rolled her eyes at him. "Be careful, you might not be able to squeeze that fat head into the car."

Adam let out a hearty laugh and gave her another peck. "And just so you know, I've got a detail on your place and the cafe. If he sneaks around either, they'll see him."

That put her mind even more at ease. She might be able to relax after all.

―――

Oceanside, California was only a thirty-minute drive, but it felt like hours to Danielle. She had been so happy to leave that it hadn't sunk in where they were going. She had never met a boyfriend's parents before, and even though Adam wasn't really her boyfriend, she was still all the more nervous. What if they didn't like her?

It doesn't matter if they like you, idiot, this isn't *real.*

"Are you sure this isn't an inconvenience for your parents? I mean, this is so last minute, and what if this puts them at risk? I'd die if anything—"

He started laughing, which didn't amuse her. "Sweetheart, I'm going to need you to chill out. Do you really think I would take you there if I wasn't sure?"

She let out a deep breath, "No, I guess not. I'm sorry, I'm not trying to doubt you or anything. I'm just kind of nervous." Oops, she shouldn't have said that aloud. Maybe he won't ask.

"Nervous about what?"

Shit. Might as well say it, she decided. "I've never met someone's parents before," she said, as she fidgeted in her seat.

"What about Carrie's?" he teased.

"You know what I mean," She let out another uncomfortable sigh. "I've never met any *boyfriends'* parents."

"Well, I guess there's a first time for everything," he replied, his tone still light. She noticed that he didn't remind her that this was just a farce.

"Do your parents know?" She didn't have to clarify—he knew what she was asking.

"Yeah, they know."

Unfortunately, Interstate 5 was completely clear of traffic, which may have been due to the fact that they'd left early in the afternoon during the middle of a work week. The masses were still at work, punching the clock for their eight to five jobs. Danielle was glad that she had the freedom to work when and how she wanted to. She put in even more hours and had a ton of responsibilities as a business owner, but her love for the café made her feel so lucky that she was getting to do what she was most passionate about. Not everyone had that luxury. In fact, most didn't.

When Adam and Danielle pulled up the front drive—yes, they had a circular drive—she couldn't help but stare with wide eyes in awe. The house was huge, much larger than any she'd seen back home. She could hear Adam chuckling, which she could only assume was at her expense, but she didn't care.

As they made their way closer to the front door, his parents came out to greet them, and she thought she was going to go into cardiac arrest, her heart was beating so fast. Adam, who was carrying their bags, shifted hers so that he had both in one hand. He laced their fingers as he whispered, "Deep breaths." Aside from her extremely rapid pulse, she was also on the verge of hyperventilating—her lungs trying to match the panicked speed of her heart.

"Hello, welcome, Danielle!" his mother said with tons of cheer. She pulled Danielle in for a motherly hug, the way her own might have.

The Harvester

The affection took her by surprise, but felt completely natural. She had really needed that.

"Thank you, Mrs. Burke."

"Please, call me Genevieve, and we're so glad to have you."

Genevieve Burke was a woman with a classic beauty and elegance that you couldn't help but admire. Her soft brown hair was pulled up in a chignon, and her deep blue eyes matched the dazzling sapphire earrings she wore. Her tailored blouse and pants were fitted perfectly to her form, and Danielle was sure there was a designer label inside. Her pearly white smile was so warm and inviting, and you couldn't imagine an unkind word ever escaping her lips.

"And you can call me Alden," Adam's father said, as he took Danielle's hand in both of his, not for a shake, but rather a soft clasp. "Please, come inside."

Alden Burke stood with a stature of such nobility that he looked like a king. It was obvious that Adam physically favored his father more. His salt and pepper hair—which was less salt and more pepper—had the same deep, dark brown and his eyes that same steel gray. Adam could have been an exact replica of Alden back in his day.

Danielle stepped into the large entryway, and once again, her eyes conveyed her awe. "Your home is so beautiful."

"Why thank you, we like it," Genevieve said with a wink. She then turned to face Danielle and grabbed her hands. "You poor dear, I can't even begin to imagine what you must be going through, but he'll answer for his crimes. If anyone can catch him, it's my son," she said with deep concern for Danielle, but great pride for Adam.

"Mom..." Adam said with a mix of warning and annoyance.

"I know, I know, I just needed to say my piece. Now then, Danielle," Genevieve said, as she hooked their arms, "I hear you're a chef." She led Danielle through the house to the kitchen, chattering away.

Adam was still in the foyer with Alden and the luggage, standing near the base of the mahogany spiral staircase. "It's good to have you home, son," his father said, as he gave a firm pat on the shoulder.

"Thanks, Dad. Sorry, I know it's been a while."

"No worries, we're always happy to see you."

"Well, I guess I'll take this stuff upstairs—"

"Oh no, Adam honey, you two are staying in the guest house," Genevieve called from the kitchen, which was near the back of the house. It shouldn't have taken Adam by surprise, but since it had been a while since his last visit, he'd almost forgotten about his mother's Superman-like hearing. It was so good, that growing up, Adam and his siblings didn't even bother trying to backtalk her. She always heard them, so it was futile.

He looked at Alden with confusion and called back to Genevieve, "What do you mean? Why would we stay in the guest house?"

His mother came strolling back in with Danielle by her side. "It's far too cramped in your old room for the two of you to stay in there. The guest house will be far more comfortable."

"I wasn't planning on us staying in my room. I was going to take Dean's and give Danielle mine."

"Honey, don't be silly, you're still undercover regardless of where you are, and it would only make sense for you to be staying together."

"Yeah, but—" Adam was starting to squirm in his words.

"No buts, Adam, and besides, Dean is coming home this weekend from Pendleton."

Adam's older brother, Dean, was in the Marines and was fortunate enough to be at Pendleton base so close to home. Of course, Genevieve and Alden were very pleased with the possibility of having him home. Any parent would be grateful to have their child safe from the dangers of war.

Alden jumped in, "I believe the twins are coming home, too, isn't that right, Gennie?"

"Yes, and Warren and Caleb are going to be staying in their old rooms, so you see, the guest house is the only real option."

Adam thought for a moment about putting Danielle in his sister, Erin's room, but quickly dismissed the idea. It was clear his mother wasn't going to relent, and he really didn't feel like taking her on. He wasn't going to win that debate, and the more he opposed Danielle and him staying together, the more he sounded like a jerk. As per usual, Genevieve Burke's strong will won out, and Adam couldn't be certain, but he thought he saw the slightest smile form at the corners of his mother's mouth. She knew she had won. He wasn't sure what to make of Danielle's expression, though. It looked like a combination of discomfort, nervousness, and... anticipation maybe?

Rooming together shouldn't be a big deal. After all, he'd been living with her at her apartment for weeks, and he even slept next to her last night, but for some reason he felt like the temptation was greater here, the temptation to take her and...

"Adam, why don't you show Danielle the guest house and then we'll all have lunch?" suggested Alden, cutting into his thoughts. Adam was glad for that. The last thing he needed was to get aroused in front of everyone.

Danielle felt like she might have a panic attack. Adam was easier to resist back in La Jolla, but here, she was out of her element, and if he tried to seduce her here... Holding on to her willpower would be extremely challenging, what with a soft, sandy beach practically in the backyard, and didn't he tell her to bring a swimsuit? She was going to have to be very careful.

The guest house was connected by a lattice overhang that was built off the north side of the main house. This place was almost as big as her apartment and was filled with beautiful arrangements of fresh flowers. It was a two-story loft house with crown moldings, mahogany stair railings and banisters, and an elegant décor that Danielle couldn't quite decide on the period. It appeared Baroque, but a little toned down. The downstairs floor was smaller with a powder room, a love seat, and a matching chair. On the stairs wall was a flat screen television with surround sound speakers, the only bit of modernism in the place.

The upstairs was big and open. The bathroom was huge with a freestanding garden tub with claw feet and matching sink, and a lavish vanity made of the same mahogany, but topped with marble and adorned with intricate carvings all over the wood. This was a bathroom that Danielle could have only dreamed about.

She finally took notice of the large king-sized bed that had the same beautiful embellishments in the wood that made up the four tall posters and headboard. A skylight was positioned right above that was perfect for watching the stars at night while tucked into the smooth Egyptian cotton sheets—which had to be at least eighteen hundred thread count—and to top things off, the adjacent wall was a long line of windows with the center being two large French doors that opened to a balcony, overlooking the Pacific Ocean in the distance. Yep, it was official, she had died and gone to heaven. This place was absolutely incredible, and she could feel herself getting giddy inside, like a little girl in a palace.

Neither Danielle nor Adam opened the discussion of sleeping arrangements, which was okay by her. She didn't want to think about that right now. Was he going to sleep in the bed with her? Probably not, since he'd seemed quite determined earlier to keep them separated from each other. She felt disappointed. She shouldn't, but she did.

Lunch was served out on the veranda, which was bordered with a beautiful garden full of large flowering bushes, all producing sweet scents that danced lightly in the air from the ocean breeze. They ate simple turkey club sandwiches with slices of Honeycrisp apples and peach iced tea.

"Danielle, tell us about yourself," said Alden.

She knew this would come sooner or later, so she swallowed her nerves and started. "Well, I grew up in La Jolla with my mom and dad."

"Do you have any siblings?" asked Genevieve.

"Yes, I have an older brother and a younger sister."

"Ah, so you're also a middle child, just like Adam." Based on Genevieve's tone, it sounded as if she were purposely pointing out a commonality between them.

Alden started again, "Tell us about Mon Félicité. Adam mentioned you own it."

"Yes, I do." Danielle told Adam's parents all about her café. She included the fact that she'd had the ambition for it since she was little—the joy it had brought her from spending time with her mother and grandmother and the sparks of creativity that it inspired—the culinary school she attended, and everything in between.

"I must say, it's quite impressive that you have such a successful business at just twenty-eight, and I can tell how passionate you are about it," said Alden.

It just occurred to Danielle that she'd been talking about it for nearly twenty minutes. "I'm sorry for rambling so long—"

"My dear, never apologize for the things you love," he said, as he patted her hand and gave her a smile.

"What is it that you do?" Danielle asked.

"I, too, began a business of my own from a young age. I started my own contracting firm in the early eighties. The real estate market was booming at the time, and I was lucky enough to land several good clients. Like you, I saved up money for years to start my business, and this beautiful woman to my right stuck by me through the poor beginnings and uncertain times to help me with my dream."

The way Alden looked at his wife was magical, and their exchange was anything but subtle. They gave off an affection that commanded recognition of their unwavering and everlasting love for one another. The love in his eyes was deep and ageless—absolutely beautiful.

Alden went on to explain the housing market crash that hit a few years later through the end of the decade and its effect. He had kept his business small, saving as much of the money it earned as he could, so when the real estate plummeted, there was plenty for his family to get by and stay afloat. Many others didn't have the same sense as Alden and went bankrupt. This, in turn, brought what little business there was to him. Soon, his contracting firm was the most sought after, and by the early nineties, the largest profiting in all of California. Alden Burke had accomplished so much in his life—if he put his mind to it, it happened. Danielle had so much respect for him and his ethics, both personal and business.

The Burkes gave Danielle the grand tour of the house, room by room. When they came to Adam's room, she couldn't help but wonder how many girls he'd had in there, and she could feel the jealousy kick in again.

Good Lord, woman, they were probably girlfriends from high school, chill out.

That didn't stop her from wondering. When the tour was over, they ended up in the kitchen. "Oh, I almost forgot, Danielle darling. I went to the market today and bought some things for dinner. I was going to make something with pork tenderloin, but I haven't decided on a recipe yet. Would you mind helping me?"

Before Danielle could answer, Adam cut in, "Mom, she's here to relax—"

"Actually, I would love to help you. Cooking helps me unwind," she said, as she shot a look to Adam that said to butt out. "And I really am glad you asked."

"Wonderful! I was thinking we could eat around six o'clock, what do you think?"

"I'd say it sounds like a plan."

Danielle had Genevieve show her where everything was in the kitchen, from pots and pans to spices and utensils. Alden and Adam had decided to leave them alone and go down to the beach to fish. The women talked and laughed as Genevieve told stories about Adam when he was a child, including a few that he probably wouldn't want his mother telling people.

After the tenderloin was in the oven, Genevieve poured them each some wine. It would be another twenty minutes before Danielle had to start the side dishes. Before she could stop herself, she said, "So, I bet

Adam's had a lot of girlfriends." Danielle was trying her best to appear aloof.

"Yes, he's had his share," Genevieve replied with the same nonchalance.

"Were there any in particular that you didn't like?"

"I can't really say."

She should have kept her stupid mouth shut. She never should have asked her that, and the immediate regret swirled through her. "Oh, I'm sorry if I overstepped my bounds."

Genevieve just let out a laugh, "No, no, dear, that's not it. I can't say because Adam hasn't brought a girl home since high school, and I don't really count them."

A mix of emotions hit Danielle. She was relieved that she didn't have any competition for his parents' approval. There was no one to compare her to, which made her feel special, but then again, did *she* really count? She wasn't really his girlfriend. This was just part of the job. Now it was disappointment's turn to confuse her. This was getting ridiculous, all of this up and down, back and forth with her feelings.

Danielle decided she would think of this positively, because after all, he could've taken her anywhere, and he chose here. Doubt was still trying to nag at her, though. For all she knew, he chose his hometown because he knew the layout of the city and the surrounding land—tracking someone would be easy. She let out a small sigh. Once again, the latter claimed victory.

"Is there anything wrong, dear?"

Apparently, she wasn't so aloof anymore. "No," Danielle said with a little smile, "not at all." She decided to take a swig of wine from her glass. It seemed that filling her mouth with things was becoming her method for avoidance. "Since the side dishes are ready and waiting to go, would you like to help me prepare dessert?" Cook to escape.

"I would love that. What should be done first?" Genevieve looked elated to help Danielle.

"We'll start with the dough," she said and proceeded with the steps of the delectable dessert she had in store for them.

———

Adam and Alden stood barefoot in the wet sand with their pant cuffs rolled up to their calves. The evening sun was glistening on the water, creating a yellow twinkle. The two men had fished in silence for a long while before Alden spoke. "So, what's new?"

Adam laughed at the question. His dad was always good at jump-starting a conversation. "Oh, you know, not much, just a narcissistic serial killer on the prowl with a dangerous obsession for my—" He cut himself off before he could finish saying *girlfriend*. Even though his plan was to play the part full force, he still needed to keep his sights on reality. Besides, here at the house, it wasn't necessary to refer to her that way, just in town.

"So, tell me, how bad is it? The media hasn't given much to the public."

Adam was glad his father decided to let his comment go. "That's because we haven't given them anything except for the basics. It's pretty bad. He's completely sick," he said and continued with some of the details of the killings, including the M.O. and the letters. "The picture is what sent Danielle over the edge. Up to that point, she had been pretty brave." Adam spoke with pride in his expression, but it changed to one of anger. "But the fact that he had been in her office—and is clearly spying on her—broke her."

"The whole thing sounds pretty twisted," said Alden, as they both kept their attention on the ocean.

"I know this was last minute, but I had to get her out of there."

"Think nothing of it."

Another moment of silence went by when Adam's anger started bubbling up. "I'm just so... pissed off." He threw his pole down onto the sand. "He slipped right past me. He could have waited for her and taken her and done *things* to her, and I wouldn't have known. Instead,

I was too busy nodding off like some rookie up at the front, not doing my damn job." He ran a hand through his hair and clung to the back of his neck.

Alden turned to face him and put a firm hand on his shoulder, "Son, you can't control everything." It sounded funny to Adam since he'd just accused Danielle of being the same way this morning. "Sometimes, things must happen so that we might come to our revelations."

"If I was going to have one, I'd prefer it to not happen like that," Adam said. "What kind of revelation should I be having from this?"

Alden didn't answer, but instead just turned his grip on Adam's shoulder to a generous pat, smiled, and began walking back up to the house. Adam stood there for a minute. He hated when Alden went cryptic on him. Without turning around, his father said, "Pick up your pole, dinner's probably ready."

Nothing was left of the pork tenderloin or the roasted thyme-new potatoes and pan grilled asparagus. Within twenty minutes of dinner being served, the four of them managed to clean their plates without leaving a morsel. "Danielle, I must say, this was fantastic," said Genevieve.

"I hope there's dessert," Alden said with enthusiasm sparkling in those same gray eyes.

Danielle gave a small chuckle. "Of course there is."

"She makes the best desserts. They all taste like heaven." Adam shot her a smile. The compliment made her heart swell, and she held a smile of her own.

A few moments later, she came back out to the dining room with baked caramel apple tarts. The crust was folded in like a closed flower concealing the fruit inside. When everyone cut into their tarts, apples and both crispy and gooey globs of caramel came flowing out like lava from a volcano. There were collective sighs all around the table, even from Danielle.

"Danielle, do you cater? I'm having a party in a few weeks for a fundraiser, and I want to show off your food. Oh, it will be such a hit. Everyone will be talking about it!" Genevieve's excitement was growing. "What do you say? Please?"

Danielle hesitated for a moment as she considered the offer. No one was going to say what she was thinking.

Sure, if I'm still alive.

"It sounds amazing, I'd love to," she answered, and Genevieve leaned over and clasped her hand tightly.

She glanced at Adam, and he looked as though he was thinking the same thing she was, but he didn't protest his mother's request. He didn't say anything.

It was ten-thirty when Danielle and Adam headed back to the guest house. She was exhausted, but nervousness jittered inside her like too much coffee. Adam went up the stairs first. He was always on alert. She followed and could feel a knot tying in her stomach. They still hadn't talked about the sleeping situation.

"Alright, everything looks good. Get some sleep, okay?"

He turned to walk away when she asked, "Where are you going to sleep?"

Ugh, did she really just ask that? How desperate did she sound?

"I'm sleeping on the couch downstairs."

"Adam, that's not a couch, it's a love seat. It's way too small for you."

"It's fine, trust me."

And with that, he went downstairs and left her alone. She washed her face and put on her nightgown, which happened to be one of the sexy articles of clothing she'd packed. She crawled under the covers and turned out the lights. She could see the stars through the skylight, and she felt a wave of peace flow through her.

Chapter Thirty-Three

Where the FUCK is she?!

    A loud crash echoed through the room as he rampaged. A chair went flying as it knocked into a table. Anger was boiling hot inside him as he continued his destruction. He couldn't give his angel her present until she was back, and her disappearance was hindering his plans. The window in his timeline was beginning to close for whore number three. Normally, he would've already made his move to lure her, but now he was having to wait and watch. He was praying that she wouldn't meet someone else soon. Otherwise, he would have to start from scratch and find someone new to take her place, and he really didn't want to do that.

    It's that fucking cop! He took *his* angel away—just snatched her up and made off with her to God knew where. How did she expect him to rescue her if he couldn't find her? There was no telling what that lecher might try to force on her, and what if she couldn't fight him off? No, there was no way he was going to let that perverted asshole corrupt his angel, and he didn't care who he had to take out in the process.

    "Don't worry, angel. I'll bring you home." The demented smile that curled at the corners of his mouth said he had already begun forming a plan for Danielle's homecoming.

Chapter Thirty-Four

The faster he tried to run, the farther he became from reaching her.

"Danielle! Run!"

She didn't hear him shouting at her. Why? Why wasn't she running? Adam's legs were burning from the exertion, but he refused to slow down. He had to get to her first. Finally, he was getting closer. He was going to make it!

A shadow leapt out from the darkness and stood in front of Danielle. Why was she *not* running? He was a mere ten feet away when the shadow figure disappeared. She was still standing as he approached. Thank God, she was fine. He noticed then that her white satin nightgown was turning crimson. Adam panicked as he grabbed for her. Danielle's eyes were screaming her pain, and blood-red tears streamed down her cheeks. Her arms were reaching out to him, but he couldn't touch her. Something was holding him back, yet he wasn't bound.

The dark tears were pouring as she hysterically sobbed, her arms still reaching for him. He couldn't hear her cries, just as she hadn't heard his warning. He could only see the agony on her face as she bled out. He was frantic as he desperately fought to touch her. Somehow, their fingers met, but only for a moment, when Danielle was yanked out of his grasp and went flying backwards into the darkness. That's when he heard her blood-curdling scream. It pierced his eardrums and dropped him to his knees.

"No!" he screamed.

Adam went flying off the love seat. He was dripping in sweat from head to toe. His heart was beating out of control. It was the same nightmare he'd had last night. It was all he could do not to run up the stairs like a thundering elephant, but walk instead. He had to make sure she really was safe.

Danielle was sleeping soundly, starlight softly touching her skin. He sat on the edge of the bed, careful not to wake her. He couldn't help himself as he reached out to touch her hair. He had to be sure this was real. His heart had slowed, but was still rushing.

She was the most beautiful woman he'd ever seen. He had already decided that the first night they'd met. Under all the dirt and blood smears, she was incredible, and every encounter after she became more and more lovely. Adam started thinking about the little red dress from their dinner with Carrie, and his arousal began to grow. He'd wanted to rip it to shreds. The thought of it made him start to salivate with a hunger to taste her, made his hands tremble to caress her, his thickness aching to feel the heat of her.

He started to sweat again, and his breathing became more labored. He needed to walk away now before he lost control.

Chapter Thirty-Five

What should have been his one evening off turned into a night full of phone calls, issuances of orders, warrants, explanations, and just general frustration. It was after ten-thirty when Ben got a call from the officers on the detail he'd assigned. Trevor Whitman was missing. It was a good thing the kids were in bed because a string of expletives was his response to the news.

Trevor's detail had been tailing him ever since he was released from custody. They watched his every move and knew his routine. He was scheduled to leave for the clubs by eight p.m. Being labeled a suspect for multiple homicides hadn't slowed him down when it came to picking up women. He had brought plenty back to his apartment over the past two weeks. Ben wondered if he was trying to sleep with as many women as he could, while he could.

Eight rolled around—nothing. Nine, nine-thirty, ten… no sign of Trevor. Was it possible that he was staying in tonight? Not likely. It was a Friday night, and a playboy like that wouldn't be sitting at home, especially when he already went out to pick up women on weeknights. Something wasn't right. Acting on their unease, the officers went into the parking garage attached to Trevor's apartment building. The designated parking space was absent of a red corvette, Trevor's car.

"How is that possible?" Ben had demanded.

"It shouldn't be, sir. We have had eyes on his place twenty-four/seven, as ordered."

"I want a BOLO and an APB issued immediately. I want him found."

"Right, we're on it."

Where the hell could he have gone? This wasn't good. Ben decided to give it another hour before he broke the news to his partner. By eleven forty-five and no leads, he made the call.

Chapter Thirty-Six

Every day they had done something new. Thursday morning, Adam had taken Danielle to the Oceanside Farmers' Market that had some of the best produce she'd ever seen. The fruits and vegetables were all perfect—their size, condition, flavor... She'd better not tell Neil about this place. It might hurt his feelings, and she didn't want to do that. After all, he was very good to her by giving her a discount for using his produce, which was always great, but this place was pretty fantastic, too.

She picked out enough produce and meats, plus fresh herbs and spices, to last through the weekend, and Adam refused to let her pay for any of it. "It's my family you're having to feed, so I'll take care of it," he'd said.

Friday, they'd spent the entire day at the Buena Vista Audubon Nature Society Center. They saw the bird sanctuary, and the featured animals ranging from all types and the lagoon that was simply gorgeous. Danielle felt like she was on a real vacation, and it was great. She felt so relaxed and happy. She could tell that Adam was doing his best to distract her from the problem back home, and she appreciated it.

Before she knew it, Saturday morning was creeping into her windows, and she could hear the spray from the shower, which meant Adam was awake... and naked. She began biting her bottom lip as she started imagining the water trickling down his pecs and over his abs... She was getting flushed and needed to think about something else.

Adam was always up before her, which made her feel a little lazy, but hey, she was here to unwind, right? That should entitle her to sleep in to seven forty-five if she wanted to. And, yes, that was sleeping in for her. It was funny, though, because he didn't seem like the early bird type. In fact, the more she thought about it, he'd seemed a little sluggish over the past few days.

Danielle was so lost in thought that she didn't hear the water cut off, so when he emerged from the bathroom in nothing but a towel with beads of water delicately clinging to him, she nearly choked on her breath. Droplets took their time sliding down his muscled body as they tried to keep their hold on that gorgeous male physique. His abs were tight and developed, and she could imagine licking honey from between the valleys that formed from the roped muscles. Her eyes continued to trail to the V shape that carved between his hips, which acted as an arrow pointing southward, like a sign promising magnificence. She felt flushed again and could feel a heat burning in her core that was starting to dampen her underwear.

"Danielle?"

"Huh? What?" She had completely spaced out and didn't realize he had been talking to her.

"I was just asking how you'd slept?"

"Oh, fine, thanks," her voice still had some daze lingering in it. "How about you?"

"Great," he said with a polite smile. Every morning since they first arrived, he had asked her that question, and every time he gave the same response, but something told Danielle that it was wrong. If he was getting such great sleep, then why did he have dark circles under his eyes? Something was up, and she was going to find out what. Anything she could do to help him, she was going to do.

She was surprised to find three extra faces at the breakfast table. She had completely forgotten that Adam's brothers were coming for the weekend. Clearly, Alden's genes were quite strong because all four sons looked just like him. The only exception was that the twins, Warren and Caleb, had their mother's sapphire blue eyes, but Dean and Adam were the spitting image of their father.

All three brothers and Alden stood from their seats when Danielle entered the room. *Wow, this family wrote the book on etiquette.*

"Danielle," Alden started, "this is Dean, Warren, and Caleb." They individually shook her hand across the table.

"It's a pleasure to meet you all," she said, as she took her seat. On cue, the men all sat down.

"Trust me, the pleasure is ours," Caleb said with a flirtatious smile. It seemed that the smooth talk ran in the family, as well—at least among the sons.

"Where's Erin?" asked Warren.

Genevieve came into the room and answered, as the men stood for her, "She couldn't make it, unfortunately. She has a big test Monday that she needs to prepare for." Genevieve turned to Danielle next, "Erin is working on her master's degree in chemistry."

"I'm surprised you didn't find a way to get her here. You told *us* we didn't have a choice." Warren stuffed a fluffy biscuit in his mouth with a smirk as he chewed. By the glare in his mother's eyes, she would've been happy to shove that biscuit for him.

After more breakfast table conversation, Danielle was pretty sure she had the guys pegged. Warren was clearly the instigator, the joker, always teasing and getting everyone riled up without crossing *too* many boundaries. Caleb was the ladies' man, big time. He winked so much Danielle had to wonder if it had become second nature. Maybe even a permanent twitch? Dean was the stoic one, which reminded her of Alden. He didn't lack a sense of humor, he just wasn't as much of a cut-up as the others.

Lastly, there was Adam, and after seeing his brothers, she knew him. Adam was the emotional one, the chameleon. He was made up of pieces of the rest of his family, from the outrageous jokes, to the alluring charisma, to the silent, and sometimes not so silent, strength. The tenderness definitely came from Genevieve, and his chivalry from Alden. Danielle wondered what attributes of Erin's were mingled with the others?

The entire family spent the day at Oceanside Harbor that was lined with little shops and eateries, and even a lighthouse. Danielle couldn't remember the last time she'd laughed so hard. The way they interacted and razzed each other was hysterical, which they were polite enough to include her in the jeering. She saw the angry look on Adam's face when the first joke aimed at her was fired, but he cooled when she took a few shots of her own.

"So," Caleb directed at Adam and Danielle, "the two of you are a make-believe couple, right?"

"Yeah," Adam answered. For some reason, it really bothered her the way he responded so casually—that he even acknowledged it at all.

"So, I guess that means you're actually single?" Caleb had his full attention on Danielle.

She flashed a smile at him. "Yes, I suppose it does."

"That's very good to know." Caleb was silent for a moment, then with such carefree ease, he added, "Maybe after the case has been closed, we could get drinks." That smooth smile was doing its best to woo her.

"Maybe," she said with an agreeable smile.

"Danielle!" Genevieve called to her as she walked over and took her hand, "Come, dear, I want to show you this exquisite dress at a boutique down the way."

Once the women were out of earshot, Adam laid into Caleb with a ferocious punch in the shoulder. "Ow! What the hell, man? What was that for?" Caleb rubbed his left shoulder tenderly.

"You know what that was for."

Confusion and cinched brows took Caleb's face. "Dude, I was just kidding around, relax. Jesus, when did you get so possessive? *And*, might I point out, you're not really with her. Doesn't that make her fair game?"

Caleb had a point, and when *did* he become so possessive? He'd never had to be in the past because he'd never had to question those women's feelings for him. They'd always let him know how nuts they were for him, usually to the point of being clingy, and Adam couldn't handle clingy.

Caleb and Warren exchanged glances, then with Dean, and Adam wondered if they were conspiring to give him an ass beating later for being such a dick. Oh, well, he didn't care—it was worth it. When this was over, he couldn't stop Danielle from dating other men, but he'd be damned if it was going to be one of his brothers, especially Caleb, the playboy.

Just then, his phone rang. It was Ben. Still scowling at his brothers, he turned and walked away. He didn't want anyone listening in on the conversation. He answered after he'd put some distance between the group and himself, still keeping his back to them.

"Did you find him?" Adam had to force himself to keep his composure. After his partner's call last night, he had been on the razor's edge. The little bit of sleep he did manage to get was disrupted, again, by the recurring dream. He was exhausted, but the adrenaline and four cups of coffee were getting him through.

"No, not yet." If Ben wasn't calling with news on Trevor, then there had to be something else.

"What do you have?"

"The second victim's name is Sheryl Gibson."

It had taken longer than expected to ID her, but once they figured her out, it was easy to get her entire background. Unlike Ashley Cairnes, Gibson was more of a free spirit. She was a spontaneous, fly by the seat of her pants person, so it wasn't out of the ordinary for her to be out of touch with people for days or even weeks on end. Cairnes and Gibson had absolutely no ties to each other besides their physical likeness to Danielle. This time, Adam made sure Ben gave him every piece of information they had.

"Douglas confirmed that the weapon used on Gibson matches the type used on Cairnes."

"Color me surprised," Adam said with a monotone.

"He was also finally able to determine what the weapon was, and get this..." Ben had Adam waiting in anticipation, but only for a moment. He knew how impatient his partner could be. "It's a hole saw."

Adam's brows furrowed, "A hole saw?"

"Yes, and based on the bruising of the skin and blood hemorrhaging, the saw was used antemortem."

"You mean..."

"Both women were alive, and judging how demented the killer is, they were probably conscious." He needed more confirmation from Ben. He had to be sure that he was hearing him correctly.

"Conscious when he started cutting into them?"

"Yes, Douglas said that if they had been dead first, the blood would have coagulated and there wouldn't be any bruising. It's his job to know." Ben knew Adam too well. He knew Adam would ask if Douglas was positive.

Adam ran his hand through his hair. His eyes squeezed shut, and he could feel disgust and rage building inside himself. They had to catch this sick son of a bitch before he hurt Danielle, and they had to find Trevor.

"We're trying to see if there's any way we can determine the manufacturer of the saw used and a way to trace purchasers."

"That could take forever." There was defeat in Adam's voice.

"I know, but it's all we've got."

"Does Jimmy have any new insights?" *Please, God, let someone have something, anything.*

"He said that the killer is cunning and probably very charming. Since there aren't any injuries to the women, aside from the cause of death, it's more likely that he lured them, rather than using physical coercion. Jimmy said that this is not a game to him, and he's clearly not done."

Adam wasn't sure how cunning Trevor was, but he was definitely charming—to women anyway. He cursed into the phone and ended his call with Ben, feeling even worse than he did before. The frustration and ire were taking him over, and there was nothing he could do.

The Harvester

Danielle had been in charge of dinner again, and it was just as much a success with the brothers as it had been with Genevieve and Alden. The men raved over her cooking talents and volunteered to be her tasting consultants anytime she needed them. All of the praise was making her blush, but Adam looked distant, like he was distracted by something. What was going on with him?

Genevieve brought her out of her thoughts when she asked, "Danielle, did you happen to bring your swimsuit? Tonight would be a wonderful night for a swim, it's quite relaxing."

"Yes, I did. Adam suggested it."

A smile twitched on Genevieve's lips as she quickly looked at Adam. "I'm so glad that he thought about it ahead of time. So, it's decided then. We'll clean up in here, and you can go for a dip."

"Aren't the rest of you coming?"

"No, no, we go swimming all the time. I insist."

Danielle hated leaving others to clean up after her, especially when she was the one dirtying the dishes when cooking, but everyone was telling her lately that she needed to learn to relinquish control, and Genevieve insisted.

"It does sound pretty nice, thank you so much," she said, as she hugged Genevieve. "I guess I'll see you all tomorrow morning then."

Danielle was prepared to walk away when Genevieve stopped her, "Oh, no, darling, you can't go swimming by yourself. We always swim with another for safety. It's beautiful out there, but unpredictable."

"I'll go with her." As Caleb started to stand, Adam shot up out of his chair and was at Danielle's side. It seemed his attention was back to the group. As he nearly dragged her out of the dining room, she looked back and saw everyone passing around what she was sure were grins.

Seriously, what was going on with him? Earlier, he acted like he couldn't give a damn about her having drinks with his brother, and now he was ripping her away from the table at the mere mention of Caleb being her escort? He was acting like a child. A child who had a toy that he had no interest in, but when someone else wanted it, oh no, he couldn't allow it. *And* he wasn't even consistent with *that*. Where was this big baby this afternoon at the Boardwalk? Danielle was sick of this. She was no one's damn *toy*, especially not his. He could just go suck it, she decided.

———

Adam was waiting for her on the beach, watching the soft waves roll in until the water gently tickled his toes. This was his mother's fault. Why did she suggest this? He couldn't really blame her, though, now could he? He was the one who told Danielle to bring her swimsuit, so this moment had already been planned in the back of his mind. And then, of course, stupid Caleb volunteering to accompany Danielle. He may have been just joking, but it still pissed Adam off anyway.

This was going to be torturous. Danielle would be as close to naked as she could get, and Adam was going to have to keep his hands off. He heard her walking down the sand, and when he turned to face her, he was rock hard. Her hair was blowing in the soft ocean breeze, and the moonlight was caressing her skin, which was barely covered by a delicate lavender bikini. It looked as if it had been made for her body, the way it shaped her breasts and lightly clung to her hips—and damn, those legs.

His pulse was racing, and he felt like a teenage boy looking at his first pin up picture. There was a lump building in his throat as she came closer, and he felt like he was about to break out into sweats… until she passed him by without a word and headed straight into the water. What just happened? He stood frozen on the beach, confused, as she waded through the waves. Really, though, what had he expected her to do, strip and throw herself at him? The thought of it was making his blood hot.

He followed her into the water and sank as quickly as possible to disguise his erection. They waded in silence for a moment, and it was times like this that he wished he had his father's ability to break tension.

"I hope my family hasn't been too pushy. They have a habit of getting into other people's business."

"No, I really like your family. They're very nice."

Okay, now what? Adam couldn't think of anything in particular to talk about, and the silence was returning. "What do you think of Oceanside?"

Oh, that's original.

"It's very beautiful here. The farmers' market was amazing—everything is amazing."

Danielle's voice didn't match her words, and Adam couldn't figure out why. Usually, when she spoke of things like that, her eyes would light up, and she smiled while she talked. Right now, she looked expressionless.

"Is something wrong?"

She gave a half smile and with a light voice, "No, of course not." But the fact that more silence stretched for another five minutes suggested otherwise. "I think I'm going to go to bed. It's been a long day."

"We just got out here."

"I know, but I'm finished, though. Goodnight," she said with a lighter tone.

She rose out of the water and made her way to the beach, leaving him behind. She wasn't fooling him. Something was up with her, and he was going to find out what.

———

Danielle was dripping ocean water all over the staircase as she headed to the bedroom. She assumed Adam would have brought towels since he had gone down to the beach first, but he must have forgotten, and even though the house was just a short walk, she still had goosebumps all over from the night air touching her wet skin. She hadn't even reached the bathroom when Adam had stealthily entered the room.

"I know something's bothering you. What is it?"

Danielle jumped slightly, not expecting him to have been right on her heels, but recovered herself. "I told you, nothing's wrong. I'm just tired."

"Danielle, we've spent a lot of time together, and I've learned to know when you're lying, which is exactly what you're doing right now. So, tell me the truth."

"Just leave it alone, Adam," she said with sternness.

It was his turn to be sharp as he turned her to face him. "I can tell you're mad at me. Why?" When she didn't respond fast enough, he continued, "Danielle—"

Her arms shook out of his grasp, and she took a few steps back from him. "I said it's nothing."

"No, you're acting distant—"

"Wow, I can't even believe your nerve."

"What are you talking about?"

"I'm talking about what a hypocrite you are. You constantly distance yourself from me without warning nor explanation. You are the one who was distant all day. We might as well have been strangers and then at dinner, you didn't speak a word to me... or anyone for that matter." Danielle's chest was starting to heave as she became more riled up. "At the Boardwalk, you didn't so much as bat an eye at the idea of Caleb and I going out together, yet the two of us going for a swim had you in adamant protest. You think you can just toy around with me—"

"No—" he tried to refute, but she wasn't stopping. Everything had been building inside of her, all her frustrations and confusion were rising to the surface.

"You touch me and look at me like you want me when we're alone with no one else around, with nothing to prove, no show to put on. Then, just like that," she said, snapping her fingers, "you act like you couldn't care less about me. You are the very definition of hot and cold. Do you have any idea how that feels?" She could feel her eyes welling up.

Don't cry, damn it! Not for him!

The Harvester

Adam's expression was that of pain and anger, something Danielle hadn't seen from him before. "That's what you think, that I don't care about you? Let me tell you something, Danielle, you don't even know how you've affected me. Do you think I enjoyed Caleb flirting with you or you flirting back? It made me jealous as hell. I have never felt this out of control in my life. It's so damn hard to be around you and *not* want you!"

She was stunned into silence, unsure how to respond to his admission. Before there was even time to configure a thought, he pivoted and stalked off downstairs. She was left standing in the middle of the room, still dripping.

After a long, hot shower, she was still replaying their fight in her head. Her brain was all over the place. So much so, that she wasn't tired at all. She decided to blow dry her hair, hoping the warm air would make her drowsy, but alas, she was still as wired as before. She slipped on her little satin nightgown that barely made it halfway down her thighs and went out onto the balcony instead of crawling into bed. She wanted to see as much of the stars as she could. She needed to breathe.

It had to have been past midnight when she heard a noise. She was still on the balcony, sitting and gazing at the sky. For once, the breezy air was soothing. It was mentally cooling her off, even though her fight with Adam had been hours ago.

There was a light creaking sound coming from the stairs, and a moment later, it was a stampeding horse gone wild through the bedroom. Adam went flying through the French doors onto the balcony. His chest was rising and falling rapidly, and his body was glistening with sweat. His head jerked in all different directions in search of something. Frantic words came rushing out as he spotted her.

"What are you doing out here?"

She was completely caught by surprise, so it took her a second to respond. "Nothing, I was just—"

"You can't disappear on me like that, Danielle."

Disappear?

He was still trying to catch his breath, "You're supposed to be in bed, asleep." He wasn't making sense.

"What are you talking about?" She finally saw the panic in his eyes as she stood.

"You're not supposed to be out here—you're never out here."

"Adam, I don't understand."

"I check on you every night, and every night, you've been in bed. Tonight, you weren't and..." He raked a hand through his sable hair. "You just can't scare me like that." His breathing was beginning to steady as she stepped closer to him.

"Adam, what's going on? What do you mean?"

―――

He hesitated. He didn't want to tell her that Trevor was M.I.A. He would tell her the other reason for his panic, though. He released a big sigh. "I've been having the same dream night after night that..." Adam turned his head away. He couldn't look at her. "He hurt you, and I couldn't get to you in time. I didn't save you." Pain replaced that panic, and he felt utterly tortured. "So, every night," he reiterated, "I wake up and check on you. I have to make sure that it was only a dream, but tonight you weren't in bed and..."

He couldn't finish the thought out loud. *And I was scared.*

"I'm alright," Danielle said in a soft, soothing voice.

He grabbed her and pulled her into him, his arms wrapped tightly, threatening to crush her. His head rested in the hollow of her neck, and she began to gently coo him. "They're just bad dreams. See, I'm fine, I'm right here with you."

―――

Adam lifted his head and stared into her eyes with such intensity. He put one hand on her cheek and gently stroked her jaw with his thumb, then captured her in a kiss that was so deep and all-consuming,

Danielle had never experienced anything like it. True, he had given her some amazing kisses up to this point, but this one was different. It wasn't about the façade or even teasing her, like he sometimes did. It was real. She could feel it. Moisture instantly pooled between her thighs, and her blood was rushing, pulsing through her veins.

His fingers tangled through her hair as he gently pulled her head back and kissed a trail down her neck. Her breathing became heavy, and her eyes rolled back in her head as she felt his hands make their way down her back, needy in their exploration. Adam gave her ass a firm squeeze, causing her to let out a moan of pleasure. And that's when the frenzy began. A low growl came from him, and he hoisted her up to wrap her legs around him as he made their way back inside.

Danielle's arms were locked around his neck, and their lips met again, tongues thrashing and desperate for each other. They blindly made their way through the dark with nothing but the moonlight to guide them to the bed. Adam laid her down, her body still pressed hard into his. He released her hands from him and pulled them high above her head, their fingers intertwined.

Oh God, was this really happening? Had she fallen asleep out on the balcony and ended up in one of her fantasies? No, it felt too real to be a dream—too good.

Adam broke the kiss, panting as he searched her eyes. "You have no idea how long I've wanted this."

"Yes, I do," she panted back.

His face turned serious, as he asked, "Are you sure you want to do this? We don't have to—"

"If you even think about stopping, I'll shoot you myself, understand?"

He grinned, "Yes, ma'am," and he moved his hands down her arms and past her hips to slip under her lingerie.

He shifted his weight to straddle one of her legs, so as not to crush her. She could feel his long erection pressing into her, and the thin fabric of his boxer briefs didn't leave much to the imagination. He caressed her thigh, moving from side to side, and nipped at her breasts through the satin.

Holy shit. She had never been this wet in her life. No one had ever made her this hot before.

Adam's hand stroked up her stomach to the middle of her breasts and then back down to the lacy edge of her panties. He played with the waistband, lightly tickling her skin, then moved further, inserting his fingers inside the treasure trove between her thighs. Danielle moaned as he slowly worked his fingers in and out, torturing her with his leisurely pace. Her hips began to rock encouraging him to hasten his speed, but he kept it slow.

"I'm going to take my time, sweetheart. We'll get there soon enough," he whispered.

He inched her nightie up and planted kisses on each newly revealed piece of her flesh until he removed the gown completely. With his hand still working her, he drew a soft pink nipple into his mouth and rolled it around with his tongue between his teeth. Danielle's hands came off the bed to squeeze his shoulders.

"I want to taste you," he said, as he peeled off her panties and lowered his head between her legs.

Adam's lips touched her, and Danielle thought she was going to go crazy. Oh God, it felt so good. His tongue lapped up her wet arousal, constantly moving and licking her clit. She started squirming, and he had to hold her hips in place so that he could keep drinking her in. She fisted her hands in his hair–she had to grip onto something, as his tongue massaged her relentlessly, until she couldn't stand it anymore and release exploded through her. She let out a cry of passion. That didn't stop him, though, and Danielle swore she could feel him smile as he continued sucking.

He surfaced and noticed that she was biting her bottom lip. "That's my job," he said and began kissing and nibbling her lips again. He palmed one of her breasts and gently tweaked the pearled nipple with his fingers.

"Mm, Adam," she mumbled through their kiss, "I want you... now. I need to feel you inside me *now*."

"Okay, give me a second, I need to protect you. I'll be right back." Then, he took off downstairs.

Danielle's body was angry with her for letting him leave, but he was back in the bedroom within seconds. That had still been too long. He had lost the boxers downstairs and was now standing in front of her, naked and looking like a god. His shoulders looked even more broad than usual, and his chest, which had the same dark soft hair, was tight. His abs roped over each other so perfectly it looked like they had been chiseled from marble. His cock was strong and thick, and she felt her mouth begin to water.

Adam's eyes swept all over her as he crawled back onto the bed, and she started to feel self-conscious.

"My God, Danielle, you're exquisite. Do you have any idea how beautiful you are?" There was awe and amazement in his voice, and he leaned in for a tender kiss as he stroked her cheek. "You're perfect."

"Take me, Adam," she commanded.

———

He nudged her thighs apart and slowly sank inside her. She was so hot and tight that he almost came instantly. A shudder ran through his body, and he let out a ragged sigh. Danielle's back arched off the bed, and Adam couldn't resist the urge to suck on her breasts again. They were so soft and supple. He could feel fingernails gingerly digging into his back as he glided in and out, careful to take his time.

Suddenly, two long, luscious legs wrapped around his hips, locking at the ankles, and squeezed him with a vise-like grip. She used the power of her thighs and calves to yank him down, forcing him to plunge hard, deep inside her.

"Ohhh!" she cried out, "God!"

Fuck slow.

He couldn't do it anymore, she had sent him out of control, and his need, his burn for her wouldn't allow him to hold back any longer. Adam pumped his hips so hard that the force of his strokes were moving Danielle up the bed. Eventually, she had to put her hands out, bracing herself to avoid banging her head against the headboard. Her breasts jiggled wildly with every thrust of Adam's cock.

Danielle's moans grew louder to the point of shouting as she rode the wave of another orgasm. Some sort of primal beast arose from within Adam. He sat back on his heels and grabbed her hips, slamming her into him so that her sheath swallowed every bit of his shaft. He couldn't get deep enough, though. He wanted to meld into every fiber of her being.

———

Danielle's arms were splayed out, her hands clutching the sheets desperately. She had *never* had sex this good. No, not good—fantastic, amazing, mind blowing!

Adam stopped, but only long enough to pull her off the bed up onto his lap, mashing their bodies together. His arms were tightly wound around her, and his fingers were spread wide across her skin, as if to encompass as much of her as possible.

SHe tilted her head down to nibble his ear, and he moaned as he bit her shoulder. The bite felt good and mixed with the pleasure, it sent her higher, climbing closer to reach another release. Her fingers were in his hair, tugging fiercely, and she threw her head back, her long waves swaying from side to side.

"Yes... yes... *yes*!" Her cries of ecstasy blared through the entire guest house. "Oh my God! Adam! Adam!"

———

He could feel her walls constrict as she climaxed, gripping his entire cock.

The Harvester

Her orgasm and erotic screams put him past the point of no return, and a guttural roar ripped through him, "Ah, Christ, Dani!"

Hot seed jetted out as he came... and came... and, damn, this had to be the longest orgasm of his life. Danielle's core was still gripping him, and he knew that she was still coming down from hers as well. Their chests rose and fell in sync, and their breath rushed from their lungs as if they'd just completed a marathon.

She lifted her head to look at him, and he gently pulled her in by the nape of her neck for a sweetly gentle kiss. They fell back down to the mattress, and he continued placing the fragile little gifts here and there all around her chin, and jaw, cheek, neck, and even the tip of her nose. She looked like she was lost in a euphoric state of being.

Adam rolled away and stood. "I'll be right back."

He'd never bothered to say that to any woman in the past, but his affections for Danielle were stronger. He didn't want her to think he was running off and that she was just another piece of ass, a late-night booty call.

―――

It was like he was reading her mind. When he'd turned from her to get up and walk away, she felt her chest constrict. He'd had her, and now he was ready to leave, only instead, he assured her that he would return. While he was in the bathroom cleaning up, all sorts of thoughts whizzed around in Danielle's head, and every cell in her body felt alive, humming all through her.

What did this mean? What was going to happen with them from here?

No, don't you dare think about that. This can't be anything more than it is, it's just sex. Once this killer is caught, he's going to move on, and the thrill of this relationship will be over. Your heart will break if you let this become...

Adam climbed back into bed before she had even realized he was there. She had been too distracted with her resolution. He pulled her into his side, cradling her, his fingertips lightly skating up and down her arm.

"Adam?"

"Hmm?" His voice was drowsier than she was expecting.

"There can be no repeats of tonight."

"I agree."

She cringed inside. She didn't know what she'd expected him to say, but it still stung. He didn't even protest a little bit—he just straight up seconded the motion. It's the way it had to be, though.

"So, let's not waste any more time," she said with an alluring tone.

"I thought you said no repeats?"

Danielle began to swirl Adam's chest hair with her fingers. "Of tonight, and I don't know if you've noticed, Detective, but the night's not over."

Chapter Thirty-Seven

Her hand slithered its way down his tight abs, past his belly button, and clasped around his already hardened shaft. She massaged the head, provoking a bead of his liquid to surface.

"Now, it's my turn to taste," she said, and she crawled between his legs and lowered her mouth slowly to lick the tip.

A small sigh escaped from Adam and then an even heavier one when Danielle took him completely into her mouth, engulfing him. He wove his fingers into her hair as she sucked and licked, up and down, repeatedly. He released a hiss as she massaged the sensitive spot underneath the head with her tongue.

His body began to quiver from the intense build up she was creating in him. The sensation was becoming too much for him to bear, and he grabbed her, tossing her to her back. Before he could fall into her, though, her foot came up to his chest and pushed. He fell back, and the look of stun spread across his face. The look in her eyes threatened to eat him alive, and he was more than willing to surrender. She reminded him of a deadly lioness that was coming back from the brink of starvation, and her appetite was voracious. It must have been a long time since her last meal, and to be honest, it had been a while for him, too, and he was pretty damn hungry. Danielle was the lethal predator, and Adam was her eager prey.

She damn near leapt onto him as she settled to straddle his hips, and her soft round cheeks were taunting him as they lightly pressed back against his cock.

"Christ, Dani, you have to be the sexiest—"

―――

"Shh..." she whispered, as she put a finger to his lips.

She couldn't allow any more compliments from him. It would only make their parting that much harder later on, and she knew she was already in trouble. Her heart would make her pay for this. It wouldn't be broken, but it *would* be taking a hefty beating.

Danielle replaced her finger with her lips and seized his mouth, swirling her tongue with his. She could feel his arms moving around, but they weren't on her. She didn't deem it necessary to break the kiss to investigate. His hands brushed by her thighs and around the back, and she was sure he was going to start kneading her, only he didn't. It felt like he was fidgeting with something. She heard the tear of the package and knew what it was. He must have been hoping for a second go around since he'd thought to bring more than one. Actually, the fact that he had brought any at all showed that he'd hoped they would be together.

The moment Adam was done prepping himself, Danielle's hot core ate his erection, claiming every inch of him.

———

Another hiss and shudder came from him as she began to slowly rock back and forth, that luscious derriere rubbing against his sac. Now, his hands were on her, pushing her hips down, faster and harder. Her fingers dug into his chest as her moans came spilling out. He decided they were the most beautiful sounds in the world, and the fact that he was their maker made them even more heavenly.

A deep, low rumble came from the back of Adam's throat, and he rolled Danielle onto her back, putting himself on top.

"And you said *I* was controlling," she panted with a devilish smile.

He just shrugged in response and dipped his head down and began nibbling on her neck. His speed was slower than before, but he was deep in and thoroughly grinding, making sure to hit every curve inside. There wasn't one bit of oxygen between their bodies, and their vigorous exercising had them working up a sweat.

This stallion was rocking her world, pure masculinity seeping from him and taking her high like a drug.

Then, Adam did something that took her by surprise. Putting his weight on his forearms, he was glued to her from head to toe, and he delivered another deep, sultry kiss with no end in sight. His hands were now close enough to hold her face, and he stroked his thumbs across her cheeks. What was he doing? This was too tender, too intimate... oh, but it felt so good.

Rationality left her, and she fell into it. They were making love now, and that made it dangerous. Emotions were swelling inside Danielle, and mixed with the bliss he was giving her, she was reaching a peak like no other. She'd never felt this way before. She'd never made love with anyone like this before. Her heart was already plotting its revenge. She didn't want this night to end—she wanted to do this forever.

Damn it. It was too late. She had tried to suppress it, to lie to herself, but it was crystal clear, staring her in the face, and there was no denying it any longer.

She was in love with him.

The two of them climaxed together, and it was pure rapture. A tear ran down past her temple, and Danielle prayed that Adam hadn't seen it.

Chapter Thirty-Eight

She could feel warm sunlight kissing her eyelids, beckoning her to wake up. It was morning, and that meant Danielle was going home today, back to La Jolla—back to real life where a maniacal killer was waiting for her. She let out a groan and a whimper at the thought of returning to that hell.

Her arm stretched across the bed as she rolled to her side, and her eyes popped open. She had expected to feel a warm, hard body underneath her fingers, but instead, she felt nothing but the silky cotton sheets. She remembered falling asleep in Adam's arms, and naturally, she assumed that's where she would be when she woke up, but he wasn't there.

"Adam?" she called out. "Adam?"

No answer. He must have left at some point during the night.

Tears rolled down her cheeks, and Danielle buried her face in her pillow. She had no one to blame but herself for this. *She* was the one who said there could be no repeats. *She* was the one who knew there would be consequences, and she had told herself that she could deal with the pain that she predicted would follow. She had no right to be upset, but she still felt betrayed. She felt like any other woman, easily cast aside after a one-night stand. Ugh, she wanted to throw up.

After another five minutes of crying, she wiped her eyes and walked to the bathroom to shower. She took a long look at herself in the vanity mirror.

What happened, happened. It's time to put on your big girl panties and get over it.

That was much easier said than done.

All eyes were on her as she walked into the dining room. They had been waiting on her to eat breakfast, and she felt her cheeks flush with embarrassment.

"I'm so sorry I'm late, you didn't have to wait for me," Danielle began apologizing to Genevieve.

"Of course we did, dear, it's only polite, and you have nothing to be sorry about. You're our guest."

"I just thought someone would have woken me up sooner, that's all." Danielle could feel Adam's eyes on her, but she refused to look at him.

"Don't be silly, Danielle, this is a vacation, isn't it?" asked Genevieve.

Not exactly.

"That means you can wake up whenever you damn well please, sweetheart," Warren said with a wink.

So, him, too? She was starting to wonder if he and Caleb were flirting with her just to agitate Adam. Of course, that's assuming that Adam was telling the truth last night about being pissed off that she had accepted the drinks invitation with Caleb. It sounded weird being called sweetheart by someone other than Adam. Did that irk him, too? She hoped so.

"Warren, please don't swear in front of company," Genevieve gently scolded.

"A thousand apologies, Mother," Warren said with feigned regality.

"Smart-ass," Genevieve said, as she glared at her son, and the whole family chuckled, including Danielle.

Danielle looked for her seat around the table and was surprised where she was placed. Every morning, she sat between Adam and Genevieve, but today, Dean was the one who flanked her right. Adam was wedged between the twins, like he was trying to get as much space from her as possible. She wasn't going to let that bother her, though, or least she wasn't going to let it show. She sat down and lightly touched Dean's shoulder.

"Well, this is refreshing. It's nice to see I have a new breakfast buddy;" She gave Dean a big smile.

"Actually, I think we're brunch buddies, and I'm glad."

"You are?"

"Absolutely, I'd much rather sit next to you than Thing One and Thing Two over there," Dean said, and the two of them chuckled together.

Conversation around the table was light, and it seemed no one wanted to touch the topic of the danger that was awaiting Adam and herself back in La Jolla. At one point, Danielle noticed that Genevieve was watching her intently. No, not quite watching, but more like analyzing. Her sapphire eyes were shifting from Danielle to Adam, then back again. There was a displeased look on her face. Danielle wasn't sure what to make of it, but then again, it didn't matter. She was about to leave and wasn't likely to see any members of the Burke family ever again. Actually, she would see Genevieve again for catering her party, but that was assuming she'd make it out of this nightmare alive.

―――

He really was a jerk. Hell, he was nothing short of a complete cad, an asshole, a son of a bitch... Whatever Danielle might be thinking about him, he was it. She had accused him of toying with her, which he had adamantly denied. Then, he'd lost control and spent hours making passionate love to her, only to leave her to wake up alone. The hurt he saw in her eyes and heard in her voice cut him. She did her best to disguise it, but he knew her too well at this point.

He loathed himself, but he couldn't help it. Too many thoughts and feelings were swimming around inside him, crowding him.

He had been perfectly content holding a deliciously naked Danielle in his arms, despite the coming separation of intimacy that they had agreed to. It was the buzzing of his cell phone on the coffee table downstairs that had pulled him away from the warmth of her. It was Ben. Adam had hoped he was calling with news about tracking down Trevor. In a way, he was.

Adam had stealthily made his way downstairs to answer the call, taking care not to wake Danielle. What came next, he hadn't been prepared for.

"Did you find him?" Adam had whispered, skipping over a greeting.

"In a manner of speaking." Ben let the statement hang for a moment. "Trevor Whitman is dead."

"What?" he forcefully whispered into the phone.

"It turns out he was never actually missing. He'd been in his apartment the whole time."

"What the fuck happened?" Adam growled.

"Ironically enough, it seems as though he tripped down his stairs. He was found at the bottom, his neck snapped. We had just gotten a warrant to search the apartment due to his disappearing act and were on our way when we got the call. His maid found him. Needless to say, she was hysterical. Douglas said he died the night before, after the club, based on the stage of decomposition. Given the time window, and the fact that he was in nothing but boxers, he most likely fell in the middle of the night."

Adam couldn't believe what he was hearing. Trevor was dead? "Hold on, if he was still in the apartment, then where is his car?"

"It's still M.I.A., however," Ben continued, "there was a rental car in his spot. At first, we thought someone had just stolen the space, but when we ran the plates and contacted the rental company, it was checked out under his name."

Adam paced the length of the tiny living room as he raked his hand through his hair. "But why? Why would he go through the trouble of sneaking out, getting a new car, and then going back? Why didn't he run? It doesn't make sense."

"Trust me, I know."

"Did you find any evidence from the victims inside his apartment?"

Ben sighed. "No," then he paused a moment. "Look, I know he was a piece of shit, and you didn't like the guy, but I don't think it was ever him."

"He could've been good at covering his tracks."

"You and I both know you don't believe that."

Adam sighed in defeat. He had wanted Trevor to be the killer, but he couldn't deny the simple truth anymore. Trevor Whitman may have been good at manipulating people to get whatever he wanted, but the fact of the matter was that he wasn't dedicated enough to be the killer. The fact that he was still sleeping with other women proved he wasn't obsessed with Danielle the way the Harvester was, who saw her as his sole focus. Trevor was nothing more than a douche bag with a bruised ego.

There was a long pause of silence between the partners. "When do you think the two of you will be ready to come back?"

"Tomorrow," Adam answered, almost immediately.

"If you need more time—"

"No."

They were back to square one. Fucking fantastic. They had no lead suspects, no incriminating evidence—not one goddamned clue to point them in *any* direction.

Adam disconnected his call and went back upstairs. Danielle was still sound asleep, her wavy caramel locks spilling across her pillow, the sheets twined around her like greedy hands desperate to touch her. As he'd watched her, a rush had come over him. All sorts of thoughts entered his brain, but his reactions to those thoughts were what had confounded him the most.

The knowledge that Trevor was dead had frustrated him, as it should've, from the case standpoint. Their only lead suspect was no longer alive, which put a wrench in their investigation. However, it had also pleased him, and that terrified Adam. The relief he'd felt knowing that Trevor could never touch or bother Danielle again... Adam would never again have to worry about him harming her. Trevor would never be able to take her from him...

Adam had gone still. No. He shouldn't be thinking those things. It wasn't right to be thinking those things. He stared at her for a long while, watching the beauty sleep peacefully. What was he doing, or better yet, what was she doing to him? His legs got moving again, but instead of settling into bed next to Danielle, he'd headed back downstairs

The Harvester

and gotten dressed. He silently closed the door to the guest house behind him, locking her inside. He hadn't known where he was going, but he had to go somewhere—anywhere—else.

Yep, he was irrefutably a bastard.

———

It was mid-afternoon when Adam loaded their things into his car, preparing to head out. He wanted to leave sooner rather than later. Although Trevor was dead, they had no proof that he really was the Harvester, and if for argument's sake he was truly innocent, then the real killer was still at large. If they waited until night, he would have the shadows to hide behind, and Adam didn't want to be that vulnerable.

The Burke family gathered outside to see them off, and hugs and handshakes were doled out to everyone. When Adam got to his mother, she took him in for a big hug.

"Please be careful, Adam," she said with motherly concern in her eyes.

"Always."

Genevieve took hold of her son's shoulders as she looked him square in the eyes. "And please don't take too long. You may lose your chance."

His chance to catch the killer? Adam would uncover the truth if it was the last thing he did.

Adam and Danielle swapped parents. Once again, Genevieve gave Danielle a hug suggesting they were life-long friends.

———

"Danielle, it's been such a treat having you here. I can't wait for you to come back for the party." Danielle's eyes looked to Adam, who was talking with Alden. Her expression was hesitant, and as if Genevieve could read her mind, she whispered, "I promise you'll be back. You have my son looking out for you, and I know he'd never let anything happen to you… You know it, too." That caught Danielle off guard. "Give him time, dear," and with that, Genevieve gave her a polite social kiss on the cheek.

Give him time, she thought with a mental sigh. Danielle prayed that the police wouldn't need too much more time because she wasn't sure how much more she could give.

Chapter Thirty-Nine

So, Adam thought he knew when she was lying? Well, not this time. Danielle was going to put on the performances of her life. She had to pretend to be madly in love with him—which she was—for the rest of the world, and now also had to pretend to *not* be in love with him for Adam. He had to think that nothing had changed between them, and that the other night was nothing more than hot, erotic, animal sex. No lovemaking had occurred, just pure, raw lust. This was going to be a difficult undertaking, but not impossible... she hoped.

Not a whole lot of words were exchanged in the car, but the few occasions they did speak, she couldn't have sounded more casual, keeping her tone light and laid back. She couldn't help but wonder if he was trying as hard as she was, or if it was no big deal at all to him.

It felt good to be home. Unfortunately for her, it was a Catch 22. She was glad to be back in her own familiar surroundings where she could have her control, but the reality was that there was no control for her here. There was no more comfort or safety. Oceanside already seemed like nothing more than a dream, and she was waking up into a nightmare that there was no true waking from.

After they unloaded their things, they headed over to the café. Adam wasn't too keen on the idea, but Danielle said that they needed to go back to her normal routine. What she didn't tell him was that she wanted to get to work to take her mind off him and have a legitimate excuse for avoiding him. She'd be too busy to pay attention to him, right? She hoped he would buy that.

"Boss! I'm so glad you're back!" Nina exclaimed, as she ran to greet Danielle at the door.

"It's good to see you, too. Has Ralph been driving you crazy?"

"No, why would you think that?" Nina asked with a puzzled look on her face.

"I guess I just wasn't expecting such an enthusiastic welcome." The two women began walking through the café to the back counter.

"Are you kidding me? We've missed you like crazy. Everyone's been asking about you and your vacation."

"Really, who's everyone?" Danielle grabbed her apron in the kitchen and started preparing to cook. She didn't even know what she was about to make, but she needed to do something, and cooking was the most logical thing. After all, it was one of her escape methods.

"Oh, you know, just the regulars. The Jacksons, Mr. Cline, Neil, basically the entire square... They all wanted to know where you went for your trip. Where *did* you go anyway? Ralph claimed no knowledge, but—"

"He wasn't lying. I didn't tell Ralph where I was going. I just needed some peace and quiet."

"So, does that mean it's a secret?"

Danielle looked at Nina inquisitively.

"It's just that you didn't answer my question on where you went."

Danielle detected the slightest sound of hurt in Nina's voice. She released a sigh. "I guess so, and it's not that I don't want to tell you, Nina, but it was really special to me and—"

"You don't have to explain, boss. I totally get it," Nina whispered with a smile and glanced in Adam's direction. The real reason was that she *couldn't* tell anyone where she went. It might put Adam's family in danger.

Ralph poked his head in the door, "Dani, you have a call," and disappeared back out into the café.

She walked over to the phone in the kitchen and picked up the receiver, "Hello?"

"It's about time, Danielle. When were you going to call me? I left you messages, and I *cannot* believe you didn't tell me you were leaving."

Sabotage. Ralph knew it was Carrie on the phone yet chose to omit that. Carrie probably put him up to it, assuming that if Danielle knew it was her calling, she might not have answered and stalled.

"What the hell, Dani? Since when do we keep secrets from each other?"

Ugh, it was time for damage control.

"I know, I'm so sorry Care, but I can explain—"

"You'd better," Carrie scolded.

Danielle whispered into the receiver, "Look, I can't talk to you about it on the phone, so how about we get together tomorrow night?"

"I can't. I've just been assigned to a new case, and I'm swamped with files. I'll be working on them all night."

"Okay, well, how about I come over and help you? Let me make it up to you. I'll bring all of your favorite foods, and I'll tell you everything."

Carrie was silent for a moment and then asked, "Everything?"

"*Everything.*"

"Okay, deal. I could really use some help. Come to my place around seven. Will Adam be joining us?"

"Yes, is that okay?"

"Yeah, I guess. I was just hoping we'd have some girl time."

"We'll put on a sports game or something. Out of politeness, he'll offer his help, but I'm pretty sure he wouldn't think twice if you let him off the hook. Do you have ESPN? He'll watch anything on that network."

"I think so, but I'm not one hundred percent sure. You know I don't watch sports."

Danielle was really happy with these new plans. She had no idea if Adam would even try to bring up their night together, but in case he was contemplating it, he definitely wouldn't discuss it in front of Carrie.

———

The drive back from his parents' house wasn't as uncomfortable as Adam had expected. Even though conversation was on the minimal side, he was surprised about how upbeat Danielle sounded, especially since he was sure he picked up on her anger this morning. Why hadn't she brought up what happened last night? Even though she said it was a one-time thing, he knew women, and they always wanted to talk about sex and what it meant.

Instead, she seemed carefree, almost like it never even happened. That should've been a good thing, a relief, but... Well, shit, it's not like it was a random hookup and so-so sex. It was explosive and unbridled, and he was sure that that had to be the best sex any two people could have. If there was a rating system for such a category, he knew they would top the chart. Why did he want her to care? She was being the smart one about this, and he needed to follow suit.

Danielle was hanging up the phone when Adam walked through the kitchen door.

"Who was that?" he asked, hiding all concern.

"It was Carrie, and I hope you don't mind, but I promised her we'd go over to her place tomorrow night and help her with some work."

He raised an eyebrow.

"Don't give me that look. You're more than welcome to stay home."

His eyes narrowed, suggesting that she knew damn well he couldn't leave her alone. "No, it's fine. Whatever you want to do is okay with me, as long as I get to be with you," he replied with a tone that completely contradicted his stare.

———

Danielle could predict the swoon that was seconds away from spilling out of Nina.

"Aw! That is so sweet! Danielle, you are so lucky that you have the perfect boyfriend," and she followed it up with a dreamy sigh.

"Yeah, I know," Danielle said with a smile and stars in her eyes. She closed the distance between them and gave Adam a soft, lingering kiss.

The Harvester

This time, he was the one blushing. Why on earth would he be blushing over that?

"So, Adam, do you have any brothers?" Nina asked with hope.

He chuckled. "Actually, I do—"

"Are they single?" Nina asked, as she leaned across the island, like she was trying to capture something.

"Yes, but—"

"I see," and then Nina began to daydream.

Adam looked to Danielle for help. After all, she'd met them and knew what they were like. Nina was far too young for Dean, which left either Warren, who was an instigating wise-ass and would probably put his foot in his mouth that would result in pissing her off, or Caleb, the flirtatious playboy, who might end up breaking her heart. Caleb wasn't cold or even a womanizer, but she was certain that he was not looking for a serious relationship, and Warren was an acquired taste. She wasn't sure if Nina could handle his sense of humor.

And on top of everything, all of these mushy gushy sentiments were not something Adam normally said to women, Danielle was sure. Poor Nina really was living in a daydream, but she wasn't going to be the one to burst her bubble.

―――

Danielle spent the rest of Sunday baking and cooking while Adam holed himself up in her office making calls. Once he had gotten updated on everything, which wasn't much, he worked on how to break the news to Danielle. He had purposely withheld the information. It seemed to him that she would be able to accept it better here, and keeping it from her wasn't an option. She was going to find out that Trevor was dead, and it should come from him. He had decided to wait until closing to tell her. Trevor wasn't going to get any deader. It could wait.

Will she cry for him? he wondered. He didn't like the thought of her shedding tears over him. Even still, he should try to have some semblance of tact when he told her.

He was quiet for the rest of the day, but he made sure he engaged in enough conversation to appear at ease and mask his concern. It wasn't until the last customer left that he broke the news to her. To her credit, she handled it better than he would have guessed. She didn't fall to her knees weeping, which was all he really cared about.

"Are you okay?"

"I don't really know how I feel. Despite the way it ended between us, I never would've wished something like this to happen to him. Maybe for his penis to rot off, but not to die." The uncharacteristic admission caught Adam by surprise. He almost laughed from the shock. "There was a time when I did care for him, but..." She shook her head as she looked away, her expression reflecting her conflict.

"But what?"

She sighed as she closed her eyes. "I can't seem to find any sadness inside me. I feel like I ought to be, but instead, there's nothing—no emotions. Like it doesn't matter one way or the other." She finally looked at him again. "I'm a horrible person."

Adam shouldn't have enjoyed her words, but he did, nonetheless. Knowing that she wouldn't mourn Trevor relieved him. That undoubtedly made *him* a horrible person. He thought back to his initial feelings, the ones that scared him—being glad that another man was dead for selfish reasons. "No, you're not," he answered. "No one can tell you how you should or shouldn't feel."

"Thanks," she said with a half-smile. "So," she said, changing tracks, "does this mean he's not the killer?"

"More than likely, but until we know for sure, our situation doesn't change."

Tonight's dream was even more vivid than the others. This time, Adam's hands were coated in Danielle's blood, and her screams were louder—glass-shattering. They were piercing his ear drums, causing blood to work its way down to his jaw. As usual, she was yanked away from him into the black abyss, and as usual, he bolted up off the couch and into her room.

She was there, fast asleep. The clock read two-forty a.m. in a soft green glow. Right now, he didn't give a damn if she wanted him in her bed or not. He wasn't taking his eyes off her. The Sandman denied Adam any rest. There was no way he could sleep after that torment. Nightmares? More like night terrors.

Adam made sure not to lay too close to Danielle, which was damn hard. He didn't want to wake her, and in the morning, he'd just slip out and back to the couch.

Chapter Forty

Before she knew it, Monday had flown by, and Danielle and Adam were about to head over to Carrie's place. She went overboard and made twice as much food as necessary—even Carrie wouldn't be able to eat it all. Danielle packed cheesecake, fruits, bread, and all of the makings for the crepe Ralph had made for Carrie a while back. Back before all of this.

She was getting excited about seeing Carrie, because right now, she could really use her best friend's advice, or at least her shoulder. It was hard having to re-bottle her feelings for Adam, and she had to tell Carrie before she exploded.

Fifteen minutes later, they were standing outside of Carrie's apartment, when the door flew open, and Carrie grabbed Danielle for a tight hug.

Carrie had an amazingly spacious apartment and even had a spare bedroom. Danielle was in love with her kitchen because of the size and the layout. It was perfect for a chef like her and absolutely wasted on someone like Carrie. It had a spacious island with extra storage, granite countertops, a walk-in pantry, gas stove tops, and a hanging pot rack that dropped down from the ceiling. It would take more than a few years for Danielle to afford a place like this.

"Come in, come in," Carrie quickly ushered. "Thank you so much for helping me with my work. There are just so many documents to go through, and extra highlighting hands are much appreciated."

"Do you want me to set up dinner before we get started?" Danielle asked, as she made her way to the kitchen. The question, of course, was rhetorical.

"Absolutely, I'm starving," Carrie said with wide eyes and a smile.

It always made Danielle laugh when Carrie got excited over food. As she started prepping dinner, Carrie gave Adam the grand tour of the apartment.

"And here is the big screen TV. Now, as much as I appreciate you coming as well, you're not obligated to help. This is Danielle's punishment, not yours. I hope you like sports because I already set the channel to ESPN."

"Are you sure you don't want my help?" Adam was being courteous, but he definitely wanted to take the out.

"I insist."

"Well, who am I to argue?" He smiled. Danielle's look to Carrie was a half grin with a cocked eyebrow, to which Carrie just grinned back and nodded her head in confirmation of Danielle's earlier prediction.

The moment dinner was over, Adam was speed washing the dishes and plopping on the couch, remote glued to his hand. The women shared another look and a smirk. Danielle and Carrie got to work while Adam watched Monday Night Football. By half time, Adam was passed out asleep, and Carrie nudged Danielle and kept her voice low, "Start talking."

"I'm about to tell you something huge, but you have to promise me that you won't get upset. I had no choice."

Carrie held up her hand, making the girl scouts' honor sign. "I promise."

"Adam and I aren't really together. He's just undercover as my boyfriend. It was the police captain's idea, in hopes that the killer would get sloppy out of jealousy. They're trying to draw him out."

"Well, it doesn't seem to be working," Carrie said, as she started working on her second piece of chocolate hazelnut cheesecake.

Danielle knew better than to only bring her one. "Care, I'm just easing you in. The reason we left La Jolla was because the killer left me a picture on my desk when I walked away to the bathroom that he'd taken of me through my bedroom window. I wasn't even gone for five minutes, and he'd slipped in and out of the back door of the café without being noticed. That's when I lost it, and Adam decided to take me away for a little while."

Carrie's eyes were wide, then her brows cinched with concern. "So, where did you two go?"

"We went to Oceanside. His family lives there—"

"Wait, hold up. Did you meet his parents?"

"Yes, and they're so wonderful. His whole family is," and Danielle went on to describe the Burkes. She also told Carrie about the fight she and Adam had.

Adam could hear low mumbling that roused him from his sleep. It had been his only rest since Saturday night when he'd slept with Danielle in his arms. He wasn't sure why the females' talking woke him versus the noise of the football game, and he had considered trying to fall back asleep until he heard Carrie's question.

"So, what happened?" There was eagerness and anticipation in her voice.

"We... we slept together."

"Oh my God!" Carrie exclaimed in a whisper. "How was it?"

Danielle told her about his nightmare and the hot, steamy sex that came after.

"It was incredible, Carrie. There are no words to describe it."

He liked the sound of that. It was what he had needed to hear, but what she said next completely blindsided him.

"It was the biggest mistake of my life."

Fucking. Ow.

"What are you talking about? How was that a mistake?"

Yeah, how was it a mistake?

"Because..."

"Because..." Carrie gently pushed.

Danielle let out a sigh, "Because I've fallen in love with him."

Adam's heart was pounding. He had to admit that it felt good to hear her say that, but the real truth of the matter was that it scared the hell out of him. This was exactly what he didn't want to happen. He was going to break her heart when he walked away after the case, and the last thing he wanted to do was hurt her.

"Dani, what's so bad about that?"

"It's just too complicated, Care. The psychopath out there is the only reason we're even together, and when this is all over, what then? He has no reason to stay."

"Are you sure about that?" Carrie asked.

"Yes, I'm sure." Danielle's voice became thick, tears threatening to shed. "I guess I'm just going to have to get over it." The two friends went silent. "This is the part where you tell me what to do."

"I'm sorry, bella, but nuh-uh."

"But you love to tell me what to do."

"This is different, Dani. I can't tell you what to do this time—not with this. This isn't like me telling you what to wear or who to go out with. This is love, and you're the only one who can make that decision." Danielle didn't respond, and Adam wished he could see her face. "Will it take your mind off this if we work on more files?"

"It'll help."

The two of them went back to talking lawyer shop and focused on Carrie's court case. Adam had to pretend that he'd never heard their conversation. There was no way he could approach Danielle about it. He had to let her 'get over it'. If he asked her about it now, it would only do more damage. It would be easier for her if she believed he didn't know.

Chapter Forty-One

"Adam, wake up. It's time to go home," Danielle said, as she gently shook him. The truth was that he never went back to sleep after overhearing her and Carrie's conversation.

"What time is it?" he asked with feigned grogginess.

"It's eleven o'clock."

He didn't doubt it. It felt like hours upon hours had passed between the confession and now. Carrie walked them to the door and said goodnight, and Adam made sure she locked her door before they left. Danielle took the keys from Adam when they reached the car.

"How about you let me drive, and you can just rest for a bit?"

"I'm not that tired, I'm fine."

With a look of disbelief, she said, "Really? Have you seen yourself? The circles under your eyes are getting so dark you might as well be a raccoon. I can tell you haven't been getting enough sleep."

"Alright." He didn't fight it and just went to the passenger side, quietly and obediently. Even though his mind was awake, his body was exhausted. After almost a week of minimal sleep, he was so drained he wasn't sure how he was standing.

———

As usual, he went into the apartment ahead of her, but she didn't give him the chance to do a full sweep. She headed straight to the master bath to wash up and get ready for bed. All she wanted to do was crawl under her sheets and sleep. The less time she was awake, the less she'd have to think about Adam.

As she entered the dark bathroom, she reached for the light switch and flipped it on.

Her screams rang out like an alarm that was never ending, barely allowing her to breathe and hysteria was spreading through her like wildfire. Adam came barreling into the room with his gun drawn. The image in front of them was grotesque. Another girl—another imitation Danielle—floated in the bathtub. The water was stained red with her blood and spilled over the edge of the porcelain, leaving small streaks of crimson behind.

Danielle's entire body was shaking violently, and she began to collapse onto the floor when Adam caught her, preventing the crash into the tile. The screams turned into sobs, and rivers were pouring from her eyes. He quickly turned her around in his arms to keep her from the sight of what looked like could be her own carved up corpse.

He directed her to the bed. "Stay here."

She grabbed his arm. "No, don't leave me, please." The fear and terror in her eyes pulled at him to stay with her, but he had to check out the rest of the apartment.

"Sweetheart, I've got to make sure it's safe. Just stay here." The question of Trevor's guilt was just put to rest. It was obvious they were dealing with a different monster entirely. Adam's gun was cocked and ready—ready to blow this asshole's head off. But he wasn't there. Who knew when he'd left? There were supposed to be eyes on the apartment. Someone had to have seen him. Adam called 9-1-1 for an ambulance and then speed-dialed Ben.

"Anderson."

"It's me. It's bad—really bad."

"I'm on my way." Ben didn't need to ask for the location. He already knew where Adam would be.

Within minutes, the blare of sirens filled the night air. The second Adam had ended his call, he was back by Danielle's side. Her tears had nearly subsided, but one would stream down every few seconds. The entire world was moving around her, but she didn't seem to be registering any of it. Cops were everywhere, dusting for fingerprints, taking pictures, putting things in baggies, but they must've simply been blurs to her.

To Adam, Danielle had become eerily quiet, looking like she was on the verge of checking out. When Ben arrived, he left her again so that he could fill his partner in. Many times, the two of them would bounce theories off each other, meticulously reviewing the facts, until they customized the most logical lead and followed it. Nine times out of ten, they were right, but these murders were one of the hardest cases the two of them had had in their entire careers.

The detectives walked to the tub and looked down at the woman. Red lingerie—check. Scent of vanilla—check. Body posed, heart stolen, doppelgänger of Danielle–check, check, and check. Her eyes were open with the same frozen expression of sheer terror, just like the other two, and as expected, another love note was left behind. Adam had told CSU not to touch it yet, until he and Ben were able to look at it together. He was hoping that pulling it out themselves would make something click finally. The first note had been removed from Ashley Cairnes before he'd arrived, and when he'd pulled out the second from Sheryl Gibson, he hadn't thought to look for a direct connection with the placement of the notes—and there may not have been one—but he wasn't taking any chances this time.

Adam knelt and leaned in closer as he reached for the origami heart. The mix of vanilla and the copper tang of blood filled his nostrils, nearly choking him. Even though the body was fresh, death was never a pleasant smell. The note was dry like the others, the water beading off the paper, preventing the ink from running. If they were lucky, they might be able to pull a print from it, or at least find out what he'd been using to coat the paper and where he got it. Ben was crouched down next to Adam as he unfolded the message.

Number three vexes me
I'll make you see
YOU BELONG TO ME!

Neither of them spoke as they looked at each other, reflecting their dread and consternation. He was going to kill her. Adam had no doubt about that now. The likelihood that he would just kidnap Danielle was minimal, and he was sure that Jimmy would agree. Frustration, anger, fear, and anxiety were all rushing through him.

"He's going to kill me, isn't he?"

Both men whipped their attention to Danielle, who was standing over them. She sounded lost, defeated. Adam hadn't heard her stealthy approach from behind. Clearly, she had read the letter and had come to the same conclusion as him. Neither Adam nor Ben answered her question, but then he knew she wasn't really looking for one. It had been a statement, yet Adam wanted to give her an answer. A different answer, one that involved soothing words of comfort and hope and certainty. There was no way he could give her that, and she knew it.

"Maybe I should let him."

Adam couldn't believe what had just come out of her mouth. "What?"

"It would be over. He'd finally stop. What did she do to deserve this? Nothing—nothing except look like me."

Adam stood up to tower over her.

Her posture was slumped and coiled.

"What did *you* do to deserve this? Danielle, this guy is deranged. There's no two ways about it. This isn't your fault."

"Isn't it?"

He was furious with her now. "*No*, it isn't. If you offer yourself up to him, he wins. It won't bring them back, and if you give up, then you might as well have killed them yourself."

A loud crack resonated through the air, and all conversation came to a halt. Adam felt the fiery sting from the hand that had just struck him across the face. There was hatred and betrayal in Danielle's eyes, and he knew he could never take it back. He tried to reach out to her.

"Dan—"

"Don't!" she said, as she turned away from him and sped out of the room. After a moment of complete silence, everyone turned their attentions back to their tasks.

"Man..." Ben said, as he stood up behind Adam.

"I know, I know. You don't have to tell me." Adam needed to release the anger that was pulsating through him. "Who was on duty to watch the apartment?" There was no disguising the ire in his voice. Ben released a quick exhale, then led Adam through the apartment and out to the hallway where two officers were standing, their heads hanging low. Ben usually told his partner to cage the rage, but this time, he stood by silently as Adam unleashed his wrath.

"I want to know how that sick FUCK got in here!" When neither responded fast enough, he added, "NOW!"

"Sir, we thought it was Miss Walsh," the first one said. His answer was quick and sharp like a soldier responding to his commanding officer.

"They look so much alike—" said number two.

"NO SHIT?!" Adam shouted with sarcasm. "And I suppose you thought the man with her was *me*?"

"Sir, from afar, it was possible—" number one began.

"Possible? If you had *any* doubts, you should've called me or Detective Anderson, and right now, it sounds like you weren't too sure!" His decibel went down a notch, "Tell me exactly what he looked like— brown hair, *minimum* six foot-two?"

The two patrol officers shared a glance, and number one decided to answer again, "Actually, he might not have been quite six feet."

"Are you sure?"

"Yes sir, because if the women are the same height as Miss Walsh, then he was closer to five-ten, five-eleven."

Number two decided to step in again. "And... he was wearing a hat. The way he maneuvered in the shadows made it hard to make out the hair color, and of course, we could only see him from behind."

"We know we screwed up—"

Adam just cut him off with a loud scoff. Ben interjected, posing the most important question again to the group. "That still doesn't explain how he got her inside."

"Actually, he used a key, which is another reason we believed it was Detective Burke and Miss Walsh."

All of the anger that Adam had been unleashing on the officers vanished instantly and was replaced by utter horror. The killer had a key to Danielle's apartment. That's right. There wasn't any sign of forced entry. Somehow, he had gotten his hands on her keys... Adam remembered that first day when they were headed to the precinct to talk to Jensen. They had both assumed she had simply misplaced them. Wait, but Adam had added a deadbolt since then. Adam internally shook his head and sighed. If the killer could steal them once, he could steal them again. He could have used a mold, possibly when he left the photo, and easily had a copy made from it.

Adam couldn't breathe. It felt like someone had drop-kicked him and then body slammed him in the chest, like he was gasping for air with little success. Never in his life had he ever felt this... helpless. He didn't like it.

He pivoted toward the door, as Ben said, "Go." He wove his way through the labyrinth of police that were crowding the apartment, headed for the back of Danielle's closet, grabbed a duffle bag, and started packing. Danielle seemed to have emerged from out of nowhere. When she'd stormed off, Adam was too focused on ripping someone's head off to look for her.

"What are you doing?" Danielle asked acrimoniously.

Not even bothering to stop and look at her, "What does it look like I'm doing? We're leaving." She stood there glowering at him, arms folded. "That is unless you want to sleep here tonight?" Not that she would be allowed to anyway since it was now a crime scene, but that wasn't his point.

———

Danielle couldn't help but notice Adam's frantic packing by the way he was shoving clothes left and right into the bag. She also noticed that he'd already packed her underwear, which she felt embarrassed about, and that didn't make too much sense since he'd peeled a pair off her just two nights ago. Still...

One thing that surprised her was that he had remembered all of the items of her nightly facial cleansing regimen. She guessed he paid closer attention than she'd thought. She was impressed.

No, stop it, you're pissed at him.

Suddenly, he straightened up. "Hurry, take off your clothes."

"Excuse me?" She was flabbergasted.

"Just go to your closet and then toss out your clothes," he said, rolling his eyes at her.

"But—"

"Danielle," he said with exasperation, "please, just do it."

She went ahead and did what he asked, but she chose to continue exuding her bitterness at him. A minute later, she cracked the closet door open enough to send her clothes flying with force at Adam's face. Unfortunately for her, his reflexes were sharp, and his hands caught the articles before they could actually make contact with their intended target.

When he returned, he knocked. "Open up." His abrupt tone was adding fuel to the fire. It was like they had traveled back in time to when they first met and he had been nothing but a jerk to her. His eyes lingered on her, being that she was half naked, but only briefly, and then tossed an outfit at her.

It was a female police uniform. Adam was already dressed in one himself.

She shot him a look of confusion, but instead of explaining, he just said, "Put them on."

She shut the door in his face and got dressed. The uniform fit decent enough, but she still had to do some adjusting as she stepped out from the closet.

"Okay, pin your hair up. It doesn't matter how, just as long as you can get this on," he said and handed her a patrolman's hat. It made sense now. They were going to leave in disguise, which meant that he believed the killer might still be watching from a distance. He helped her situate her hat, tucking strands of hair that Danielle had missed back under the cap. The delicate touch of his fingers felt so good and stirred her down inside. She hated that he had the power to do that to her. She wasn't through being mad at him, damn it.

Adam threw the bag over his shoulder and grabbed her hand as they headed out of the apartment. They stopped momentarily in front of a couple who resembled them, so Danielle could only assume these were the officers they had swapped identities with. The male cop handed Adam a pair of keys, which most likely belonged to his squad car.

"Thanks again for this," he said to the pair.

"Of course, Detective," they chimed in harmony.

Ben was waiting for them out in the hall and opened his arms as they approached. Adam tossed Danielle's bag to him, and he gave a reciprocating nod. Adam didn't even pause to exchange words with his partner. It was part of their psychic connection.

He was pulling Danielle along at a hurried pace down the hall, and when they got to the elevator, he answered the question she was wondering.

"He'll drop it off at my place later. If the killer is watching us, he might be suspicious if he sees us leaving the building with a piece of luggage. I can't take that chance."

"We're going to your place?" The doors opened, and they stepped inside.

"Where else do you propose we go? I know my apartment, and I could find my way through it blindfolded. It's the safest option we have right now."

"Fine." Danielle could see Adam nervously fidgeting, which he never did. "What aren't you telling me?" Her present loathing had suppressed the fear from earlier.

"He was in your apartment, Danielle."

"I know," she said solemnly.

"How do you think he got in?" Adam was staring straight ahead at the elevator doors. She had been so freaked out earlier that she hadn't even thought about it yet. Adam continued, "He has a key."

Now, she was anxiously twitching, too. She could feel her breathing intensifying and she was starting to get claustrophobic. "How long do you think he's had it?" Did she really want the answer to that?

"I don't know." His words were clipped and tight. "What I really want to know is how he got it." She hadn't thought of that, either.

"Wait a minute, that first day I went to the station with you, I couldn't find my keys, but when we came back to Mon Félicité, they had reappeared. He's been able to get into my apartment the whole time?" Danielle was doing her best not to hyperventilate, but it was getting harder.

"Not quite. I added that second deadbolt right after I moved in. He had to wait for another opportunity to copy the new key." The fear was threatening to completely overtake her. "Breathe," Adam instructed, finally looking at her.

Their eyes met, and the look in his reminded her of the cool, soothing feeling they had evoked that first night when he'd convinced her to open the doors of Mon Félicité. Even from the beginning, he had promised he wouldn't let anything happen to her. As she tried to focus on that, she could feel her heart rate start to level out again.

Bing. As the elevator doors opened to the lobby, Adam dropped her hand, which she'd forgotten he was holding.

"Act natural, okay? Just follow me to the car—don't look around for him. I can guarantee you that there will be a crowd of spectators outside the building, and he could be one of them. If he sees you searching—sees your face—then our cover is blown, and he could follow us. Now, tell me you understand."

Danielle took a deep breath, then nodded her head. "I understand."

"Good, let's go."

Red and blue flashed in every direction like strobes at an underground rave. Danielle repeated Adam's instructions in her mind, over and over again. She worked hard to loosen her muscles and make her movements more fluid and relaxed, but still serious. She couldn't act too casual. She needed to look authoritative.

She followed directly behind Adam as they made their way to *their* squad car. Luckily, the crowd split for them without them having to ask, getting them to the vehicle and pulling away within minutes. Those few, short minutes, though, felt impossibly infinite, and even after she was in and belted down, she refused to let herself relax until they were well on their way into the city.

Adam's phone rang. "Did you see anyone?" Danielle could hear Ben's voice on the other end of the line.

"No, I didn't see anyone follow you. Hopefully, he wasn't even there, but if he was, I don't think he knows."

"Thanks, man."

"I'll swing by as soon as I'm done here."

"Right, see you later." Adam hung up, and Danielle's hand reached for the bill of her hat when he stopped her, "No, not yet."

"I thought we weren't being followed?"

"Not until we get inside."

Her hand dropped back down into her lap. This had been a hell of a day. It couldn't have started any more normal—go to work, bake, cook, see Carrie, go home... Yes, normal until she found a dead woman in her bathtub, and now the secret undercover getaway, where she's posed as a cop running from a madman. What was this, a spy movie? More like a murder thriller. Yeah, *that* was the thing to be focused on, what genre her hellacious nightmare fell under. Jesus. She was sure she'd never know normal again.

Chapter Forty-Two

Adam's second floor apartment was modest. It was limited in its décor, but still more than she'd expected. He probably got the little bit of skills he had from Genevieve. If Danielle had to guess, she'd say that he only decorated the place just to keep his mother from coming in and doing it herself.

"Would you like some water?" he called from the kitchen.

"Sure, thanks." She felt uncomfortable again, and that sucked. She missed feeling at ease and open with him.

He tossed his hat on the kitchen table and got a glass down from one of the cabinets. She could hear the slight jingling of handcuffs and realized that the sound was coming from Adam. Then, she realized that she didn't have any.

"How come I don't have handcuffs?"

He approached with her drink. "Why do you need handcuffs?"

"I don't know," she shrugged, looking off to the window. That wasn't true. There were a few things she could think of what to do with them, but that was out of the question. When had she become so kinky, and wasn't she mad at him? Her anger had dwindled while she was working to focus on their escape, but there was still some resentment.

She took the glass from him, and the water began to slosh. Her hands were betraying her façade of calm. They revealed how shook up she still was, and it frustrated her. She tried to control the movements, but to no avail.

"Hey," Adam said, as he took the glass and set it down on the end table, "you're safe now." He pulled her into his arms.

Danielle released a deep breath and melted into the embrace. She could already feel the trembling lessen, and she closed her eyes. Her lids flew back open. All she could see was that girl's dead body floating in the pool of water and blood.

Suddenly, she felt Adam chuckle lightly. "You can take the hat off now."

"Oh," she laughed awkwardly, "good." She stepped back and pulled the hat off. Before she knew it, Adam closed the distance and began unpinning her hair and tousling the locks. She couldn't breathe, and her heart was racing. He kept running his hands through her waves, weakening her and making her knees want to give out. Why did he always do this to her? She needed to get over him, and he wasn't making it easy.

Danielle saw the gale again, swirling in those stormy gray eyes. She'd seen that storm before, back at Blue Star, where they threatened to ravage her right there on the ballroom floor. No, this was bad—very, very bad. She couldn't allow this to happen. If they slept together again, there was no telling how much her heart would hurt this time. So, why couldn't she pull away from him? Adam's lips softly burned hers, as he placed a tender, full kiss on her.

Walk away, dummy. Now.

Her feet wouldn't move. Her body was refusing to listen to the common sense of her brain. He deepened the kiss, and she felt her arms slide up his chest and around his neck. Apparently, that was the signal he needed. He dropped his hands from her hair and moved them down the sides of her, stopping at her hips, squeezing them, and pulled her in, pressing his huge erection against her.

The feel of his arousal heated her core, and her breathing intensified, which must have excited him more because he moved his hands to her cheeks and massaged. God, she loved those hands. Adam's kiss was becoming more and more greedy, captivating as much of Danielle's mouth as he could.

Adam broke the kiss and took a moment to look her over. Jesus Christ, she looked hot in that uniform. Never had he been turned on by a set of blues before. His dick was hard and tight against his slacks, and the fire was building down inside him. He wanted her so badly. He needed her. When he came to her eyes, he was entranced. The last time they made love, they had had nothing but the moonlight to see each other, but now, the lights were on in the apartment, and Adam could see her passion igniting the vivid gold that expanded into the lush green. Her eyes glowed. He'd never seen any as beautiful as Danielle's.

Adam snapped out of the daze, and the beast was unleashed. He grabbed the center of her uniform and ripped it open, sending buttons flying off in every direction and revealing her simple white cotton bra that was as sexy as any lace laden one. He moved his hands inside the shirt and around to her back. Her skin was warm and soft, and he loved the way it felt under his fingertips.

———

Once again, he captured her in a deep, sensual kiss, nearly swallowing her whole. Danielle could feel herself moving backwards, but Adam's body was still pressed up against hers with his hands splayed across her back. So, where was she going?

Thump!

She smacked right into the wall, pinned by Adam and his ferocity. He had walked her across the room, and even though the meeting of her back with the drywall was loud, it didn't hurt at all. In fact, it was hot. So hot that she let out a sound that was something between a gasp and a moan. His lips traversed in a pattern-less trail all down the length of her neck to her collar bone. She could feel her shirt being untucked and pulled down her arms, followed by the *swoosh* of the garment flying through the air. One hook, then two came undone, and her bra was the next piece to fly. Now, she was sliding *up* the wall. He had lifted her to bring her breasts to eye level, or more like lip level. His hot tongue flicked her pearled nipple as he drew her breast into his mouth and sucked.

Holy shit!

It felt so damn good. Danielle could feel herself getting wetter by the second, saturating her panties with the arousal Adam was causing. Her legs were wrapped tightly around his waist to help him keep her hoisted.

Adam desperately wanted to palm whichever breast his mouth wasn't currently occupying, but he needed to keep his hands around her toned cheeks to fight gravity. Even with her pressed up against the wall, he didn't want to risk dropping her. Talk about a mood killer. Danielle's hands held his head close, removing the option of Adam withdrawing from his task, and he began to hear soft panting from her, but he had to taste her.

He stepped away from the wall and forced her to untwine as he set her down. He began unbuttoning her pants while she hurriedly removed his shirt, causing tricky maneuvering to stay out of each other's way. He had her pants yanked down so fast that she barely had time to step out of them before he slammed her against the wall again.

Adam knelt and moved in. Danielle was drenched, anticipating his touch, and he could feel his cock ready to rip through his pants. He nipped gently at her clit through the thin, white cotton thong and heard a sensual moan. His mouth was watering as his fingers moved the material over to one side and pressed his lips to hers. He lapped up her juices, drinking them in.

"God, you taste so fucking good," he said between licks, muffling his voice.

A whimpered sigh was her only reply.

Her fingers went back and forth between pulling Adam's hair and pressing into his scalp. He was stoking the fire in her core with every flick and swirl of his tongue. That mixed with the feel of his hands rubbing firmly up her thighs was making Danielle's entire body quiver. She could feel the crest of her first orgasm rising, and as he plunged his tongue deeper, the wave crashed, and she let out a cry of satisfaction. Her knees would've been knocking together if he hadn't been between them.

Adam came up for air, kissing from navel to nose as he rose to his feet. Danielle had to lock her arms around his neck to stay standing, and a cocky grin plastered itself on his face. He threw Danielle over his shoulder with his sights on the bedroom. It was like he was channeling Conan the Barbarian or Tarzan, making off with his Jane.

―――

His behavior was prehistoric, but he couldn't care less. He also couldn't help it if she brought it out in him. He could feel her hair swaying, lightly brushing his back as he carted her off. All that was left was a pound to his chest and a slap on her ass, and the caveman persona would be complete. Adam decided against the ass slap—he knew she was voracious, but was she kinky? He wasn't about to take the chance and ruin the moment. If he had to stop now, a bad case of blue balls would probably cripple him.

He tossed Danielle down onto the bed and was on top of her before her body was done bouncing on the mattress. Finally, his hands were free to roam and grope anywhere he pleased, but before he could get a good handful of anything, he felt her push against him. Shit, he was being too rough with her. Did she want him to stop?

The answer was no. She was moving him slightly so that she could get better access to his zipper. Adam decided he would let her do the work because the feel of her undressing him, of her sliding his pants, then boxers down was damn sexy. His cock was pulsating, waiting for her to grip him in her delicate hands. He rolled off her briefly to toss the clothing to the floor, but Danielle caught his pants mid-air and removed the handcuffs from the belt.

Ah, so that's why she wanted a pair.

Looks like Danielle was kinky, after all. She was one surprise after another. Adam snatched them from her and pinned her arms above her head, locking the cuffs around her wrists.

"Are you going to read me my rights?" she asked with a husky, lustful voice. Never, ever in his life had he been with a woman like her. She was every man's dream—gorgeous, killer body, smart, independent, and funny, though most of the time she wasn't trying to be. And the icing on the cake? She was a sex kitten. Yep, she was perfect.

"You have the right to scream loudly," said Adam before he attacked.

He ripped Danielle's panties off and settled onto her, letting his erection rub against her clit, providing blissful agony for them both. He enveloped her in another heady kiss, and their tongues thrashed wildly. Adam blindly searched for the nightstand drawer to give Danielle her protection, knocking a clock off in the process, which crashed loudly as it hit the hardwood floor. The two of them weren't fazed one bit. Their passion was in full throttle, and there was no turning back.

The second he was finished preparing, which had been a difficult task with Danielle bucking her hips in yearning, he plunged his thickness into her, and sounds of pleasure rang out. There was no being gentle or tender, no taking his time. He wanted all of her, and he wanted it now. Adam's pelvic thrusts drove his shaft deep inside her to the hilt, and her hot, wet core squeezed tightly around him, grasping hold.

Danielle raised her arms up and over, using the links of the cuffs to pull Adam down so that they were chest to chest. Arms braced on either side of her, Adam started nibbling on her neck, doing his best not to bite too hard. He wasn't concerned about hurting her—because at this point, he was pretty sure she'd like it—but he didn't want to leave hickeys behind like some hormone-crazed high school kids. Even though they were grown adults, he feared that if he left evidence of their eroticism, people would judge her.

There was that sweet sound again—Danielle's moans were endless and driving him insane. Adam could do this all night. In fact, he could do this every night, but he couldn't think about that right now. He needed to focus on her pleasure, on giving her the best sex of her life.

"Oh," she groaned. "Harder, harder!"

Her wish was his command. Adam fiercely pounded his cock into her sheath, and he could feel his gluteal muscles, not to mention his hamstrings and quadriceps, tremor. He didn't think he'd ever worked this hard before. He liked it. She was pushing him to rise to new challenges, challenges that he *would* meet.

———

The feel of the cuffs jingling around her wrists thrilled her. It was an entirely new experience, and one that she never, in a million years, thought she would enjoy. It was erotic, naughty, playful, and just out and out hot. It made her feel even sexier, if that was possible. She felt unabashedly wanton and oddly powerful. Her desire and passion were so extreme that she had to be tamed by this man. Sweet lord, this man…

This man that worshipped her body in ways she could only dream of. He was utterly gorgeous. Lightning crackled in those stormy gray eyes and enveloped her. Every look was a caress that she felt move over her, through her. The power of his strength as he took her, the warmth of his skin that pressed against hers. It was decadent and indulgent. Yes, this man was driving her senseless.

His long, engorged cock was taking her to new heights of ecstasy that she didn't want to come down from. Knowing that Adam could go deeper, needing him to go deeper, she pulled her legs through his arms, and one at a time, placed them on his shoulders. She was right. He sank even further into her, and now, each one of his pumps hit straight in her g-spot. Her moans turned into cries, which transformed into screams.

Her senses were heightened. The sound of his panting, the look of searing desire in his eyes, the taste of his kiss on her lips, the smell of him as she breathed him in, the feel of his body moving in and around her... Her arousal ratcheted tighter and tighter. Too much more, and she just might lose her mind.

Holy shit! Adam thought he was going to explode any minute now, but he refused to allow himself release before Danielle reached her moment of joy. Actually, he was pretty damn sure she was experiencing joy already, but he wanted to send her all the way to the moon.

He no longer felt the metal links of the cuffs digging into his neck, but instead felt fingernails scratching across his shoulder blades. There was a slight sting, and he knew he would have bright red streaks on his back, which he would wear proudly. They would be a symbol of the outstanding job he did pleasuring his woman. Wait, what? No, Danielle wasn't his woman. Was she his lover? Whatever she was to him, he had no claim to her. A small pang came with that thought, and Adam had to force it out of his mind.

"OH! GOD! YES!" Danielle shouted. Her head flailed on the pillow, and her eyes rolled back. Her long lashes fanned across the tops of her cheekbones so delicately, and he wanted to kiss those lashes, those cheeks, that cute nose...

Fucking focus!

"Adam!" Her head came off the pillow, and her eyes opened momentarily to find his lips, and in that split second, he could see a haze in them, like she was in another state of being.

When he thought he could barely contain it any longer, Danielle's head dropped back, and her lips ripped away from his as she let out a pure carnal cry. He could feel the walls of her core squeeze him rapidly and knew she'd made it to the moon. Her crescendo sent him over the edge, and he exploded with her. His pulse was pounding in his ears from the cardio workout they'd just had.

Adam carefully moved her legs down with shaky hands and then crashed onto her. The two of them were still heavily gasping for oxygen. His lips were right next to her ear, and still short of breath, he let out a sigh and whispered, "God, Dani."

He nuzzled her behind her ear and then placed a sweet kiss on her neck where her pulse was fluttering faster than a hummingbird's wings. This was the second time he'd called her by her nickname. Danielle didn't make anything of it the other night, though she did find it a tiny bit peculiar, but now, she wondered why he'd said it. She had assumed it was some sort of slip of the tongue because he heard Carrie and Ralph use it often, but not something he would actually adopt. After all, only the people that were closest to her called her Dani... Did Adam consider them to be close? Did he want—

No. No, no, no. You are not allowed to think about that. Deal with it later. You can't fall apart now, not in front of him.

Thankfully, she was too exhausted to fall apart. She could feel her eyes getting heavy, and all she could think about now was falling asleep. She heard a *click* and then another and felt the heavy metal of the cuffs release their hold on her wrists. Danielle didn't know when Adam had retrieved the keys, but she didn't care.

He rolled off her and padded to the bathroom, shuffling his feet. It's a good thing he didn't have carpet, or he probably would have static shocked the hell out of himself when he turned on the light. She wasn't sure how much time had passed since she nodded off, but when he crawled back into bed, she noticed that all of the lights were off and there was nothing but complete darkness. She could feel the coils in the box spring lightly bounce as the mattress dipped, ever so slightly, closer and closer to her. Adam barricaded her as he enclosed her into his body, spooning her like they were soldered together. He inhaled deeply, and Danielle realized that he was smelling her hair. He dragged out his exhale, and she could feel the little hairs on the back of her neck tickle her skin.

Chapter Forty-Three

Dawn was breaking through Adam's bedroom window, filling the room with a deep orange glow. He was still plastered to Danielle, encircling her in his embrace. Should she go ahead and get up? If she stayed in bed with him, he might shower her with kisses when he woke... or he could sneak out, leaving her by herself *again*. It would probably be the latter, considering he'd already done it once, and there was no way in hell she was going to be left to wake up alone twice. She wasn't going to be an occasional booty call or hook up. It may be casual for him, but to her, it was anything but. She had already admitted to herself that she was in love with him, and when she opened herself to love, she opened herself to pain. The two were bound together. Good and evil, heaven and hell, yin and yang... it was the same thing. There was no one without the other. And even if they woke up together, it was likely to be awkward. Nope, she definitely didn't want to deal with that.

She *very* slowly slipped out of her enclosure, because if he caught her sneaking out, that would be ten times more uncomfortable. She was successful and began to tiptoe to the kitchen. Danielle abruptly stopped when she realized that she was stark naked. Her eyes began scanning the room for anything, anything at all, to cover herself. Normally, she would appreciate that Adam was tidy, but right now she wished he was a slob. She had no choice but to check his dresser. It seemed to be in fairly good condition, which meant it was probably relatively new. She had no idea if the drawers would squeak or which would contain shirts, if any. She had to guess. The longer she waited, and the more drawers she opened, increased the chances of him waking up.

She decided one of the bottom drawers would be the best bet. She crouched and gently pulled on the drawer's handle. Her speed was so painstakingly slow, that a snail could have crawled across the room

The Harvester

faster than the time it was taking her to open the drawer. *Jackpot*. A small stack of t-shirts laid folded inside. She grabbed the first one on top and quickly pulled it over her head. She contemplated on whether or not she could close the drawer. On one hand, she didn't want to make any noise, but on the other hand, she didn't want him to know she was rifling through his stuff. When he woke up, he was going to see her in the shirt anyway, though, so she left it open.

Danielle crept to the door that was still hanging wide open from their abrupt burst into the room and carefully closed it behind her. She kept her grip on the knob twisted, so that as the door and the jamb made contact, the latch wouldn't click. When the two met, she took her time letting the knob twist back into place and released a mental sigh of relief.

She desperately wanted some coffee, but she wasn't going to risk waking him with the aroma. Once he was up, she'd make a pot, unless he didn't have creamer. She had to have creamer, or she couldn't bear it. Black coffee was just too bitter. Danielle decided to check the refrigerator and sighed with joy when she found the bottle of Coffee Mate. It wasn't flavored, but she could live with that. She noticed that the expiration date was getting close, and it occurred to her that even though creamer had a longer shelf life, everything else perishable was probably spoiled. Adam had spent the last month or so living with her, so the milk, juice, yogurt, etcetera, were all bad. Holy crap, had it really been a month? He had only come by his place a few times for fresh clothes. The only reason she hadn't been dragged along was due to her promise to not step one foot outside the café. Ralph and others had to be with her any time Adam wasn't.

There was no salvaging anything, and Danielle began to pout with disappointment. Cereal? No milk. Toast? Moldy bread. Fruit? Rotten. It looked as though her breakfast was going to consist of a big glass of water. She decided to raid the pantry a little more, rummaging to the back of each shelf. A short moment later, she began to jump up and down with elation. She found some apple cinnamon oatmeal, which she could definitely make with water. Her stomach was growling, and she didn't waste any time grabbing a bowl and filling it with water to throw in the microwave. Boiling the water ahead of time would keep the oatmeal from wafting throughout the apartment.

Danielle gobbled down the small breakfast and was left wanting more. Their late-night romp had completely burned off dinner, which if she was going to lose calories, she couldn't think of a better way to do it. Even after the first helping, her stomach still felt empty. The second bowl, though, started to give her sustenance.

She washed her bowl and then went over to the couch. She didn't know what to do with herself. She didn't dare turn on the TV for the same reason she couldn't make coffee. The longer she could avoid Adam, the better. Her attention turned to the front door. How desperately she wanted to bolt and go home where she could hide, although thanks to the Harvester, she couldn't go back at all, at least not without an escort.

A black bag caught her eye sitting in front of the door. It was the bag that Adam had packed before they slipped away from her apartment, but how did it get inside? Danielle's heart rate quickened as she walked over to it. The front door was locked so... A note was sitting on the top, slightly tucked into the zipper, presumably to prevent it from falling away. The note read:

Sorry I dropped by so late, but here's Danielle's stuff.
I used the key so I wouldn't disturb you two.
-B

Oh, God, what did he mean by that? He didn't want to disturb them because they were sleeping or because they were having wild, hot... Her mind drifted away, and Danielle had to shake her attention back to the present. She was turning herself on just thinking about last night and then, she thought about how she'd told Adam that Saturday night was a one-time thing. Well, everyone could see how that turned out. What happened to her resolve? It must have been smothered out by his perfectly sculpted body molding to hers. God, that body...

Again, she had to snap out of her fantasy. Actually, it wasn't a fantasy anymore. Now it was a memory—a damn good one, too.

She was extremely happy to see her belongings because she definitely needed some fresh clothes, not to mention a toothbrush. Right then, a hot shower sounded exquisite, and she crept back into the room, taking her bag with her. The hot water beating down felt fantastic on her skin, and it would have been easy to get lost in the comforting warmth, but this was another instance that called for a speed wash. Danielle didn't want to linger too long, in case Adam might... She let out a huff in her mind.

Hell, I don't know what he'll do. He's so freaking unpredictable!

Mixed signals were flying all over the place, and it was taxing trying to decode them. It was impossible to try to read Adam. Danielle thought she had him figured out, and for the most part, she did, his personality at least, but when it came to his emotions or feelings, she was at a loss. How did he feel about her, really?

Hurry up, and get out of the shower.

She didn't want him to see her naked or even almost naked, just in case he got any ideas. Even if he had ideas, she wasn't going to sleep with him again. She was serious, damn it!

The more she thought about it, the more she realized she wasn't being very crystal clear herself. Here she was, pretending to have casual sex with a man she was in love with and leading him to believe that she didn't care about a relationship. She was so sick of lying, but until this whole ordeal was over, she had no choice. Telling Carrie the truth of it all—which Danielle was sure Adam didn't know about and definitely would have objected to—gave her the tiniest feeling of freedom. She wished she could talk to her now.

She crept out of the bathroom, fully clothed, and went back out into the living room. She wasn't sure how much longer she could hold out before she'd *have* to make some coffee.

———

The red digital lights read nine a.m. as they glowed back at Adam from the floor. He remembered now that he'd knocked it off during their spicy lovemaking, and as he closed his eyes and thought back on last night, he started to get hard with excitement. Danielle was so incredible, so amazing, so… there weren't words to describe her.

The nightmare had made its appearance right on schedule, but this time, his eyes had flown open to find her tucked tightly into him, and he'd immediately eased, then drifted back to sleep. It was the first time since the dreams started that he was able to get more than a few hours of sleep, and he felt refreshed. He had woken up many times their first night, back when he had decided to stay with her.

He inhaled deeply and released a slow, calm breath as he went to glide a hand over Danielle's soft, naked skin, but his brows cinched together when he felt nothing but cotton, and it was then that he noticed his arms were empty—they were absent of a warm, gorgeous, sexy Danielle.

He swiftly rose out of bed, grabbed his boxers, and sped into the living room with gun in hand, ready for anything. She wasn't there. He heard a noise coming from the kitchen and cautiously rounded the corner of the wall that halfway separated the two rooms. Danielle was loading a coffee filter into the pot and pouring grounds in, anxiously tapping a foot as if it would make her hands go faster. He knew she needed her morning coffee, or she'd get twitchy, and her entire day would be thrown off. How long had she been up, and why had she waited until now to make the pot? As the water began to percolate, the aroma quickly filled the air, and he theorized. She didn't make any coffee because she didn't want to wake him, but the real question was did she wait out of consideration or avoidance?

"Jesus!" Danielle said sharply, as she jumped at the sight of Adam and his gun from the corner of her eye. It was a good thing that she hadn't already made a mug, or she would have spilled it everywhere.

"Sorry," he said, as he set the gun down on the table. It was all business in his voice. When Danielle kept looking at him, he knew she was waiting for an explanation for the overkill entrance. "You weren't in bed."

"So?" she asked, raising an eyebrow.

"So, I didn't know where you were. You just left."

She turned her attention back to the pot and began to pour her mug full. "For one, I didn't know I needed permission to leave the bedroom." She stirred the sugar and creamer, took a sip, and sighed as she closed her eyes.

"And two?"

"I just took a cue from you," she said nonchalantly and shrugged her shoulders. She didn't even bother looking at him, but instead kept breathing in her coffee and taking slow sips of the soothing, warm liquid.

Adam didn't need clarification—he knew exactly what she was referring to. It seemed as though she was upset after all about him leaving her in bed alone Sunday morning. She'd fooled him on the car ride home, and it was idiotic of him to think that a woman like her wouldn't be hurt. He'd completely deserted her in the guest house and then intentionally distanced them at breakfast, not even giving her the courtesy of acknowledging her. He deserved to be punched in the gut for that. And yet, even after his actions, she told Carrie that she was in love with him. It's no wonder why she thought he had no reason to stay. Did he have a reason?

He was already privately berating himself for breaking his rule *twice*. Now, he was no better than the other sleazy cops who slept with women from their cases. He'd sworn he would never take advantage of that kind of vulnerability. But... what if he had given in to his own vulnerability? The affect Danielle had on him ran deeper each day, and the longer he was with her, the more personal this case became to him. The thought of harm coming to her made him sick and enraged at the same time. Hell, it was giving him nightmares for Christ's sake. Adam felt confused about everything. He wished he could take a step back to figure things out, but that wasn't an option. Danielle needed him, and he was going to be there for her no matter what.

It was too late to apologize for Sunday. If he did it now, it would seem like he was only saying it because she had made reference. He didn't want her to think he was patronizing her, so he ignored the comment.

"It would make me feel better if you'd tell me next time."

―――

It took every bit of restraint she had not to whip her head around to gape at him. Next time? Danielle had come very close to choking on her coffee as she swallowed the beverage. Did he think they were going to keep sleeping together, sex *and* slumber? If so, she desperately wanted to refute that assumption, but she decided against it. Opening that conversation would lead straight into the one she didn't want to have.

"Please?"

She could feel Adam's eyes on her. She hadn't realized that he was waiting for her agreement. Since when did he give her a say? It scared her how accustomed she'd already become to letting someone order her around—aside from Carrie, of course. At least with Carrie, though, she did an equal amount of bossing her right back. Considering their circumstance, commanding Adam about wasn't an allowance for her. Not that she would do so purposefully, but it would be nice to have some authority of her own every now and then.

"Okay," she replied, keeping her tone light. She wasn't going to argue with him. She still was not going to open that door. She'd figure out the new sleeping situation later. And there *would* be a new one.

"Thanks." He was thanking her, too? He had never thanked her for her cooperation before. Maybe because she didn't always offer it up so easily.

No, no, she thought with an airy, sarcastic taunt, *you just offer up your body easily.*

Oh, how she loathed herself right now. Who was she? She didn't go around sleeping with guys all willy-nilly. The way she felt about Adam couldn't be classified as willy-nilly, but that didn't change the fact that she'd hopped into bed with him like a horny bunny. *And* they weren't even in a relationship. That made it worse. At least if they were an actual item, she wouldn't feel so trampy. Adam probably did think there was going to be a next time, because after all, she had put out twice now without any protests or hesitations. He had to think she was easy. She wouldn't regret it, though. No, both times had been incredible, and the pleasure he had given her made them the greatest experiences of her life. So, no, she wouldn't regret. Instead, she'd treasure those memories and lock them away.

Danielle's cell phone rang, breaking the silence, and she didn't waste any time following the sound. It led her to her pants that were still sprawled on the living room floor. Oh God, just another reminder. Before she could answer it, Adam snatched the phone from her hands.

"Hey!" Why was she surprised?

He didn't respond but gave her a serious look that said he was boss as he answered her phone. "Ralph." There was that all-business tone again. "Yes... yes... no."

She couldn't hear the other side of the conversation, and it was frustrating her that Adam was responding in his short, clipped answers. "I can't tell you that, there's too much risk... I agree, one hundred percent."

Agree about what? Danielle might as well have not been there because not once did he bother to include her.

"Yes, actually, there is. I want you to observe anyone who asks about her, which means full descriptions and names if you can manage... Yes, even if they're regulars. At this time, everyone is a suspect. Be discreet, though. I don't want anyone catching on, okay? Thanks."

"What was that all about, and why didn't you let me answer? It was just Ralph," she asked, as he ended the call.

"The call came from Ralph's phone, but that didn't mean it was him. If the killer can steal your keys, who's to say he can't steal Ralph's phone?" He had a point, she supposed.

"Okay, so what did you talk about? And thanks for including me, by the way."

"He knows about the murder in your apartment. He wanted confirmation that this was really about you and if you were in danger."

Her eyes narrowed in suspicion as she asked, "So, what do you agree one hundred percent about?"

"That you're not to set foot in the café." There was no delay with his answer or unsteadiness in his voice. He didn't care how she was going to react.

"Excuse me?"

"Not until he's caught."

Danielle let out an angry chuckle as she threw her arms in the air. "Well, Jesus Christ, you might as well have put me in a safe house after all since now I'm under lock and key. It would've saved us a lot of trouble." That was her code word for heartache.

"Trouble?"

"This whole charade of you and me being madly in love with each other. It was all for nothing, just a waste of time." She could have sworn she saw a trace of hurt in his eyes. Hell, it hurt her a bit, too, when her mind echoed the words. It was then that she noticed he was still in nothing but his underwear, those tight boxer-briefs hugging every muscled curve of his butt and thighs. She wanted to lick her lips and take a bite. The near nakedness was another reminder of last night.

"So," his voice solemn, "you think it was a waste of time?"

"Well..." Had she hurt him? Surely not. He admitted in Oceanside that he cared for her well-being and was attracted to her, but nothing more than that. "I'm just saying that you could have gotten to work on the case more like you wanted, instead of babysitting me. You could have stayed here in your own apartment, not trapped at mine. You would have been free to do whatever you wanted."

Or whomever he wanted. He wouldn't have had to be tied down to her. Danielle was trying very hard not to let the salty tears start welling in her eyes. The thought of him being with someone else, making love to them with the same ferocious, all-consuming passion that they had shared, was gut-wrenching.

"I'm not babysitting you. I'm doing my job."

Yeah, well arguably, his job probably didn't include doing *her*.

"I'm protecting you from a crazed lunatic who poses a huge threat to your right to live."

Adam's voice was devoid of emotion. It was as if he was reading a script and reciting the words to her. Danielle was in his direct path to the bedroom, and as he came toward her, she became nervous. She had no idea what he was going to do. In less than twelve hours he had comforted her, yelled at her, comforted her again, made erotic, wanton love to her, held her tenderly through the night—and the morning—and had now switched to robot mode. She had no clue, and she hated it. He was frustrating the hell out of her. She wished he'd just come out and say if he was interested or not, instead of making her guess, which she couldn't even do *that*. This merry-go-round was making her head spin, and the metaphorical centrifugal force from it was giving her a literal splitting headache. She didn't know how much more of this she could take.

Adam gently placed his hands on either side of her waist, expression still unreadable, and moved her to the side and out of his line. Not one word was uttered as he walked past her and into the bedroom. It took a minute for Danielle to realize that she had been holding her breath and she needed oxygen. The door closed behind him, and she was left standing in the living room by herself.

She took a step as if to follow him, but stopped. She felt compelled to tell him she was sorry, but then wondered what the hell would she be apologizing for? She hadn't said or done anything wrong. Even if she had hurt his feelings, he had no right to have them. Not once had he shown them to her, not his true feelings. Therefore, they were his own responsibility. She wasn't going to carefully tiptoe around, delicately picking the right words when he didn't bother.

Danielle took a deep breath. This was it, the end. It didn't matter how much she wanted him, how much she loved him. No, this was it. The cement was being poured, the stones re-paved, and the wall erected higher than ever. She had let Adam get dangerously close. He had nearly torn down her entire barrier, probably without even realizing it, and she had made it so easy. She couldn't help but think of the opening scene from *Raiders of the Lost Ark*. She pictured Adam with the iconic hat and whip, reaching out to replace the idol—her heart—with a bag of sand. He was going to steal it and leave her with nothing. She would be empty.

Danielle scoffed aloud to herself. It was bizarre the parallels between her dilemma with Adam and the Harvester. Both threatened to leave a gaping hole in her chest. Both threatened to destroy her.

Adam stood under the steamy spray, arms braced against the tile, his head lowered, allowing the hot water to cascade all around his face. Her words had hurt. They shouldn't have, but they did all the same. Danielle regretted it. All of it. No matter how incredible their nights together had been, in the end, she wished it had never happened. Last night, she'd confided to Carrie that she was in love with him. Was that truly how she felt? It didn't matter. Even if she did, to regret their time together meant she didn't *want* to love him. If she could go back and undo it, she would.

He cursed as he chastised himself. *This was why you weren't supposed to get involved with your cases. Why you shouldn't.* Why he couldn't. It was as if he had stepped outside of his body and watched as all of his discipline abandoned him, not able to do anything to stop it, to stop himself. He could smell sweet vanilla on his skin, could feel her body on his fingertips, could taste her kiss on his lips. Danielle was consuming him.

Chapter Forty-Four

He sat at the worktable as he placed strands of honey blonde hair into a small baggie and pressed his fingers tightly on either side of the track, securing the seal. The Sharpie cap squeaked as he removed it and labeled the bag slowly, making sure each letter was perfectly legible.

Number 3

He'd already added the prize onto the shelf next to the others. They looked good—no, terrific. His arrangement of the shrine was wonderfully balanced. Centered above the shelf was a gorgeous picture of his angel. She truly was a creature of beauty. To the sides, he'd positioned smaller snapshots of her in geometrical patterns, alternating between color and black and white prints, making the design very pleasing to the eye. She surrounded the entire room, enveloping him in her perfection. She comforted him and drove him crazy. He had to have her. He would have her. She *would* be his.

Black ribbon was tied around each one of the lids to remind him how black their evil hearts were. To remind him that they were infected with the poison of promiscuity. Their salacious impurity eliminated their humanity, and if they weren't human, then they didn't belong among the living. They deserved the consequence of damnation that resulted from their deeds.

Imposters. All of them.

Oh, how he missed her. His angel had disappeared again, and it was torture. He knew she was still in the city, he could feel it, but he just didn't know where. Something he was sure of, though, was that she was with that fucking cop. He wanted to drive a nail through each of his fingers and listen to him scream in pain. Oh, yes, he would allow him to scream. It would be music to his ears.

Chapter Forty-Five

Adam and Danielle walked up the steps to the precinct hand in hand. They reached Homicide and made their way through the doors of the department. Once again, every eye was on Danielle, and once again, Adam was ready to deck anyone and everyone. Their gawking looks roamed over her figure from head to toe and back again. She was wearing a pair of blue jean shorts and a plain white button up shirt that was gathered down the center. He had just thrown a bunch of stuff in that bag and hadn't paid any attention—or given a shit—about what he picked out, but she managed to make everything she wore look good. It was amazing that she'd been able to put something together out of the items he'd picked.

Her long legs made her shorts seem too short, and the gathered material of her shirt brought too much attention to her chest. Her skin glowed with the gentlest kiss from the sun and accentuated the honey in her eyes. Was there ever a time when this woman *wasn't* stunning? Nope, and she was completely oblivious to it, too. He couldn't understand how unaware she was of the way men looked at her. She was a total bombshell, and everyone knew it but her.

The leers from the other men caused Adam's fingers to thread tighter between Danielle's. Some of the perusers released their fixation when their eyes caught sight of Adam's, which threatened to burn holes into every man's skull who dared to continue ogling.

His left arm received a slight tug, bringing his attention to Danielle. Corolla had pulled her off course, jerking Adam along with her. His grubby, sleazy fingers were all over her free hand, his grin oozing of womanizer, and his perverted eyes groping her physique.

"Danielle, I'm so glad to see you're unharmed. You must have had quite a fright." Corolla's eyes were theatrically sympathetic, and his voice was so overly concerned, it was obnoxious.

"Yes—"

"I'm sorry I wasn't there to attend to you. I would have been there in a flash—all you had to do was call, but I'm sure the distress was a lot to take, mentally." Corolla was still molesting her hand.

"That's kind of you, but Adam's been doing an amazing job," she said with a soft smile.

Corolla looked at the two of them sourly, but only for an instant.

That's my girl.

Adam was giddy inside with smugness. He was loving watching Corolla get shot down.

Then, Corolla smiled. "Well, I guess there really is a first for everything. I'm still available, should you need anything." He dropped Danielle's hand and hooked his thumbs around two belt loops. It was clear that he was consciously trying to draw attention to his crotch, as if to woo her.

It took everything Adam had not to slug that jackass. He felt the déjà vu kick in when he pulled Danielle along and away from Corolla, walking with a fast, clipped pace to Jensen's office. Jensen wasn't going to like the confrontation that was about to happen, and he especially wouldn't be happy about having Danielle there to watch, but he didn't dare leave her alone at his desk again. There was no telling what Corolla would do. Adam wasn't too concerned with the other guys, but Mitch… Not to mention, he had, more or less, promised her that he wouldn't leave her after the last time.

"Adam, hold up," Ben called across the room.

Adam stopped just a few steps from Jensen's door. The look on Ben's face told him that he needed to ease the intensity in his expression before he approached the captain.

"Before you go storming in there, Jensen already told me to bring you back into the fold." Adam was glad to hear that, but he still felt pent up. "He does want to talk to you, though."

With that psychic connection, Ben told Adam that that meant alone. Adam quickly flashed his eyes in Corolla's vicinity, and back to Ben, who responded with the slightest of head nods. You would've had to be examining the two of them with a heavy stare to even notice the exchange.

———

"Come on, Danielle, let's go over to my desk. I'm sure I'm better company than this guy," Ben said, as he gave a smile and a smack on Adam's arm. "Plus, my wife, Lacey, made some lemon squares for me. She'd lay into me if she knew I didn't get your opinion on them."

"She knows I cook?" Danielle didn't know why she was surprised. Probably, because she was so used to Adam keeping things bottled up, that she'd come to expect that from every man, especially his partner. He could stand to learn a few things from Ben.

"Yeah, I pretty much tell her everything. Well, everything that I'm permitted to."

Danielle thought that was really sweet. It was nice to know that there were still couples out there who confided in each other wholly.

"I'll bet they're fantastic. I'm flattered that she wants a critique from me," she said with a smile, her eyes turning warm and gentle.

"From the way Burke here raves about your food, she's absolutely beside herself."

She kept her focus on Ben. She was curious if Adam was blushing at the reveal, but she didn't want to know. How would it benefit her? It wouldn't.

"Honestly, I think she made them in hopes that you would come by."

She let out a small laugh. "I seriously doubt it. How would she even know if I would come to the station?"

"I'd say my hunch is pretty strong since she's sent me to work with a treat nearly every day for the last few weeks."

———

The Harvester

Danielle laughed deeper. The laugh that made Adam want to smile and laugh with her—the laugh that made him warm inside, calm.

"Um, Adam," she said, snapping his mind back to the present. Adam didn't even know that he'd faded out. He had also forgotten that he still had a serious twine of her fingers with his. Holding her hand had become second nature to him. He quickly let go and watched her walk away with his partner.

He was a bit curious about what Jensen would still want to discuss, but he didn't care. He had already been prepared to have a lengthy conversation that would most definitely have ended up in some yelling and no doubt some repercussions.

Adam entered the captain's office without knocking, which he didn't normally do—no one did. Jensen didn't look up, nor did he bark at Adam for his intrusion.

"Sit down, Burke," Jensen said, head still down, eyes preoccupied with the piece of paper in front of him.

Adam did as he was told. Now wasn't the time to be defiant since Jensen appeared to be calm. That may come into play later. A long moment of silence passed before Jensen pulled off his reading glasses and gave physical acknowledgement to Adam.

"I assume that Anderson has already informed you that you are to come back onto the case completely?"

"Yes."

"Good," Jensen said, then released an exasperated sigh. "You and Anderson are the best team I have in here. I don't know what it is that the two of you do or how you do it, but together you have solved the most cases over any of the others." Jensen paused and let out another one of those sighs. "This case is different, Burke. This bastard is smart, careful. He's left us with nothing useful, nothing to figure out his next move, his next victim. The only thing we can be certain of, which in court is still circumstantial, is that Danielle Walsh is at the center of all of this." Adam didn't need to be reminded of that. He was well aware. "The commissioner has granted me permission to allocate whatever resources you need in order to catch the Harvester. You have complete agency-wide discretion."

Adam was shocked and ecstatic.

"The crime lab, M.E., and criminal profiler have all been assigned to this case as first priority. They are at your disposal and are on call twenty-four/seven. This station isn't sleeping."

Adam was still soaking in this fabulous gift when Jensen brought up the next topic.

"Now, about Miss Walsh," the captain said, gaining Adam's full attention. "I'd like for you to continue your cover story, but I can assign another to guard her during the day. We can make up a reason why someone else is with her without blowing your cover. Maybe plant some as customers. Detective Corolla volunteered for the job—"

"No," Adam said a little too forcefully. Jensen raised a brow. "I don't think she should be going back to Mon Félicité. Anyone who knows about the third murder will put two and two together, knowing that she has something to do with the killings. I want her here, where I can keep an eye on her."

"I need your best game, Burke. Are you sure you can do both?"

"Yes," he said, the force returning in his voice.

Jensen was quiet momentarily. "Alright, then we're done here." Adam stood and headed for the door. "Burke," Adam looked back at Jensen, who spoke with emphasis, "whatever it takes—by any means necessary."

Adam gave a nod to the captain and left the office.

———

"So, do you know what they're talking about?" Danielle was sitting in Adam's chair, looking up at Ben, who was leaning against the desk, arms folded. To her, it looked like Ben was casually, but cautiously standing guard. Throughout their conversation, his eyes would scan the room every few minutes, looking out for what, she didn't know.

"I know some." That was all that Ben offered, and she didn't push for more.

"Tell Lacey that she makes a mean lemon square."

"Yeah?" Ben's pride in his wife showed in his smile.

She longed for that. "Absolutely, I've eaten three already." That wasn't necessarily a good thing, but they were pretty damn delicious, and food was her best distraction, whether she was cooking it or eating it. She tried not to do too much of the latter, but she currently didn't have a kitchen to lose herself in.

"Thanks, that's really going to make her day," said Ben.

"I call it like I taste it," she said, and the two of them chuckled at the altered figure of speech. "How long have you and Adam been partners?"

"Six years now."

"Wow," Danielle paused. "How have you put up with him for that long?"

Ben erupted in laughter. "I suppose that's a good question." His sudden outburst made Danielle laugh along with him. "In all honesty, it's because we're so similar."

She gave him a look of disbelief. "How so?"

"We both believe that bringing criminals to justice is the greatest thing we could do for the world—knowing that we're making it a safer place, that we're making a difference. I know Adam can seem pretty intense..."

I'll say, she thought.

"...but, that's because he takes his job very seriously. Not everyone does."

That was probably true. As much as society would like to believe otherwise, there was always a bad seed amongst the honorable. It was a shame.

Danielle had been hoping that Ben would have something, anything, to say about Adam that would make her see him in a different light, but he didn't, and that beautiful light that he was in presently shone even brighter. Her need to find a kitchen was growing, especially if she was going to avoid gaining ten pounds from Lacey Anderson's lemon squares.

Adam strolled out of Captain Jensen's office looking pleased. As he neared, Danielle popped another lemon square into her mouth. *Hello, ten pounds.*

"So, what else did Jensen have to say?" Ben asked.

"I've got carte blanche."

"Really? Damn, I'm a little scared now."

Danielle didn't need to ask Ben why. She could tell by the look in Adam's eyes. She had just finished swallowing the tart dessert when Adam's hand reached out to her face. His thumb lightly dusted across her lips, taking a few sprinkles of powdered sugar with it. She felt hot, not from embarrassment of having the sweet, white speckles lingering, but from the tender stroke of his touch. She decided not to acknowledge the favor, but rather to ignore it as if it were nothing. She couldn't show him the effect. This wall was going to take forever.

―――

Adam couldn't stop the impulse. It had been a natural reaction, not even thinking about what he was doing or the significance of it until after the fact. It was what a *real* boyfriend would do for his *real* girlfriend.

He also couldn't stop the fantasy that sprang into his head—and his pants—as Danielle self-consciously licked her lips after his touch. He was kissing the snow white sugar from them instead, tasting the sweetness. Papers were flying from his desk as he swept his arm across its surface to lay her down. Their passion was fierce, but not hurried. Every kiss and touch were filled with pure sensuality and pleasure. The things they were going to do to each other…

Adam needed a cold shower to douse his lust, and a good smack in the face to bring him back to his senses. His desk phone rang, and he leaned across the desk—and Danielle—to pick it up. Why did she have to smell so good?

"Burke," he answered and listened to his caller. "Yes, but I need you to come down to Homicide." He hung up the phone and moved out of Danielle's space. "Jimmy's coming down to talk to Danielle," he said to Ben, then turned to her, "Jimmy Tharp is our profiler. He wants to speak to you."

She looked as though she was swallowing a lump in her throat and would have killed for a glass of water. He could see the anxiety that had popped up in her.

"You don't need to be nervous, Jimmy's a good guy."

Her only reply was an absent nod of her head and a fidgety squeeze of her hands.

———

Jimmy Tharp was a tall, lean man, late-thirties, with dark brown eyes that matched his dark hair. He wore a simple black suit with a skinny black tie, and if his glasses had been horn-rimmed instead of thin wire frames, Danielle would have thought he'd stepped straight out of the nineteen-sixties. Instead of sitting directly across from her at the unoccupied desk, Jimmy sat on the same side, face to face, one on one with a very casual body language. Danielle, on the other hand, was sitting ramrod straight in her chair.

"So, I hear you cook or something like that?" Jimmy's joke immediately eased her as she chuckled and released some of her posture.

"Yeah, something like that." She expected him to have a note pad and a pen ready to jot down her every word, but he didn't bring anything with him. He just sat leaning back in his chair, hands folded in his lap, and a leg leisurely crossed over the other.

"You seem fairly young to have your own restaurant."

"Actually, it's just a little café, and I get that a lot. I've scrimped and saved nearly every penny since..." Danielle paused, "since forever, I guess."

"Did you always know you wanted your own business?"

"It wasn't about having my own business. It was about getting to cook and create new dishes, master the classics, and share them with other people. Food can be more than just about consumption. It can create feelings and memories. I know that if I don't see a smile on a customer's face, then I didn't do my best."

"Ah, a perfectionist."

"So I'm told."

"Do people give you a hard time about it?"

"Sometimes, but not too much. Besides, I'd rather be a perfectionist than a lazy slob, half-assing everything." Her eyes grew a bit. "Oh, I'm sorry, I didn't mean to swear."

"I'm not a priest, Miss Walsh, although, I do have something in common with them. Everything is confidential between us, unless you tell me otherwise, but that would really only matter if I was your doctor, and this was a session."

"Isn't it, though?" The nervousness returned to Danielle's expression.

"Nope, I just wanted to get to know you a bit. I'm not analyzing you," his joking smile returned, "unless there was some sort of personal problem you wanted to discuss?"

Danielle laughed again. "Well, there is this one thing…"

―――

Adam and Ben sat at their desks, trying to figure out what the next course of action might be, when Detective Randall appeared out of nowhere. He must have been booking it.

"Burke, I've got a young woman on the line reporting a missing person. She says it's her roommate, and when I asked for a description, it matched the other victims and Miss Walsh."

"Patch her through to my line."

"Already did, she's on hold. Line two."

"Thanks, Randall." Adam exchanged a look with Ben as he reached for the receiver. "This is Detective Burke."

"Please, you have to help me. My roommate is missing, and before you ask me if I'm sure, I'm sure. She wouldn't disappear like this, I know it. I know it."

"Miss, what's your name?"

"Ana Esposito," the girl rushed.

"And your roommate's?"

"Bailey Van der Veer. Please, you have to help," she begged with so much pleading in her voice.

"Miss Esposito, can you come down to our station right now and possibly bring a picture of Bailey?"

"Yes, yes absolutely. Oh God, thank you so much. Thank you," she choked out.

"When you get here, tell the clerk at the front that you're here to see me, Detective Burke, and they'll bring you straight up, okay?"

"Yes, got it."

"You think her roommate's the one?" Ben asked grimly after Adam hung up.

"I know she's the one," Adam said, just as grim.

Barely fifteen minutes passed before a young girl, whose appearance suggested she was probably a college student, entered the doors to Homicide, wildly eying the room. She had to be Ana Esposito. She continued searching for Adam, even though she wouldn't be able to identify him without the help of her escort. You could see the desperation in her expression. The escort pointed to Adam, and hope bloomed in her eyes. She sped down the aisles to his desk in a matter of seconds. Adam and Ben both stood to shake her hand and pulled up a chair for her to sit in.

"Thank you, Miss Esposito, for coming so quickly."

"Of course," she said, then she bowed her head like a guilty child. "Actually, I was speeding pretty bad to get over here. I'm surprised I didn't get pulled over. I brought a picture like you asked," she said, pulling her phone out of her purse and browsing through it until she found what she was looking for.

She handed the phone to Adam. It had the two girls posed in a hug, both wearing shimmery tops with colored lights in the background. They had probably been out at a dance club. The girl next to Ana in the photo was flashing a bright white smile, and her hazel eyes glittered from the lights. The array of neon colors glowed around the girl's straight, dirty blonde hair.

"Does Bailey have naturally straight hair?" Adam asked.

"No, it's usually more wavy. She straightened it that night since we were celebrating our exam scores. We had been inside the apartment every night for two weeks straight studying, and we were so excited to get out and have some fun."

"How long ago was this picture taken?" Ben asked.

"Saturday night."

Fuck.

"Tell me exactly what happened that night, right down to the smallest detail. Nothing is insignificant, even if you broke a nail, used the ladies' room, whatever it is, okay?"

Ana nodded.

"Start from the beginning," Ben said.

"Okay, so we took our chemistry exam Wednesday—it was our midterm final—and got the scores back on Friday. We had both aced it, which was nothing less than expected, because we studied our butts off. We wanted to go out Friday night, but we were still so exhausted from all of the late nights, we decided to rest up and go out Saturday instead."

"What club were you at?" asked Adam.

"The Cheshire Cat."

He had heard about that place. It was known for its bright colors and crazy décor. Even the staff wore funky outfits. It had a good reputation with the police, too. The club was excellent about checking IDs, and Adam couldn't recall ever hearing about fights breaking out there. Ben took the next question.

"What time did you get there?"

"Um, ten o'clock, I think. We had eaten dinner at the apartment to save money for the club."

"Did Bailey have a boyfriend—was she dating anyone?" Adam cringed inside because he realized that he'd used the past tense in reference to Bailey, but Ana didn't seem to notice.

"No, neither of us are dating anyone."

Ben continued, "So, you got there around ten—what did you do next?"

"We ordered some drinks and danced."

"Did you, at any time, leave your drinks unattended?"

Ana strongly shook her head. "No, absolutely not. The Cheshire Cat is a nice place, but you can never be too careful."

Adam was glad that this girl was sensible and not naïve about the real world and the degenerates that preyed in it.

"Oh, yeah, then there was that guy—"

"What guy?"

"This guy bought us both a drink, but he was definitely into Bailey." Finally, this may be the clue they needed.

"What did he look like?"

Ana paused and thought back. "All of the colors made it hard to tell about his eyes, but I'm positive he had blond hair."

"Can you remember, roughly, how tall he was?" Ben asked.

"Um, I'm not very good at guessing height, but I know he was taller than both of us."

Okay, so at least the size of the guy might be matching up. "Did he give you any creepy vibes or say anything that seemed odd?"

"No, he was very charming and gentlemanly. Oh," she piped up, "wait, there was one thing that seemed a little strange. She had already agreed to go on a date with him."

"Why is that strange?"

"Well, for one, Bailey didn't set up dates right after meeting guys."

"What do you mean, right after?"

"I mean, he wanted to take her out on Monday night."

Son of a bitch. This was bad.

"Bailey said that he'd told her he couldn't wait until next weekend to see her, so she agreed to go out with him. She thought it was romantic, and I did, too, but it still seemed weird to go out on a weeknight. I'd never met a guy that was *that* eager, or least openly eager to see a girl so soon. When she didn't come home last night, I got worried. It's not like her to take off without telling me."

Adam had to contain the intensity that threatened to overtake his voice. "Did he tell you his name? What was his name, Ana?"

Her brows cinched tightly trying to concentrate. "I... I can't remember," she said, as she shook her head. "I can't remember. I'm so sorry."

Ben offered her words of comfort, "Don't be sorry, you've given us a lot to work with."

"So, does this mean you'll be able to find her?" The hope in her voice was painful to Adam's ears. God, he hated this part.

"Miss Esposito, we can't be one hundred percent positive without a conclusive DNA result, but based on the information you've given us, we believe we've already found Bailey."

"I don't understand. What do you mean?" She knew what he was saying, but it was clear that denial was already setting in. Adam always kept his desk fully stocked with tissues, for precisely what was coming next.

"A girl was killed last night—"

"No," she said, as she started shaking her head.

"I'm sorry," he said softly.

"No. No, you said you couldn't be sure. You said you needed DNA proof." Ana's volume started to increase as she stood from her chair. Adam stood up as well. He could tell that she was going to be one of the hysterical ones.

"The information we've gathered so far lines up too closely with your timeline. Plus, the picture you've given us all but confirms it."

"No!" Ana screamed, releasing a torrent of sobs. "Oh God, no!"

Chapter Forty-Six

Danielle was startled, as she heard a woman wail through agonizing tears, and she turned quickly in her chair to find the source. A young woman was hysterically falling apart in Adam's arms. She was sobbing the word *no*, and it made Danielle's heart hurt for her. This had to have something to do with the girl the Harvester left in her apartment. For as long as she lived, she would never forget the compassion that she saw in Adam's eyes. She could see the sorrow that he felt for the young woman.

Ben ticked his head to the side at Danielle, but she wasn't sure how to interpret the gesture. "Danielle," said Jimmy, "what do you say we take a walk?" It seemed he knew.

"Sure," she responded slowly. It was hard to look away. Jimmy offered his arm and led her in the opposite direction from the scene. After they had rounded a corner, she asked, "Why did Ben suggest we leave?"

Jimmy answered in a very straight, analytical tone, "Assuming that that young woman is connected to the latest victim, and based on her reaction to the news that Burke and Anderson just gave her, seeing you would only make it worse for her."

Danielle silently nodded in agreement. Even though she was caught up in this hell, she still had no idea what that girl was going through. She'd never lost anyone. Not like that.

The two of them found another empty desk and continued their chat. Jimmy was very easy to talk to, and Danielle found herself enjoying his company. They talked about anything and everything… everything except the murders. He was giving her a small sense of normalcy, and her tension eased. Jimmy looked at his watch.

"Wow, it's already noon. Are you hungry?"

Danielle's stomach let out a loud growl answering his question.

"I'd take that as a yes." She blushed a bit from the 'tell.'

"What would you like?"

"Normally, I'd just make something for myself at the café, but since that's no longer an option…" She had to think about it. "A hamburger sounds pretty good."

"Now you're talking," Jimmy said with a smile, "I'll call it in. I know a great place that makes some of the best burgers in town. I'll go grab a menu."

"We're eating here, I presume?"

"You presume correctly."

He poked his head from around the corner. The coast was clear, and she followed him as they made their way back to Adam's desk. Once Adam and Ben had calmed the young girl down, they'd asked her if she would be able to sit with a sketch artist. Once she was finished, she was sent home with an escort. With the Harvester still at large, they wanted to keep tabs on her, since she could possibly ID him. She was their best, and only, lead, and they couldn't afford to lose her.

"Would either of you like a burger for lunch? I'm going to call in an order for pick up." Both men answered with a resounding *yes*, and Jimmy headed off to get the menu. Twenty minutes later, Danielle was chowing down on a fabulously unhealthy lunch. She had never tasted a burger that good before. It hit the spot, satisfying her starving stomach. She wolfed it down and didn't care who saw her.

She spent the rest of the day, with the exception of a few phone calls that she couldn't put off, sitting in a chair next to Adam, as he and Ben collaborated and reviewed every report and every picture from the crime scenes, trying to piece together anything they could. They had created a few theories to follow up on and were deciding on how to divide the allotted man power. Adam looked at her every now and then, probably to see if she was dying of boredom.

She tuned out their conversations as best as she could. She probably should have been listening, because after all, she was always complaining about being left out, and it might be good for her to know as much of the facts as possible, in case there was anything she could contribute, anything that might trigger some sort of connection. Two minds were better than one, and three minds were better than two, but she just couldn't. She couldn't keep hearing the gory details over and over again.

―――

Danielle sat quietly to herself all day, and Adam couldn't help but admire her. Not once did she complain or whine about being stuck there. Eight o'clock had rolled around, and he decided that he needed to take her home. They had the sketch that Ana had provided them, but without a name to go with it, it still didn't give them much to go on. There wasn't a point in staying any later tonight.

Home, he thought again. The word made him smile.

"Are you ready to go?" he asked, as he offered a hand to her. She took it and rose to her feet, looking tired and glazed over.

Releasing a sigh, she responded, "Yes."

The moment they got into the car, she conked out and slept all the way back to the apartment. Instead of waking her, he decided to carry her up. Adam had found his shirt from this morning that she had used before he'd woken up. He took her to his bedroom and changed her clothes. He didn't know if she would be okay with him undressing her, but he didn't really care. He'd already seen her naked and tasted every square inch of her body on more than one occasion, so to him it wasn't a big deal.

He wasn't concerned about waking her, either. Danielle was completely dead to the world. He envied how easily she could fall asleep and how soundly. A marching band could have paraded around the room and she would have slept straight through it.

He gently removed her shorts and shimmied them down her legs, until he could pull them off. Her top was a little more difficult. He carefully unbuttoned the blouse and pulled her arms from the short sleeves. Adam slid his hand between the bed and her back, unclasping her bra and sliding down the straps. He stopped for a moment and admired her. Even though his pants were getting tight, he wasn't overwhelmed with lust. It was adoration. He softly stroked her cheek that felt like silk to his fingers.

After he got her into his T-shirt, which he really liked to see her wear—in fact, it turned him on even more—he pulled the sheets over her and tucked her in. He wanted to sleep beside her, but he didn't want her to feel awkward again tomorrow. Now he knew how she had felt in Oceanside. It hadn't just worried him when she had left the bed this morning, but it had also hurt to find her gone. He had expected her to be in his arms when he woke, but instead found them empty.

He ordered some Chinese food to be delivered and ate dinner by himself. After eating and watching some television, he decided he was pretty tired, too. He stretched out on the couch and tried to turn off his brain. That was easier said than done.

Chapter Forty-Seven

The last verse and chorus played through the room. The notes of the piano keys floated through the air as Ana lay on her bed. Her eyes burned from the continuous stream of tears that wouldn't stop. Her spiky lashes felt heavier from the weight of the salty water. Ana hadn't stopped crying since the detectives had given her the horrifying news about her friend's death. Her murder. The violent sobs came in cycles and so often that her entire abdomen was sore from the convulsions. The song began again. She had set it to repeat, and she couldn't count how many times she'd listened to it by now. Today had been the worst day of her life. This song had been the only source of consolation she could find, and it was still minuscule at that.

It was one thirty in the morning, and she was wide awake. She desperately craved sleep, her body exhausted, but her mind wouldn't allow it. She uncurled herself from the tight ball she had been positioned in, feeling stiff from the hours of total stillness. Ana had only gotten up once to use the bathroom and hadn't eaten lunch or dinner. Her appetite was completely diminished. Every light in the apartment she had once shared with Bailey was on.

She was too scared to be in the dark. Bailey's killer was still on the loose, and her fear and sadness overwhelmed her. She had shuffled into the kitchen where the girls kept their vitamins. Among them was a bottle of a natural sleep aid that they used every once in a while when they had needed to go to bed early. Usually, it was because they had a test of some sort in the morning that required them to wake up at the crack of dawn and they wanted to have a fresh mind.

Ana popped open the lid and shook one into her hand. One was all it took. If she swallowed two, she'd sleep through the entire day. Right now, all she was looking for was a bit of rest to escape her new reality. Even though she had e-mailed her professors—there was no way she would've been able to speak intelligibly over the phone—that she wouldn't be coming to class, she didn't want to be comatose tomorrow. Correction, today.

A swig of water washed down the pill, and Ana headed back to her bedroom. Crawling under the covers, she closed her eyes and waited for her relief.

Chapter Forty-Eight

Danielle thought back to the telephone conversations she'd had to endure yesterday. She didn't know which one had been worse, talking to her parents or talking to Carrie. After lunch, Adam had gone back into the zone and had temporarily forgotten about her.

Her parents were absolutely sick with worry. They had begged her to come stay with them, but she'd refused. It was too dangerous. She explained that she was better off staying with her 'boyfriend,' the cop. They still believed her cover story. Carrie was the only person who knew the truth. They eventually relented, but it had taken fifteen minutes of convincing, and that didn't include the time they had spent exchanging the phone back and forth to each other, taking turns freaking out on her.

Carrie's phone call was melodrama to the nth degree. Danielle couldn't blame her, or her parents, for their reactions, but it was still more than she'd wanted to handle. She wasn't prepared for Carrie's greeting when she had placed the call. Carrie didn't answer 'hello,' but instead was bawling her eyes out to the point where her words weren't even discernible until five minutes into the call.

"Dani, I'm so scared," she blubbered.

You think you're scared?

"You have to leave."

"Carrie—"

"I'm serious, Dani, run. You have to run away!"

"Carrie, I can't."

"Yes, you can. He's not going to stop. He's not going to stop until… until…" A new wave of near unintelligible words came out, "Until he kills you!"

"The safest place I can be right now is with Adam."

"Jesus, Danielle. How can you sound so calm about this?" Carrie began scolding.

Danielle was reaching her limit. "I'm not calm, *Carolina*," she gritted her name through her teeth, "not by a long shot, but I don't have the luxury of falling apart—I already broke down last night. I'm not being blasé or cavalier about this. I have to keep my sanity together. I have no choice." She was struggling not to yell at her friend. She was sure she wasn't doing a very good job.

Carrie was quiet for a minute. She knew that Danielle only used her full name when she'd been pushed to the point of snapping. "I'm sorry, Dani. It's just... the thought of you... being gone..." Carrie couldn't even stand to say the words *killed*, *murdered*, or *dead*. "I don't know what I'd do without you. You're my best friend. I couldn't bear it." Danielle was getting choked up. Carrie was good at that.

"I love you, too."

"Promise me you'll call me tomorrow."

"I promise."

Today, Danielle's focus turned to Adam. When she had woken up this morning, she noticed that he'd changed her clothes, but he hadn't stayed with her. Wasn't that what she wanted, to sleep separately so that she could start closing herself off to him? Hell, she didn't know what she wanted. No, that's not true. She wanted to be with him, but she *needed* to let go of him.

She wished she *could* run away, like Carrie told her to, but it wouldn't solve anything. The Harvester could end up tracking her down. Look how close he'd come already? She'd never be safe. She'd spend the rest of her life paranoid and in a state of permanent neurosis, always afraid that he'd find her. Plus, she could never leave her family behind, and that included Carrie, Ralph, Nina, every customer, the café... She loved them too much, and she'd worked too hard to give everything up.

Another reason running away would be pointless was that it wouldn't change her feelings for Adam. The change in geography wasn't going to make a damn bit of difference, and she knew it. Danielle felt like she was stuck floundering in a pit of noxious tar, the fumes suffocating her and the sticky liquid pulling her under to drown in a thick pool of black. And she'd have to drown silently, because like she'd told Carrie, she didn't have a choice. Now that Adam was lead detective on the case again, they'd go down to the station and she'd sit there all day, going through the motions, pretending to be okay.

———

Adam still didn't have any food in the apartment since they were at the station all day yesterday. They'd just swing by a coffee house or donut shop on their way back to chaos central. He had everyone from nearly every department working on this case. He was planning on hitting up Douglas to see if there was any progress. He knew that if there had been, Douglas would have informed him right away, but he was going to go down to Autopsy anyway. He was especially glad that Douglas believed in his theory about some sort of poison being involved. It pissed him off, though, that they couldn't find it.

They left the apartment relatively early and headed straight to the nearest coffee shop. He ended up laughing at Danielle by the time she had finished ordering her breakfast. She had gone a tad overboard and walked away with two bags full of muffins and pastries, not including her coffee.

Adam was trying to lighten her mood, but she wasn't going along with it. She wasn't the same. Her emotions were too well in check. He didn't want her to be a basket-case wearing everything on her sleeve, but he missed seeing all the different sides of her. She was putting on a brave face, and he admired her for that, but he wanted Danielle to be herself again.

The moment they reached the station, he was back in the zone. His focus was solely on finding the Harvester. As planned, he eventually headed down to Autopsy to see Douglas and look over Bailey Van der Veer again. He was hoping that somehow she'd be different and there would be something to find. Before leaving, he put Danielle in Ben's charge, not just for her safety, but to keep the dogs away.

Adam pushed the heavy door open, and as predicted, Douglas greeted him without laying eyes on him. "Right on time, Burke."

"I try." Adam made his way to the table where Douglas already had victim number three laid out in anticipation of his arrival. She was laying peacefully with her eyes closed. The last time he'd seen her, she looked anything but peaceful. Her eyes had screamed at him. All of their eyes had screamed at him.

Like the other two, Bailey's skin was pallid from head to toe, and her hair, which was now dry, waved across the metal slab. The water from the bath tub had reversed the work of the flat iron, revealing the true texture.

"Alright, Douglas, hit me."

The medical examiner grabbed his chart and started the list off. "Our killer is methodical to a T. The same type of weapon was used to cut through her chest, similar rope fibers and burns—"

"Did she struggle? You said that the other two didn't put up a fight."

"And I still believe that. I think that the rope burns have more to do with how tightly he was tying them than the women resisting." Douglas continued with the breakdown, "There was no water in her lungs, so we know he didn't drown her."

"And that whole hemorrhaging thing?"

"Yes, the hemorrhaging of the blood in the skin shows that the lacerations were antemortem."

"Here's what I don't understand, why didn't anyone hear them scream? If they were alive while he was cutting into them, wouldn't they have screamed?" Adam folded his arms across his chest. "I can see how maybe no one heard Sheryl Gibson since she was in the park, but Ashley Cairnes was outside the café, and Danielle was right inside, and Bailey Van der Veer was inside Danielle's apartment with plenty of neighbors above and below. How is it possible that no one heard? And what about the saw?"

"The sound of the saw could easily be covered with the noise from a large crowd or a stereo, perhaps playing music as a disguise. However, your question in regards to the screaming is precisely why I know some sort of substance had to have been used on the victims. I just can't prove it yet. Plus, there's still the question of why *aren't* there signs of struggle, because again, there's no blunt force trauma, so how in the hell is he sawing into them alive with no resistance of any kind and no screams? I examined their throats, and they're not raw or even strained." Douglas sighed deeply with exasperation. "I still have some more work to do, but I'm pretty damn stumped, Burke."

"What about Chloroform?"

Douglas shook his head, "No, I already ran that test, too—actually, the moment each of them were brought to me—and there was no trace of it whatsoever in their blood, fluid samples, or lung tissue. I'm telling you, whatever this guy is using, it's highly uncommon and not something that is normally tested for."

"Thanks, I appreciate everything you're doing."

"Just doing my job," Douglas responded, as they shook hands.

Shit. They weren't any closer. Adam could feel his mood becoming more and more tumultuous by the second. He needed to calm down, and the only way he could think of was to see Danielle. He didn't like leaving her alone for too long, even though she was being supervised in a police station chock-full of cops.

His cell phone rang, and it seemed that he would have to wait a little longer to get back to her. Jimmy wanted Adam to come to his office to discuss some things from the case. He left Autopsy and headed a few floors up until he reached a door that had the name *Dr. James Tharp* on it and let himself in, skipping the formalities.

"Okay, so what do you have?" he asked, as he made himself comfortable in a chair across from Jimmy at the desk.

Jimmy looked up from his pad of paper that Adam could only assume were notations that he'd jotted down. "I wanted to talk to you about my assessment of Danielle Walsh. Well, my assessment of the Harvester based on what I learned about her."

Adam felt nervous about what Jimmy would say, not that he could say anything bad about her, but he was anxious anyway.

"Starting with her outer appearance, she's considered to be highly attractive. Her body type and features would classify her as ideal to most men."

She was more than ideal, and Adam detested the fact that other men knew it. He did, however, appreciate Jimmy's tactful and professional statement of it.

"The fact that she has a successful business shows that she's smart. Now, going deeper, her personality is very well-rounded. After speaking to her, I see that she's modest, but still confident, considerate, and definitely exudes passion in the things that matter the most to her. I would say that she's easy-going and laid-back, and in a romantic relationship, she would be categorized as low maintenance."

"You could tell all of that from a little conversation?"

"Well, yes, but it also helped that our little conversation lasted a few hours. You were engrossed in the case with Anderson for quite a while, which is why you don't recall the actual amount of time."

Adam was glad that Jimmy couldn't tell what a vixen Danielle was in the bedroom. That would make Jimmy very talented, which is always good for the department, but that's also more than anyone needed to know. Adam was the *only* one who needed to know.

"The relevant conclusion is that she greatly lacks a social life, which results in a lack of boyfriends. Danielle is low-key. She doesn't go out and party. In fact, most of her life seems to revolve around her café. If she doesn't ever go out, then she doesn't meet many men, meaning she doesn't have any romantic relationships, with the exception of Trevor Whitman. If she's not bringing anyone home, then it's discernible she's more or less abstinent, at least somewhat. In the killer's eyes, she's practically a nun, pure and wholesome. Throw in her innate kindness, and I believe these are the backbone to the angel metaphor."

Jimmy paused and leaned onto the desk, his forearms resting on top, his hands clasped together. A look of dark imminence covered his expression.

"The goal of your cover story was to make the Harvester jealous, to make him believe that the two of you are romantically and intimately involved, with the hopes of drawing him out. If he has fallen for it, he'll no doubt believe you've taken her purity," Jimmy's delicate way of phrasing sex, "ruining her. He *will* try to kill her, Burke. The question isn't *if*, but *when*."

Chapter Forty-Nine

It was two in the afternoon, and Ana had slept for a good twelve hours. She was glad she hadn't taken two pills because that would've been overdoing it for sure. Simon and Garfunkel was still playing on her stereo, bringing her back to the ugly truth. She could feel the tears starting to well up in her eyes again as she headed to the bathroom. A nice hot shower would feel good. She caught sight of her reflection in the mirror. The girl that looked back at her was haggard. Her eyes were bloodshot and her entire face was puffy and swollen, almost unrecognizable. She couldn't give a crap what she looked like, though.

While she waited for the water to get hot, she stripped out of her pajamas and tossed them into the hamper. After a minute or two, she put her hand between the curtain and tiled wall to test the water temperature. Climbing in, she dipped her head back and let the water soak down her hair. The heat felt good on her head—it soothed the headache she'd gotten from those hours of crying.

Ana's movements were slow and drawn out as she reached for the shampoo. She was a zombie just moving through the motions, barely registering the feel of the substance in her hands or their movements as they began a lather in her hair. "Bridge Over Troubled Water" could still be heard coming from her bedroom, and her ears listened. Then, her mind listened. There was something there in the song, something her brain was trying to grasp. She kept listening.

"I remember! I remember!" Ana couldn't get out of the shower fast enough. She fiercely rinsed the suds out of her hair—skipped conditioner and soaping down altogether—and grabbed a towel, running back to her bedroom where her phone was.

Chapter Fifty

Jimmy's prediction echoed loudly in Adam's head, and his stomach was churning, but seeing Danielle waiting for him at his desk brought him some ease. Unfortunately, it didn't provide a whole lot since she looked utterly miserable and continued to keep to herself. When her eyes found Adam, she gave a smile that looked partially forced, but at the same time relieved.

"Is Ben boring you to death?"

Danielle cracked a more sincere smile. "No."

Adam's phone rang just when he reached his desk, and he leaned across Danielle again to answer. "This is Detective Burke."

"I remember his name!" Ana Esposito was nearly shouting into the phone. She had his attention.

"What is it?" Adam asked.

"It's Simon. Simon Schuler."

"Excellent, Ana, you did a great job," he said with praise. He had had situations like this before, where a key piece of information was provided by a civilian, and you had to give them recognition for their contribution. They deserved it and needed it, especially people like Ana who were greatly affected.

"I want you to sit tight, okay? Do you think you can manage to stay inside today? It's only a precaution."

Ana complied, and the conversation was over as quickly as it began. Finally, at last, Adam was going to get this asshole and end it. Danielle would be safe and could go back to living her life. She could be happy again.

"We've got him. We've got the piece of shit." Adam tried not to swear too much around Danielle, but that wasn't the greatest concern on his mind at the moment. "Let's run his name through DMV and get his address, then I want to put a team together."

"Right, how many?" Ben asked.

"Four or five."

The minute they had Simon Schuler's address, Adam enlisted five others to join the ambush, devised a plan of entry, and started gearing up. Everyone was informed of their roles and positions. Schuler was to be apprehended using extreme caution during engagement and taken out if necessary. Adam was so fixated on the upcoming siege that her voice brought him back to the whole.

"What should I do?" Danielle asked softly. She sounded oddly meek, and he detected nervousness. Looking into her eyes, he saw confirmation of her anxiety.

"You're going to stay here. I don't even want you to leave my desk. If you have to use the restroom, ask for a female officer to escort you." He waited for the protests, but they didn't come.

"Adam…"

Ah, here's the disagreement, he thought.

"Please be careful—promise me you will." Her eyes were pleading with him, and now he knew the source of the anxiety. She was worried about him. Adam wanted to lean in and kiss her and tell her everything would be alright, but he couldn't. He nodded his reply, and with that, he rounded everyone up and prepared to head out.

Chapter Fifty-One

Knock, knock, knock.

"Simon Schuler, this is the San Diego Police Department. Open up," Adam called with a raised voice outside of Apartment 317.

The building was located in a run-down, low rent side of the city. Adam and his team had kept their sirens off so that the suspect wouldn't be alerted. They wanted to eliminate any possibility of evasion.

"Schuler, open up!"

Adam gave the nod to Ben and then kicked in the door. With guns raised, they filed in and began the sweep. The apartment was small, much smaller than Adam's in comparison. If they weren't so well coordinated, it would've been easy for him and his team to trip over each other. There was a tiny hallway that had nowhere to lead but to the one and only bedroom. With his partner close behind, Adam burst into the room.

Lying against the far wall was a thin man, his head hanging low. Adam and Ben continued to advance, searching the room for anyone or anything else. Lowering their guns, they walked up to the lifeless body. The blood and slits across his wrists proved it. It was obvious that too many of those red cells had abandoned him to sustain his life. On his right was a piece of paper written as a letter.

Shit!

Adam knew what that piece of paper was, and as he picked it up, he began reading the suicide note:

Angel,
I only did it for you. They weren't good enough, and I had to punish them for pretending, for lying. It hurts me now to see that my attempts to protect you have actually hurt you. I never wanted to hurt you. I know

now that you will never love me the way I love you. I can't accept that. Forgive me.

"Fuck," Adam hissed and handed the letter to Ben. As his partner read, Adam turned his attention to the walls. They were covered with Danielle. Photos of her spanned the room from ceiling to floor, some of the shots from distances and others that were eerily close. A few had been clearly cut out of newspapers, but the majority were snapshots taken with an amateur, run of the mill camera. How long had he been stalking her? Adam's anger was swirling around inside him.

"I definitely didn't see this one coming," Ben said, capturing his focus.

"Tell me about it," he growled.

"Burke, Anderson, we've got some things in here you'll want to see," one of the team members called from the bathroom. Lying on the counter were three baggies that were labeled in permanent marker *Number 1, Number 2,* and *Number 3,* each containing strands of blonde hair.

"We found these in a drawer, and this was in the medicine cabinet," the cop said, as he picked up a bottle and handed it to Adam. This may be the poison that Douglas was struggling to find.

"Hey," another said, as he entered the doorway, "we found a stack of receipts from Mon Félicité on the coffee table. Man, don't you love that the bastard gave us everything we needed *after* he killed himself?"

Yes, that was pretty fortunate but... "Did anyone find the victims' hearts?" Everyone looked to each other and then gave a final headshake. They were still missing. The fuck-head wanted to keep one last secret. Adam released a huff of exasperation. "Alright, someone get CSU in here to finish up processing."

Adam looked at Simon again. His face matched the sketch that the artist had rendered based on Ana's recalled memory. So, this was the guy. The man who had led them on a chase for nearly two months— the man who had such violence inside him, that now sat slumped against the wall, exiting the world so quietly and discreetly. Adam exhaled harshly in frustration. The prick didn't deserve the right to leave so quietly. Not after everything he'd done.

Danielle wasn't a nail biter, but she was ready to chew them off. What if the Harvester killed Adam? What if he's apprehended and Adam brings him in for questioning? Would Danielle have to see him? Her heart rate was out of control.

"Here you go." Jimmy sat down at Ben's desk across from her and handed her a stress ball.

She looked to him, snapping out of her flurry of thoughts, and began squeezing the holy hell out of it. "Thanks," was all she managed to say, and her attention went back to her worries.

"How do you make quiche?"

Danielle looked at Jimmy again, but clearly befuddled. "What?"

"How do you make quiche? I've always wanted to know, and I have it on good authority that yours is outstanding."

Was he referring to Adam? Had he actually told Jimmy about the ones she had made for him their first day as a couple? Had he boasted about her without requirement?

"Um," she fumbled, "well, it's fairly easy. What kind do you like?"

"The kind with ham and cheese."

"Okay," she said, still taking her time getting her words out, "that's Quiche Lorraine, and for starters, you'll need eggs, butter, cream, ham, Swiss cheese, onion, salt, pepper, nutmeg," she listed off. She told him the entire process from scratch. When she had finished, he asked her for another cooking lesson—then another. She had instructed him on everything from shrimp scampi to crème brûlée, which led to blow torches and other unique kitchen gadgets. Her anxiety had decreased immensely. If she could, she'd carry Jimmy around in her pocket, that's how good he was.

An hour or so had blown by, without Danielle realizing it, when Adam—alive and unscathed—walked through the door. Her heart thumped wildly in her chest. Where was Simon, though? Did she really want to know? Yes. She had to know that he'd been captured and that he couldn't hurt anyone else.

When he reached her, she couldn't stop herself, and she stood, throwing her arms around him. She was so glad he was unharmed, that she didn't care what anyone thought about her intimate hug. She wouldn't be surprised if Jimmy was analyzing her behavior. What did surprise her was the way Adam half-heartedly patted her back a few times and removed himself from her embrace. She could feel the shock and confusion in her eyes.

"So, where is he? When do you want me to speak with him?" Jimmy asked, immediately detracting from the palpable tension that would have enveloped the entire room had he not stepped in.

Adam's face was stone. "You won't be. He's dead." Both Jimmy's and Danielle's mouths dropped. "Suicide."

"Suicide? But that doesn't make sense."

"He left a note for Danielle. He wanted her forgiveness." Adam's voice was laden with disgust.

Jimmy was utterly bewildered, as if he couldn't process what Adam had said. "I... I can't believe I was wrong."

Danielle wanted to burst into tears. She couldn't believe it was over. The Harvester was dead, and she was safe. There was no more wondering when he'd come for her, no more suffocating from the constant fear... but that wasn't the reason tears were threatening to spill over. She was relieved for Simon Schuler's demise and finally felt like she could take a deep breath. It wasn't that she wanted him to die, she was just grateful that it had come to an end. It was the nature of his ending that wasn't a concern of hers.

No, the overwhelming sadness came from the knowledge that she wouldn't be with Adam anymore. Danielle knew this day was coming. She had tried to embrace it, to actually speed it up by shutting him out, but nothing could have prepared her for it, and the fact that she thought she could erect that barricade again made her a damn fool. There hadn't been enough time—the damage had been done. Attempting to repair her shattered heart would take a lifetime.

And shattered it was because it was clear to her that Adam had already let go. It wasn't his feelings that had been hurt Monday morning, but rather his ego. And even with all the hurt that throbbed inside her now, she still loved him. She couldn't blame him for the fall. That had been her own doing. He had had an assignment that involved thrusting the two of them together into an unconventional situation, and they both let passion get the better of them. It was her fault, though, for taking that extra step off the ledge.

You stupid idiot, her voice trembled inside her thoughts. She had to get out of there.

Chapter Fifty-Two

"I've got a present for you," Adam said, as he tossed a bag labeled *evidence* to Douglas. Opening it carefully, Douglas looked at the vial.

"Do you think you'll be able to find it in the girls' blood samples?"

"Most likely, however, that doesn't necessarily mean that I can find the answer right away. It will still take me some time to figure it out. Having the actual substance on hand, though, will make it easier."

He was pissed the entire elevator ride back up to Homicide. Adam had been hoping that Simon Schuler just had dumb luck with evading him, but that wasn't the case. The bastard was smart and clever, and he'd obviously done his research. When Adam approached his desk, a tiny olive-skinned woman with dark espresso hair, looking like a clothing ad model, was standing next to Danielle. She really was always dressed to impress.

Carrie was smiling and crying at the same time, squeezing her best friend's hands while hugging her intermittently. Danielle hadn't exaggerated about the petite emotional roller coaster that was Carrie. The two women looked up at him. He slightly towered over Danielle, but he dwarfed the dark fashionista.

"Hello, Carrie, it's good to see you again." He was trying not to sound so formal, but he didn't know how else to greet her. For some reason, he felt almost as awkward with her now as he did with Danielle.

"You, too," she smiled. The discomfort was now spreading to her as well. "Uh, Dani, I'm going to go pull the car around. I'll meet you out front?"

"Sure, I'll be right down," said Danielle, and Carrie swooped in for another hug like it might be the last, then took off, swishing her hips like a runway model as she walked, catching the eyes of every male in the room. Adam thought Danielle's strut was sexier.

The Harvester

"You're leaving?" He tried to keep his tone casual and less disappointed.

"Yes, Captain Jensen said I was a free woman. I'm going to stay with Carrie until I find a new place. I love my apartment, but there's no way I can stay there anymore."

"Makes sense," Adam said, bobbing his head and shoving his hands in his pockets. He was bombing at playing it cool.

"When would be a good time for me to get my stuff from your place?"

It felt as if he'd just been sucker-punched, and all of the oxygen had been forced out of his lungs from the blow. Adam tried to recover. "Tomorrow night if that works for you. I'm probably going to be tied up here pretty late tonight."

Danielle responded with haste. "Sure, tomorrow's fine. Thanks."

Awk-ward.

"Okay, well I guess I'll see you then."

"Yeah, see you then." She gave him one last smile and then walked away. Her strides were long, and she stood tall and confident, but there was no trace of that sexy sway. Watching Danielle walk away wasn't the hard part. What really hit Adam was that she didn't look back.

Danielle couldn't look at him as she walked out the department doors. It took every ounce of strength she had to not erupt with tears because she swore to herself that she'd make it out of the building with her dignity. It was tempting to see if he was watching her walk away, but she resisted the urge, because if he hadn't been, her heart would have been irrevocably shattered.

She made it down the front steps of the station, where Carrie and her blue Audi were waiting for her. She climbed in, buckled her seatbelt, and was holding it together until Carrie's soft voice asked, "Are you okay, bella?"

The floodgates opened as Danielle buried her face in her hands.

Chapter Fifty-Three

Danielle and Carrie arrived at The Strata, the luxury apartments that Carrie called home. They had gone by Danielle's place to gather as much of her things as they could, the majority being her clothes. Everything else would have to wait. Her hands had trembled just slightly as she'd entered her home, but it wasn't home anymore. It would never be home again. The landlord let her out of her lease—considering the circumstances—without any penalties, which she was grateful for. She'd tried talking her into staying in a different apartment, but Danielle declined. She couldn't do it. The apartments were all designed the same, with the exception of the larger corner ones, which were too expensive for her. It wouldn't matter which one she switched to, they'd look exactly like her old place, and every time she went into her bathroom, the girl's dead body would be the only thing she'd see. No, there was no going back.

She helped Carrie make up the guest bed and put away her belongings. Being her best friend, Carrie knew how badly Danielle needed to cook. They went to the grocery store where she purchased enough food to feed an army again. The moment the girls got back, she hit the kitchen and didn't stop. She cooked for a solid four hours, baking, sautéing, chopping, you name it. She got especially good use out of the knives as she sliced and diced—butchered, really—the vegetables, and the stinging tears in her eyes from cutting the onions didn't make a difference. They were already red and irritated.

Another tool Danielle found therapeutic was the meat tenderizer, as she repeatedly drove the spikes into the poultry. Carrie watched her friend from the safety of the island as she slammed the little hammer down, picking up speed.

"I'm afraid to offer you a glass of wine," Carrie said, as she sipped hers.

"Actually, I'd prefer a bottle," Danielle replied, still swinging.

"Coming right up, but after you put down the weapon."

Danielle stopped, realizing she was unleashing hell on the chicken breast, and looked up to meet Carrie's gaze. For the first time today, Danielle laughed.

After dinner and dessert—and the start of Danielle's second bottle of wine—Carrie got serious. She had spent the evening laughing with Danielle, doing her best to ease her friend, but now it was time to lend her shoulder.

"What happened, Dani?" They sat on the couch, turned toward each other with their legs crossed, like a couple of teenage girls having a sleepover and dishing their secrets. Danielle released a sigh, and her shoulders slumped.

"We slept together again." Danielle's eyes were looking down at her glass that she was holding in her lap.

"When?"

"Sunday night."

"Wait, the night you two were over here and that girl was murdered?"

"Ugh, I know, I know," she said with disgust, as she fell back onto a pillow. "It's totally messed up."

"That's not really what I was going to say. I guess I'm just surprised you were able to get in the mood."

Danielle lifted herself back up and gave a thankful look to Carrie for her non-judgment.

"Me, too. He was just so sweet, Care, and comforting. The way he looked at me, the way he touched me..." Danielle continued with her description of their night together and everything up to their goodbye. "I thought maybe..." she paused, "but it wasn't real for him. There were times when I felt sure, but..." She just shook her head. "And now I have to go see him tomorrow night to get my stuff and face him." The tears started to collect again. "I don't know how I'm going to do it."

His apartment felt empty. Not a thing had changed in the years that he'd lived there, but now that she was gone... Adam had spent the last seven weeks with his life turned upside down. He'd never lived with anyone before, apart from his family. Then, all of a sudden, Danielle was tossed into his life, and he was living with his *girlfriend* like it was a piece of cake. The crazy thing was it *had* been easy with her. Hell, their fake relationship lasted longer than any of his real ones. Adam felt more serious about his job than he had for any woman. Without fail, every one of them would end up feeling neglected, and he eventually got to where he avoided the situation completely. He dated, but he was no one's boyfriend.

Then, just as suddenly, Danielle was out of his life. There was no time given for adjustment—she was there one minute and gone the next. Seven weeks with her, spending every day together, and he had liked it. He knew every habit and nuance of hers, likes and dislikes, and even started developing the ability to predict her reactions. That was, until the end.

Adam was exhausted. Today had been filled with disappointment. It had started with him still standing at square one, then the break they needed came from Ana Esposito when she had given him a suspect, but misfortune kicked back in when they found that fucker dead. Adam had wanted to beat the shit out of him, and he didn't care if it fell under police brutality because he deserved it. He knew the rest of the team would have looked the other way. Finally, to top it off, he had let Danielle walk out without saying... what? He had no idea, but he should've said something instead of leaving it like that.

Adam had eaten pizza at the station while he worked on the report with Ben, and now he was ready to crash. As he stripped down and climbed into bed, he smelled Danielle's shampoo on his pillow—pears. Her vanilla was gone since she had been forbidden to go back to the café, but the scent of pears still lingered. He inhaled deeply, filling his nose with the sweet smell. Needing to fill his arms, he grabbed the other pillow on the bed and held on. Maybe he could pretend.

Chapter Fifty-Four

Red. Everything was red. It surrounded him from all sides. He hated it—hated the vivid color. Her hair was stained with it. Her cheeks were streaked with it. Her skin was splattered with it. Her gown was saturated in it. Her eyes were devoured by it. No more green and gold. No, those colors didn't exist here.

Just. Red.

There were no screams this time. Just silence—just death. She lay lifeless in his arms. Her lungs didn't breathe, and her heart didn't beat. There was no heart *to* beat. There was no rise and fall of her ribs or flutter of her lashes. Her lips were the only part of her that were absent of the bright pigment, revealing the depletion of her vitality.

Gone. She was gone.

Adam was trapped in a void. There were no doors or windows, just empty space. He couldn't leave. He wouldn't leave. He would never leave her here. Ever.

Adam sat up in his bed with a jolt. He shivered from the cold sweat that covered him, his skin wet with perspiration and covered in goosebumps. He could feel a weight on his eyelashes—they, too, were wet. The sweat must have trickled from his forehead down onto them, although, his eyes didn't burn from the salt. Was there any salt? Could he have been...

No, it was sweat, it had to be sweat. He rejected the possibility of it being anything else. And why was he still having these dreams? The Harvester was dead. It was over, done with. Why was his subconscious continuing to torture him? Would it ever end? If this kept up, he was likely to die from exhaustion. Adam fell back onto his pillow and stared at the ceiling. He craved sleep. Real sleep without seeing her death night after night. A dreamless sleep was preferred. Was that too much to ask? Sunlight entered his window, and Adam sighed.

I guess so.

Thursday dragged on at the precinct. There was so much work to do, but it was a fog to him. His concentration was completely shot from the lack of sleep, and everything took longer for him as a result. Just absorbing people's words were a task. He was able to nod off a few times at his desk until the motion of his elbow giving out woke him.

"You okay, man, because you're looking kind of wrung," Ben said, noticing the nap.

"What? Oh, yeah, I'm just a little tired, that's all," Adam said, as he adjusted his slouch in the chair.

"Really? It looks like you're a lot tired. I was trying to spare your feelings, but you look like shit," Ben teased.

Adam laughed. "Screw you."

"So, how do you like being *single* again?"

———

Adam's attention was fleeting, and Ben was trying to bring him back. It worked. Adam's eyes regained focus, no longer looking into an invisible distance.

"It's fine. Same as before." Instead of looking at his friend, he stared down at the paper in front of him, passing off the question as insignificant.

"Good... that's good," Ben said.

He was slowly trying to work his way to the real problem with Adam. Knowing his partner, Ben couldn't just out and ask him about Danielle. He knew it had to do with her, and he definitely couldn't tell him what he saw as fact. Adam was prideful, sometimes to a fault, especially if it got too personal. He refused to let anyone tell him how he felt or how he should feel. Ben was surprised that he actually got along with Jimmy, considering he was a psychologist. It was Tharp's job to tell people what was inside their minds and emotions.

"Because, you know, once you find someone, you have to get ready for a lot of changes."

Adam turned and raised a brow.

"For example, you're the exterminator. Women expect you to be the free bug killer, even if it's a gnat. Hugs and kisses are to be delivered multiple times a day *without* being asked for. Let's see," Ben continued, "the couch is for cuddling and the bed is for snuggling, and whatever side you prefer doesn't matter anymore because they'll wrap their entire bodies around you and take the whole thing." He could see Adam mulling over his words.

"So, are you saying you wish you didn't have to deal with any of that?" Adam asked, confused. Apparently, his brain still wasn't functioning properly.

"Oh, no, no—not at all. No, I love those things," Ben replied with a smile. "I like that Lacey makes me feel needed. It actually makes me feel more like a man, you know? My woman needs me. I know that sounds totally lame, and kind of caveman-like, but it's instinct. It just comes out of you. No, I was just saying that it's not always for everyone. The word bachelor exists for a reason. Some men are just happier being alone. No one to have to take care of or spend time with—no obligations." Ben gave Adam a tap in the arm. "You know what I'm saying, you're pretty solitary."

And his job was done. He saw a flicker of offense in Adam's eyes.

"I'm not that damn solitary," he snapped in a defensive tone, as if Ben were making an accusation.

"Oh, sorry, I didn't realize. I just assumed that you didn't care about those things."

"Well, you shouldn't assume." There was still plenty of bite in Adam's voice.

Ben knew not to push any further. If he did, Adam might catch on to what he was digging for, and that clam would shut tight. Adam would be on complete lockdown.

———

"Boss, I'm so glad you're back!" Nina shouted across Mon Félicité as she ran to hug Danielle. "Oh my God, I was freaked out of my mind. I had no idea what was going on until I read it in the *Tribune*, and Ralph decided it was safe to tell me. Were you scared? I would've been so scared, like super totally freaking scared."

Nina was rambling at hyper speed. Danielle had kind of missed it. She had missed this place so much.

When she'd left to go to Oceanside, it had been the longest she had ever been away from the café, and even though she'd only been gone for two days this time, altogether it felt like an eternity. This place was her sanctuary, where she could do what she loved and be herself. It was her sanity when everything else in her world got crazy.

Danielle had begun tuning Nina out until a question caught her by surprise. "So, does this mean you and Detective Burke broke up?"

There was a moment of pause. "Sort of. We were never really together in truth, so I don't know if I would actually call it a breakup—it was all for show. We had to have a viable reason for him to be hanging around me so much."

Hold it together, Dani.

"Wow, that's crazy. I got used to him being around every day. It's going to be weird not seeing him here anymore, you know?"

Yeah, she knew.

"You think you'll miss him?"

Goddamn it, Nina! Shut the hell up.

As much as she wanted to say it, Danielle couldn't be mad at her. Nina had no way of knowing how much she was hurting inside. She was just being her usual, inquisitive self, and she couldn't fault her for that. Instead of answering her question, though, she went ahead and moved on.

"Catch me up on what I've missed. Where's Ralph?"

"I'm right here," Ralph said, smiling as he came through the kitchen doors. Reaching Danielle, he gave her a big bear hug. "We missed you, kid." His eyes turned from a twinkle to worry. "Are you sure you're ready to come back? I can hold it down a little longer if you need some more time—"

"No," Danielle rushed, "trust me, I'm ready to get back to work—dying to, actually."

"Alright, if you're sure," he said with hesitation and a bit of doubt.

"Oh, I'm sure."

After she was filled in, she got to work in the kitchen and decided to save the business end for tomorrow. She still had the cooking bug and needed to get some of it out. She cooked for hours, and every time she stepped out into the dining area, a customer stopped her to ask how she was dealing with the whole 'ordeal.' Was she traumatized? Was she suffering from anxiety? It was sweet how much they cared, but it got old fast.

She finally tired herself out and decided to take a break while she waited for Carrie to call. Carrie didn't want her to have to be alone while she waited for her to get back to the apartment. She was so worried Danielle would have a nervous breakdown. Instead, she had to wait for Carrie to let her know she was close to home. Relaxing on the couch in her office, Danielle nearly fell off when she heard an unexpected knock on the door frame.

"Hey, stranger." It was Neil.

"I'm guessing you're here to ask me how I'm holding up."

"You caught me," he said, his hands in the pose of surrender.

"Sorry, that was rude of me. That's been the question of the day, and—"

"Say no more, you don't have to explain," Neil said, and then in a not-so-subtle way added, "I heard you and that detective aren't an item anymore. Well, actually, I heard you were never an item."

Nina and her big mouth. "Yeah, well, it was for the case. I'm sorry I had to lie to you but…"

Neil just held out his hand to stop her. "I get it."

He smiled at her, and Danielle felt a bit relieved. He had been concerned with her rash decision of living with Adam, but in the end, he was always upbeat and kind. She couldn't recall ever seeing him in a bad mood. That must be nice. Just then, her phone vibrated with two buzzes. It was a text from Carrie that she was leaving the D.A.'s office and would be home soon.

"Neil, I'm sorry, but I'm going to have to cut our conversation short. I have to go meet Carrie," she apologized, as she gathered her things and headed for the door.

"Don't worry about it. I'll see you later."

———

Nina, Ralph, and Neil stood by the kitchen door as Danielle took off. "She says she's fine, but I don't totally believe her," Nina said, turning to the guys.

"What makes you say that?" asked Neil.

"Ralph, you can back me up on this. I've noticed from working with her for a while now that whenever she's stressed or upset, she cooks until there's nothing left." Nina pulled open the door to the pantry that looked almost bare. "Am I right, or am I right?"

"Yes, that's true," Ralph confirmed with an additional head nod.

"I also noticed that when I asked her about Detective Burke, she quickly changed the subject. I know she thinks I don't pay attention to details, but I do. I mean, I am a psych major, after all. It would be pretty sad if I *didn't* notice."

Nina crossed her arms and leaned into the guys, as if to keep anyone from overhearing, even though there was no one to overhear. "If you ask me, I think she really did have feelings for him. She would deny it, of course, but I'm telling you, as a hopeless romantic, I know what I see. I don't need my degree to tell me that."

Ralph raised a questioning brow, and Nina looked exasperated. Men were so clueless.

"Love, I see love."

Now it was Neil's turn to raise a brow.

"Come on, you guys, she just spent almost two months living with that man, who in no way is just any man. He's tall, strong, handsome, a complete dreamboat." She was beginning to get starry-eyed. "And since he's a cop, he's totally heroic. That is a plus in any woman's book." The two men rolled their eyes at her. "Ugh, whatever. I know I'm right."

Chapter Fifty-Five

Finally, a peaceful night. It was what Adam had been praying for. A complete dreamless sleep had been granted to him, and he slept through the entire night. He didn't even change positions. When he had awoken, he was lying in the same spot as when he'd gone to bed. No nightmares about Danielle. He didn't care if he dreamed, just as long as it wasn't about her—as long as he didn't have to see her like that. That's all that mattered.

"It's about damn time," he said aloud.

He was actually surprised that he hadn't dreamed about Danielle. He figured that she would have been lingering in his subconscious since he'd been thinking about her before he'd gone to sleep. He'd felt shitty yesterday but had become a mix of anxious and excited the closer it had gotten to six p.m. He was going to go home and relax... and he was going to see her again. Danielle was going to come over to pick up her stuff. He'd had no idea what he was going to say to her, but he was going to see her. He had insisted to himself that his anticipation was due to her sudden absence. He'd gotten used to spending every day with her, so it felt strange that she was instantly gone. That's all it was, a wrinkle in his routine. He'd go back to normal soon.

Twenty minutes after he'd gotten home, there was a knock on his door. She was there. Adam had felt his nerves getting stronger as he headed to the door. When he opened it, he had been surprised at what he'd seen—or more at who he'd seen. It was Carrie, not Danielle. As usual, not a strand of that espresso hair was out of place.

"Hey," she said with a chipper tone, "I'm here to pick up Dani's stuff."

Adam had quickly tried to hide the disappointment. Had it been obvious? He hoped Carrie hadn't seen it. "Oh, um, yeah, it's right over here," he said, as he walked over to the couch and grabbed the bag. Why he hadn't had it waiting by the door, he didn't know. He should have.

"She couldn't make it."

He must have been wearing his confusion. He gave her an easy smile. "Yeah, but it's always nice to see you." There was no flirtation in his voice, just a good-hearted compliment.

Carrie smiled bigger. "Why, thank you, sir."

"Here you go," he said, as he handed her the bag.

"Thanks, Adam," she said with less pep and more sincerity. "Take it easy, okay?"

"You, too," he replied, reflecting Carrie's sentiment.

It was more than just his ego that was bruised this time. He felt somewhat... slighted. He shouldn't, but he had all the same. She'd sent Carrie in her place. That's how much she hadn't wanted to see him. Adam no longer had any doubts—she wanted to forget. He knew that now. After Carrie had left, he opened a few beers, ate some pizza, and watched a movie filled with guns and testosterone. He hadn't wanted anything to do with anything feminine or girly that might make him think of her, but after the TV was turned off and he'd fallen into bed, that hadn't stopped his thoughts from going back to her.

So, yes, he was shocked he didn't dream about her.

———

"Kali ma, Kali ma!" A bald-headed man with red paint approached her with his hand reaching out, grasping.

She couldn't run. Why couldn't she run? Danielle looked to her sides and realized she was trapped in a cage with her entire body restrained, denying her the ability to struggle, and was being slammed with heat all around, the majority coming from the fire below.

"Kali ma, Kali ma!" he repeated.

Danielle screamed. She screamed her head off, but no one came. Then, his face changed. He was no longer bald or wearing ceremonial robes, but instead was dressed in all black. He was tall and muscular and felt as ominous as Baldy, but she couldn't make out his face. It was hidden in shadows that had no origins—they simply formed on their own. She didn't need to see his face to know who he was. It was the Harvester. He'd come for her—come for her heart. Her screams became more frantic, and her lungs and throat began to burn. He reached through a hole in the cage, his hand just inches from Danielle's chest, the part that housed the vital organ, and prepared to dig into her flesh. Her chest heaved as her breathing became rapid, her heart beating at an incredible speed, like that of a rabbit cornered by a hungry predator. Her eyes were wide, and she was finally able to form words.

"Please, please don't do this," she choked through sobs. "Please stop. Please! PLEASE!" Her eyes followed as his fingertips gently landed on her skin. She shot her attention back to her captor, but he was gone. It was Adam who stood in front of her. He'd heard her. He was here to save her! A dull pain grew quickly from below, and Danielle looked down to investigate the cause. Fingers were penetrating her flesh, submerging deeper and deeper. They were *his* fingers—it was Adam.

Tears rolled down her cheeks, and anguish took hold. It wasn't from the tearing of muscles or the breaking of bones, though. It was from betrayal.

"Adam, what are you doing?!"

He didn't answer. His eyes were cold and dead. No sympathy, no emotion lay inside them. They were completely empty.

"Why?" The question was uttered in a whisper of defeat. The tears kept rolling down, but Danielle didn't struggle. She didn't fight. She knew it was futile, for she had lost this battle before it had even begun. Her tears were not for the pain. In fact, she couldn't feel it anymore, instead her body felt numb. Had she gone into shock?

The tears were for the heart he was breaking.

Adam showed her the life force that he'd ripped out of her. Danielle was no longer numb. As he squeezed, her body was wracked with unbearable pain. The agony shot through her like lightning, and she prayed for death, or least unconsciousness. Nope. How was she alive? She should be dead. She wished she were dead.

Music entered her ears, and Danielle slipped back into awareness. She blinked a few times, confused on her whereabouts. As her mind began reasoning, she realized the music was her alarm and her location was the guest room at Carrie's apartment. It had been a dream, thank God. She thought back and recalled every moment—the fear, the pain, the loss. Danielle's emotions were still running high, and she had to calm herself down. She forced herself to be analytical and scrutinizing in breaking the dream down. The more she convinced herself of the ridiculousness of it, the better she felt. It eventually dawned on her that her nightmare was pulled from *The Temple of Doom*. What the hell was with her and Indiana Jones references? She wasn't sure, but she knew she'd never see the movies in the same way again.

Chapter Fifty-Six

Friday was almost as bad as Thursday. Adam was slightly refreshed, but one night's sleep didn't make up for two weeks without. Things had steadied back out at the station, no longer a high alert rippling through all of the departments. Exhaustion had taken hold of him yesterday, but something different plagued him now. He couldn't quite put his finger on it, but he felt uneasy. Every time he closed a case, he was always ready to move on to a new one, ready for a new puzzle to solve. Not this time. He wasn't ready. Why, though? The killer was dead. They had finally found the asshole that had eluded them for so long, which did indeed mean he was clever.

That nagging in Adam's brain began to take form. Why would a guy who worked so hard to stay hidden leave so much out in the open? It didn't make sense. Adam realized that that was part of the reason he'd been so sour when they'd found Schuler. It had been a lackluster ending. Did he want a shootout, no, but dealing him the justice he deserved would've been nice. Instead, he'd gotten away on his own terms and left them a pretty package, so nice and neat. He'd never left them anything to go on before, and now he hands it all over? This wasn't right. This didn't feel right.

Ben was sitting at his desk reviewing documents when Adam cut through his concentration. "It's not right."

Ben communicated his confusion with a raised brow.

"I know this is going to sound crazy, but it just doesn't fit."

Adam presented his case to his partner, and by the end, Ben was agreeing.

"Do you think Jensen will go for it?"

"I don't know, but I have to try." Adam stood from his desk and headed to Jensen's office. The captain was hard to read sometimes, and Adam honestly didn't know which way he was going to land on this. He gently rapped on the door and waited for admittance. He was going to do everything he could to start off on Jensen's good side.

"Come in." As usual, Jensen's head was down, paying no attention to his visitor until he was ready. "Burke? What can I do for you?"

Adam sat down in one of the chairs in front of Jensen. He wanted to present himself on an even level and not come across as hostile. "I've been thinking about the Harvester case—"

"What about it?" The interruption was annoying, but Adam let it go.

"I don't like it, sir."

"What's there to like?"

"Captain, I don't think we're finished."

Jensen pulled off his glasses and gave Adam his full attention, his eyes narrowing. "What do you mean you don't think we're finished?"

"I don't think Simon Schuler is the killer," Adam said directly. He didn't see a point in beating around the bush.

"And what makes you think that?"

"Let's look at the facts—the killer left no trace evidence at any of the crime scenes, keeping us in the dark with our heads up our asses looking for the light switch. He out-witted us with his drug of choice that he used on the victims, proving that he has a brain and isn't just some dumb-ass with a hard-on and a power tool. He managed to sneak in and out of places under our noses undetected, remaining hidden for seven damn weeks—"

"What's your point, Burke?"

Again, Adam had to tell himself to let it go. "It doesn't make sense that someone with that kind of cunning and intelligence, that kind of determination, is just going to off himself at a sudden moment's revelation of the wrong he's done and leave us everything we need to pin it to him. There's no way this guy could have had remorse. It went on for too long and then the receipts and hairs and poison are conveniently laid out? And what about the hearts? We haven't been able to locate them. If he was going to give us everything, why wouldn't he give us those? This was too easy."

"Douglas has not confirmed yet what, or even if, that was poison in the bottle you bagged at Schuler's apartment."

"Sir, it has to be."

"And so what if it is? That doesn't change anything. It's merely an explanation to a detail of his methods. As for the hearts, maybe that was his last *fuck you* to us. Still keeping his trophies to himself. Honestly, Burke, you know better than anyone else that this was anything but easy. You should be glad that it's finally over. We got the son of a bitch."

"Captain—"

"The case is closed, Burke. Don't go chasing ghosts." And with that, Jensen went back to his work, silently dismissing him. There was no sense in disputing it anymore. He was going to have to do this on his own. Adam left Jensen's office with resolve fueled by exasperation. He didn't know how, but he was going to prove he was right.

Ben was awaiting Adam's return at their desks. Adam answered the question before it was asked. "I'm on my own."

"*We're* on *our* own," Ben said with a smile and a fist bump. Adam was grateful to have a partner like Ben. There were plenty of other cops that merely tolerated their partners, not really giving a shit about each other. "So, where do we start?"

"Jimmy. He's the first one who saw something wrong with this." Adam was gathering up files to take to Jimmy when he heard someone approach from behind.

"So, Burke, how was she?"

Adam didn't say a word, but continued collecting his things. He couldn't let Corolla get the best of him. He had to keep his temper in check.

"Oh, Mr. Holier than Thou doesn't want to talk about it, huh?"

Still, Adam said nothing.

"Why she would get it from you is beyond me. I definitely could have shown her some fun."

Adam's rage was roiling. He was already pissed that Jensen wouldn't believe him, forcing him to continue the search by his own devices, and now listening to the way this dick was talking about… Already ramped up with anger and frustration, the last thing he needed was Mitch Corolla even breathing near him. He could feel his blood surging through his body with such intensity he thought blood vessels would pop.

"You don't know what the fuck you're talking about."

"Come on, Burke, you think I don't know you were tapping that sweet ass? I could tell by the way she looked at you. I guess the saint is like the rest of us sinners now. Welcome to the club," he grinned.

"I'm nothing like you, Corolla."

"Oh contraire, mon frère, you're exactly like me. Tell me, choir boy, how does it feel falling off that high white horse of yours?"

"Shut the fuck up, Mitch," Adam gritted through his teeth. He needed to walk away now. Ben needed to pull him away *now*. Still, Corolla kept on. He clearly didn't have the good sense to know when to stop—or to not have started.

"I guess now that the case is over, and you're done with her, she's available. I don't normally do sloppy seconds, but to bang her, I'd make an exception."

Adam couldn't hold it in anymore, and there was no way anybody was going to stop him. Corolla was grinning like the disgusting, sleazy prick he was, but his eyes went wide as he saw the delivery. It all happened in a split second, but the result was impossible to miss. Adam's arm drew back, and his fist cracked into Corolla's face, and like the power of Thor's hammer, he sent Mitch flying over the desk behind him. Adam felt the snap of Corolla's nose breaking as it collided with his knuckles. Blood began trickling from Corolla, shock and pain all over his face.

"What the f—" He didn't have a chance to finish. Adam was around the desk in a flash and yanked him to his feet, throwing him down onto it.

"Hear me, you piece of shit, you say one more fucking word about her, and your nose will be the least of your problems—got it?"

"Someone get him the fuck off me!" Corolla shouted. The entire room's attention was on the brawl, but no one came to his aid. Ben stood near Adam, in case anyone thought about interfering. Adam shook him harder, still fisting Corolla's shirt.

"Got it?!"

"Jesus Christ, yeah, I got it!"

Adam released his grip, letting Corolla fall the few inches of space that was between him and the desk and backed away as the pig stood and rearranged his rumpled clothes. The crude cop's eyes glowered, but their anger paled in comparison to Adam's fury. His eyes were raging like a bull seeing red. It was hard to walk away, but Adam turned his back before he got himself into any more trouble, and there was definitely going to be trouble over this. He wasn't sure what the repercussions would be, and he didn't give a shit. He knew, though, that he was going to have to calm down.

He was struggling to tamp his ire, but his efforts were shot to hell when he heard Corolla mutter under his breath, "Must be damn good pussy to make you go fucking psycho."

Adam no longer had control. He pivoted on his heels and delivered a weighty haymaker right into the side of Corolla's face with supreme force. It was the ultimate T.K.O. Adam thundered off with Ben flanking him, as Corolla's unconscious body hit the floor with a *thud*.

As the partners made it to the elevator, Ben spoke, "It's a good thing we're going to see Tharp." The bell on the elevator rang, signaling the opening of the doors, and the two men entered. Turning to face front, Adam hit the button.

"Why is that?" he asked, absently.

"So, you can tell Jensen you're already seeing a shrink for your anger management," Ben's voice was filled with amusement.

It was ten-thirty, and Danielle was bored. She had been so efficient Monday on catching up with all of the business, that it barely took her

The Harvester

an hour to perfect everything. She even went as far as to color code. There was nothing left to do. Her only option was to cook to distract herself from Adam and her dream. She was actually agitated with him because he'd bestowed his wonderful gift of nightmares upon her. She pulled her apron off the hook on the wall by her office, tied the strings, and got ready. Today, she was going to do something different. Today was about no structure.

She was having fun. It had been so long since she'd played around like this, and some of her experiments came out so well, she decided she was going to feature them on the menu. She felt like she was already getting back to her old self... some of the time. The MP3 player was going, and she was jamming while she cooked—her own personal brand of therapy.

"Hey, boss," Nina said, as she poked her head through the door.

Danielle waved a hand at her, beckoning her to enter.

"There's someone here to see you."

Danielle felt herself hold her breath. "Who is it?" Was it Adam? What would he be doing here?

"I don't know, but she is so elegant, I want to take her picture. She looks straight out of *Glamour* magazine."

She had only one guess of who that could be. She dusted her hands on her apron and headed to the front of the dining area, and there she stood, looking so lovely and proper.

"Danielle, darling, I'm so glad to see you," she said through a perfect pearly white smile.

Danielle smiled back. "Hi, Genevieve." Just as before in Oceanside, the divine Genevieve Burke pulled her into a warm hug and even threw in a little rocking motion. "What are you doing here?"

"My dinner party, dear, remember? I decided I would stop by and discuss when we wanted to start planning." With everything that had happened in last five days it seemed her memory had been offline.

"Oh, that's right. I'm so sorry I forgot about it. I do apologize—"

"Danielle, sweetheart, what on earth are you apologizing for?" Her eyes looked at Danielle like she was loony.

Danielle also noticed that Genevieve always threw in an endearment when she used her name—it made her smile.

"If anyone should be apologizing it should be me, after all, I just dropped by unannounced—"

"No, not at all, I'm still very touched that you even considered me to do your catering."

"Well, I know good food when I taste it, and yours is absolutely top notch."

Danielle could feel herself blushing. She wasn't used to getting so much praise in one dose.

"I would've thought a woman of your talent would be used to compliments," she said with a wink.

Apparently, the blush was showing through.

"Is now a good time for you?"

"Now is fine." Danielle led Genevieve into the kitchen where they sampled her *talent*, earning her lots of *oohs* and *ahs*.

"Like I said, top notch." Together, the two women narrowed down a list of dishes to serve for the party. "Dear, I am so thrilled about this event," she said, beaming and clutching Danielle's hands. "How about I call you in a few days after I get some more details ironed out?"

"That sounds great."

Suddenly, Genevieve's expression changed, concern blending with her smile. "I'm so proud of you. Your strength is incredible."

Danielle was taken aback.

"I don't think there's anyone who can say they understand what you went through. Your spirit and poise are just astounding."

Danielle was beginning to become misty-eyed as Genevieve pulled her into one last hug, and they said their goodbyes. Collecting herself, she went back to the kitchen to work some more. As much as she adored Genevieve Burke—partly because she reminded her of her own mother—seeing her also brought Danielle a small tinge of pain. Her presence made her think of Adam, whom her heart was trying to forget. She sighed, because she knew she couldn't forget him, but maybe she could repress him into the depths. It would be a start.

Chapter Fifty-Seven

"If you want my professional opinion, I'd say it's more than probable. I'd say it's highly likely. I know it's technically a hunch, but I believe your argument is very valid, to the point of continuing the investigation." Jimmy Tharp was leaning against his desk while Ben sat in one of the guest chairs and Adam paced up and down the room.

"Yeah, well, unfortunately, it doesn't mean shit to anyone else," Adam spat with frustration.

"So, what is our next step?"

Ben and Adam both looked at Jimmy with a hint of surprise.

"I'm in on this, too. He's still out there, and Danielle Walsh could still be in danger. Plus, I have to prove that I was right. My reputation is stake here."

"Right?" Ben asked.

"That he wouldn't kill himself—that he'll go after her, that he won't stop until she's dead... take your pick." Adam glared at Jimmy for his last comment. He knew Jimmy didn't want to actually see Danielle harmed, it would just redeem his assessment of the Harvester. He didn't like being wrong. Regardless, that didn't mean Adam had to like the prediction or that Jimmy vocalized it.

"The next step is to talk to Douglas. There has to be something we're missing. Jimmy, you can look over Simon Schuler's body, and maybe Douglas can provide you with some information that would discredit the guy as the Harvester. Maybe then, Jensen will let us re-open the case."

Ben stood up from his chair, ready to head out. "Okay, let's do it."

"We'll have to wait until tomorrow," Jimmy said, bursting his bubble. "He's already gone home for the day."

"Do you want to call him, see if he'll come back up? He's on call."

Adam shook his head. "Not anymore, he isn't. With the case being officially shut, he's back to his regular assignment schedule. He'll be coming in here early tomorrow for some more analyses, and it's already late. We technically don't have any proof to back us or a legitimate reason to think Dani's in immediate danger."

Ben and Jimmy shared a look of piqued interest that had passed under the radar of Adam's attention.

The trio called it a night and went home. Adam had kept his composure with the guys, but inside him, a beast was rampaging. He didn't need definitive proof or viable reasons to believe Danielle was still at risk. He knew it... he could feel it.

———

Sleep hadn't come easily for Adam. It was one in the morning the last time he looked at the clock, meaning he didn't fall asleep until about two. They were back—the dreams. It was different, though. He was still sitting in a sea of red with Danielle's blood-stained body in his arms. Again, the hate and anger and sorrow consumed him. It was the same until...

She blinked. Adam blinked—repeatedly—as well, to be sure that his mind wasn't playing tricks on him. Yes, she was alive! "Dani, sweetheart, can you hear me?"

"Adam..." she whispered, filling him with relief. He couldn't be any happier. It wasn't possible. She was conscious and breathing, speaking, living. That was all that mattered. "Why didn't you save me?"

His breath caught in his chest. "What do you mean? He's dead, and you're safe."

"You and I both know you don't believe that," she whispered with a few coughs. "Why didn't you try?" There was so much hurt in her expression, but he knew it wasn't from her present physical condition.

"Dani, I did try... I mean, I *am* trying—"

"You took too long," she said, choking on blood, "You're too late, Adam..." She gasped for air, then said, "Too late," and she released her last breath. Two final crimson tears trickled from the outer corners of her eyes, and he saw the change. They were empty now. Their light was gone, and the image was now burned into his brain, never allowing him to forget.

Wet droplets fell and left polka dots on Danielle's cheeks, cutting through the blood that smattered them. The streams flowed stronger as Adam pulled her into him, rocking back and forth. His mother's words entered his thoughts, *"Don't take too long... you may lose your chance."*

How prophetic? He *did* take too long, and he *did* lose his chance. He hadn't caught the true Harvester, and now Danielle was dead. He'd failed her. There was a crushing pain in his chest. It was his heart, and it was more than crushed—it was obliterated... beyond repair.

Adam woke up with a new resolve. His dreams weren't nightmares, they were messages from his subconscious that he'd been refusing to acknowledge, but after last night, he wasn't going to deny it anymore—he was done fighting. The thought of being without her hurt more than anything he had ever felt, and that could only mean one thing—he was in love with Danielle.

Adam and his cohorts met up in Autopsy with Douglas. "Gentlemen..." Douglas said, looking a bit confused, "what can I do for you on a Saturday?"

"We need to see Simon Schuler's body." That was all Adam offered him.

"Alright, any particular reason?"

"I wanted to take a look at him myself," said Jimmy.

"Ah," Douglas said, as he began putting on a pair of gloves, "You don't think this your killer." Douglas's intuition still surprised Adam sometimes.

"We're not completely convinced," said Ben.

Douglas crossed the room to where he kept all of his residents and opened the compartment currently occupied by Simon Schuler. The four men congregated over the body that was lying on the pull-out slab of metal. He was pasty and looked so vulnerable. Adam's initial reaction was to despise him, but if he was right, then this dead guy was just another innocent victim slain by the Harvester.

"You have a theory?" Douglas asked.

"Yeah."

"Got any proof?"

"No."

"Okay," the M.E. said to him, "let's hear it." Adam knew he didn't really care about proof; he was merely collecting information from him. He knew that Douglas believed if someone had a hunch, it was for a reason. He was always willing to help provide the facts that were needed. Whether or not it proved people right or wrong wasn't in his control. Facts were facts, and he presented them that way. Adam caught Douglas up to speed, and their theory definitely sparked his interest.

"Jimmy, is anything jumping out at you?" Adam said, looking impatient. He did his best to keep his speech at a normal speed.

"Well," he said, Adam hanging onto his every word, "he seems kind of scrawny." Ben and Adam looked perplexed, while Douglas appeared intrigued. "I expected him to be bigger. This guy doesn't look like he had the strength to string up Sheryl Gibson."

"He could have used a ladder," Ben suggested, initiating collaboration among the group.

"No," Adam said, as he rubbed the stubble on his jaw, "there would have been imprints in the ground from the legs. We've gone over those photos a million times, and there were no signs of any imprints from a ladder."

Douglas chimed in, "I concur with Tharp's assessment. Now that I have a body to look at, it's not likely with his bone structure and muscle mass that he could have pulled Gibson's body into a tree."

"Even using rope to haul her up?"

"Doubtful."

Adam excused himself from the group to step into the hall. The more they disproved Schuler as the killer, the more anxious he became about Danielle. He needed to call her and make sure she was okay. He needed to tell her he was sorry... he needed to tell her a lot of things. Danielle didn't answer, though. He tried again but got her voicemail. He left her a message in the off chance she decided to listen to it. Hanging up, he sighed. She was probably pissed at him. Hell, she may even hate him. It didn't matter, though. He wasn't going to be deterred. He would win her back no matter what it took.

Adam rejoined the group. "What did I miss?" he asked, as he put his phone away.

"Not a whole lot," Ben answered, "just that we're sure he isn't our killer."

"Fuck." Adam raked a hand through his hair. "I knew this was too goddamned easy."

"Do you think we can take this to Jensen now?"

"No," Adam shook his head, "this is still just circumstantial. There's no way he'll reopen the case without hard evidence." Then, it hit him like a punch to the head. "Ana."

"What?" Jimmy asked with a furrowed brow.

"Ana Esposito. She saw the killer in the club with Bailey Van der Veer. We have to get her down here now and identify this guy."

"Schuler matches the sketch that was rendered from her description, though. He has to be the guy that was there, not to mention the fact that she was able to provide his name from meeting him at the club."

"I don't care. I want her in here. If it's a negative ID, it may be enough for Jensen."

This time, Adam didn't bother excusing himself, as he furiously dialed Danielle's phone. No answer. Adam called Mon Félicité's phone, which rang four times before Nina finally answered.

"Mon Félicité, this is Nina."

"Nina, it's Adam. Where's Danielle?" He wasn't concerned with pleasantries right now.

"She's not here. We're crazy busy today, and we ran out of some things, so she went to the store."

"Will you call her cell phone?" Adam still thought she might be ignoring his calls, so maybe she would answer for Nina.

"I would, but she went off and left her phone here. She was trying to rush out and forgot it."

Damn it.

"Nina, I need you to tell her to call me the second she gets in, okay? I really need to talk to her." He couldn't stress it enough.

"I'll definitely let her know. Ooh, I'm sorry, but I've got to go. I have a customer flagging me down." The only silver lining to Adam's frustration was that since Danielle had left her phone, maybe she wasn't ignoring him. That silver lining wasn't enough to put him at ease, though.

———

Ana Esposito's reaction to the phone call had been mixed. She was apprehensive about looking at a dead body, but the thought of Bailey's killer still being on the loose gave her the push she needed to get past it. Luckily, she had been at home studying, so her E.T.A. should be short.

Adam's limbs fidgeted, and his brain turned the gears faster and faster. He paced around Autopsy, never stopping, like a shark swimming in the ocean for survival, only in his case it was for sanity. Time was moving at a snail's pace, yet he felt like he was running out of it. He had no idea how much of it he had to work with before the real killer emerged. Would he? After all, he went to great lengths to make the case close. He knew this was wishful thinking, but he couldn't help it. He hated thinking of the alternative.

"Jimmy, are you sure, and I mean absolutely sure, that he's going to—"

With a grim expression, Jimmy nodded, "It's like I said, the question isn't *if*, but *when*." The phone rang in the frigid, cold room, echoing louder than usual due to the silence that had fallen in the wake of Jimmy's prediction. The news was good—Ana Esposito was being escorted down to verify if their Simon Schuler was her Simon Schuler. They were about to know for sure.

The young woman meekly entered the doors behind her escort. Adam envisioned that she had probably once been a vibrant girl enjoying youth and college and life with hopes and dreams, but she looked aged with the weight of tragedy and real-world endings. That's not too surprising when your best friend was murdered.

She wore a pair of hole-y jeans and an oversized sweatshirt with the San Diego Chargers logo on the front that was probably a decade old. Her dark hair was thrown into a messy ponytail, and her face was absent of make-up. He wondered if that was from being at home studying or if it was an effect from recent events. The dark circles under her eyes hinted to the latter. Neither were relevant, though. All that mattered right now was the accuracy of her memory. Ana stopped a few steps after entering and eyed her surroundings. Her posture was curling inward as if to provide a place for her to retreat, should it be necessary. Adam approached her with a gentle voice and a steady hand.

"Are you ready, or do you need a moment?"

Ana gathered a strong determination in her features, gave a little nod, and said, "I'm ready."

The two of them walked together to the table where Simon Schuler's body lay, and Adam could barely contain himself. Each step was unbearably slow. He didn't take his eyes off Ana, though. He studied her face with great intensity, watching for any changes in her expression, anything that would give him a clue as to what she would say.

"Yes, that's him," she said with emotion.

"Are you sure?"

"Yes, I'm positive." Adam raked his hand through his hair, struggling to keep the slew of expletives to himself. "I wonder if his friend knows what a psychopath he was."

Adam's head snapped to Ana at full attention.

"What friend?"

Her eyes widened, "Oh my god, I completely forgot about him. I'm so sorry, Detective." Her eyes pleaded for forgiveness, and Adam must've looked like he was going to explode to cause such a fearful expression.

"It's okay," he forced himself to say calmly. "You're remembering now. Tell us about him."

"Well, it was obvious he was Simon's wingman. He whispered some things to him when they were standing at the bar, right before Simon came over to us."

"Did this guy interact with you at all?"

"No," she said, shaking her head, "he stayed away. I guess he didn't want to risk Bailey choosing him. He was pretty good-looking. Actually, he looked a little similar to Simon."

Adam was nervous and excited at the same time. He could be their man—the real killer. "Can you describe him to the sketch artist?"

"Sure, when?"

"Right now." Ana must've detected the urgency in his voice because she nodded her head at a rapid pace repeatedly. "Ana, are you positive that Simon is the one that Bailey went out with?"

"Well, no," she said more slowly with a cautious tone, her eyes focused sharply on Adam, indicating she suspected there was something more to his inquisition. "She went to meet him at the restaurant."

Could the friend have really been the one waiting for her? It was entirely possible.

"What was the name of the restaurant they were to meet at?" Ana's gaze left him, and her eyes searched through empty space, looking for the answer, her concentration tight on her face.

"Um…" She began pacing, her fingers placed tightly on the top of her head, her palms pressed against her temples. "I remember she told me they were going to have Italian…" Another minute of pacing, then, "Oh!" she said, coming to a dead stop. "Buona Sera. That was it!"

They had a real lead at last.

"Ben, see if the restaurant has any security cameras and if they have footage from that night." Adam turned and gestured to Jimmy. "Ana,

The Harvester

this is Dr. Tharp. He's a psychologist, and he can help you with any memory problems you might have." The young woman wore a look of determination as she headed out of the morgue with Jimmy, allowing Adam to relinquish his composure. He wanted to scream and throw things, but the most he could do was curse and pound his fist on the table. He knew it. He knew this had been wrong. Whoever this mystery guy was, he was the killer. Adam had no doubts.

"Fucking fuck!"

"Adam—"

"I love her," Adam said, as he looked up at his partner, fists still in contact with the metal table.

"I know."

"I love her, and I didn't tell her. He could already have her, Ben. He could have already..." Adam clenched his jaw, grinding his teeth.

"Hey," Ben said, putting a hand on his friend's shoulder, "you can't think like that, not right now. That won't help her."

Adam released a deep exhale. Ben was right, he had to get his shit together, or else he was no good to her.

"And, Burke," Douglas started, gaining Adam's attention, "I finally figured out the poison that was used. What was in the girls was the same as the substance in the vial you brought me."

"What was it?"

"Belladonna. It's a plant. It's genius, really."

"Why? Tell me exactly why."

"Okay, I'll break it down." Douglas walked over to his desk and grabbed a piece of paper. "When we run toxicology screens, there are certain substances that we check for. Rohypnol—a.k.a. G.H.B.—and any of the typical drugs that might be used to incapacitate someone, especially women." He scrolled his finger down the list as he showed Adam the categories. "If belladonna was a common method of drugging, we'd probably have a screen developed for it, but since it's *extremely* rare—if not unprecedented—to see it used like this, it made identifying it a real son of a gun."

Adam's hand raked through his sable brown hair for the thousandth time. "Where would he have gotten it?" He toned his fidgeting down to weight-shifting instead of pacing.

"Well, the only place I can think of would be an herbal or holistic shop. In small doses, it's used as a natural sedative or sleep aid. I believe it's usually applied to a beverage like tea or something."

"What about wine?" Ben asked.

"Sure, it would hide any flavor the berry might have."

"So," Ben began, "that's how he did it. He spiked their drinks."

"And he would have to know precisely how much to administer, otherwise, if he added too much, it would be lethal and would easily kill the women, and we know for a fact that the victims were all alive when he cut into them," Douglas added.

"Okay, so we're looking for someone with a bigger build than the real Simon Schuler, who might have knowledge about herbs and plants, although I suppose it's possible he was just thinking outside the box and did his homework."

Adam's brain pored over Ben's last assessment, and the light bulb came on. Actually, it did more than that—it blazed hot and bright, nearly scalding him. Without a word, he turned around and took off.

"What is it?" Ben called after him, as he followed.

Adam didn't respond. He was too blinded by that light bulb to think about anything else. He didn't wait for the elevator, either. He dashed up the stairs, flight after flight. He could hear Ben's footsteps behind him. He reached his floor and burst through the door from the stairwell. He marched down the hall, looking for them. Mike, Ana, and Jimmy were all sitting at a desk, looking at something on the sketch pad.

"Hey, Burke, we were just about to call you. Mike and Ana are already finished with the rendering—"

"Let me see it," Adam rushed, nearly snatching the pad from Mike. He held his hand out in an impatient manner, and everyone became silent with wide eyes as the picture was passed to him. It seemed that they could see and feel the intensity radiating off him like a blast wave pushing them back. He clutched the pad of paper tighter by the millisecond as his face contorted into fury. "That son of a bitch!"

Chapter Fifty-Eight

Danielle's head was throbbing. This had to be the worst headache she'd ever had. Maybe it was a migraine. Crap, was she going to start having migraines now? She had never experienced one herself, but she'd heard about how agonizing they were. Your skull felt like it was going to explode, your eyes were sensitive to light, ears sensitive to sound, and it was painful just trying to move your head from side to side.

Yep, she was having... Wait, that wasn't quite right. Her head wasn't going to explode. The pain was centralized to a specific area, and it was coming more from the outside rather than the inside. In fact, there was a heavy stinging sensation. She carefully moved a hand to investigate when it was stopped by something. She tried again, and heard metal clang together. This time, she pulled harder with both arms, and more metal clanged louder. Danielle's eyes shot open. Her vision was a bit blurry, but images began to clear. She wasn't in the café. She wasn't at Carrie's. Where the hell was she? *Think, think.*

Danielle had gone to the grocery store to pick up some things for the café. She knew she wasn't there because she clearly remembered paying and leaving... right? She tried moving her arms again, but this time she looked to see herself restrained by... shackles. Shackles and chains—they were the source of the metallic sounds that were echoing in the tiny room. She began scanning her surroundings, but nothing was recognizable. It was dark and a little damp, with just a soft light illuminating overhead.

It was chilly, too. She felt her entire body break out with goosebumps, and the cold air swept over her bare arms... Bare arms? Danielle was wearing a three-quarter sleeve peasant blouse and some jeans today. She turned her head back and forth, and sure enough, they were lacking the soft, teal cotton. Her legs also felt a breeze. Danielle looked down at herself and gasped. She was no longer wearing her clothes. Instead, she was wearing a long, white satin gown. The material was thin, allowing the air to pass through easily and touch her. Her nipples budded from the chill, and she became very self-conscious... and scared. Someone had undressed her... someone had chained her up.

Someone had kidnapped her.

A door across the room squeaked as it opened, and a man appeared. "Neil! Oh my God, Neil, help me. What happened—where are we?" The blond haired, brown eyed man crossed the room and knelt, placing a hand to her cheek.

"I'm glad you're awake," he said with warm eyes and a smile.

"Neil, what's going on? Come on, help me get these off," she said, as she pointlessly rattled the chains.

"Shh, angel, it's okay."

Angel? Neil had never called her that before. It was weird, if not a little creepy. It was the way he said it. Danielle wore a look of confusion. What the hell was happening, and why was he so calm? As she continued to look at him, she noticed something different about him—something had changed. The warmth she had seen in his milk chocolate eyes altered and became eerie. His smile mutated into one of malice. Realization expanded Danielle's eyes and quickened her pulse. She pulled harder at her restraints as her brain finished catching up.

"Angel, you'll hurt yourself if you keep doing that." His voice was sweet and tender, and she had never heard one scarier. She couldn't stop herself from trying to break free, though. It was animal instinct. No creature sat idly while being trapped by a predator.

"I said stop struggling!" he yelled, dropping his hand from her face. Correction, *now* she'd never heard a voice scarier. She flinched in reaction to the sudden outburst. Panic and fear were making her chest heave, and her breathing was too rapid.

"It's you. You're him. You're the Harvester."

"I suppose I am, but I'm not too fond of that name." He spoke cool and calm again, and then chuckled, "Although, I did tell you it was the perfect time for harvest. What beautiful symmetry."

"Neil, why are you doing this?"

"Because, angel, we're supposed to be together," he said, thick and sweet again. "Didn't you read my note I left with Simon? I told you I couldn't accept being in a world where I can't have you."

She swallowed a lump in her throat. "Why didn't you just take me from the beginning? You didn't have to kill those women."

He released a sigh. "Clearly, the police didn't show it to you. I explained it all."

"They were innocent."

He erupted again, "No, they weren't! They were whores committing a crime!"

"What crime?"

"Masquerading around as you, angel, and that sin is unforgivable. They were trying to tarnish you. Really, you should be thanking me."

"What?" she asked, entirely flabbergasted.

Neil ignored her. "I even disposed of your ex for you. You're welcome."

He had *killed* Trevor. "The fall..."

"I helped him with that," he said, smiling.

"Why?"

Neil moved closer to her face. "Angel, when I found out what he had done to you, I couldn't let him continue to breathe. Besides, what was one more whore to kill? He had it coming."

Danielle couldn't believe what she was hearing. He was completely and utterly insane. How had he pulled off appearing normal? How had he fooled her, fooled everyone? The more important question was what was he going to do to her? Never in her entire time of knowing Neil Ghering had she thought him to be violent... or homicidal. She thought back to the first murder when Adam had interviewed her.

"I know the majority of the people that were here, and it couldn't have been any of them."

"In my line of work, Miss Walsh, that doesn't mean anything. You never truly know what someone's capable of."

Metal on metal echoed again, and she looked to her left to see Neil pulling on the chains, decreasing the slack, and forcing her arm to rise. He did the same to the right. She had found herself sitting on the floor when she had first come back to consciousness, but now it seemed she was meant to stand. Her arms were now positioned in a high V, and her bare feet were chained. Shit, there went any ideas of kicking him in the gut or kneeing him in the groin. He deserved both and much, much more.

"Would you like to see my shrine? You'll see how much I worship you, angel," Neil said, smiling. Ugh, he was proud of himself, and it was sickening.

She didn't respond to his rhetorical question. It wouldn't matter what she said, he was going to show her regardless. Neil walked to the right wall and turned on a switch that produced light from an installed track lighting system that was meant for the sole purpose of showcasing his disturbing display. With the extra illumination, she could see everything much clearer. A large master chair was laying on its side, as if it had been thrown in rage, and there were photos of her everywhere laid out in patterns on the walls.

In the center was a mantle that was absent of a fireplace, and three mason jars wrapped in black ribbon were evenly spaced across the surface. Danielle narrowed her gaze to study the contents of the jars, and it only took a moment for her to identify them. Bile rose in her esophagus, threatening to breach past her throat, and her body heaved in reaction. They were the missing hearts. They were well preserved in a clear liquid that, if she had to guess, was formaldehyde, but she had no idea how he would have gotten a hold of it.

"What do you think?" he asked, wickedly grinning.

Danielle wasn't just afraid anymore, she was angry. "I think you're sick," she spat at him.

His eyebrows pinched together in sadness. "That's so hurtful. Why would you say such a thing?"

"Because it's true," she said, glaring. "You're a monster."

Neil walked back over to her, standing too close for comfort. "Angel, I'm your protector, your warrior—don't you see?"

Danielle scoffed at him, "How so?"

"I smite anyone who would think to tarnish you or your name." He began pacing in front of her. "I ran into whore number one at a farmers' market. I went to taste the competition. When I saw her, I couldn't believe my eyes—the resemblance was uncanny. I was intrigued, so I pursued her, but when she was willing to give it up, she had to be punished. I should have punished her sooner for even daring to walk around as you. After that, I decided I should find other impostors, which brought me whores number two and three." He shook his head. "Number two was worse than the others. She made it known she would've spread her legs for me. Fucking slut—she had to go. I hadn't counted on that dick cop moving in with you because of it, though. It's okay. I know you did it just to make me jealous, but you scared me when you took off. I had to bring you back."

So, he had also killed Trevor to give them a false sense of security—to lure them home.

"I couldn't keep an eye on you and make sure he didn't take advantage of you."

Danielle kept her mouth shut. She wasn't sure how he'd react to the truth, and she didn't want to find out. It was clear now that he was unpredictable, and there was no telling what he'd do to her. Suddenly, Neil stopped pacing and stood with his shoulders squared off, once again, too close. His expression turned sour, and his dark eyes focused on hers.

"Nina said something yesterday that disturbed me greatly. *She* believes that your show wasn't just a show. She believes that you are, in fact, in love with him." There was only a brief moment of silence, not nearly enough time for Danielle to decide what to do or say, when Neil continued, sighing, "You disappoint me, angel."

Danielle's head flew to the side from the force of his palm. It surprised her. She'd never been slapped in the face before, and it hurt like a bitch. The sting felt sharp and stabbing, making her skin burn, and her eyes tear from the pain.

"Ugh, now see what you made me do?" His tone carried the weight of affliction. He sounded remorseful... in a psychotic sort of way, of course. "It seems that Nina was right. I'm afraid this doesn't bode well for you."

She was terrified into silence. Fight or flight instincts were playing tug of war in her head. She didn't want to die. She wanted to live and breathe and be free. She wanted to see her family again, wanted to start a family of her own. Regret made its debut. Yes, she now regretted putting off those things—love, marriage, children. She had always told herself there would be time for that later. She didn't have 'later' anymore—that was gone. Neil was going to kill her, she had no doubt about that. Danielle knew there was no turning back for him. No changing his mind, especially if he found out about her and Adam.

Chapter Fifty-Nine

Adam stormed his way to his desk, his eyes locked on his destination. He tore through the drawers, grabbing two extra magazines for his Glock. Adam wasn't taking any chances. He would put as many bullets in Neil Ghering as he needed to take him out.

He looked at his watch. Nina said she expected Danielle to arrive in fifteen minutes… that was over an hour ago. Adam harshly punched in the number to the café on his cell phone as he began accessing the DMV database for Neil's home address. He was confident that if he had Danielle, Neil would keep her in his home or at his shop.

"Mon Félicité, this is Nina."

Once again, he didn't waste any time. "Is she back? Is Danielle there yet?"

"No, not yet, but she should've been now that I think about it. Should I be worried?"

Adam didn't feel like dealing with another female freaking out. "Let me talk to Ralph."

"He's in the middle of grilling—"

"I don't care, let it burn. I need to speak to him *now*."

"Yes, okay, I'll go get him."

Adam could hear the anxiety in her voice. He hadn't meant to cause it, but she needed to understand the urgency he was commanding.

"Ralph, here."

"Ralph, it's Adam."

Ralph picked up immediately on Adam's stressed tone. "What's wrong?" he asked, just as serious.

"Danielle is in danger. The real killer is Neil." He walked and talked at the same time, and just before he made it to the door of the department, Jensen called out to him.

"Burke, where are you going?" he asked with authority. Adam pushed the door open and went straight out without a response. "Burke!"

Adam went back to his conversation with Ralph.

"What? Are you sure?"

"One hundred percent positive."

"Oh my God."

"Have you seen him today? Is he at his shop?"

"I'm not sure, hold on." Ralph paused, presumably walking to the front window of the café. "I don't see his car in the front, but he could've parked behind the store. What do you need me to do?"

Adam could hear the concern a father would have for his daughter. He didn't know if Ralph had any children, but it was clear that his relationship with Danielle resembled just that. "Is there any way you can check without being seen?"

"Yes."

"Good, find out and call me back. No, wait, scratch that. I'm going to call Danielle's phone, and I want you to stay on the line with me. I'm heading your way."

"Okay, got it."

"Is there anyone you can send to the grocery store to see if she's still there?" He was already in his car buckling the seat belt and tearing out of the parking lot.

"Believe me, I'll find someone." Ralph was quiet for a moment as he scanned the room for a candidate. Then, Adam heard, "Mrs. Cline, can I speak to you?" Adam could only hear Ralph's side of the conversation. "I need a huge favor. I need you to rush over to the supermarket and let me know if Danielle is there. I'm having a kitchen crisis, and I can't leave, and she went off without her phone, so I can't contact her. Can you please do that for me?" She must have complied because Ralph gave her the cafe's number and reiterated how dire the *situation* was.

The two men disconnected and began again from Danielle's cell. Adam sped down the city streets as Ralph crept over behind Neil's shop.

Whispering into the phone, Ralph said, "His car's here."

"Great, thanks, Ralph. I want you to go back to Mon Félicité and tell no one. We don't need a panic spreading. If for any reason Neil comes in there, stall him."

"You got it."

"And call me the second Mrs. Cline gets in touch with you." Adam prayed as he drove like a bat out of hell toward La Jolla. Ben was probably going to be pissed with him for taking off without him or any backup, and he knew he would get an earful and some sort of punishment from Jensen. That was all trivial. Danielle was the only thing that mattered to him.

Chapter Sixty

How long had she been there? Danielle didn't know anymore. Fear and fatigue clouded her ability to think clearly. Her body was already beginning to let go, slumping lower to the ground because of the unnatural position it was forced to maintain. The lactic acid build-up burned in every muscle group in her arms, and her knees bent under her, no longer able to stay straight to stand.

Her cheekbones hurt from the abuse. She was all alone now after Neil flew out of the room in a rage a few moments ago. She thought back to the terrifying encounter that had just taken place.

"Be honest with me." Neil stood at the mantle, eyes fixated on the morbid keepsakes. "I'll know if you're lying, so be honest." He had paused briefly, as if he were trying to force the question out of his mouth without choking on the words. "Did you sleep with him?"

What was she supposed to say? How could she answer that? If she lied, he might believe her, but if he saw through it, there was no telling what he'd do. If she told the truth... well, there was still no telling what he'd do.

"I asked you a question. Did you have sex with him?" Neil gritted through his teeth and a clenched jaw.

Danielle's brain was frantic, still struggling to make a decision. Suddenly, Neil whipped around, pure malice emblazoned in his eyes.

"DID YOU FUCK HIM?"

Her silence must have been enough of an answer, because like a flash of lightning, he was in front of her. She saw it coming this time, figured it would, but that didn't make her any more prepared. His right arm crossed his body then swiftly swung back in her direction. The back-handed slap hurt even more than his open palm, probably because she could feel his knuckles this time. Bone on bone. He'd slightly curled his hand on purpose to inflict more damage. Psychotic bastard. She could feel a bruise already taking form, and a tear escaped her. Maybe he planned to beat her to death.

His expression turned to anguish as he brought his hands up to cup her face. "Do you think I enjoy this?" he said, softly, practically cooing her.

She remained silent, but the glare in her eyes told him what she thought.

"Well, I don't."

He stroked his thumbs across her stinging red cheeks, flaring up the already present burn. Some fresh tears ran down, making contact with his skin and smearing across her face by the pads of his fingers. He moved in closer, eyeing her mouth. His head tilted as he prepared to kiss her, but before his lips could make contact, Danielle snapped her head away from him. His hands pressed hard against her, the pressure threatening to crush her skull. His thumbs dug into her cheekbones right under her eyes and his fingers into the bones just past her temples, as he forced her to look forward again.

This time, instead of pressing his lips to hers, they settled next to her ear. He inhaled deeply, taking an intense whiff of her hair. "I'm going to miss smelling you," he whispered. Neil pulled away, and Danielle saw pure hatred burning in his eyes. His face contorted as he tightened his lips, clenched his jaw, and narrowed his eyes.

CRACK!

One brutal delivery after another landed on her face. Her flesh felt raw with the potential of peeling off at any moment, and her neck took some serious whiplash. Just when she thought another hit was coming, Neil pivoted and took off out of the room, slamming the door behind him.

Now, there was nothing she could do but ponder about when he would come back and if anyone had taken note of her absence. Surely, someone would have—Nina, Ralph? Like an idiot, Danielle forgot her phone at the café, so there was no way for anyone to get in touch with her or worry that she wasn't answering it. Plus, everyone believed the

Harvester was dead, making there no reason for anyone to think she was in danger.

Danielle thought about Adam and what a coward she had been sending in Carrie to retrieve her things from him. She wished she could've seen him one more time. She had walked away from him without looking back, and now she would give anything to go back and change it. She wasn't exactly sure what she would have done instead, but nonetheless, she so badly wanted to change it. She wanted to believe, pray that he would figure everything out and come for her, but she didn't dare. She had to accept her inevitable fate.

Adam parked his car around the block corner. He didn't want Neil to see or hear him coming. He had received the confirmation call from Ralph, who got it from Mrs. Cline, on Danielle's whereabouts. She wasn't at the market.

His gun was loaded and ready to go for the worst kind of fire fight. He didn't know if Neil had a firearm, but he had to consider every option. This man was dangerous physically and mentally. He could probably hold his own in a fight based on his size, and then add his deranged state of mind, and you've got a lethal cocktail of psycho killer.

From the back pocket of his blue jeans, Adam pulled out a tiny tool kit that's sole purpose was for quiet entrances. He was glad he thought to grab the lock pick out of his desk before he left the station and probably his job. He stealthily crept his way down the back alley to the back door of Neil's shop, moving with such swift precision that it was simple to remain undetected. He jiggled the thin pieces of metal, maneuvering them into the nooks and crannies of the door lock with determination. He was getting into the shop one way or another. He hoped he could enter the silent way, but he'd break down the door or a window if necessary. There was more risk to Danielle if it came to that, but he wasn't going to sit around and wait just to find out that she was killed during his stakeout.

He worked more vigorously until he heard the *click* he was waiting for. He gently opened the door and slipped in, closing it just as quietly. He drew his Glock from his shoulder holster, safety off, prepped for lethality. He moved in a low crouch as he swept across the floor and rose to a stand as he assessed and rounded the corners. Not a sound. It was dark inside, and Adam could see the *Open* side of the door's business hours sign. Neil was making a point to keep people away.

Adam stressed his senses to heighten. He willed his vision to sharpen and strained his ears to hear something, anything. He searched every square inch of the store. There was no sign of Danielle or Neil. Could he have been wrong? Holstering his weapon, Adam whipped out his cell and sent a text to Ben.

1813 Darlene Ct., SD
PWC

It was Neil's home address. Ben would know to look in the city and to proceed with caution. He knew Ben could get there faster at this point, and he wasn't going to waste time with Danielle's life on the line. If his partner could find her, then that's all Adam cared about—getting Danielle back alive.

The door of the musty, dank room opened, and Danielle's demented captor returned. His expression was unreadable. The look of malevolence and amusement mingled together, forming something that she had never seen before, not even in movies. That made sense, though. Actors were merely playing a role—Neil wasn't. No one could possibly duplicate such evil without being precisely in that state. She noticed a large metal bucket in his hand. By the slight lean of his body, she could tell the contents were heavy enough to make him compensate for the weight. She swallowed a lump in her throat. What was in the bucket?

Her tears had dried when he'd left her in solitary confinement, but his presence caused her eyes to begin to well again. He stopped directly in front of her.

"I didn't want it this way," he said and then tossed the contents at her.

She held her breath and closed her eyes to prevent any of the substance from entering. She had no idea what was about to crash into her.

Something wet splashed over her, cold and viscous, stray droplets ricocheting onto her cheeks. She inhaled again and blinked her eyes back open and saw red. It was blood.

Oh, Jesus!

Danielle's breathing became heavy, and she twisted and wriggled in her confines. Her eyes no longer welled but flooded. Whose blood was this?

"I loved you, angel. I could've made you happy," he said with pain and hurt.

"Neil, please—"

"But you let him ruin you. You let him make you his whore," he spat.

"Neil," she began to plead, with the strategy of using common sense. "You know I've had boyfriends before him, before Trevor. You had to know I wasn't a virgin—Jesus, I'm not perfect."

"You were to me."

"I never asked you to believe that. I never asked you to put me on some pedestal," she stressed.

Neil just ignored her. "You're just like the others now. You're not my angel anymore."

Disgust and sadness made up his tone. Neil reached behind his back after tossing the bucket to the side and pulled out a gun that he pointed right between her eyes. Fresh streams of tears ran down Danielle's face as she squeezed her eyes shut. Nothing happened. She was waiting for the sound of the bullet leaving the chamber and the gunpowder igniting, but nothing happened... just silence. She opened her eyes when she felt cold metal caress her cheek. Neil was softly running the barrel of his gun across her skin.

"You know, Danielle, even though my angel has fallen, a tiny part of me still loves you, which is why I think I'm going to let you keep your heart. How does that sound?"

What did he expect her to say, thank you?

"It sounds like I'm dead either way."

He ran the gun down her neck and over her collarbone to trail down the cleavage of the white and red-stained lingerie. "I expected more gratitude from you."

"For what, kidnapping and murdering me?"

He breathed deep—deceptively calm—and with the lightning speed of a viper striking, he grabbed a chunk of her hair at the back of the crown and yanked down with an angry force so strong that it made her body move and her chains rattle from the wake of the action. Danielle cried out in pain.

"For sparing you the torture of having to watch me kill you," he gritted loudly through his teeth. "But now," he whispered in her ear with sick pleasure, "I think I'll take your heart after all, and don't worry, I'll still use the gun to make it quick. Once I have it, you'll be mine forever."

Under other circumstances where she thought she stood a chance of surviving, Danielle would've kept her mouth shut, but she was as good as dead—her executioner itching to end her—and she wasn't going to die without saying it, so she gathered the strength to steady her voice and let him have it.

"I love Adam. I love everything about him, and he's one hundred times the man you are. Actually, you're not even a man—"

"Shut up."

"You're evil incarnate—so twisted, and demented, and completely screwed up."

"I said shut up!" he yelled, as he released her hair and punished her face. That didn't stop her.

"Just the sight of you makes me sick! If I truly was an angel to you, then how could you think I would ever love you, a monster, a devil?" Danielle locked eyes with Neil, who now stood in front of her, and she snarled, "I detest you, I loathe you... I *hate* you." She was conscious just seconds long enough to see him swing the pistol and make contact with her skull.

Chapter Sixty-One

D's not here. On my way.

Adam pressed send on his cell phone and began making his way to the back door where he'd broken in. He hoped Ben would get to her in time. Neil could have taken Danielle in her own car, explaining why his was still parked out back. Why hadn't he considered that? Because he was so damn worried that his usual focus and rationality went out the window in his haste. He reached out for the door's handle.

That's when he heard it. It was faint, but unmistakable. Somewhere, a woman released a painful yelp. Adam stopped breathing. She *was* here! He ran back into the main room and turned in circles, his eyes darting and scrutinizing everywhere and everything. He saw nothing. There was only one option that ran into his mind—there must be a hidden door. He started combing the perimeters of the walls, but there was no trick book or jar—no handles, buttons, or levers. He began searching the floor. Adam reached a refrigerated section that had rubber mats at the base which would typically be used as a preventative measure to avoid any slips or falls from possible liquid spills or condensation. One of them was askew. He ripped the mat up off the floor, and sure enough, there was a tiny trap door with a handle. *Bingo.*

Finger poised on the trigger, Adam pulled back the door swiftly and carefully positioned himself to avoid anything that may be awaiting him. All clear. He tiptoed down the wooden steps—praying they wouldn't squeak under his weight—and made his way down the little hall. Adam was amazed. How could someone have built this underground lair without anyone noticing? It's not like you could knock it out in one night, and what about the money it would take?

He moved along the wall until he came to the first of the three doors. Two were directly across from each other and the last faced him at the end of the corridor. Which one was Danielle in? If he busted down the wrong one, he could alert Neil to his presence. He listened. He needed a sound or noise of any kind, just something to indicate where he should go. Remaining completely still, one minute passed, then two. Finally, he got his answer. It was the door straight ahead. Adam heard what sounded like metal making contact with a wall—the loud echo was a blessing, and he was raring to go. He approached the door in just a few long strides and halted. How should he enter? There wasn't time to contemplate.

Fuck it, here we go.

A loud crack resonated in the air as Adam's foot met the wooden door, splintering it and forcing it to fly open. He took a step forward and then froze. Time stopped, and his entire world came crashing down as he blinked in disbelief at the sight in front of him.

Danielle's limp body hung from chains in the wall that pulled her arms high, nearly out of socket. Those long caramel locks curtained her face from the drooping of her head, and the blood… Oh, God, all that blood. She was covered in it.

His heart lurched and then sank to the pit of his stomach. Devastation hit him like a Mack truck, and he couldn't breathe, couldn't think… and that cost him. He heard a *click,* and felt a barrel press against his temple.

"Well, if it isn't Detective Burke. I must say, I'm surprised you found me."

"Why is that?" Adam asked, remaining still where he stood.

"Oh, I don't know—maybe because you and the other morons all ran around with your heads up your asses for almost two months. You'd still be looking for me if I hadn't handed you that kid, Simon." Neil pushed his gun harder into Adam's head. "Toss your gun over there."

Adam had no choice but to comply. He needed an advantage, and right now, Neil had the upper hand.

"So, how *did* you find me?"

"You're not as fucking smart as you think you are."

Neil just chuckled, then abruptly ceased. "I see. I guess I should have killed that slut's friend from the club, after all. She's the only reason you were able to identify me, wasn't she?"

"You left your calling card with the belladonna." Adam wasn't about to confirm that Ana was the nail in the coffin.

Neil laughed humorlessly at himself for his error, then addressed Adam again. "She was so beautiful," he said, quickly looking to Danielle, and sighed. "It's your fault, you know?"

Adam was silent, allowing Neil to continue the one-sided conversation, injecting his anger.

"You seduced her and then corrupted her. You *ruined* her," he gritted, then exploded into a full shout. "She was mine! She was mine, and you took her from me! You stole her!" An angry, hysterical laugh escaped him. "So, I had to punish her... she had to be punished." Remorse joined the other emotions flying out of Neil.

Adam's eyes were fixated on Danielle, and Neil's psychotic commentary made the scene all the more horrific. "You're so fucking stupid."

"What?"

"This is *your* fault. If you hadn't started the killings, I never would have met Danielle. You're the one who brought us together, fuckstick."

"No," Neil shook his head. "NO, NO, NO! I loved her! I was proving my love for her!"

Adam finally had his advantage. Neil's emotions were running rampant, completely unstable, which took away from his ability to keep his mind sharp, including his reflexes. Adam made his move. He pivoted and grabbed the hand that wielded the gun. The second Neil brought his other hand around to regain control, Adam took it, crushing his fingers into highly sensitive pressure points, and sending Neil to his knees, who vocalized his discomfort on the way down. The debilitating pain from Adam's fingers caused Neil's other hand to release his hold of the gun, and it fell to the floor. Adam let go of his grip on that wrist,

The Harvester

and still crushing the pressure points, used his free hand to slam his fist into Neil's face, knocking him to his back.

It was probably a good thing that Adam was here by himself because if anyone dared to stop him, he couldn't guarantee their safety. Using his shins to pin Neil's arms to the floor, Adam unleashed havoc on his face. The blinding rage erupted from him like the most cataclysmic volcano the world had ever seen, and as his fists wailed on Neil, his words came spilling out as dangerous and deadly as the lava raging in his blood.

"I'll kill you," *punch!* "you sick," *punch!* "fucking," *punch!* "piece," *punch,* "of shit!" Each punch of Adam's fist brought more damage. Blood was shooting from Neil's nose and slicked his teeth. Bone shattered under the brutal force of Adam's strikes, mainly from Neil's cheek and jaw bones, but Adam would be lucky if he walked away from this without a broken hand. Adam's features were ferocious as he landed blow after blow and let out a roar of true, raw, undiluted wrath of loss—of heartbreak so severe, it was maddening. His mind had left him to be consumed by darkness.

Neil Ghering's eyes were flooded with blood from the broken blood vessels that popped under the strength of Adam's power. He gasped for air as he choked on the thick, red liquid that ran down and coated his throat. He might also have been choking on a tooth, because between punches, Adam noticed at least one incisor was missing. Finally, Neil's eyes rolled back in his head and closed. Was he dead? No, he was still breathing, although the breaths were shallow. In fact, Adam could barely see his chest rise and fall.

Adam gasped for air. He had to calm himself down before he really did kill Neil. It would be hard for him to use the excuse of bashing Ghering's skull in as self-defense when he could have easily rendered him unconscious without killing him.

He patted Neil down until he found the keys he needed and went to retrieve his gun, sliding it back into its holster. He looked at Danielle, and his heart wrenched. He hurried to her side and began unlocking her restraints. Adam couldn't bear to see her like that. Once her feet were free, he released one arm at a time, draping her over his shoulder so she wouldn't plummet to the cement floor. He held her tight in his arms as he declined with ease to a sit.

His nightmare had come to life—Adam couldn't believe it. Once again, his parents' words echoed into his mind, only this time he was awake.

"Some things must happen, so that we might come to our revelations." It had taken a large dose of cold-blooded tragedy for Adam to wake up and realize his love for Danielle.

"And please don't take too long. You may lose your chance." At the time, he had thought she was talking about catching the killer. Now, looking back, he was certain that his mother had meant that he would lose his chance with Danielle to another man—one who was smart enough to hold on to her and never let her go. In a way, he had, and now he found the harsh blending of the two. He had taken too long to solve the case, and now she was dead. He'd lost his chance… lost her forever.

Chapter Sixty-Two

The correlation of his dreams and reality was startling to Adam as he rocked her gently in his arms. Neil had been right about one thing—she *was* beautiful. She was always beautiful, no matter what she wore or how she looked. Danielle was incomparable.

Droplets rained down from him onto her skin, and he combed her hair away from her face. He began to question how he would come back from this, but he pushed it out. He couldn't think about the future, especially not one without her. He just wanted to be there with her, holding her—nothing more. Danielle had been Adam's enchantress, casting her spell on him. She was his undoing, and even in death, he couldn't resist her. He brushed his thumb over her lips, and then pulling her in to meet him, gave her one last, sweet, tender kiss.

Something tickled his cheek like butterfly wings dancing on his face, and Adam drew back. Long, dark lashes fluttered at him and confused, hazel eyes searched for understanding. Steel gray eyes met them back, widening with shock in response.

"Adam?" she spoke softly, smiling, closing and opening her eyes slowly as if her spiky, tear-fused lashes were fighting against molasses. "You came. I can't believe it."

He was stunned. How was this possible? He looked her over again and made a few discoveries that he'd somehow missed. For starters, there was no gaping hole in her chest. In fact, she didn't have any cuts whatsoever. Parts of her face were purple, though, a combination of the red stinging skin and the blue bruises forming underneath. It was clear Ghering had beaten her several times. Adam's hunger to kill him flared up again. But where had all this blood come from? It was obvious now that it wasn't hers, so for the moment, it wasn't important.

Danielle let out a deep sigh and her expression became sad. "I'm dead."

That surprised him. "No, you're not."

"I have to be."

"Well, sorry to burst your bubble, but you're very much alive," he smiled.

"But..." she stuttered, "he was about to... about to kill me. There's no way you could've known... you couldn't have found me."

"Sweetheart, come on, give me *some* credit. I'm not a *complete* idiot."

"I didn't mean... I know you're not an idiot."

"Actually, I am. I should've told you..." Adam paused, searching her eyes, lost in their beauty.

"Told me what?"

"How much I love you."

Danielle's eyes rolled back in her head. "Oh, God, I *am* dead."

He laughed.

Preoccupied with her physical state, he hadn't heard Neil get up. "NO! SHE'S MINE!"

Everything morphed into slow motion but was over in a flash. Danielle saw a bloodied Neil staggering on his feet, his weight fluctuating in a swaying motion from foot to foot, and his gun was pointed at her and Adam. His face was barely recognizable from the swelling and the disproportion of the broken, lopsided bones. The red blood that engulfed his eyes made him look like the disturbing, malicious demon he really was. His breaths were raspy and heavy from struggling for oxygen and the volatile rancor that surged from him in a powerful force.

Like the fastest cowboy in the Wild West, Adam ripped his Glock from its holster, and still holding Danielle tight into him, straightened his arm out to the side and pulled the trigger. There was no hesitation or warning for Neil, no precautionary *"Put down your weapon"* speech. Danielle began to count the bullets that ripped into his chest.

One, two, three—straight into his heart with deadly accuracy. She wondered if Adam had intentionally chosen that target.

Four, five, six. According to Newton's first law of motion—an object set in motion tends to stay in motion—the inertia from the force of the bullets from Adam's gun should have sent Neil's body thrusting backwards, but instead, it jostled back and forth.

Someone else's bullets were plunging into his side and back. The convulsing action of his body from the hail of fired ammo caused the gun to shake loose from his grip, and he dropped to his knees, crumpling to the floor. Blood pooled as it flooded from his body. One thing was for certain, there would be no rising from the dead. It really was over this time. Danielle didn't have to be afraid anymore, no more wondering, *'what if?'*

Stepping through the doorway was Ben, followed by a small contingent of officers.

"Are you okay? Is she..." Ben asked, putting away his weapon. There was uncertainty in the second question, uncertainty of wanting to know the answer.

"Yeah, we're fine."

Ben sighed in relief. "Alright, I'm going to get a medic down here to check you two out, just to make sure."

"No, have them meet us at street level. I don't want her in this room for another minute." Adam stood, scooping Danielle up with him, and headed for the door as Ben made the call. She caught what was more than just a glimpse of a dead Neil lying in his own crimson puddle. It was his last expression—surprise—frozen onto his face. Relief and tears overwhelmed her. Adam stopped walking at the feel of her body shaking.

"Dani, what's wrong?" His brows were cinched tight with concern.

"I really am alive," she said softly through the crying.

"I told you so," he responded lightly with a soft kiss on her forehead and began walking again. That meant Adam had really told her that he loved her. She hadn't imagined it, it wasn't a fantasy, and she wasn't dead. Now, she could lead the life she had wanted.

An ambulance waited for them topside with a paramedic standing by. Adam sat her down on the edge of the truck and requested a blanket to cover her with. He knew she would be cold from the light breeze meeting the still wet blood that dribbled down her. Plus, anyone who came to check out the commotion would see her drenched in the blood, not to mention her near nakedness, and he wanted as few eyes on her as possible. That was easier said than done, though.

―――

Adam wrapped the blanket around her and began rubbing her arms up and down in comfort. The medic had a damp cloth in her hands, ready to clean her, but Adam took it over. He gently wiped the blood splatters from Danielle's face, and the tender way his eyes swept over her made her breath catch.

"Sweetheart, what can I do?" His voice was as warm and soothing as the blanket he'd wrapped her in.

"You've already done so much... I can never repay you, Adam," she said meekly. It was true that he had told her he loved her—she was sure of it now—but this was an intense circumstance where emotions and adrenaline were running high. He'd probably thought she might still die at that time, compelling him to say it. She wasn't about to hold him to it.

"I think I know a way," he said sweetly.

Oh God, no. She couldn't handle another relapse in sleeping with him again. The consequences...

"Marry me."

Whoa, whoa, whoa, whoa... She couldn't have possibly heard him right.

"What?" she asked, leery and confused. Adam set down the cloth and took her face in his hands.

"Marry me."

Danielle couldn't believe what he was saying. "But—"

Those gray eyes were calm and steady, smiling of their own accord as they searched hers. "Dani, I'm crazy, stupid, head-over-heels in love with you." Her heart thundered like a stampede of wild mustangs racing across the open plains. "When you left, it was hard... harder than I expected. I thought I could let you walk away and live your life," Adam shook his head, "but it hurt not having you with me, not getting to see you every day. That was nothing, though, compared to today. Nothing could've prepared me. When I thought you were gone, that you were dead and that I'd failed you and lost you... Dani, I wanted to die. The pain..." Adam grimaced and shook his head as he caressed her face. "It was unfathomable. I'm so sorry you were hurt, and I want to spend the rest of my life making it up to you."

Wow. For all of those times when she'd wished he'd just say how he felt, he was finally opening up. No, opening up wasn't the right term—more like pouring out everything in a flooding rush. It was surprising and slightly overwhelming. It was like a seal breaking on the dam around his heart and releasing a powerful flow that was going to overtake her—drown her. Danielle wanted that. She wanted to drown in him.

Adam let go of her face and took her hands instead, as one knee, then the other, rested on the paved asphalt. Danielle thought she might hyperventilate.

"Oh, my God!" she heard a girl squeal. She turned her attention to the direction of the voice to see Nina grinning from ear to ear, bouncing on her toes and yanking on Ralph's arm.

"Dani," Adam said, drawing her attention back to him, "I'm on *both* of my knees, begging. Please marry me? I don't want to live without you. I was a fool to think I could because I can't. I won't. I refuse to."

Nina and Ralph weren't the only ones observing anymore. They had a street-filled audience, and though he wasn't shouting, Adam's professions weren't in a whisper, either. Some pretended to do their work, but their eyes were shifted to the sides, staring intently. Ben, however, didn't bother faking it. He stood a ways back, arms folded and smiling with pride for his partner.

Danielle's gaze locked again with Adam's as he waited for her answer. He actually looked nervous. "Well, it sounds like I don't have a choice," she said, smiling.

"Not really, no," he smiled back. He stayed down on the ground, though, apparently waiting for that official word.

"Yes," Danielle said, smiling and giggling through tears.

Adam popped up instantly, pulling her into him and off the back of the ambulance for a deep, passionate kiss, followed by a multitude of tiny ones all over her cheeks and jaw. He took care not to hurt her tender spots, which wasn't too hard—it was obvious where they were. His arms were warm and strong, but still gentle in the way they encircled Danielle. Cheers and applause surrounded them.

"I love you," he beamed, and his steel gray eyes sparkled. Her heart melted for the millionth time. It did that a lot with him.

"I love you, too." More kisses rained down on her. He held her so tight against him, not even a crowbar could wedge between them.

With a respectful approach, Ben said, "Let me be the first to congratulate you." He and Adam shook hands, then did a bro hug, patting each other on the back two to three times, synchronizing their movements. "Not to ruin the mood, but I thought you might like to know whose blood is all over your fiancée."

The word fiancée sounded foreign and wonderful to Danielle... the blood part, not so much. She cringed as she waited.

"It's pig blood."

"What?" she asked simultaneously with Adam.

"Well, Douglas will still have to do a test to confirm it, but we found a butchered swine that was drained of its blood in one of the other rooms down in the *dungeon*." It seemed the basement under the shop had already been nicknamed. Danielle was relieved to know it wasn't human hemoglobin covering her, but that didn't mean she liked being drenched in the alternative.

"That poor pig." No one was spared from Neil Ghering's brutality.

"Better Wilbur than you." Adam's face had turned serious again.

He definitely had a point, and Danielle nodded in agreement. She looked over her shoulder to find Ralph and Nina again. Ralph was occupied in a phone conversation, but Nina was standing with her hands clasped tightly together, shifting around like a child doing the potty dance. Danielle smiled and waved her over, and Nina practically sprinted across the street. Her arms began to open for a hug, but retracted when she saw the red smears.

"Oh my God, boss, are you okay?" Nina was on the verge of sniffling.

"I'm fine. It's not mine."

Nina let out a sigh of relief, then glanced away. "What about Adam?"

Danielle scanned Adam, who had a toned, muscled arm wrapped around her waist. He was also gory looking. His cotton t-shirt was stained with the same sacrificial pig that marred Danielle's clothes, only on him, the outline of her body was sponge painted from their embraces. Her eyes kept perusing him, as she answered Nina, "Also, not ours." She loved looking at him. Then, the hand that hooked around her caught Danielle's eye. It had a dried brownish-red substance on it. It was definitely dried blood, but it looked different from the swine's. "What's this from?" she asked him.

He was still discussing the whole showdown with Ben. She knew it couldn't have come from the pig blood on her because it looked different. Adam cut himself off immediately to see the source of Danielle's inquiry. He looked at his fingers and knuckles, then back at her. "Remember Neil's face?"

How could she forget? It looked like someone had run him down with a car... a few times. Adam raised a brow, and it clicked. She responded with a silent, *Oh*. Oddly, she felt herself smile. Adam had bludgeoned Neil's face to mush over her, and even though Danielle didn't consider herself an advocate for violence, she fully supported it in this case. Neil Ghering had deserved it. Adam must have read her mind because he smiled back, then leaned in for another soft kiss.

Ralph strolled up next to Nina, still speaking into the phone—Danielle's phone. "Here she is," he said, as he winked and passed off the device. Danielle knew exactly who was on the other end of the line.

"Hey, Care." Danielle gave her a quick run-down of the insane events and, of course, had to include a lot of reassurances of her well-being. Now, there was only one more thing to tell her, and it was the best news Danielle had ever delivered. It was short and simple.

She barely got out the words, *'Adam asked me,'* before Carrie forced her to hold the phone six inches away from her ear. Everyone laughed as they heard high-pitched screams erupt from the tiny speaker. Soft, warm breath tickled Danielle's other ear.

"I can't wait to get you home."

Keeping her voice low, she said, "And why is that?"

"Well," Adam whispered, seduction coating his words, "you're pretty dirty right now, and I'm going to invest as many hours as it takes—"

"To soap me down and lather me up until I'm clean?" she asked, equally alluring. She knew how to play this game with him.

"No, until you're filthy. I guess we can do both, though." He placed a light kiss on her ear.

Now, a whole other part of her was melting. A flood of images entered her mind of all the things she wanted him to do to her—all the things they would do to each other. Her mouth went dry. "How soon can we get out of here?"

Adam laughed quietly enough for only her to hear. "Are you ready to go?"

Danielle's breathing deepened with her growing anticipation. "Actually, I'm ready to—"

"So," a voice cut in, reminding Danielle that she and Adam weren't alone, "why don't you two go get cleaned up, get some rest, and I'll take care of this." It was Ben who had brought them back to Earth. "Adam, I assume you can collect Danielle's statement on your own?" He was giving them their out. The smallest smile just barely formed at the corners of his mouth.

"I think I can manage it," Adam said, returning the sly look that only these partners could pull off so discreetly.

They couldn't get to Adam's car fast enough. They jumped into their seats and threw their belts on. Adam turned and looked at Danielle. She knew what he was waiting for.

"Take me home."

Adam flashed one of his devilish, irresistible smiles. "Sweetheart, I'm taking you to the moon," he drawled out, as he put the key in the ignition and turned the engine. "All the way."

Epilogue

The sand was soft, and the water was crystal. The late-October sun in Cabo San Lucas was warm and rich. The feel of it kissing Danielle's skin was heavenly, but it couldn't compare to his kisses. Nothing could.

Adam's lips danced across her neck as the pair lay sprawled in the hammock, gently swaying. So, this was what vacation was like? Captain Jensen had given Adam some time off from work—paid time off—which according to Lacey Anderson, who heard it from Ben, Mitch Corolla wasn't too thrilled about.

"Adam?"

His eyes were closed as his head was nuzzling hers. "Hmm?"

"How come Detective Corolla got so bent out of shape about you getting to take vacation?"

"Where did you hear that?" he asked casually.

"Ben told Lacey."

She felt Adam chuckle. "Why am I not surprised?"

When he didn't follow up with a response, she prodded, "How come?"

"Why is it so important to you?"

"I'm just curious. The times I saw the two of you together, I could feel the tension in the air," *and the testosterone*, she thought. "I got the impression that he doesn't like you too much."

"We definitely aren't the best of friends, that's for sure. I barely tolerate him."

After more silence, Danielle reached around and poked Adam in the side.

"Okay," he started laughing, "okay, he's pissed at me because of a disagreement my fist had with his face. He was even more pissed that I didn't get suspended for it."

Getting out of possible suspension hadn't been hard. Adam had followed his gut, which Jensen privately praised him for. It helped that Adam had stopped Neil, otherwise the captain might not have been so supportive. Ultimately, putting an end to the Harvester trumped Mitch Corolla's bruised ego—and face.

"Do you go around fighting everyone?"

"Only when it comes to you." He kissed her temple.

Danielle remembered the way Mitch Corolla incessantly hit on her, offering his *services* every time she was at the station. Yes, Corolla was a major sleaze bag, and God only knew what he'd said to set Adam off, and she was sure she didn't want to know. Besides, Adam would never tell her anyway, so she left it at that.

The scents of plumeria and hibiscus flowers blew in the breeze and mixed with the ocean air, joining in the perfection. Fingers began skating up and down her skin as a pair of lips found her jaw and ear lobe, and a husky, purely masculine voice—saturated in the promise of pleasure—filled her. "Did you bring it?"

"Yes, and I'm glad it's almost Halloween or else I'd have felt a little embarrassed about getting it."

"Well," Adam continued seducing her ear, "the good part is you won't have to return it."

"No," she drawled, "the good part is now I have my own pair of cuffs."

Thank you for reading *The Harvester*! Please consider leaving a review on Amazon or Goodreads. Every review helps bring more visibility for new books.

Keep reading for bonus content, including a soundtrack for *The Harvester* and a sneak peek into book two, *The Siren's Storm*!

Find *The Harvester*'s soundtrack on Spotify!

Stay tuned for a sneak peek into book two: The Siren's Storm...

She's a siren, calling me to my ruin. And I just can't resist her song.

After three tours with the Marines, all I want is to settle into my new, quiet life.

Then, my brother calls to ask a favor—a favor that will change everything.

Carrie Marossi is the opposite of quiet. Not only is she bubbly and outspoken with a larger than life personality, she's gorgeous—absolutely stunning—with a quick wit to rival anyone who dares to challenge her.

She's the kind of woman a man would risk everything for. The kind of woman I had risked everything for.

I told myself never again, but the more time I'm forced to spend by Carrie's side, the harder it is to resist her charm and allure—to resist the passion burning between us... to resist falling under her spell.

And what shakes me to my very core is the realization that saving her life... might just cost me my heart.

Chapter One

Damn. 8:07 p.m. She was supposed to be there at 7:45. Of all the days to be late, this was not one of them. Carrie's best friend in the whole world was getting married to the man of her dreams, and their engagement was finally being celebrated. Both the bride and groom-to-be had insisted on waiting until all siblings were able to make it back to San Diego for the soirèe—and a soirèe it would be. The groom's mother was a prestigious event planner, and Carrie had no doubts that the party would be nothing less than fabulous.

It was only three short weeks ago that Carrie's best friend had been kidnapped and almost murdered by a lunatic serial killer. Danielle Walsh had been the center of the psychopath's disturbing obsession, his sick and twisted distortion of reality that had cost the lives of so many others. He was nothing short of a monster.

Thinking about it made Carrie shiver. Her short, sleeveless dress didn't help, either. Frustration was building inside as she idled in her Audi, stuck between 5th and 6th Avenue. From what she could see, some idiot tried to turn right onto a one-way street. The same street she was on, and it just so happened the direction of the one-way was not the same as that driver. Carrie let out a huff. Cars were moving at a snail's pace. Everyone was being forced to one lane in order to get around the accident, and not all of the motorists agreed on the same method of executing said detour. You had some drivers that were letting *everyone* over and some that refused to take pity. They had the *'sucks to be you'* mentality.

Carrie's thoughts ventured back to the harrowing events that still felt like yesterday. Had it not been for Adam, Danielle would be dead today—just another victim of a tragic story. Detective Adam Burke had been assigned to the case when the murder spree began. He and Danielle had fallen for each other, though they both took their sweet time admitting it. In fact, it took near death for them to realize they couldn't live without each other.

Carrie shook her head lightly and smiled to herself. It was ridiculous to her how hard they'd made something so obviously simple. She looked at the clock again—

Double damn.

She was officially thirty minutes late now. Just as she was about to call Danielle, her phone rang.

"Hey, Dani, I'm still stuck."

"Don't worry about it, Care, just get here safely."

"Thanks, I'm so sorry. Even though it's creeping along, I think I can make it in ten minutes, fifteen tops."

"Do you want me to go ahead and order a drink for you?" Carrie could hear the music and laughter at the lounge, Belo, through the phone. Her apartment was only a mile—one freaking mile—from the sophisticated club, but an accident on Market Street had forced her to take this alternate route, which proved to be just as bad. It seemed all of the bozos were out tonight.

"Sure, get me a Sex on the Beach... with extra Sex."

Danielle burst into laughter. "I'll see what I can do."

"Alright, ciao, bella."

Danielle was still chuckling, "Bye."

———

Foam fizzled as it slid down to the bottom of the now empty pilsner glass. Dean signaled to the waitress for another beer, but couldn't quite get her attention. She'd been snatched by another patron just before her line of sight would have caught his gesture.

"You're not tapping out already, are you?" Warren asked, as he nudged his elbow into Dean's arm. "That'd be pretty pitiful," he continued with a smirk. One of the younger Burke brothers, Warren was the instigator of the family and the biggest smart-ass. Dean didn't feel like humoring him.

"I'm trying to flag down our waitress."

Warren took an assessment. "It looks pretty swamped over there.

You may be better off going to the bar yourself." He was right. There were now two other men vying for the young woman's attention. It may have had to do with the fact that she was attractive.

"If you want, I'll go grab her," said Caleb with a devilish smile. Warren's twin was the ladies' man, and the ladies definitely agreed with that moniker.

"No, I'll get it myself," Dean said, as he put his hand to Caleb's chest, blocking his movement, as he was already preparing to take off after the pretty young woman. "You don't need to *'go grab her.'*"

Caleb's face took on a look to say, *"I don't know what you mean,"* as Dean gave his own look of *"Yes, you damn well do"*.

Danielle, his soon to be sister-in-law, jumped in. "Oh, Dean, are you going to the bar? Would you please order a Sex on the Beach?"

Normally, he would have felt a little ridiculous ordering such a girly drink, but not for Danielle. She was an amazing woman and perfect for his other brother, Adam. They'd just been through hell and back, and Dean was glad to see his brother pull his head out of his ass and snatch her up before someone else did. And someone else definitely would have. Plenty of men's eyes were on her, and he witnessed Adam's possessive hold on her tighten, well aware of their looks.

Dean wasn't a mushy kind of guy, but even he had to admire their love. The passion, the devotion, radiated off of them. Just the way Adam looked at her said everything—and Danielle was certainly something to look at. Her long, caramel waves flowed from the top of her head to the bottom of her shoulder blades. Her green and gold eyes—the colors melding into each other—sparkled at her fiancé.

"Sure."

Danielle flashed him a sweet, appreciative smile. "Thanks," she said in a sing-song voice. She could probably tell that this favor wasn't his favorite one to execute. He cleared a path to the bar. Most people got out of his way on their own, but there was a cluster in front of him that wasn't breaking up. The swarm of men seemed to be staring at something, dumbfounded. Make that some*one*.

Dean pushed his way through the horde only to run smack straight into the siren. He quickly snaked an arm around her waist to prevent her from tumbling backwards, pulling her into him. The gorgeous creature, even in her three-inch stilettos, barely came to his chin. Dark espresso hair cascaded down to the middle of her back, the multitude of layers framing from her chin all the way down her slender, petite little body.

Her dazzling emerald eyes were accentuated by the vibrant green, beaded dress. Jewels, sequins, and crystals covered the short little number, which revealed most of her tanned legs. It was no wonder why every man in the vicinity was ogling her. The sexy cocktail dress covered only from her breasts to the top half of her thighs, with plenty of cleavage to admire. She felt good pressed up against him. After the surprise left her features, the beauty gave him a heart-stopping smile.

Chapter Two

Carrie had finally made it to Belo and began making her way through the lounge. She could feel the gawking from the opposite sex as she strutted across the floor. Ordinarily, she would take her time—she wasn't ashamed to admit that she liked the perusing. It boosted her confidence and made her feel sexy.

Tonight was different, though. She was agitated that she'd already missed a bit of the engagement party, so she lengthened her strides as she headed to the back toward the VIP area where the Walshes and the Burkes were waiting. A small congregation of men were in her path, staring her down, but Carrie didn't slow. She knew they'd part for her. Suddenly, a tall brick wall in a handsome black suit slammed into her, nearly knocking her off her feet. In a flash of speed, a strong arm wrapped around her, saving her from the floor. The six-foot-three hottie clutched Carrie tightly to his hard body, leaving her momentarily breathless.

The look in his eyes shifted from surprise to something heady, intense. Those steel gray eyes... Carrie had only seen one other pair in that beautiful shade. This had to be one of Adam's brothers. There was only one thing to do—she had to mess with him.

With a flirtatious smile, she said, "Wow, tiger, you're fast. Do you tackle all of your prey this way, or am I just lucky?" Carrie could see the bewilderment, then fluster in his reaction.

"Sorry about that," Hottie said, huskily. He released his hold on her slowly, almost reluctantly, as he righted her on her feet. Carrie liked the feel of his hand sliding across her lower back.

"Don't worry," she said, still seducing him with her smile, "I'll let you make it up to me later. See ya." She touched Hottie Burke's arm as she walked past him, sashaying her way through the room.

Dean stood in the middle of the floor, perfectly still, as he watched the siren's hips sway from side to side. After she disappeared into the throng of drooling men, he continued his trip to the bar. He placed the order with the bartender, and as he waited, his thoughts went back to what that beautifully seductive voice had said.

"I'll let you make it up to me later." What did that mean? The tightening in his pants had its own theory.

Dean arrived back to the tables with a tall glass of amber beer in one hand and the fruity vodka drink in the other. As he was about to hand off the beverage to Danielle, a delicate, tan hand reached across him to retrieve it.

"Thanks, tiger. I knew you'd come through."

He looked to his left, and there she was, his siren. His confused expression made her chuckle and wink at him.

"Tiger?" Adam asked, his gaze shifting back and forth between Dean and the bombshell in green. Danielle didn't seem surprised, though. She just grinned.

"Your brother just about pummeled me a moment ago. Luckily, he's got the reflexes of a cat, but based on what I see, no ordinary, domesticated house cat." Her full, glossy pink lips began sucking on the tiny straw, sipping the cocktail down slowly. Dean couldn't seem to pull his gaze away.

"Dean, I'd like you to meet Carrie," Danielle introduced with laughter in her voice, making Dean get a hold of his wits.

"Nice to meet you," he said, extending his hand out to hers. Carrie reciprocated with a firm shake. For someone so delicate-looking, she had a strong, confident grip. It impressed him. He'd have taken her for the kind of woman who gave the *princess shake*—light and fragile, like you might break her hand.

"Right back atcha." Their hands remained clasped longer than they should have, and Dean broke the contact at the moment of that realization. Her smile was sly and playful. Those full lips looked delicious. He did a subconscious shake of his head. He didn't need to be thinking of her that way.

"Oh my God, Carrie, that dress is amazing—super sexy!" Danielle's younger sister, Alaina, rushed over from one of the tables where she'd been mingling. She grabbed Carrie's hands and spun her in a slow circle to show off the sparkling garment.

"I'll say." Smooth-talking Caleb joined the group. Did he ever take a rest? This was the first time that his brother's incessant flirting actually bothered Dean.

"Why, thank you," Carrie said with a coquettish smile. It was clear to him that she was a flirt herself, making her and Caleb two peas in a pod. In fact, Dean was sure at any moment Caleb would sweet-talk her into a dance. Why did that bother him?

"Come on, tiger." Carrie set down her drink on the table and grabbed Dean's hand. He certainly wasn't expecting that. Her skin was soft and warm. A romantic Paul McCartney tune filled the lounge, and she was taking Dean to the dance floor, whether he wanted to or not.

She delicately placed a hand on his shoulder as he repositioned his hold of their joined hands, and they began swaying. Dean could feel the soft brush of Carrie's hair on his arm, as he took hold of her waist for the second time tonight.

"I think my brother may be a little disappointed in your choice."

The corner of her mouth pulled up as she turned her attention back to the party. "I think he'll get over me." Dean's gaze followed and saw Cassanova already chatting up Alaina Walsh. He grinned to himself as he shook his head, and Carrie let out a soft chuckle. The gentle laugh seduced his ears.

Paul McCartney continued to croon his romantic ballad over the lounge's sound system, casting an amorous spell over the couples on the dance floor. You could feel the weight of it in the air—could see it in their movements. Carrie's eyes were staring deep into Dean's, as the two sweetly moved across the floor in circles. Those emeralds were hypnotic. Carrie didn't say a word, only smiled, and the trance was all-encompassing. He had to do something to stop the tightening in his chest.

———

"So, what do you do?"

Carrie was a bit surprised by Dean's question. It sounded more like an interview than a sincere interest. "Oh, just boring stuff."

That wasn't quite true. A high-profile trial in criminal court was anything but boring, but she really didn't want to talk about work. She had put in a lot of long hours this week, and she wanted to enjoy her time away from it. She wanted to absorb the happiness all around her and enjoy the party, her friends, and a dance with a handsome man. Out of courtesy, though, she countered the question.

"What do you do?"

Dean lightly grinned. "Boring stuff."

Carrie just laughed. "Okay."

She studied Dean. Aside from a few smiles, his features remained expressionless. She felt she was good at reading men, but this one was proving to be more difficult. She did, however, notice that he refused to keep eye contact with her for more than two seconds at a time. Did she make him nervous? It was hard to tell. His gaze shifted subtly from point to point, not erratically all over the place. Either Dean Burke was determined not to look at her, or she wasn't of enough interest to hold his attention.

Carrie was intrigued. She needed to tamp it down, now. Dean was not someone she should be intrigued by. Curiosity would get the better of her and she'd... Nope, not a path she could venture down. After all, her only intention was to have a bit of fun at his expense. Why should she care if she made him nervous—or if he found her uninteresting? She didn't, she told herself. But that didn't stop her nose from crinkling and brows furrowing.

———

The bridge of Carrie's nose cinched, and her pink lips tightened as they pursed together. She looked mad, and she was staring right at him. Was she angry with him? Dean wasn't sure what he might have done, but that wasn't too surprising. He didn't spend much time with women, and when he did, he kept it short. He didn't know how to read them the way Caleb did, and he didn't want to. For some reason, though, it bothered him—the thought that he possibly upset this woman. Why? He decided not to dwell on it. What did he care? He didn't.

Suddenly, as if she realized her expression, her face turned sweet. Pulling Dean down by the nape of his neck, Carrie met him halfway, rising onto her tiptoes, and placed a tender kiss on his cheek. "Thanks for the dance, tiger." Her voice was laced with seduction, and her eyes twinkled at him, that sexy smile taunting him.

Dean remarked with the safest response he could think of. "Sure."

She chuckled again. Damn, she was sexy. Dean's chest was starting to constrict *again*. A siren, indeed. One little laugh, and he was a mess in the head. He didn't like it. She flashed him one more smile as she headed back to the group, leaving him alone on the dance floor. He hadn't even realized the song had ended. He had been so focused on Carrie... *Damn, she's good*, he thought. Good at the game. Plenty of women had tried to get him to play, but he left them wanting. He didn't do games—he didn't do relationships.

Dean felt a firm slap on his back. "Hey, you alright?"

Adam was to his right. Dean hadn't noticed his approach—not good for someone with honed observation skills.

"Yeah, fine. Why?"

Adam took a sip of the fresh refill in his pilsner glass. "You just kind of had an intense stare focused on our tables. Plus, you're standing on the dance floor by yourself, looking creepy." He grinned, as he sipped the lager, when his comment got a narrowed glare from Dean.

Before he got the chance to throw some name-calling at his brother, a beautiful, sexy laugh cut through Dean's thoughts, calling him to attention.

Carrie's long, espresso hair swayed as she tossed her head back. The light shone on it, gleaming ribbons across every strand. She was holding onto Danielle's hands, as though if she were to let go, she might fall over from her laughter.

"So, are you just going to stand here all night and stare at her, or are you going to come back to the party?" Dean shot another glare at Adam before the two walked back to the tables. As they approached, their waitress appeared, tray and drinks in hand. She delivered everyone's order, then placed a drink in front of Carrie.

"Oh, I didn't order this," Carrie said, apologetically.

"It's from the gentleman at the bar," the girl said with a smile. Everyone turned to get a glimpse of Carrie's admirer. His blonde hair was parted and slicked back, and based on his suit and skinny tie, it was clear he'd been watching too much *Mad Men*. *What a tool*, Dean thought. The man flashed a "dapper Dan" smile at Carrie as he raised his glass to her. That aggravated Dean, but what bothered him more was that Carrie reciprocated the gesture.

"Is there something I can get for anyone else?"

"Yes," Dean replied, as he grabbed the drink out of Carrie's hand. "I need another Sex on the Beach—you can take this one back," he said, placing the glass back on the tray, "and a scotch, neat."

The waitress looked to Carrie for approval, but Carrie's eyes were on Dean, stunned and perplexed by what had just happened. The young woman only hesitated a moment before she headed back to place the new order. Dean turned his attention to *Don Draper* at the bar. He could see the displeasure on the douchebag's face and then his forfeit as he turned his back on Dean.

Adam nudged Dean in the arm as he raised a brow and whispered, "Scotch?" He knew Dean only ordered scotch when something was on his mind. Dean didn't respond, but instead clenched his jaw for a visible tick. "Okay," Adam said, along with an indifferent shrug of his shoulders.

A sharp finger stabbed Dean in the chest. "Excuse me, but would you care to explain yourself?" Carrie was mere inches from him, hand on hip, and a challenge in her eyes. Was this woman ever *not* sexy?

He gave it to her straight. "You were going to drink a beverage from a perfect stranger."

"And?"

"And nothing. That's reason enough."

She didn't back down. "No, it's not."

"You don't know him or what he could have done to your drink." Dean kept his response very matter-of-fact.

"It's not like he made it himself. It came straight from the bar."

"Can you prove that?"

Carrie was quiet with rage brimming in her eyes. Dean knew that technically, no, she couldn't prove that it hadn't been touched by anyone other than the bartender and waitress.

"Really?" she asked with exasperation, looking to Adam for help.

"He has a point."

Her eyes narrowed and scrutinized them in disbelief. Dean knew Adam would back him up, regardless of how thin his case was. Working for the police department, Adam knew how easy it was for women's drinks to get spiked.

Carrie scoffed loudly at them. "Well, I'll make sure I call you the next time I need a lecture on *'stranger danger.'*" Dean noticed that she hadn't backed away from him. She was still in his face—or with their height difference, as close to his face as she could get. The sound of a woman's throat clearing interrupted the staring contest.

"Here are your drinks," the waitress said, as she placed them on the table and quickly left. This time, she didn't ask for more orders. It was apparent that she felt the tension between Dean and Carrie, and she wasn't the only one. They had developed a small audience from their group. Multiple pairs of eyes shifted back and forth in anticipation.

Acknowledgments

Consider this my acceptance speech for the Oscars, because I have an absurd amount of people to thank. To start, I want to thank my husband and family for believing in me. To my coworker, Christy (here's your shoutout), for letting me brainstorm *to* her, whether she wanted me to or not. To Nury and Jenn, for being tremendous friends by reading the story many times over and giving me their feedback and support. I'd like to thank my editor and cover artist for both helping me bring this dream into fruition. To the readers who took a chance on me, I'm beyond grateful to you. Lastly, I'd like to thank the Academy… just kidding.

About the Author

Hi, everyone! The hardest part about writing is writing about yourself, but I'll give it a go. I started out like everyone else: I went to school, went to college, got a degree, got a job that had absolutely nothing to do with that degree, stayed in that job out of convenience, so on and so forth. A tale as old as time, as they say.

One of my favorite past times was reading. I read a lot. Eventually, I had an epiphany: why not write my own stories? It was a hobby just for fun, but the more I wrote, the more I thought, "Wouldn't it be cool if I could be an author and have people read my books? Then, I could do what I love all the time!"

It was a fun dream in the back of my mind, but after many years, I finally came to the conclusion that it didn't have to be a dream. It could be a reality, but *I* had to make it a reality. All I needed were the right tools to publish myself. So, that's what I did!

Printed in Great Britain
by Amazon

ed4aad12-e746-4c17-a2a0-5d57776c84e8R01